TIDINGS

Also by William Wharton

Birdy
Dad
A Midnight Clear
Scumbler
Pride

TIDINGS

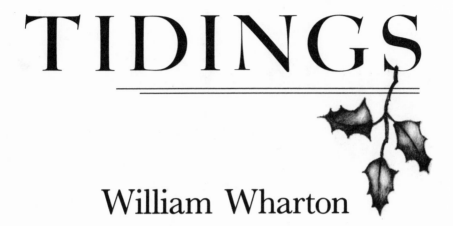

William Wharton

HENRY HOLT AND COMPANY
NEW YORK

Copyright © 1987 by William Wharton
Published by Henry Holt and Company, Inc.,
521 Fifth Avenue, New York, New York 10175.
Published in Canada by Fitzhenry & Whiteside Limited,
195 Allstate Parkway, Markham, Ontario L3R 4T8.

Library of Congress Cataloging in Publication Data
Wharton, William.
Tidings.
I. Title.
PS3573.H32T5   1987   813'.54   87-7483
ISBN: 0-8050-0532-3

First Edition

Designed by Jeffrey L. Ward
Printed in the United States of America
1   3   5   7   9   10   8   6   4   2

ISBN 0-8050-0532-3

To Saint Nicholas

I swept and slept
Through promise
Not kept.

TIDINGS

I

A Partridge in a Pear Tree

There aren't many holly berries this year; the leaves are dark viridian green, deeply dented, sharp-pointed; but virtually no berries.

The damp, cold air shifts between fog and mist. Drifting, light, incipient snowflakes float from the darkening sky.

I have my arms full of berryless holly now, so I start down toward our heavy stone and wood ancient water mill at the bottom of this French Morvandeau valley. The streams are gushing with water; a thick, black thrust; tumbling, rounded, moss-covered stones roiling in rocky streambeds.

There's no one up and about in our village. Those who are there, sit huddled in oldness and cold, alone, beside wood fires. Even at four thirty, all shutters are closed.

This is the year's shortest day; the sun's declined to its nadir. Tomorrow we can watch it be born again, redeeming life for a new year.

Rounding the downhill curve, I see our own light at the mill; pink, inviting. It gleams through a small west window incised in a two-foot-thick, rough-cut, three-hundred-year-old stone wall. It's a great window for watching late sunsets in July, also a good window to be coming home to on a near-freezing, earliest winter evening.

I go in through our cellar which opens directly onto the road. This cellar has damp, dark, cold, humid, hand-hewn granite floors.

It houses the giant cogs, shafts and flywheels of the defunct mill machinery. It's now pungent with birch sawdust from this morning's work; sawing wood, piling it by the fireplace upstairs in a probably futile effort to heat this mausoleum for our family Christmas celebrations.

This year, our two daughters are coming from America to join us. Our youngest child, a boy, still lives at home. Our older son is spending Christmas this year with his French girlfriend; she riding on the back of his motorcycle; the two of them eating miles of desert dust in far-off Arizona and New Mexico.

But then, after all, the first Christmas *was* in a desert. Our Michael-cum-Joseph guides his 500-cc Yamaha donkey, with, I hope, a not-too-pregnant Geneviève-cum-Mary in postillion. There *will* be room at *some* inn, no doubt.

Our older daughter and oldest child, Maggie, hasn't been in France for seven years. She has left behind her five-year-old son, our only grandchild, with her husband in Arizona. She's also considering leaving her husband.

Our other daughter, Nicole, spent a Christmas with us here at the mill three years ago. She froze, missed hot water, showers, rock music, a place to wash her hair, and a man. This time she brings a man with her. All the rest remains practically the same— easy to miss.

Our youngest, Ben, will be fifteen on the eve of Christmas Eve. He's our only child who seems to share our atavistic, pagan Christmas feelings. For us, just being here is fulfilling. We revel in the confines of this closed valley. We are happy encircled by

rolling, wooded hills, rounded sometimes with slanted pastures
for hardy sheep.

Ben doesn't particularly like to shower, wash his hair, *or* listen
to rock music. He far prefers animals to people, and animals
outnumber humans by at least a hundred to one in this valley.

In a vain effort to approximate somewhat the ease and comfort
of Western-states American living, and because I had no classes
after I gave midterms at ACP, the American College of Paris,
the school where I teach, I came down here from Paris three
days early. Lor, my wife, who also teaches and has problems of
her own, insisted it was probably the best thing after all, considering everything.

With me, I transported an additional heater—that should help
with the freezing part. I'd also hoped to haul down a water heater
and install it but there was no more room in my car. This car's
a small sports Fiat with thirteen hundred cubic centimeters of
power. One might well fit it in the back of an American station
wagon. It's the only sporty thing I own, that is, if you don't
count my underwear or jogging shoes.

I transported down with me thirty meters of two-meter-wide
material purchased at the Marché Aligre in Paris. Ten meters
of it are bright red. With this I hope to camouflage some of the
more rugged, ragged, crude aspects of the mill.

I spent the first day sweeping, dusting, knocking down cobwebs,
washing windows, wiping, mopping; nailing down or supporting
various idiosyncratic elements which might offend.

I swept up a fair mound of rat, or dormouse, shit and two
wheelbarrow loads of general dirt, mostly *chaum*, fallen from chinks
in the walls. These walls are slowly disintegrating; very slowly
though; with help they're good for another two or three centuries.

I also cleaned out about ten years of accumulated ash from
our fireplace, the remains of perhaps one medium-sized forest.

I then, using my red cloth, made drapes for our windows. To
be honest, I only stapled them to the heavy oaken lintels over

each window. I used strips cut from the ends and made tie-backs to let in what little daylight there is. I even used a remnant of red cloth as cover for our eating table in the center of the room.

Now, it all looks very Christmasy, will be even more so with my dark green, although berryless, holly.

The second day, again with my trusty stapler, I climbed up to the loft where our girls, plus the imported man, will be sleeping.

There's fiberglass insulation up there; more or less in place, but hanging somewhat indiscriminately. For reasons I don't quite understand, our dormice like to hibernate in this fiberglass; perhaps some remnant "looking glass" memory. They shred it, shape tiny nests. Probably they'll all die of silicosis—no great loss.

I stapled twenty meters of my brown material, rafter-to-rafter, right over the fiberglass, dormice included. They won't notice till spring (the dormice that is).

Not a creature was stirring, not even a dormouse.

With the rest of the material, I gussied up our tiny toilet room, considered by our neighbors a marvel of American ingenuity, and probably unhygienic. Our toilet was the first in town. I also braced this toilet so it won't rock when one tips to wipe. The john's now jammed tight by a small electric heater. This gives some solidity and welcome warmth where it counts.

Unfortunately, one needs to turn off a heater in the main room before one turns on the toilet heater, or a fuse will blow. There's only fifteen amps of 220 volts coming into the mill. This is mostly a summer place for us.

The flushing system is much too complicated to describe; also "less used" toilet paper is saved to be burned in the fireplace. This is not an energy conservation measure; although, normally, I'm a great energy conserver; could be part of *my* problem; which seems to be at the base of *all* our problems. It's just that our septic tank can only handle so much; it's almost thirteen years old now.

I trim and arrange my holly in vases. Then cook up for myself a quick meal with cassoulet from a can. I soak this up with bread, wash it down with red wine. When I'm alone, that's about the extent of my culinary effort.

Next, I'll be going out to cut a few branches from a nearby planted pine forest. This part requires the total darkness now upon us. The past twelve years we've stolen our whole celebration Christmas tree from this forest. Daytime, we'd hunt till we'd found the perfect tree, then mark it. In the night we'd sneak out, saw at ground level, cover the stump with dirt, drag our tree from the forest, through this sleeping town, and into our mill. There's nothing quite so soul-satisfying as a stolen Christmas tree.

In general, it's a good trick putting together the precepts of Christianity with the *ordinary* American way of celebrating Christmas. It's even more difficult with *our* particular family celebrations. We concentrate on the fantasy, the wonderful drama of Santa Claus and Christmas tree; yule log and gift giving, emphasis on star, snow and domestic animals; pure paganism. And, to top it all off, we steal our Christmas tree.

But now those trees, our *old* Christmas trees, in this planted forest, are tall and thick around as telephone poles. No one in the family will help me with the cutting, sawing, dragging home and hiding. That wonderful forest outgrew us. So, this year, we'll probably be reduced to *buying* our tree in Nevers. We'll be there, with hordes of others; pawing through tree cadavers looking for just the right size, and fullness.

I dress in my duffle coat and woolen hat again, pick up the saw and flashlight, drop down through our trap door carefully feeling in the dark with my feet. Before I'm even in the cellar, I'm met by a breathtaking blast of cold. I know cold air *can't* flow up. Maybe the molecules are so cramped in this freezer of a cellar they're forced up by sheer pressure of numbers into the light, airy, open space of the warm upstairs room. I pull shut the loose, swinging, hingeless trap door, stumble down the last steps and walk out into the blackness of night. There should be a crescent piece of moon up there somewhere, I think, but I move in virtual total blindness.

Does the road seem to glow? I don't know if the paleness I see is wet road or only something I want to see. The mind is a powerful force. I feel the hard surface through my rubber boots so I should sense if I wander left or right off the road. I can always flash my light, but then I lose what little night vision I have. Also, I don't want the villagers to know I'm out stealing pine branches.

Ahead is a halo around our next town, a ghostly haze of whiteness fills the misty air from the single town street lamp. I watch as forms loom out of the all-surrounding gloom. The light creates visions different from ordinary daylight scenes; it's like snow, muffling, at the same time defining new shapes. I stare, entranced, at stone buildings standing bare in the night.

I pass through the other side of this light and my shadow stretches ahead. I finger my flashlight briefly walking along, waiting for the road to curve. At the turn I step off into the forest, wading through broken branches. They're so rotted, so damp, they don't crack when I step on them.

I begin cutting pine branches with my small handsaw till both arms are full. I stumble out onto the road, and scurry downhill through the dark wet air, back to my nest.

Inside, I take off my coat and hat, staple my branches across beams and over windows to hide those staples in the drapes.

Tomorrow I'll drive into Nevers to pick up Loretta and Ben. They're taking the seven A.M. train down from Paris. We'll do our Christmas and food shopping there in Nevers then come back here to the mill. I hope we can make the trip home before dark. French country roads at night are treacherous, especially if this weather turns to snow.

The girls and guest arrive the day after tomorrow, Ben's birthday. Ben was our Christmas surprise baby, born the eve of Christmas Eve. In a certain way, each of our babies was a surprise, a minor miracle. Maybe that's why Christmas means so much to us.

Next morning, I wake at six. Whorls and swirls of snow spin through the path of my flashlight out our window. The "powers that be" have miscalculated; snow was supposed to hold off at least one more day. So now I'm in for a sixty-kilometer drive in the snow, in the dark; driving a car with no snow tires, no chains, a malfunctioning heater and a driver's-side window that won't really close. Also, there's no third gear on this four-speed, all slow, car, and the clutch started slipping irrevocably on the way from Paris. Fancy, new sports car, my car is not.

Then again, perhaps I won't need to drive my wreck to Nevers. The battery has been failing. There are white encrustations on the zinc plates when I look through its translucent sides. Maybe if I shake it I'll have a miniature snowstorm in there, the way it snowed with the tip-toys I loved so when a child.

As a precaution, I brought down my battery charger. This is based upon several frustrating, Herculean, early morning efforts in Paris. Ben and I pushing the car with Loretta steering; she throwing it into gear then chug-churring down to nothingness. Finally, we'd have a frantic dashing off to the metro, book bags flying, tempers fraying, while I'd unhook the dead battery, haul it upstairs to the apartment and charge it. Gradually, morning's cold grip would let up some and after two hours' dialysis, I'd reinstall the battery and drive off to my ten-o'clock class. Normally, Loretta and Ben drive the car while I take the metro.

So now I dress hurriedly in the clothes I'd set out on a chair the night before. I pull on gloves and hat, check my flashlight, lower myself carefully through the trap door into our granite tomb of a cellar. Mill machinery looms mute and massive in the dense molecule-packed darkness. I press the door latch, go up the few stone steps into wild, twisting whiteness. The street already has four inches of fresh, untrammeled snow. Icicles hang over the opening to our lower grange where I keep our car. Inside spread the remains of at least six motorbikes surrounding our car like an escort. These represent Mike's progress from 50-cc pedal bikes to his current 500-cc love. Here in dusty, rusting machinery is revealed the remnants of one man's personal passage through mechanized puberty displacement.

In the car, I check that the lights and heater fan are off before turning the key. I pull the choke out a finger length, press down hard on the accelerator slowly, twice, following carefully the instructions of the man from whom I bought this car, a Mr. Diamant.

Then I turn the key. The starter motor sings in merry glee: "Here we go! Here we go! Here we go!" The engine remains stone deaf (maybe that's steel deaf), hearing nothing, not responding.

I switch off, wait, in quietly surging panic, despair. I try again. Again: "Here we go! Here we go!" But we *don't*.

I jam the accelerator once more to the floorboards, *against* Mr. Diamant's explicit instructions.

This starter motor has no working relationship with the engine, lives a liberated, futile life of its own. Or maybe it's the engine's fault, it might not want to be turned on by this particular little starter motor. Gradually we move from "Here we go!" to "I'm not making it" to "I can't make it" to "I give up, quit," the last in the slurred, tired tones of a staggering drunk or perennially discouraged lover.

I'm ready to quit myself; at the same time my mind's spinning. I have an hour to recharge the battery. I'll move the new butane heater down here in the grange to heat the car. I also have jumper cables. Maybe I'll wait till Philippe, our neighbor, gets up, then cable-jump from his battery.

I give it one more turnover and there's an embarrassed sniggle from the motor, a flirting response, a hobbling hopscotch skipping of almost going, then nothing.

I wait two full minutes in the dark, exercising my pagan excuse for prayer; creating appropriate expletives against fate, humbling myself with beseechments and benedictions to the engine. I promise I'll give it an oil change a thousand kilometers early; I'll give it winter oil, maybe even have the transmission repaired.

No, that doesn't make sense, it'd cost more than the value of the car. I suppress for a moment the treacherous, wonderful, obvious truth; I'm going to *junk* this car and get another. In fact, I'm already courting several possibilities.

Get thee from me, Satan!

I clear my mind. I twist the key as if it's a July day and this is a new car. It turns over, starts, roars, before I even *hear* the starter motor! What's the secret? I sit there in the dark, glowing, floating, freezing, listening, as all four cylinders begin to synchronize, mutually warming each other. I pull back the throttle and climb out to swing open the huge grange doors before I asphyxiate myself with carbon monoxide. It'd probably go down as just another unexpected Christmas suicide.

"None of us noticed anything, but then he was always secretive. It was hard getting close to him, even his wife was very reserved. Philosophers are a weird bunch. You know, he wasn't even sure the world was real. Can you imagine that?"

Now I leave the car running, my effort at Christmas suicide self-aborted. I dash back through our cellar to the still warm room. I make the bed, unplug the transformer for our American electric blanket, quickly brush my teeth, wash up; listening, always listening, to hear if the car's still running. I clean out the fireplace ashes, body warm; set up twists of paper, faggots, thin twigs, dry branches, all overlaid carefully with two split logs for an easy fire start when we get back. I'm listening; the car's still running.

I leave matches by the fire, turn the butane heater down to minimum; butane bottles cost seventy-eight francs each and it means a five-mile drive into Chatin to buy them. I check wallet, checkbook, car papers. I pack expansion wrench, screwdriver, pliers. I pick up a coal scoop in case I get stuck in the snow. I'll shovel gravel under my wheels from the piles along the road, if I can *find* gravel under snow in the dark.

I'm ready as I'll ever be. I leave the single light on over our table. I hate leaving; it all looks, feels, so cozy, just right for a long winter's day before a fire, sipping frozen vodka, thinking, pondering, speculating along my usual well-worn tracks; what's it all about? Why am I here? How can one actually *know* anything? What would make Lor happy? I think I know, but am I really ready? Boy, the heart and the mind are hard to compromise. Just what the hell is love? How much of it is respect, admiration, how much passion? How can I hold it together, or keep it apart? One or the other.

Down in the grange, my car's still purring. There's even some interior heat. I push in both choke and throttle. At the entrance to our grange, outside the door, just under snow, it's deep frozen mud. In reverse, I power my way out and onto the road, front-wheel-drive spinning. I brake skiddingly, stop just before crashing into Madame Le Moine's snow-bedecked blackberry patch, where the old stable used to be.

I get out, and, from inside, close the large interlocking grange doors, pull down and engage a huge hasp; there's a small hobbit kind of hatchway cut in the left door for mere humans. I go out, pull the latch to, and step out softly, trying, ineffectively, to avoid cracking through the new snow and thin ice into thick mud.

The first two kilometers of my journey will be the test. Since we are at the bottom of a bowl into which three streams flow forming the mill pond, there is no way out but up, rather steeply up. In each direction there's an unrelenting slope of at least two kilometers. Summer jogging here calls for a reserve of foolhardy courage.

I'm back in the car, auto heater more or less keeping ahead of steam condensation, snow and ice on the windshield slowly melting. I lean out and brush the side-view mirror; look at my watch. It's seven ten. They'll arrive two hours from now; I'm obviously postponing the obvious. I force the clutch, get into unsynchronized first, then start grinding up the steep hill to Vauchot.

I make it fine up the first tough pitch, the part where I enjoy making my brave *downhill* finishing sprint, summers. I stay in first, rounding the banked curve, past where Monsieur Pinson has a gate to his lower field. The back end of my car tends to veer left and right samba-style.

I slalom up the hill, knowing if I stop I'll never make it. Finally, I arrive at the top in Vauchot. It should be really exciting going *downhill*.

I glide-slide through Vauchot.

Now there's a long curving downgrade twisting toward the town of Corbeau. Going up this hill on a motorcycle is where our Mike would practice speed-shifting while slanting his machine at a forty-five-degree angle to the ground. That desert trip of Mike's begins to seem like a quiet, sane and peaceful way to spend Christmas.

I stay in first gear. The car slips twice but holds and I'm on the straight stretch to Corbeau. I shift up to second for the first time. The next ten kilometers are twisting ascending and descending curves but none worse than the five I've just negotiated. I begin to hope I shall actually make it to Nevers; never-never land of the Bourgogne.

The first light is beginning to glow gray through the falling white when I intersect Route Nationale 978 toward Nevers. I see that, on this well-traveled road, the snow has been squeezed to slush on the sides so the dark road surface is visible. I ease out carefully, speed-shift from second to fourth, past that nonexistent third, switch my lights to low, fight down the window and wipe off my side-view mirror. The rear window is fogged from the steam of anxiety.

The French have a bumper sticker saying AU VOLANT LA VUE C'EST LA VIE. I was never sure if it meant "While stealing, visibility can mean your life," or "While driving (actually steering) vision is life." This gives some idea of my high-quality French.

Even though I did my master's thesis on Albert Camus' concept of "cherish your illusions," my French is weak, to say the least.

I wrestle my window up again to half-mast and wipe mist from the windshield. The snow seems to be slowing down some. I sneak a peek at my watch in the rising light. I have almost an hour left and only forty-five kilometers to go.

It's five till nine when I roll through Nevers. The medieval stone buildings crisscrossed with half-timber wooden beams, lean over narrow cobbled roads. I work my way to the train station; park and check the station clock. I'm fifteen minutes early, my watch is five minutes fast.

I go into the station restaurant; order a black coffee and a croissant at the bar. I pay and sit down at a table. There's clatter all around me as a French boys' school group, wearing school ties and school jackets, struggles with skis and ski equipment, preparing to board the train from which I hope to see Loretta and Ben descend.

The smell of my coffee, the first sip, sends me on a search for the restaurant toilet. I find it, a shared sink and mirror with separate bisex johns. It's a sitter not a squatter. There's no light and I assume it's one of those French *logique* affairs where the light comes on when you turn the latch. There *is* the right kind of latch but when I turn it tight nothing happens. I reopen the door to locate: seat, toilet paper, flusher (chain), paper (individual-sheet, slippery). I grab a handful of the paper, get all my angles, vectors and locations set, then prepare to shut the door.

A woman in a fur coat comes out from the other john and is fluffing her well-cut hair. I wonder if there's a light in that one, consider dashing in behind her, instead, elect for gallantry, maybe modesty, close my door and settle down in the dark.

When I'm finished, after some dark fumbling with buttons, hooks, snaps, I grope for the latch. I'm wearing long johns over regular underwear, then black ski pants, two long-sleeved undershirts, one waffled, guaranteed against arctic cold (but not too effective against Morvanic), a sweater and my jacket. I never do quite manage my jacket zipper in the dark.

I come out, gratefully, to an empty room. According to my reset watch, there's still five minutes till the train arrives. In the bright neon light over the sink, I can see all the mill dirt I've hauled with me. I use a dirty handkerchief to brush off the worst. My new L. L. Bean crepe-soled shoes are covered with goop from in front of our garage. I run trembling fingers through my crazy looking shock of white hair. I hate being nervous, so nervous my hands shake. It seems to happen more often lately.

I started graying seriously at thirty-five, had a white streak in front when I was only in my twenties. There's something about those of us with a premature white streak, gray, or white hair which causes other people to distrust us. I think they feel we're crazy or have had some terrible trauma which has permanently disabled us. Maybe that's how I became a philosophy major. I *look* like someone who worries about things. I am.

Now I'm fifty-two it isn't so bad, white hair is more appropriate but none of it will fall out. They'll bury me still looking like a slowly fading, washed-out boy. That's not far off the mark either. I've been waiting over fifty years to feel like a man. I might as well get used to it, it's probably never going to happen.

I stare ten seconds at unsure cerulean blue eyes surrounded by somewhat bluish flesh, as I wash my hands. It's really weird, as I get older, my eyelids keep drooping so now my eyes look as if they're peering out from the ends of side-by-side pup tents.

I should have shaved this morning but there wasn't time; also, I didn't think of it. My beard, strangely enough, is still dark, at least the stubbles are. Once I let it grow a little to see how it would look. I looked as if I had my head on upside down.

The train is five minutes late so I have time to make a momentous discovery, for me, that is. It's far from original, this insight, but it's creative within my personal limits. I discover why croissants are made that way, wrapped as thin layers into a crescent form. It's so they can be dunked in coffee, easily, with virtually no crumbs dropping in the cup. I luxuriate over my croissant, my lukewarm coffee and my idea, feeling genial and very cosmopolitan. The anxiety of the trip is dropping off like that slush from the Nevers road.

Coffee usually makes me hyper, but this time I'm soothed, perhaps because it's almost cold, or perhaps something chemical happens when it combines with a dunked croissant; or probably this is only a letdown after the mad, desperate rush. I don't know which, but I'm mellow, very Santa Claus–Christmasish, wishing I had a bell and sleigh. It would be great fun to *really be* Santa Claus. Maybe next life.

So, when I hear the train from Paris come into the station, and I go out onto the *quai*, I'm the international man meeting his loved ones at the start of some story in a book. Probably a book by John O'Hara or J. P. Marquand about unrequited love. Better not to think about that; not now anyway. I'm still not ready.

II

Two Turtle Doves

Out on the *quai*, I've just about given up, I'm beginning to think of phoning Paris. My mind's spinning wildly through all the bleak alternatives; then I see them, the last ones off the train.

I should have known. It's not Loretta's way to fight through a crowd just to be first or tenth or thirtieth, or three hundredth. She'll sit unruffled till everyone's struggled, fought, scrambled themselves away with their luggage; then, unhurriedly, graciously, as if it's her private car, as if there were no such thing as time, she'll dismount, nice smile for the conductor on the way out. Ben's the same, I'm not. I'm a pusher-shover. The two of them drive me nuts; I hate to imagine what they think of me.

So there they are, lightly luggaged, drifting dreamily along behind the crush. They find me and I think we're all glad to see each other. Christmas is actually beginning. I sneak some looks at Lor to see how she's holding up, but she has her "isn't the world lovely" smile pasted on her face so I can't tell anything. Mike has a smile like that, too; but his is amateurish and childlike compared to Lor's.

First we drive out to a large market, two kilometers from town, called Carrefour, French for intersection. It's almost like an American supermarket, huge parking lots, grocery carts, Christmas music playing. We'll stock in the bulk of our perishable groceries here and perhaps buy some gifts for our neighbors.

The big purchase will be the turkey. It needs to be large enough for six with enough left over for turkey soup and a hot turkey sandwich meal.

I've already bought all the nonperishables in Paris and carried them down in the car, extra goodies such as Nova Scotia smoked salmon, chocolate bars, several cookies: Russian cigarette, chocolate chip, oatmeal raisin. Also a bottle of Cointreau, some Poire William, Cognac and Champagne. These are the superlatives. There are also eight hundred francs' worth of the necessities, apples, flour, rice, cheeses, sugar, butter, canned goods, onions, matches.

Lor, Ben and I push our cart through the aisles, agreeing, disagreeing, picking, weighing, gradually filling up. We buy more tangerines, oranges; walnuts for the Christmas cookies. A sack of peanuts in the shell, endive, lettuce, tomatoes; celery, stalk and root, for the turkey stuffing. That turkey isn't the only one who's going to be stuffed.

I also buy a ten-liter can of spar varnish and a new paint brush. This costs over three hundred francs right there. My mind glistens just thinking about that varnish.

I sneak in a Cuisinart food processor for Loretta. We also fulfill Ben's greatest Christmas wish, a Russian-built, clip-loaded .22-caliber rifle with a seven-power telescopic sight. Rifles are a minor mania with this peaceful, shy, almost fifteen-year-old last child of ours. He, through his *Guns & Ammo* magazine, is our only contact with a whole world to which neither of us relates. Lor is concerned about the appropriateness of a rifle on a festival of peace. But it's also a festival of love. A good part of love, to me, is respecting the uniqueness of another, especially when his preferences are different from yours. God, I'm a great one to talk about love!

Ben is as much concerned with trajectory, accuracy, optics as anything. A rifle to him is a magnificent tool for projecting an object at high speed over a considerable distance with accuracy. It isn't far removed from his passion for model airplanes and gliders. He has a horror and fear of actual hunting, or flying in a real plane. Hang glider, or hunter, or soldier he'll most likely never be.

We also buy log cabin logs, two dolls, baby doll carriers, a spinning top with a tiny train inside which goes around and whistles when the top spins, plus a sack of grain to feed the ducks on the pond. For Madame Le Moine we buy a potpourri of plants all in one pot. For her son, Philippe, thirty-seven years old and unmarried, a set of small glasses, each with a different fruit sealed in eau de vie, also one of those dogs which wags its head when you put it on the back shelf of an automobile.

On the way out of the market we see some Christmas trees. These trees are small, none taller than six feet, but they're cheap, only eighteen francs. They're unloading the truck with a new supply. We choose the bushiest, tallest tree. Ben's in a state of shock as I tie it to the roof of our car.

"Gosh, Dad, that's not a Christmas tree, it's a branch."

I assure him I've found a stand of most beautiful trees in the woods near Mike's cabin. Philippe told me this part of the forest is owned by Monsieur Boudine and I can probably make a deal with him to cut down one of the trees for us. All year we let him pasture his donkey, Pom Pom, in our field when we aren't there, so we should come to some arrangement. Paying to have someone cut down a tree for us in plain daylight is a long way from stealing one in the secret of night but a sight better than what we're hauling on our car.

We drive into central Nevers, it's almost two o'clock and the traffic is a muddle. By sheer luck we see a woman with two kids coming out of a parking place on a one-way street behind the post office. We're on the wrong end of the street. I gallantly let the woman out, then wildly start backing up the narrow passage between close-parked cars. I am notoriously one of the world's worst backer-uppers. I've always considered it a special skill like juggling or tightrope walking and *I* don't have it. Some people can safely back up at full speed using only the rear-view mirror. I need to twist all the way around and look directly back to have even half a chance.

Loretta's up on her knees; rubbing the rear-view window clean, trying to give directions in a calm but clear tone of voice so she won't spook me. Ben is scrunched down in the seat beside me, avoiding flying glass. I'm going fast as I can, twisting my bad back, rushing to get to that place before a car entering the correct direction gets there. We just beat out a Peugeot 505; the driver smiles grimly and waits while I make a messy four-swing park, then he zooms down the street past us. We sit a moment while I recoup my calm.

Shopping in Nevers is always fun. The old streets are decorated, but nothing too gaudy. There are no loudspeakers playing Christmas carols. The main streets are blocked so there are no cars. The stores are old-fashioned, mostly with creaky, shined hardwood floors. The elevators are wire cages which jiggle, then bounce when they stop. They only take people up; you walk down.

We go our separate ways, agreeing to meet by the car at three. That way we can hope to get home before dark. At this latitude, this time of year, with clouded skies, five is almost night. I find a good, practically prebuilt, but put-it-together-yourself, rubber-band model of a Sopwith Camel World War I airplane. I buy a waffle iron for the family, and an electronic game of Battleship for Ben. We'll leave the waffle iron at the mill where there's always time for leisurely breakfasts. I find an easy-to-operate Polaroid camera for Lor and buy two packs of film. I buy some holders and candles for the Christmas tree.

I've arranged with a painter friend in Paris to paint portraits of the girls. He's good, they're the right age to be painted and he could use the money; a triple-threat Christmas present.

Ever since the girls reached thirteen, I've had no chance at all of buying them a present they like. Buying any clothing is catastrophic, witness the orange raincoat I bought Maggie for her fifteenth birthday, the knee-length boots for Nicole on her fourteenth Christmas. Apparently I'm the same problem for them. I'd hate to be buying anything for me, I can't think of one thing I want; at least anything someone could buy. Nobody can buy time, or love, or understanding. They're too perishable, difficult to transport.

We congregate at the car. Even Ben's bought a few things so we're almost as packed as *I* was coming down from Paris. Loretta climbs in the back seat and we pile packages on her; Ben with his long legs can't fit back there and Lor's afraid of the suicide seat in a car.

When we turn off the main Nevers road into the back country it's past four o'clock, darkness is coming on and although the fields and trees around us are still covered with snow, the narrow roads are relatively clear. I switch up to my high beams, not because it's that dark yet, but to compensate for my lack of horn going around curves. The local driver in this area still thinks he's the only automobile within fifty kilometers and hogs the crown of the road. Death by *deux chevaux* is far more common than impalement by wild boar around here.

We happily come down the icy Vauchot hill and pull up in front of our place. The mill is unique in that it's built *into* the dam forming the pond; this road on which we're arriving is about fifteen feet below dam level. The grange-cum-garage and the cellar open onto the road. The portion of the mill we've converted for living, where I've spent the past three days hustling, trying to get it into living order, opens onto the *top* of the dam. Our door up there is only ten feet from the pond itself, practically level with it.

We start unloading. Ben helps me untie our mini–Christmas tree. I delay putting our car in the grange so I can be inside the mill when they first see all my refurbishments, drapes, rehung cabinets, general cleanup, holly, pine boughs, decorations.

Loretta and Ben walk around to the damside door with some of the provisions. I dash through the cellar, up those steps through our hingeless trap door, into the main room. I turn on the lights, put a match to my preset fire and turn up the new butane heater before they arrive. I open the damside door from the inside and step back without comment.

Ben moves to his guns which I've hung beside the fireplace.

Lor is wonderfully appreciative; makes it all worthwhile, remarks on the drapes, the clean windows, "even in the dark they glisten." She exclaims over the decorations, comments on the general order and cleanliness. I was lucky enough to marry a woman who has good nesting feelings. But I still have the uneasy feeling she's only going through the motions, play-acting, pretending, trying to make me happy. I hope I can hold onto her somehow. I hate to think of life without her.

The fire took on perfectly with one match and isn't smoking. Lor even notices I cleared out those damned ashes.

Ben and I haul the rest of our things from the car while Loretta puts them away. I make my mad, sliding run through the snow and slushy mud, maneuvering our car into the garage without hitting any motorcycles or motorcycle gas tanks, carburetors, extra wheels or rusting tools. I manage to match and close the interlocking device securing the big doors, wiggle through the small door and miss the greater part of the mud. On my way through the cellar, I gather an armful of dry tinder to start our fire next morning.

It's a strong, good feeling having the nucleus of our family together again. Stone walls, heavy wooden beams, even a glowing fire, a shimmering pond and a splashing waterfall, can never replace or compensate for feelings of love and loving. I know my sleep tonight will be different than it's been these past three nights. When I sleep alone, I sleep deeply, dreamlessly; the night

seems to just disappear. Sleeping with Lor, I dream, I wake for brief periods. I know I'm sleeping and I don't feel alone.

After dinner, we light the red candles in a silver candle holder I found and shined. They look beautiful on top of our new red remnant tablecloth. Lor and I sing Christmas carols; Ben listens. I've jammed the small Nevers tree into the center hole to one of the reserve millstones. This stone is flat on the floor just to the left of the door as you come in from the dam. Once there were two stones in that place, one on top of the other; but I moved the upper stone as a base for our fireplace.

It took three automobile jacks, two levels, several inclined planes and half a heart attack moving that stone against the wall, then constructing our fireplace on it. The fireplace is heavy, more or less squared-off stone, rounded, projecting into the room, sort of a Dutch oven, with a throat resembling the entrance to a cave.

The smell of the fire, our mini-tree, the pine boughs, burning candles fills everything. The second night of Christmas is upon us. And I still don't know what to do. I've got to tell Lor, it isn't fair to just let it go on like this.

Later, when we're tucked in bed listening to the roar of the waterfall from the pond, the crackling of our fire, the deep breathing of Ben sleeping on a cot in front of the fire, Lor does her usual just-before-going-to-sleep "sigh" and says "I guess we'll hear from the girls tomorrow; they should be in Paris today."

I think to myself that in less than an hour Ben will be fifteen. It won't be long before we'll be having all our Christmases alone, if we're lucky enough to stay together. Right then, for the first time, I realize I've lived with Lor almost twice as long as I've lived with anybody else in my life. Since my parents are dead, and I'm an only child, I've known her longer than anybody else. She's the closest thing to a "reality" I know.

The day after Christmas will be our thirtieth anniversary.

Next morning, while we're having breakfast, Madame Le Moine peers into the damside door and knocks. She's come all the way around up onto the dam and down our narrow, slippery, stone steps. I'd made arrangements for her to get the number if anyone phoned and tie a dish towel on her door handle. I can see her door easily from our west window and I've been checking regularly for it the past few days.

Madame Le Moine recently celebrated her eightieth birthday. Five months ago, she had a stroke which left her partially paralyzed and with failing memory. She's almost completely recovered now, but definitely shouldn't be running around delivering phone messages in this mud and snow.

We're bullheaded about not having a phone. We dislike the invasion of privacy a phone, a TV or a radio allows. We were the first to have a toilet but are now the only ones without a TV, a phone or a radio. We've given Madame Le Moine's phone number exclusively to our kids and a few friends. I know it has to be one of ten people when Madame Le Moine stutters out— "Tell-ey-phon."

I invite her in. Loretta skims along the dam to Madame Le Moine's house. It almost has to be Nicole just as Nicole knows it's Lor who will answer. I could go into my aversion to answering phones here, but I won't. I think it has to do with voices from anywhere out of nowhere.

I seat Madame Le Moine in the rocker before the fireplace beside our miniature tree. I give her a cup of tea with two lumps of sugar, whip out my cuff and take her blood pressure. Madame Le Moine is rocking and smiling.

Lor introduced tea into this village. Before we arrived, it was coffee, strong, or, *un canon*, a glass of wine, also strong, or *naöle*, super-strong one-hundred-proof alcohol made from fallen fruit; a regional version of marc de Bourgogne.

When the villagers did get hooked on tea, only the women, I should say: that is, Madame Calvet, Madame Le Moine and Madame Rousseau; Lor was shocked to find they were pouring her Christmas gifts of Twining's Earl Grey breakfast tea into the

bottom of a teakettle, and *boiling* it. They'd all be dead in a few years from tannic acid poisoning.

After that, Lor initiated the village women into the entire routine: start with cold water, stop just as it comes to boil, rinse out pot with hot water, dry pot, the correct amount of tea, three minutes steeping. She's even got them drinking it straight, without sugar or cream, something she hasn't even seduced me to, a very seductive woman in many ways, but not *that* seductive. Next thing she'll have them knitting tea cozies.

My contribution to the village, besides toilets and septic tanks, has been "blood pressure." Every day, whenever we're here, I have informal morning clinic, taking blood pressure, pulse, listening to old hearts rattling along behind shriveled titties. Once in a while, one of the men, Pierre Rousseau, Claude or Philippe will sit for me. I think they feel it's good for them, healing; therapeutic blood-pressure measuring.

Madame Le Moine is convinced she wouldn't have had her stroke if I'd been around that summer instead of off in America. I do feel somewhat guilty.

Whenever she'd be more than eighteen over ten (the French measure in centimeters not millimeters) I'd pop her with a five-milligram Valium and a diuretic. It'd usually bring things around in a day or two. It'd also bring around other things; eggs, a fresh-killed rabbit, lettuce, potatoes, tomatoes, string beans. It's hardly worth our running a garden. Pumping a rubber blood pressure machine bulb's a hell of a lot easier than hoeing hard earth and hauling water.

I roll down Madame Le Moine's sleeve, give her the good news— *dix-sept sur huit*, 170 over 80 (maybe the stroke helped), look up and see Lor come smiling through the door, humming and singing.

Anyone who didn't know Lor, would assume she is the bearer of good tidings. After years of experience I'm reserving judgment. Loretta could interrupt a little song to announce the fall of Rome, the death of the president, the onset of terminal cancer or the end of a marriage. She tends to sing when she's scared, depressed or confused, to buck up flagging emotions. The trouble is, she *also* sings, hums, skips when she's *happy* about something. It can be very disconcerting. It's *skipping* which gives the real clue; she came down those stairs rather light-footedly for a woman in her late forties, so I'm not expecting the worst.

"It was Nicole. They're all fine. But Nicole's luggage got lost in the transfer at Frankfurt so they won't be down until tomorrow morning."

I'm sorry they won't be here for Ben's birthday but perhaps it's better this way. We can give all our attention to him.

Actually, at the functional level, Ben is an only child, he has practically no remembrance of the other kids living at home. They're more in the order of distant aunts or uncles.

It's tough for Ben having his birthday jammed up so hard against Christmas, especially with our anniversary the day after.

Also, it's good they'll be late because I want to varnish; I feel a strong varnish mania coming on. I varnish the way some people clean out garages or attics, wash cars or windows, shine shoes or silverware. It's a way to smooth life, straighten raging emotions out when I'm mixed up.

And I know I'm really confused. Right up to lately, I thought I was handling things okay, that it was going to be all right, but now I'm not so sure.

I keep telling myself it's only because I don't want to hurt Lor. But it's more than that. I don't even want to think what my life would be like without her.

At bottom, I'm very selfish. I'm afraid of the words, the words that will be said. I know they can never be taken back. I'm not sure I can trust myself and I don't really know what Lor has on her mind, what she's thinking.

Something in me just doesn't want to close in on the reality of what's happening. I hate to think of myself as a coward but I guess I am. Lor seems to be taking all this so much more easily than I; I'm sure she's suffering, it's more than I can bear, just watching her. It would be so much better if she'd bring it out, talk about things with me. That's more the way she usually is. I'm the one who's usually evasive, who can't bite the bullet, or whatever you're supposed to do.

I pry open the lid on the varnish can. The thick, virtually clear varnish is like concentrated glass. I'll be spreading it, making the surfaces seem permanently wet, as if it were all new, not old and crumbling.

I sweep and clear out the area by our beds and the wash table. I begin brushing away. The varnish sinks into the dull, dry, roughened wood and brings out the warm colors, the natural grain. My soul glows again; I stroke with the length of the boards, long even sweeps.

I'll only be doing a portion of the floor at a time. This is a fast-drying varnish; I might finish in one day.

As I carefully brush varnish into the corners, I realize varnishing is much like my personal ethic and aesthetic. It's a way of taking what's there, or seems to be there, and making it more visible. I don't know how this fits into the Camus theme of "cherish your illusions," but somehow I feel it does, in an American sort of way. I'm protecting the surface of things, preserving; at the same time making things look better than they really are. That can't be all bad, can it?

I work my way around the room in bliss. I varnish the ragged dish cupboard I built a dozen years ago from wood salvaged while tearing down an old shed beside the mill. I varnish our bread holder, the barometer, the millstone boom. Long ago it was used to lift and move the millstones, and is now supporting a suspended five-light chandelier.

I do the mantel over our fireplace. I varnish the huge table we built across the original millstones, still in place. I varnish our food cabinet; the door to the upper grange and, of course, all the floor; putting down planks so we can go from one part of the room to the other. I'm varnishing one of the supporting beams when Ben taps me on the shoulder.

"Hey, Dad, look here, you forgot the firewood."

That does it. The knot in my psyche is loosened up a little;

also I've run out of varnish. We'll have one half-shiny beam for Christmas.

Now, the mill smells like one of the ateliers around our place in Paris, where they fake original Louis Quinze and Louis Seize furniture.

After we eat lunch we give Ben his airplane. He's thrilled. Together, we get it constructed by three o'clock. He says he wants his birthday dinner at Madame Le Page's, the local restaurant up on the hill, but his dessert must be a real mother-baked cake down here in the mill. His preference for the main dish, if it's possible, is *pintade*, French guinea hen. Lor goes across to Madame Le Moine's to phone and see if it's possible. She comes back smiling, humming, singing and *skipping* so I don't even ask.

"They're also going to have french fries and *jambon du Morvan* for him. Madame Le Page is so considerate."

Ben and I are up on Maggie's hill adjusting angles of wings, turning ailerons and finger-winding the rubber-band-driven propeller, when Monsieur Boudine comes along the path up to us.

Actually, at that moment, I'm on a ladder trying to detach Ben's airplane carefully from the high branches of an oak tree. As a result of bitter experience we always have a ladder and long stick up there with us. The stick has a forked V on the end of it to push gently up under the airplane and dislodge it. Trying to shake a fragile model plane out of a tree or pull it down through the branches can have disastrous effects.

In summer, we design and build our own, both gliders and power-driven. We've experimented with motor-driven planes, free-flight and U-control, but the noise, the smell of the gasoline, the thrust and speed of the machines weren't what we wanted; our planes must be as much like birds as possible.

I'm up on our ladder with the stick, nudging the plane loose when Monsieur Boudine arrives. Ben is afraid of heights, so the really high hang-ups are usually for me. Finally I get just the right leverage and the plane comes fluttering down. Ben starts to run after it.

"Wait a minute, Ben; let me down off this ladder first."

Ben's been holding the foot of our ladder so it won't slip from the tree crotch where it's wedged. I'm not too crazy about heights myself. I jump the last two rungs, walk over and shake hands with Monsieur Boudine.

I'm always uncomfortable with this man. Loretta is afraid of him and I understand why. There's something wild there, something untamed, a slyness, secretiveness like a hunting animal. Loretta told me once he's the archetype of what all women fear in all men, a genealogical throwback to a maleness which can't be conditioned to society.

His family lives in the next village. He's fathered nine children; seven girls and two sons. One of the sons, a really likable boy, would, every summer, give Ben and other children of the village, rides in an old-fashioned donkey cart. His name was Thierry but he was killed six months ago in a motorcycle accident.

When I first contacted Monsieur Boudine about our Christmas tree, I tried commiserating with him. The worst thing in the world I can think of is outliving any of our children. It's ten times worse than what's probably about to happen to us now.

Monsieur Boudine lifted his hat, a weather-beaten old-time brown felt hat with a light part where there was once a silk band. He wears it brim down, all the way round, so you can scarcely see his soft, deep-sunken, yellow-brown eyes. It's as if he's perpetually protecting himself from either the sun or a rainstorm.

He ran his hand over his full head of wavy gray hair and shook his head once, the way Pom Pom, his donkey, would shake off a single fly in his eye. Sometimes I think Monsieur Boudine's feeble-minded, a fecund throwback of some kind. Lor might be right, she usually is. This head shake was his only response.

Mike claims Monsieur Boudine's the original nature boy, knows every bush, tree, root, mushroom along all the paths through all the woods in the area. He spends entire days tromping alone through deserted countryside.

At this point, I can see Monsieur Boudine might know his plants, but he doesn't have much idea what a Christmas tree's all about. He's dragging behind him a two-foot-high spindly pine spine that wouldn't make a proper table ornament. He's all smiles, for him. Most times his face is set in a passive, resistant mope, like a mule. He and Pom Pom are a natural pair.

I take the Christmas tree branch and try to act enthusiastic; Ben has turned away in total disgust. I try to give him some money but he declines because Pom Pom uses our fields. *Uses* is right. He ate the only sweet corn crop I've ever been able to grow and nibbled to bare sticks three young apple trees, two peach trees, an apricot and a cherry tree.

I take his olive branch of a tip to a pine tree. After all it is Christmas. But my mind is racing. Where can I get a genuine eight-to-ten-foot Christmas tree at this last moment? Can I con poor Ben on his birthday eve into a treenapping? It doesn't seem fair, also he's deathly afraid of the dark.

But, can I present a bush, a branch, a twig, as Christmas tree to our two daughters after transporting them six thousand miles, away from California and Arizona sunshine, their parties, their friends, their comfort and ease; dragging them unwillingly into this cold, winter-dark, lonesome valley in a stone-hard, wood-heavy, primitive mill beside a pond?

Something must be done! Monsieur Boudine clumps off into the woods, self-satisfied with his gift. I decide tonight's the night and it's probably best if I do it alone.

We are about a thousand feet above sea level here in the Morvan. About two-thirds of the hardwood forests, birch, ash, beech, has been cleared for pasturage; the rest, in steeper, less accessible sections, has been left intact. Formerly these woods were used as a source of wood for burning. Now, however, most of the people in the valley have shifted to oil for heat, very few still burn wood, even in the kitchen stove.

Recently, entrepreneurs, mostly Parisians, have been buying up the woods, bulldozing out the hardwood, selling it off to paper mills, or as firewood, then planting these woods with Douglas fir for Christmas trees. This had been going on for over fifteen years now.

Five years ago, to protect the area from this and other depredations, one of the first large parks in France was established. Le Parc Régionale du Morvan. Our mill is just included on the western edge. West of us, the forests are still being massacred. Young pines, five to ten years old, abound. The Morvan is becoming known as the Christmas-tree capital of France.

I've decided to snitch my tree from one of the Christmas-tree farms outside the protected park. I've worked up a whole rationale to defend my action; however, I don't think it would hold in a French court.

But I'm desperate.

When I show our Monsieur Boudine "Christmas Tree" to Lor she's as disgusted as Ben and I are. Already we'd decided to trim our wings from the usual fourteen-foot monster we've always had jammed in the corner on the *right* side of the fireplace. It was impossible to trim, blocked the food cabinet, and overlapped the steps up to the toilet. This year we'll have a smaller tree, maybe ten feet, and set it in the millstone on the other side. Right now, we're not even close to ten feet.

Loretta says she'll drive into Château Chinon and look for a tree. She also has some shopping to do. Fat chance, the French idea of a *large* tree almost reaches the navel. While she's gone, Ben and I get out the decorations, wipe off the balls; unwind garlands, untangle electric lights. We're preparing to decorate a giant tree no matter what. Irrational persistence can be a powerful force.

We also clean off and set up our crèche on the sill of the west window. I string one set of lights around it. Ben goes out to gather moss from trees and rocks for the inside and roof of the stable.

What we're doing doesn't have much to do with religion in a Christian sense. We're playing dolls, acting out our husbanding, parenting impulse, making sure *that* baby is cozy and warm, surrounded by father and mother, warm breathing animals, the steam of urine and manure-soaked hay giving off the heat of fermentation. We live with it, this is not too far removed from the life all around us here.

When Lor comes back, no singing, humming; no skipping. No tree. There wasn't a tree over three feet tall in the whole town. She says she almost stopped and gnawed down a tree beaver-style on the way home. I tell her I'm going out tonight to liberate a tree for us. She isn't fighting me too hard. Loretta for all her seeming airs of gentility is a practical, pragmatic person when the going gets tough. It's what makes her an effective first-grade teacher. It would also make her a good president or chairman of the Ford Motor Company.

That night we walk up to Madame Le Page's for Ben's dinner. It's dark as it was when I went out to cut pine branches. All the better. On the way out from the mill our thermometer shows three degrees and there's moisture in the air. I tell Ben it could easily snow again. He wants snow more than anything else for Christmas. I'm hoping it will hold off till the girls get down here. They're driving our *other* car, a 1969 Ford Capri. This wreck makes my failing Fiat seem like a new Cadillac.

The meal is terrific; the *pintade* cooked perfectly. Ben has an entire liter of lemonade to himself while Loretta and I splurge with a 1976 Pouilly Fumé. The dining room is all ours; heads of deer, *sanglier* mounted around us. The restaurant is called La Fin de la Chasse and its main clientele are local hunters.

We walk down in the overwhelming dark and get home at about nine o'clock. I push the wood around in our fire to get it burning again, throw in another log, slip on my boots and prepare myself for the great adventure. Ben knows what I'm about to do but doesn't volunteer. I don't press; who wants to spend the evening of his fifteenth birthday in a French jail, and besides he'd probably spook me with *his* jumpiness. *I'm* bad enough, myself. With Ben along we'd probably wind up jumping into each other's laps simultaneously.

I take our car key from the nail over the mantel, pick up a flashlight, let myself down into our cellar through the trap door, grab the saw from where I've hung it over the wood pile. I go out the door and slush my way through mud to open the door into our garage.

This time I wouldn't mind too much if the car doesn't turn over; but that engine has its ear tuned directly to the starter motor and coughs into life on the second try. The engine has become as easy to arouse as a nymphomaniac. But how would I know? My sexual experience so far indicates that even a certified nymph would just ho-hum me into insignificance. But I can get that Fiat going now, maybe it's a good sign of things to come. That's an accidental joke.

I get out to open the big doors, hoping the motor will conk while I'm doing this, but it keeps humming away. I back out slowly, maybe I'll get stuck in the mud but those tires grip like tractor wheels. All the omens say I'm in for it.

I drive up through Vauchot and out toward Corbeau. Five miles along I turn toward Monçaron. On my left looms a young pine forest, trees planted about two feet apart, mostly only about twice the size of the tree we already have, but several approach my ideal. I turn down the car lights to just parking indicators. It's dark. I can scarcely see the road. I shut off my motor and coast the last fifty yards or so. This is a road with practically no traffic. Just ahead is a bridge so narrow *one* car can barely pass over it.

I sit there in the dark. I roll down both windows and listen; nothing but wind in the trees, the dripping of water from branches,

and, now and then, the mew of a night hawk or the *whoo-whoo*
of an owl. Maybe we should just use that Nevers tree, tie Monsieur Boudine's tree to the top for extra height.

I reach back and get the saw. I let myself quietly out the car
door, gently easing it closed.

I have Ben's flashlight in one hand. It's still so dark I can't
see anything. I'll need to do everything by feel. I stumble, creep,
crawl, crouch, my way off the road between trees. I try not to
step on the smaller ones, while feeling left and right for high
trees, higher than my head. I can't be sure of anything.

I stop and listen. Would anybody actually be hiding in these
woods in this wetness, in the dark, just to stop a failed philosopher
from snitching a tree? I believe it! But I've *got* to flash my light.
I should have come out earlier and marked a tree as usual but
with that damned Monsieur Boudine and his branch there wasn't
time.

I put my hand over the flashlight so just a beam escapes
through my fingers. I spin slowly around, carefully scanning for
a proper tree. I see one, just the right size, and bushy, twenty
yards to the right. I switch off my light, expecting a voice from
the dark, or the sound and feel of buckshot. I work my way over,
doing the last ten yards on all fours. I hand gauge the thickness
of the trunk, give one quick flash to make sure. It's the right
one, over ten feet tall. I scrape and clear away pine needles, dirt
from the base of the tree, till I'm below ground level. When I'm
finished cutting, I'll spread dirt, pine needles, leaves over the
ground-level stump, expert testimony to years of experience in
knavery.

I pull out my saw, then lie on my back quietly, listening,
looking up into the gloomy night. There's nothing to be heard
but those hawks, owls and the wind. I start sawing. It's soft pine
and not more than four inches in diameter; I saw through in less
than a minute. Nothing like when we took down the last one, a
veritable ship's mast. That time, Mike and I took turns cutting
and leaning back on the tree to keep our saw from binding. We
were definitely pushing our luck. When we got home, Mike,

vehemently, almost in tears, swore he'd never go treenapping at Christmas again.

As the tree starts to wobble, I steady it with my left hand and take the last two strokes one-handed. It falls over easily—right onto me. I lie back and smell greenness, feel cold drops of water, ice and snow drip onto my face. I'm totally sweated up, not so much from exertion, from nervousness. I'm also experiencing a sudden, deep sense of depression. Why am I here, what fear of life drives me on with this ritualistic fantasy? Where did I lose contact with reality as others perceive it? What can I do to make things right or, at least, learn some tolerance when they seem wrong to me? I drift back to my real situation under the tree. I'm trying not to cry.

I'm not even sure just which way it is to the road. I think it's slightly downhill but I'm not positive. I can't make out anything in the dark. How am I going to stuff this monster tree into my tiny car and drive home without anyone seeing me? I'll take the back roads, past where Mike's Geneviève and her family have their home.

I start crawling through the small trees, dragging my tree behind me like Little Bo Peep's sheep's tails. I flash my light once to make sure I'm going downhill. I'm totally lost and am convinced I'm going deeper into the forest.

Finally, I feel a strong decline and know I'm coming onto a road, some road at least. But the car isn't there! I must've come out at a different angle from the one I went in. I can't imagine anybody stealing that car without my hearing them start the motor. Yes, right, I even have *that* thought. I might be the world's biggest worrier, the least effective one too. Or maybe I don't worry enough. I know Lor is convinced I don't pay enough attention to things; I probably don't.

Is the car to the left or right? Is it even on *this* road? I peer into darkness. I stash my tree in a ditch. It's most likely getting smeared with mud but I'll wash it off later.

I peer and think I can make out a dim shape to my right. I walk along the road in that direction till I'm sure it is the car.

Then I come back for my tree. I can't find *it*. Right here is when I make my final decision never to go in for bank robbery, or murder, or anything serious.

But, I do finally find the tree, a bulge in the ditch, without flashing my light. I drag it and the saw behind me in a low crouching rush to the car. Now I'm vulnerable. If a car comes along, or anybody turns a flash on me, there's no excuse I can think of for being out here running to my car along a road with a fresh-cut tree in one hand and a saw in the other.

I have no rope for tying this tree onto the car roof; that's my kind of careful planning. I open the offside door and push the butt of my tree back in; over the seats, as far as I can into the back. I bend the top of the tree so it sticks out through the window and I can close the door. I carefully squeeze all the branches in, then ease the door shut. I lean the door tight closed and the inside floor light of the car goes out. I'm in the dark again.

By feel, I know the tip of the tree sticks out three feet past the windshield. I start edging around the other side to get in; I trip over my saw where I've left it leaning against the car. If I hadn't tripped over it, I'd have left it there, driven off without it. Two wrongs do sometimes make a right, like negative numbers in algebra; that is, if stealing a Christmas tree can ever be considered a right.

I start the car, no problem, thank God, or whomever. I drive a hundred meters with just my parking lights on, then turn up my highs before I get to the narrow bridge. Now I'm away from the scene of the crime. I'll just *blind* anybody who gets in the way with my highs. Ruthless, that I'll be.

I cross the bridge, turn off onto the back roads, only slightly more than paths; twist, turn, up and down through what we used to call the enchanted forest, a veritable fairyland of ancient, hoary, moss-covered oaks, now a barren wasteland of three- or four-year-old Christmas trees. The shutters at Geneviève's house are closed as I go by; but the grange door is open and some light seems to be coming from one shutter. Geneviève's mother must be there, it's going to be a tough Christmas for her. I just don't have the guts to do what she did; I hope Lor doesn't either. Maybe continuity means too much to me. I'm too inertial, not courageous, creative. It explains a lot.

I speed by and promise myself I'll walk over the hill soon to wish her a Merry Christmas. I power my way in first gear up to Vauchot. There's almost no snow on the road but some places are icy. I stay in first and glide down those last two kilometers to the mill. I've left the grange doors open; I'll swing the car straight on in.

I get into town without seeing anyone. I twist and slither through mud into the grange; stop, turn off the motor, turn out the lights and sit a moment, quiet in the dark, giving my blood pressure a chance to arrange itself.

Then I get out, close the grange doors. Using my flashlight, I wend my way through motorcycles past and present, to the other side of the car, open the door; free the top of my tree from the window, and carefully work the bushy part from inside the car. I stomp the stump on the grange floor, holding it by the middle.

I open the little door-in-a-door to see if anybody's out in the street. No one. I skip over the sill, through the mud, clutching the tree under my arm like a bride. I get through the cellar door and start pushing the tree backward up our steps ahead of me. I don't want to break any branches going through the trap door. Lor holds the trap and pulls the lower end of our tree; helping me through. I come along behind and take it from her; the pillaging, rampaging, returned, conquering hero; crumpled, dripping, bristled, tousled, white hair in a flying mane.

I lift that mini-Nevers tree from the millstone, push it out the damside door onto our porch, then jam my newly cut tree into the millstone hole. It fits perfectly, tightly, stands straight up, buttoned-top tip almost touching the log ceiling under the loft; branches, glistening wet, spread to fill the space. It's not too bushy and hasn't a bare part; somehow there's no mud either.

Ben stares, he flashes his pulled-together squint which serves for a smile.

"Now that's a *real* Christmas tree, Dad. It makes me want to believe in Santa Claus again."

Lor puts her arm around me, gives me a hard hug.

"It's okay with us if you want to, Ben, there probably *is* anyhow you know, just ask your father; he's the expert."

"No, I don't think I could do it any more, it's too hard. People don't really want fifteen-year-old boys to keep believing in things like Santa Claus. It isn't fitting."

Lor pours me a small glass of Poire William. We light the candles on our table and turn off all the other lights. There's only a glow from the two butane heaters and the light from our fireplace. It's warm enough so we don't need the electric heaters any more. Our inside thermometer on the newly varnished barometer says twenty degrees. The outside thermometer registers two above, still snow temperature. In my varnishing mania, I varnished the plastic match holder by the sink, including the striking surface on one side, so now we have a hard time striking matches. But we do get the candles lit.

Slowly, softly, Lor and I begin singing Christmas carols. Ben hums along with us. He has a deep melodious voice, perfect pitch, but it's the first time he's actually joined with us in singing. Only last year, he would've quietly absented himself, going out in the grange, or for a walk. Ben has a horror, an intense dislike for overt performance. It's a feeling I understand, appreciate. There's something sad, hard to be around, when people perform in a desperate attempt to prove that they *are*. I often cry at concerts or in a theater. It has nothing to do with the music or the play. I'm feeling sorry for the musicians, the actors, all those for whom that public performance of private fantasy is a way of life.

The temptation is strong to comment, congratulate, thank Ben for his participation on these, the last moments of his fifteenth birthday. But I don't, it would be a violation. *Not* doing those things is most of what I'm trying to learn. I seem to lack a certain sensitivity, respect, for the inner needs of others; Lor always seems to know just what to do. It might be a part of what makes me a piss-poor philosopher and her an outstanding first-grade teacher. She almost always seems to do the right thing without trying.

We continue through the carols, very low-key, whispering, and I'm surprised how many of the words Ben knows, as he begins to sing with us; convinced it isn't a competition or a command performance, but a mutual expression of good will. The tree stands mute, deep, dark green, mysterious; our representative from the great outdoors; an unwilling martyr to our desire for expression of oneness with the world, with all living things.

I feel calm inside. I resolve to hold tight the promise I made Loretta and keep my mouth shut when our daughters start working their thing off. Both our girls are heavily committed to the emancipation of womankind. Brothers and fathers are automatically guilty and are expected to absorb the brunt of the assault. Assault I can usually handle but directed insult triggers me if I'm not careful. The problem is, after twenty-five years of philosophical nit-picking, I'm a veritable demon at dispute, and it's frustrating for the girls, especially Nicole.

This is what happened two Christmases ago in California. Loretta walked away and went to bed, she refuses to let herself get involved in nonproductive, noncommunicative conflict situations. I wish I could be so smart, I think it's the contentious Irish in me. Nicole gets especially hostile after she's had too much white wine. She's so much like Nora, Loretta's late sister, it can be frightening.

That Christmas, Nicole started insisting we'd "fucked up" her life. I guess all parents are shocked, concerned when one of their children comes to feel this. But having evolved from difficult backgrounds ourselves, Lor and I'd convinced each other we'd honestly tried not to do just that. It's so hard to show love, especially when you really love, respect and admire the loved one. It's almost as if they *want* you to violate them, force them to behave by some standard of your own not related to their desires. Maybe they want a chance to manifest their love for you by submission. I don't know. It's beyond me.

So, there, in the pleasant dark, I reaffirm my determination to listen, not to be provoked, to make the most of this which, I'm convinced, will be our last Christmas together. I feel a pang again because Mike won't make it, but then again, we can't have everything.

Before going to bed, I heat some water and scrub myself thoroughly in the washbowl. I stink from nervous perspiration and it'd be no fun for Lor sleeping beside someone who smells like an escapee from a metro or a zoo. I even shave. Ben sets up his bed before the fire, then when everybody's settled in, I blow out the candles and crawl into bed.

As I'm going off to sleep, wrapped close to Loretta's back, I think again what a big mistake our species made when we started building houses with sleeping, eating, cooking, washing, all separated into different compartments. Virtually everybody in this village lives as we do, in one room. It's surprising how comforting this can be. I won't try to defend that one with the girls. There's no reason to.

I wake at about seven thirty for a pressing morning piss. I don't usually take a diuretic before sleeping, but last night I did, along with my usual Valium. I could feel signs of elevated blood pressure, a slight tightness under my left arm, a throbbing in the temples.

Two good things came of my medicating. One, I got up twice during the night and each time threw a good-sized log on the fire to keep it going, so now it's burning merrily. Starting a new fire in the ashes on a freezing morning with cold, damp wood, is not my idea of a great way to begin a winter day.

I let my eyes drift around the room, enjoying peace and the coming dawn.

The second good thing is the blood pressure is down and I'm feeling very content, undisturbed inside, in tune with the world.

I run through again what has to be done, as I see it, and my only concern is for Lor. But it's a concern, not an anxiety.

For me, Christmas Eve day is even more important, more exciting, than Christmas Day itself. The sense of anticipation, of expectant readiness, is magic. I hear, feel, Lor breathing beside me. Ben is stretched out, overlapping his cot by the fire, arms hanging over the sides. He sleeps deeply, calmly, no tossing, no teeth grinding, no startled nightmares, no thumb or finger sucking. We like to think it's because we never let him cry himself to sleep, never left him alone in the dark when he wanted to be with us. Until he was seven, he spent at least half of each night in our bed, usually cuddling with me. I didn't mind, I liked it; I don't think sleeping alone is natural. With our first three we were young and foolish enough, vulnerable to rigid conditioning theories then prevalent, to insist they stay in their own beds, so now each is an erratic sleeper. I myself only became capable of deep, full, refreshing sleep when I was about forty. I can't always manage it, now, even with meditation or Valium, but then things have been hard lately.

The skylights in the ceiling are beginning to lighten. It almost looks like blue sky, clear, behind tree branches hanging over our roof. The room is starting to quicken with light.

I ease myself out of bed, slide my feet into cool slippers, adjust for the failing clasp on my pajamas, turn the butane heater up to high, fill the tea kettle with water. I love filling this kettle through the spout, might even be a sexual thing, some compensation for my failure as a lover to my loved one.

I light the stove and put on water for washing. I sneak past Ben, turn over the log burning in the fire and jam another log next to it. I check the inside temperature, fourteen Celsius, we should have that back up to twenty within the next hour. I go to the door and pull back my thick red drapes so I can look at the outside thermometer.

I'm startled by a white, just lightening sky over the frosted trees, blending to a fragile, transparent white-blue overhead. I'm transfixed in wonder.

I break my eyes away enough to look at the outside thermometer through the frosted window. Twenty-two degrees *below* freezing. The sun still hasn't risen. I'm torn between waking Lor and
Ben or enjoying this special moment to myself. They'll be up
late tonight with the Reveillon at Madame Calvet's, plus all the
excitement of the girls arriving; they need their sleep, so I take
the selfish decision.

I dress quietly, turn off the stove under the hot water, slip on
boots, jacket, gloves, wool knit cap. I carefully open the door,
let myself out, then pull firmly so it latches behind me.

I look left and there is magnificent ice sculpture from the falls.
Every splash, every flowing current is frozen in twisting glossy
forms like transparent, clear toy candy. The ivy growing along
the sides of the sluice gate is wrapped in ice, inches thick, drooping gracefully with the weight of each leaf captured green in
transparent ice cages. There are giant icicles, four feet long, three
inches thick hanging from the stone, temporary stalactites. I walk
across the frozen, ice-creaking wooden porch, up the slippery
steps onto the dam to look out over the pond.

It's frozen absolutely clear without a ripple. If you didn't know
it was winter, if there were green leaves to reflect on its perfectly
calm surface, you'd think it was five thirty in the morning of a
June dawn; halfway around the calendar from now.

The glow of the sun is still hidden by the eastern edge of our
valley-bowl. There are no clouds. It's so empty, one could easily
wonder if there ever had been, ever would be a breath, a breeze
again.

I do my usual thing, the summer ritual, standing on tiptoe,
reaching up high as I can, pulling myself out of myself, trying
to let some of that glorious empty sky come into me. In the
interest of my sleeping family and the neighbors, I repress the
desire for a grunting howl.

With one boot toe I kick loose three small, flat stones from
the dam surface, two smooth, one ragged. I pick them up; they
feel like ice even through my leather gloves. The first, the ragged

one, I throw full-force directly down at the ice. I'm standing now on the small wooden platform from which, in summers, I slip quietly into the water for my after-run-before-breakfast swim.

Those summer mornings, I slide in quietly so as not to disturb the fishermen halfway around the pond. This morning, the platform glistens with ice crystals, but doesn't seem slippery under my boots. The stone glances from the ice, making a small crazed dent, then bounces and skims another thirty or forty feet. The entire pond surface screeches and echoes from edge to edge, hallowed, hollow, deep-throated. A scientist friend told me once how the crackling howling sound is due to ice cracking along the surface faster than the speed of sound, so it causes a mini-sonic boom. That's hard to believe, but it *is* a magic sound.

Holding onto an overhanging tree branch, I ease one foot over the edge from my platform to test the ice. It cracks slightly, the cracks spread crazily in all directions away from my toe. The ice appears to be about an inch or so thick. I take one of the smooth stones, cock my arm and skim it underhand across the incredibly water-clear ice. It bounces, slides; almost without friction, seemingly endlessly, accompanied by echoing reverberations of the ice. It continues; until, almost out of sight, it enters the cattails, marshland and reeds at the far end of the pond, then stops against one of the domed muskrat dens out there.

I'm about ready to skim the last stone, feeling it icy cold, smooth, sucking heat through my gloves, when the sun begins to glow white fire over the eastern edge of our valley. It shines almost pure white, like a communion wafer painted by a Spanish eighteenth-century painter.

This is time, happening. I can feel it passing through me. When one thinks about time, and I do too much; it's part of what makes me a philosopher I guess; but when one thinks about it, it's the most mysterious phenomenon we know.

We try to define it with clocks and calendars which are, more or less, based on movements of sun, earth and moon, but that's only measuring. All we can really guess about time is it's probably related to space and matter, whatever they are. If space and matter just became, it's when time began. But time can't begin because "begin" is a time word, beginning-ending.

But this sun seeming to come over those hills, time or not, is practically pure light, cutting through ninety-three million miles, the source of virtually all earth's energy.

I feel it already warm on my cold face before it's halfway over the hill. It lights my soul. I put the last stone back in my pocket, take off my gloves, allowing my hands to be healed by these magic rays. I close my eyes, face the sun directly. I can feel, see, the red insides of my eyelids, lighten; redden; warm with the blush of life. I want to hold my breath or sing; dance; something, some way to say thanks.

Instead I put my gloves back on; open my eyes and watch till the sun is finally detached from the earth, free-floating, a heavenly body again, giving us all for nothing. I vow to express my thanks by showing love for my loved ones. I wish I could somehow transmit to Lor, to the kids, my intense joy in them, the way they are. But dumb events, happenings, keep getting in the way, blocking my true feelings. But I'm going to try.

But first I want to walk, to hear, feel the crunch of frozen grasses under my feet. I walk around the pond toward the Rousseaus'. The trees are coated with ice, thick, clear, natural varnish, crackling in the sunlight as rounded prisms, a myriad of colors reflected from hoarfrost on the ground.

Last year's blackberries, most still unpicked, now dried, hardened on the frozen bushes, are, each one, surrounded, enveloped in an irregular-shaped, perfectly clear ball of ice, like insects caught in amber. They hang their heads the same as they did in summer when filled with sun-sweetened purple juices.

I turn and look back over the pond to see our mill reflected, frozen, in the still ice. Even on a perfectly breezeless day in spring or summer it is *never* so completely mirrored. It has the look of someone in a tintype, long dead.

I stare transfixed by this temporal transmutation, then stamp my chilling feet and start back, jogging lumpishly along the top of the dam to our mill. I'm ready for this year's Christmas Eve washup. I'm having my two daughters arrive today, I want to look my best which isn't much, but what I've got, what I am. Oh how I wish I could be different, be what Lor wants, what the kids want. It's a terrible feeling inside when you're seen as a "flake," a "wimp" by others when you're personally convinced you're not one.

Everybody's still asleep. I turn up the water to heat again. I strip down to my long johns. The water, already warm, heats quickly. The room temperature is now seventeen degrees. I pull back the drapes on our east window to let in the sunlight. I pour hot water into the washbowl, regulate it to just right with cold water from the pitcher. I wash my face, scrub soap into my hair. I hang my head over the sink, pour the rest of the cold water from the pitcher over my hair to rinse it. If I weren't completely awake, aware, before, I am now.

Then I strip off the top part of my long johns and do a good soaping and rinsing off of my whole upper body, not just under the arms. I scrub up a good lather in the hair on my chest, arms and back.

I dry vigorously with a towel, then strip off the bottoms to the long johns, scrub all my vital parts. I actually lean over the bowl on our table to let them float in the water so I can do the job properly. I think this part of a man has less density, floats more easily, than other parts. It should, there are no bones, despite romantic claims to the contrary. I stare at these complicated organs of mine and wonder what music they should play to be heard. I rinse and towel myself off again, pull the long johns back on, mostly for Ben's sake. He's at an age where nudity bothers him. He even goes into the cold toilet room to dress. The new heater in there might save him from pneumonia.

Now I put the bowl on the floor and the towel beside it. One at a time, I carefully wash my toes. No wonder the washing of feet is such an intrinsic symbol for so many religions. There's such comfort in it.

I resist overstimulating a minor case of athlete's foot on my left foot between the little and next toe. No sense starting something.

I carefully dry each foot and slide on the socks, the ones I washed last night, along with my underpants. I'd hung them on the mantel to dry. They're somewhat crinkly stiff, but still soft and warm. There are some small luxuries in life, hard to describe, but which give it texture, and for me, having washed the socks and underwear by hand, myself, drying them by a fire I kept burning all night, makes it a better, deeper experience. I've got to be careful not to try forcing the ones I love to love the things, the ways of living, I love. It's an easy mistake to make. It might be called the philosopher's folly, or maybe everybody's folly. It would be so great if we could show our love by enjoying those we love for what they are, not what we want them to be. It would be the ultimate *mutual* emancipation.

I'm just exploring that thought, pulling my dark blue Shetland wool sweater over my head when I hear Lor waking up; yawning, *mmmn*ing, lip sucking. She gave me this sweater for my birthday, she knows the kinds of things I like. She should, after thirty years, but some women wouldn't. I don't really know what *she* wants sometimes; I hope she really wants the girls here for Christmas. I hope she even wants to be here herself. She has every right, every reason to want to be somewhere else right now. But it all came about so fast.

"What time is it, dear?"

I look at my watch tipped sideways on the table, beside the bowl of dirty water.

"Quarter to nine. Wow, is it ever beautiful outside, Lor. Look at that sunshine, and it's twenty-two below! Everything's frozen. Except for the sun coming up, it's almost as if time's stopped."

Lor rolls over on her stomach, props her chin on her elbows, looks past me out the new washed window into the icy world. I think there are tears on the outsides of her eyes. It could only be from sleep or the strong light from the window. She quickly wipes them away with the backs of her wrists.

"You should have wakened me. What a beautiful day. Happy Christmas Eve day, darling."

"Happy day to you too, Lor. There's still plenty of hot water to wash up if you want."

I look at the inside thermometer.

"It's between eighteen and nineteen now, practically like California."

She's turned over and is sitting up; spreading covers, making the bed as she slides out. She's wearing a dark blue flannel nightgown. Sexy sleeping gowns are not her thing. Lately Lor has been much more sexy in the clothes she wears and the way she makes up and does her hair, but she still sleeps in old-fashioned flannel, usually dark blue.

"Not quite California, dear. I'm not complaining; I think it's wonderful how you keep this place warm but for a Californian this is arctic hardship. Gosh, I wonder how the girls are going to manage? I did tell them to bring plenty of warm clothes."

I dump my bowl of dirty water into the sink, wipe it out with a paper towel, fill it with steaming hot water and some cold, while Loretta makes the freezing trip up to the toilet. I stretch out on the made bed. She doesn't have time to unplug and plug heaters, just one quick morning piss, or maybe with a woman that's pee. I know a man's piss and a woman's pee sound different; in a toilet bowl anyhow. It's amazing how much stronger piss smells in the cold. I wonder if she notices that too, probably it's in the great area of things too vulgar to discuss.

When she comes back, she walks past me, pulls her nightgown up over her head, splashes water over herself, toweling dry as she goes. I try not to let her know I'm watching, but this is one of the best parts about being at the mill. Her skin is still smooth as when we married, transparent pink, no moles nor warts, her stomach bulges slightly under the belly button from four kids but her body is odalisque, especially her back. Ingres, Matisse, Cézanne would love to paint her. Our relationship is such that I find myself more aesthetically pleased than sexually aroused. I don't know why. I don't really think either of us wants to rock our boat; broad-beamed, slow-moving, hard to tip over, or at least I always thought it would be hard to tip.

I've come to believe nothing fouls up a successful long-term man-woman relationship more thoroughly than rampant sex. One or the other, or sometimes both, sooner or later, get to using withheld intimacy, physical satisfaction, as a weapon; sexual blackmail. Even now, with everything that's happened, I still feel that way. Maybe that's part of what's wrong with me.

At school, over the years, I've had many chances at flirtations with students and fellow teachers. I always back off, the rewards don't seem to match the involvements, the complications, the expectations. I just don't seem to have the sexual drive needed. I'm much more the romantic than the stud.

Lor squirts herself with deodorant and starts dressing. I get up, push logs around on the fire, then snuggle another one in. We have enough logs cut to get through the day but not enough for tonight. It's probably time for me to induct Ben into the art of hauling and cutting wood. It's a very Christmasy thing to do. I hope he'll see it that way.

Behind me, Ben has wakened. He reaches for his glasses on the table beside him and looks at his digital watch, also on the table. He's very nearsighted. When we go back to Illinois next time we'll try fitting him with soft contact lenses.

He's weird with his watch and his sense of time. He has a flat credit-card size combination computer-watch. He can't even tell time with a regular handed analog watch. Don't ever tell him it's quarter to three instead of 2:45. That's sacrilege.

Ben swings his feet out of bed and slides them into his slippers. These slippers are the largest size made in France. He stares into the fire. He's a slow waker, coming from some deep place of rich, imaginative dreams which he'll sometimes share with us at breakfast, but not now. We all know better than to try much communication with Ben at this point. He told me once he doesn't mind getting up but he hates to stop dreaming.

"Morning Ben, have a good sleep?"

"Uh uh."

"It's a beautiful day out, clear and cold. The pond's frozen."

"That's good. Did it snow?"

"No. It's too cold to snow now."

"Uh huh."

Ben's a bit of an old man in his ways. Each night he carefully folds his clothes and stacks them on a chair beside him. It's hard getting him to surrender clothes for washing. He's not enthusiastic about change of any kind, even changing his socks. If happiness is being satisfied with what you have, then Ben's the happiest person I've ever met.

He gets up, stretches, pokes the fire with his favorite stick poker, gathers together his pile of clothes and heads up the small, steep, four-step stairway toward the bathroom.

"Ben, you can turn on the heater in there if you want, I'll turn this one off here."

"Thanks. That's all right. I don't get cold."

But I turn off the heater anyway. With the fire blazing away, we're almost up to twenty. Lor's dressed. She dumps her water into the sink, wipes out the bowl, puts the bowl and pitcher on the dresser.

"Dearest? I wish Ben would wash in the morning. He's beginning to smell like a dog kennel from playing with all those dogs in the village. That, combined with his own smell, it's enough to turn anybody's stomach.

"I snuck in new socks last night. It was one of the times you got up and went to the toilet. What'd you do, take a diuretic *and* your Valium? Is it that bad?"

"Not really, just getting ready for the onslaught; bracing myself, packing in reserves of passivity, nonresistance, paternal permissiveness, mellowness, coolness. I'm okay. What're we having for breakfast?"

"How about pancakes? I have syrup already made and there's Roland's honey. How's that sound?"

"Great. I'll straighten things up and sweep while you're whipping them together."

I'm tempted right here to reveal the Christmas waffle iron.

Waffles would be great this morning. I roll up Ben's sleeping bag and spread it at the bottom of our bed. I haul his mattress up the stairs and tuck it in his old toy corner out in the upper grange. I come back and fold his cot, store it under the stairs going up to where the girls will sleep. I guess I should wait for Ben to come back. He always puts his bed away, carefully, slowly, but I'd like things cleared away for breakfast.

Actually, the stairs are more a ship's ladder than a staircase and not so sturdy at that, but they've lasted almost fifteen years now.

I built the first step two feet off the floor so Ben couldn't climb up it when he was little. I've been meaning for the last seven years to put in this missing step but never have. It's little things like that I tend to let get by, or maybe it's because putting in that step will be one more proof we don't have a baby any more, aren't going to have any, any more.

The grandchildren thing doesn't look so hot either, both Mike and Nicole say they're not going to have kids and Maggie seems in the process of terminating the father of the one she does have. I'm not about to wait for Ben to come through; although he's physically precocious in his sexual development, he doesn't show much interest at the *functional* level. The things young girls do to attract young boys all seem silly to him. He told me once he'd really like having an interesting girl to talk with but the girls at school are only boy crazy.

"They aren't dumb, Dad, they just act that way."

Could be in his genes. Maybe we'll have a sequel, "Son of the Vanishing Man." This is one of Nicole's inventions that caught on. She claims I'm really invisible sometimes, that when things get tough, I turn off my mind and vanish inside myself. She could be right. I don't know.

But I'd probably better nail in that missing step anyway; the girls would appreciate it since they'll be sleeping up there.

Lately, I've been trying to work out some semantic progression through all the steps, conditions, *below* satisfaction. Right now it goes something like: acceptance, tolerance, accommodation, acquiescence, resignation, resentment, surrender, revolt. I've been practicing, trying to figure out just where I am.

I'm not sure that last one belongs there, but building that step on the stairs fits pretty well with accommodation or maybe acquiescence. I do actually *have* to build the step, find the wood, nails, hammer, saw; cut the wood, fit it, hammer it in place. Accommodation. Yes, we have accommodations. Or, "No, we have no accommodations, you may sleep in the stable."

I find our broom and start sweeping over by the firewood corner to the right of the fireplace. Loretta's pouring pancakes on the griddle, the smell of them fills the room. She talks to me over her shoulder.

"Dear, could you hold off sweeping until after breakfast?"

"Honest, Lor, I promise I'll just take little six-inch strokes; I won't raise any dust at all. Promise. Besides, Maggie's even worse than you are about dust; if I don't get it done now, we'll be walking around in dust up to our ankles before they leave."

"Peg, dear; remember it's Peg. You know how upset she gets. Anyway I don't think she'll stay more than three or four days at most. She's always hated the mill."

Lor turns over the pancakes, puts syrup and butter on the table. I continue sweeping with mini-strokes trying to keep the dust down. I sweep off the front of the millstone in front of the fireplace, sweep up my first pile, throw it into the fire.

Ben comes down the steps from the toilet, his pajamas carefully folded. He goes over and tucks them under his sleeping bag.

"Oh boy, pancakes. That's one of the best things I like about the mill, we always have time for a *real* breakfast."

He stops, pauses.

"Thanks for putting away my bed, Dad. I would have done it though."

He goes to the dish closet and pulls out dishes to set the table.

"Ben, dear, I've got the dishes there warming on the heater. Be careful you don't burn yourself."

Lor pushes another batch of pancakes into the oven to stay hot. Ben fastidiously lifts the dishes off the heater, spreads them on the table each to our accustomed spot, me facing the fireplace, Loretta on the side with best access to the kitchen, Ben, his back to the fireplace. I wonder how it will work out when the other three arrive. I can take any place and Lor can move over a place to make room, but Ben will be immutable.

Generally he doesn't even like to eat with other people; says it's hard to concentrate on the taste of the food, and he doesn't like the sounds of people chewing, swallowing, banging forks and spoons against their teeth.

Normally, on non-school days, Ben finishes two or three books a day. I say finishes because he's often reading four to five books at a time, something like Nero Wolfe. He told me once he likes to be reading one funny book such as *Mad* or *Mash*, one violence book like an *Executioner* series or MacDonald, one science fiction and one serious book, a technical book on airplanes, or automobiles or geology, botany, anything. He's also usually reading or rereading one of the perhaps five-hundred old National Geographic magazines we have stacked around the mill, or the apartment. Oh yes, I forgot, he's also a dedicated reader of the wonderful French hardcover comic books, *bandes dessinées, Tin Tin, Astérix* and *Obélix, Lucky Luke*. He says that's where he really learned French, not at school. I believe it. Ben's one of those wonderful people who doesn't need school. He's a natural learner-thinker.

But he does generally accommodate and share meals at the same table with Lor and me. *We* accommodate, too. I've learned to eat the way I've learned to sweep; small, short, inconspicuous bites and swallows. Actually the food does taste better that way and I don't eat so much. I can be a real gulper if I'm not careful, and it *is* amazing how many times a fork bangs against the teeth if one doesn't make an effort.

Then, also, Loretta and I are great chatterers during a meal and Ben's made us very self-conscious about speaking with food in our mouths. Tucking it over to the side, hamsterlike, is *out*. I must say, all the careful chewing, swallowing, mouth clearing,

slows down conversation; but then, it'll probably keep our diges-
tive systems functioning properly a little while longer.

I look out the window at a car going past. It's still incredibly
beautiful, blue sky—white, icy trees drawn against the heavens.
Except for the cold, the girls certainly can't complain about the
weather, not today anyhow. I notice Loretta looking out the
window, too. We're both nervous. Even if they started at eight
in the morning, which is well within the range of the impossible,
and drove the entire trip in only three hours, which *is* within the
range of the *possible*, but *not* in that old Ford, not if it's driven
by anyone with two cents worth of common sense. But then, the
friend might be driving, so who knows.

No, we'll have time for our breakfast. I don't think the girls
are exactly breaking their necks to get down here in a hurry.
After all, they've already missed Ben's birthday. Maybe they'll
only come down for Christmas Day. Who knows? It could be
better that way. Then they can have fun in the apartment up in
Paris while Lor and I try to work things out. Ben will stay out
of the way or not pay attention. War could be being declared
right beside him and he most likely wouldn't even notice.

III

Three French Hens

I'm just finishing my second pancake when I hear the unmistakable front left brake squeal of the Capri. I stand up, straddling my chair and it's they all right.

"Here they are, Lor, safe and sound."

We both move to the west window, Ben leaning over behind us. Nicole's out first from the passenger side. She's wearing a padded eiderdown vest and a long, wraparound, red wool scarf. I have unwelcome thoughts of Isadora Duncan, one of Nicole's all-around favorite people. Nicole has a wool hat pulled down low over her forehead and ears, the jacket and scarf across her mouth. She's waving her arms wildly, although she probably can't see us through the curtained, narrow window. The boyfriend climbs out the other side. He shocks me. He looks like an older, balding, bearded version of Mike. I never thought this was the kind of man Nicole would hook up with. Her other men have tended either toward the emaciated-kook-musician, dirty, smelly type or the unbelievably handsome aspiring moviestar variety; nothing in the middle.

"Geez, Lor. That guy sure looks a lot like Mike."

Loretta's dashing past me pulling at the trap door.

"Who else do you think it is, dummy? Of course it's Mike. What a wonderful surprise; we'll all have Christmas together after all."

I can see now she's right. It's so wonderful to hear the excitement in her voice. Mike's doing his after-a-long-drive stretch, very similar to my morning sunlight reach. Then he slightly cocks his left leg to let off a Jack-Kerouac-on-the-road fart. I wonder where Geneviève is. Maybe they got their signals crossed and she's in California waiting to be picked up at LAX.

I hurry down the cellar steps behind Loretta. Madame Le Moine has opened her door and stands with hands clasped, radiating pure joy at our joy. Mike has Loretta in a big bear hug. I go over and hug Nicole. We exchange French style cheek-to-cheek kissing. She feels, looks heavy even discounting the padded jacket. But she looks healthy, bright-eyed, good color, better than I remember her two years ago.

"Did we surprise you?"

"You sure did. What happened? Where's Geneviève?"

"Mike will tell you. It's his story. Let me get inside, I'm freezing."

Now Maggie is working her way out from the back seat. She's even more bundled up than Nicole and looks truly miserably cold. She's been covered by all kinds of packages and luggage. I give her a hand to help her out over the lowered back of the front passenger seat. We share a good, hard hug. She's exactly the same height as Loretta but thinner. She's been working at keeping slim and looks wonderful. After Seth was born she took on weight, but now she looks like a girl again, younger than Nicole, although she's five years older. She's wearing the afghan alpaca-type coat she left with us in Paris.

"Hi, Dad. Holy mackerel, your hair is practically pure white and are your eyebrows naturally that dark, or do you dye them?"

"White in the head only, Maggie. Getting older's just as bad as I thought it would be."

She hugs herself, tucks her mouth under the neck of her sweater.

"God, I'm freezing. Mike had to keep the window open so he could signal. The left turning signal wouldn't work."

"I know."

Mike shouts over the car.

"Really, Dad, you ought to get a real car for a change; this thing's a menace; it starts shimmying at eighty kilometers an hour so it almost shakes your teeth out. My arms are still vibrating."

"I know. The frame's bent; was that way when I bought it, makes a good automatic governor, but it wears out tires. How are you, Mike, other than being tired?"

"I'm pooped. I'd like to sleep for about three days."

Maggie reaches in to get her stuff from the back. Lor is hugging Nicole. Mike comes around front of the car through the bumpy, frozen mud to me. His eyes look red-rimmed as if he's been smoking pot for three days. Probably it's all the sleep loss flying over, then driving down. Coming this direction is deadly. Mike's shaking my hand, has his other hand on my shoulder.

"Did we surprise you?"

"Sure did. With your new beard, and not expecting you, I thought you were Nicole's boyfriend. By the way, where is he?"

"He decided not to come after all. We finally convinced Nickie the mill isn't big enough for six people in the winter time, especially if one of them's a complete stranger. Remember, I lived down here through one winter. Boy, am I ever strung out; driving that car wore me right down; you know the left front brake is grabbing."

"I know. Where's Geneviève?"

Do I imagine it, or does he give me one of those quick looks; the look I've learned to live with, when quite by accident, I start mucking too much in my kids' lives.

"She decided she had to stay *here*, couldn't come to the good old U.S. of A. after all. Her mom would be down for Christmas by herself most of the time. Her dad's coming down too, for a few days, so they can divide things up. It'll be tough for both of them and Geneviève felt she couldn't leave now. Besides I didn't want to pass up the chance for a Christmas with us all together at the mill, like old times."

He stares at me closely again, almost as if he's looking to see if I believe him. It's uncomfortable and I can't figure it. Mike's one of those people who give off vibrations. I can usually feel them but I'll be damned if I can interpret them. He leans close.

"I had to spend my school tuition money on a plane ticket. Is that okay?"

"Sure, no problem. I'll write a new check and we'll get it right off. The deadline is January fourth, isn't it?"

"Don't worry about that, Dad. I'll work it out."

How's he going to work it out? Does he have a job? Hidden resources, computer access? Maybe he'll explain later.

I wish either I didn't have antennae or I had better ones. Mine work just well enough to let me know when something is wrong, but not *what's* wrong. I spend too much time in an emotional dusk. With Christmas mail and all; with the holidays, January fourth seems like cutting things close.

"Is it okay if I borrow your one-twenty-five, Dad? Geneviève's over there now and I want her to know I'm here. First we can unpack all this crap, then I'll buzz over."

"Sure. Does she know you're coming?"

"No. It'll be a surprise for her, too. To be honest, I didn't know I was coming till just the day Peg and Nickie were leaving. It was only luck I had that blank signed check for the tuition. I packed my stuff in about half an hour."

"Well, whatever the reason, it's great you're here. This might be our last chance for a big Christmas get-together."

I know I'm not with it somehow. But then I never am. I also know better than to ask why he just doesn't drive over in the Capri. I'll wait till Lor can do some investigation and translating.

Lor's still on the other side of the car gabbing with Nicole and Maggie. Maggie's definitely jumpy; I can feel it right over the car roof. She's probably expecting me to talk about her leaving George and Seth. Not me; what good does it do? Besides, I have to live with my wife. There's no use explaining those things; Kelly's first law: when it comes to emotions, everybody's wrong.

We start unloading. They all only have sleeping bags and banana bags. The girls say they left their big suitcases up in Paris at the apartment. Mike's even more careless with clothes than I am. All his stuff is in the smallest of those banana bags, nothing in Paris. He's the one who should be freezing. He's only wearing that blue sweater Geneviève knitted him last Christmas. Unless he has some magic collapsible down coat in that little bag, no socks, no underwear, no change of shirts, shoes, he's going to need clothes. I search through my mind for whatever extra warm clothes we might have stored in the upper grange. We'll find something. Actually, I have the duffle coat I haven't been using much. With my Bean catalogue long underwear I don't get cold.

Finally Ben comes down and drifts around the groupings. He's trying to see everybody, participate without being seen. I'm worried how he'll react when the girls greet him. He's only this year gotten up his nerve, his tolerance, enough so Madame Le Moine can kiss him on the cheeks when we arrive. Mike's the first to see him.

"Holy Jesus, Ben! You've grown another six inches since I last saw you. Now I'm *your* little brother. How tall are you anyway? And that's some beard you've got there."

He goes over and puts his hand out for Ben to shake. Ben, hands to match his feet, long thin fingers, strong hands, gives a good shake; but he can't get himself to look into the eyes of any person with whom he's shaking hands. It's too personal, too intimate. He tends to look down, or at an oblique, about two feet beside and three feet behind the other person. Mike knows Ben enough to respect this.

"He's somewhere over six-two now, Mike. I had to stand on a chair to cut his mark on the post for the millstone boom. He passed both of us last summer."

Nicole and Maggie see Ben. Nicole comes over, she swings the dangling end of her scarf across her neck, shakes her head to get her hair over her ears and behind her shoulders.

"My God, Ben; you're a *giant*. You can't be my *little* brother. Holy cow, *I'm* the baby in this family again, for sure. What happened?"

She closes in on Ben with her arms out. She doesn't even come up to Ben's shoulder. He lets himself be hugged, hands limp at his sides and his head too high up for her to try a kiss. She steps back, staring at him from head to toe.

"My God, I can't believe it; he even has the beginnings of a straggly beard there. Maybe you'll be the new Santa, you and your hairy brother can fight it out for first elf."

Maggie's standing behind Nicole. She puts down her banana bags on a snow spot, all the rest is mud.

"Hi, Ben. You're getting so handsome, I almost wouldn't recognize you. I'll bet the girls at school chase you all the time."

She gives him a brief hug. She doesn't try to kiss him although she's tall enough. With a valiant effort, she might manage a shot at his beard. But from the way Ben leans out from her hug, she gets the message.

Ben takes the banana bags from Maggie and Nicole. They carry the sleeping bags. Mike has his stuff under his arms. There's nothing left for Loretta and me to carry except some wrapped Christmas presents from in back of the car and a duffel bag full of something, maybe extra warm clothes, I hope. We pack them under our arms; I'm praying the Atari set is there and that the cassettes are the ones Ben wants, *Combat* and *Space Invaders*. He definitely doesn't want any of the sport ones, soccer, Ping-Pong, tennis. I'm sure it's okay.

We decide to go around onto the dam. With all this junk it'd be hard to get up the narrow stairs and through our trap door. Besides, I want them to see how beautiful the pond is, also, how I've cleaned the ivy from the roof, swept the leaves off the porch, tied the roses to the wall.

On the dam side, it almost looks like a *real* French country house, with French doors opening from the upper grange onto the dam and a stone terrace along its length. The other side, the road side, where the car is parked, looks square, hard, high and cold. Nicole and Maggie are still rattling away a mile a minute with Loretta. Just before they go down the stairs, Lor stops and turns.

"Look at this, girls, have you ever seen anything more beautiful?"

The two of them hug their sleeping bags to their chests and look out over the pond. For some reason there are small crystalline outgrowths, growing in tiny clumps like butterflies all over the surface of the pond. There must have been some condensation that froze. Each crystal reflects like snow and refracts so it's almost blinding with the direct white light, sprinkled with tiny spots of blue, red, purple, even yellow.

"Good God. It's like Disneyland or Fantasia or some kind of sci-fi flick. It's practically psychedelic."

That's Nicole, I mean Nickie. Maggie stares entranced.

"It's so beautiful. We used to have it like this up in Idlewild, California; in the mornings sometimes. But let's get inside, I'm freezing."

Ben and Mike behind me stand as if hypnotized. Both of them have bare hands and both hands loaded. They don't put down their loads, only stand there.

"My God, Dad! I forgot how beautiful it is. It's so easy to let things get out of your mind. I've been sort of afraid to come. What with Thierry having his accident and Henry Carron dying of cancer and then Madame Le Moine almost dying with a stroke. I was worried if I could handle all those changes, if it would ever be the same.

"But *look* at this."

"Madame Le Moine's fine now, Mike. She has her memory back and most of her strength. She's been asking about you. She was just over to see us yesterday. She was even out there watching when you all came in, but didn't want to interfere. She's still the same wonderful woman."

"You mean she was *there* and we didn't even say *hello?*"

He stares into my eyes, then starts as if going right over to make up for it. Ben steps forward.

"It's all right, Mike. She understands. You can go see her later."

Ben walks past Mike.

"Don't worry. I looked up at her and made a sign with my hand to show I saw her and she pushed down with both her hands as if she were shushing me, didn't want to interfere. Madame Le Moine understands things, Mike."

Ben goes past me and down the steps. Mike comes close. "Jesus, Dad, he's so serious. Is he always this way?"

"Most of the time. He's a very serious person, Mike. He's so conscientious he makes me, the mad compulsive, feel like a blithe spirit."

We step carefully down the cracked steps into the mill. I'm sorry I missed the girls' first reaction when they went in, but I'm glad to've had a moment somewhat alone with Ben and Mike. For some reason I'm a better father for boys than for girls. At least it seems that way to me. It's hard to know if this is true, but I get more complaints from the girls, or maybe girls complain more than boys.

Lor's expert in the way she complains, no whines no bitches; just a constant niggling; reminding me about things that need to be done, keeping me in line, watching over; like automatic drive. She's always saying "Let's do this," or "I think *we* ought to do that," but mostly these are projects for *me*. Maybe that's the way it is in all marriages, I don't know, I probably don't care. God, I wish I had a better grip on things. Mostly, I wish I had a better grip on my marriage.

When I come in the door, I can barely close it behind me. There's a fairly narrow gap between the table built over the millstones still in place, and the millstone with the Christmas tree jammed in its center. Three sleeping bags and three banana bags have been straight dropped, plugging the gap. I don't know whether they walked through and dropped the bags behind them or dropped, then stepped over. Actually it's as good a place as any. They'll need to take the bags upstairs sooner or later and the bottom of the stairs is right there.

I think for a minute before I say it, the idea seems so natural, so logical.

"Okay if I put your bags and things upstairs?"

There's a two-second beat of silence; they look at each other, then all, all three of them, begin laughing. Lor glances at me. Ben is confused as to what's so funny; what's wrong, what was said that he didn't hear, didn't understand. Nicole steps, trips over the bags, falling toward me.

I *know* why they're laughing and it *is* funny. Nicole gives me a daughterly kiss on the nose, a child-love equivalent to "Good boy, Rover, well done."

"Dad, you wouldn't believe it. We were talking about this on the way down in the car. It's so weird having an old maid for a father. We were in hysterics about how you were always sweeping here at the mill or vacuuming up in Paris or even helping old Frau Berger scrub on Saturdays in Bavaria. Remember how you'd lock us out of our rooms if we didn't make our beds or hang up our clothes?"

She's having a hard time talking, between laughing and giggling. I have a strange feeling the laughing isn't real, only some kind of cover-up for deep feeling. Maybe neatness isn't something daughters want in fathers. The other kids are quiet; I sneak a quick look at them, they seem as uncomfortable as I feel. Lor is frozen. Here it is, just inside the door, Christmas Eve and we're already on the edge of a scene.

"I don't know, Nickie, maybe I'm just a garden-variety anal compulsive. You know the story of how my mother trained me. Every time I dirtied my diapers she wouldn't breast-feed me. Then, I was strapped onto a training potty before I could sit up straight; used to keep slipping through the hole. I was seven years old before I managed a turd that didn't look like rabbit pellets."

Maggie puts her fingers in her ears.

"Come *on*, Dad. Don't start grossing me out in the first five minutes. I thought you'd at least wait till we were eating. Between you and Mike; him with his burps, belches and farts, and you with your gross stories I'll swear I almost starved to death as a kid."

"I'm sorry Maggie. I was only trying to explain. I'll shut up."

The interesting thing is I'm *only* neat, *not* clean, and I'm definitely *not* a classy dresser, distinctly sloppy. But I'm not comfortable in a disordered environment, I feel insecure and I've never been quite sure if my mother did it to me, or the U.S. Army, or it's some deep personal fault. I tend to live my life as if there's a Saturday inspection always just around the corner. It must be a drag for others to live with but I don't think it is for me. Some of my most pleasant, joy-filled, anxiety-free hours are after I've cleaned the apartment, everybody's off somewhere and I have it alone to myself, neat and quiet. It could be part of the "Vanishing Man" thing again. Maybe I'm trying to make everything around me vanish into nothingness.

Mike breaks the spell.

"You're right, Dad. That's a dumb place for us to drop the bags. We were just so glad to be here, to see it all clean and beautiful, so much like home should be, we didn't think. Let me give you a hand with that stuff. You go halfway up and I'll pass them to you."

I go up four steps so I can push the bags onto the floor. Mike and Nicole hand them up to me. I'm glad my head's out of sight. Lately, the smallest things, can make me fill up. I guess if daughters don't want an "old maid father" they sure as hell don't want a "crybaby." Maybe it's only the strain of waiting, wondering, preparing things, preparing myself. The strain of not knowing what's going to happen.

It's also part of getting older for me. Or maybe philosophers are supposed to cry easily, at least philosophers without a working philosophy.

Loretta's keeping the ball rolling. I can hear she's got the kettle on for some tea, her all-time, all-purpose remedy, her Irish version of Jewish chicken soup.

"You girls should see how your father's got it fixed up there. It's so cozy, with a cloth-lined roof and bed lamps for each bed. He even has a nice rag rug on the floor. He washed it in that icy pond by hand. You'll see; it's all so snug and comfy."

Thank God, Lor's backing me up. If she falls apart we're dead. I know she won't. In an emergency she has nerves of steel, or rubber. I've never been able to make up my mind which.

The bags and sleeping bags are at the top of the steps now. I climb the rest of the way and distribute bags at the heads of beds where I think each of them'll be sleeping. Maggie comes up behind me. I give her a hand on the last step. She holds onto the guardrail I built to keep Ben from falling over when he was little.

"Dad, can you guarantee me no rats are going to nibble at my toes or run across my face?"

Maggie's half funny, half in earnest.

"Well, Peg, I've had traps out the last three days, three kinds of rat poison and no rats, so I guess you're safe."

I keep quiet about all the rodent shit I swept out up here and down in the kitchen cabinet. They even ate the greater part of a bar of soap, thin teeth scourings all around it in a beautiful decorative pattern, almost like coral. They also ate their way through a plastic lid into a jar of mustard, must have been a terrific disappointment.

I keep all this to myself. It'd only "gross her out," ruin her sleep for nothing but a little gratuitous honesty. I've gotten to distrust myself when I play with the idea of honesty. Too often, it means I want to hurt somebody, sometimes myself. The fruitless flirtation with truth and honesty, each and both arrogant delusions, has caused more misery to mankind than almost anything I know. The inquisition, the Hundred Years' and Thirty Years' wars, the Crusades, most of the other wars, killings of man up to and including the European holocaust of Hitler fame, were based upon a conviction of "truths" and a desire to be "honest" by acting them out.

I'm beginning to think man will be happy, will be fully realized, only when we can all accept the tentativeness of life and *all* around us; the tenuousness of seeming reality. We need to revel in speculation without expectation of answers, only other questions.

The search for surety, unassailable security, in the physical or emotional sense is a retreat from our essential humanity. If our species has a reason, it's to *guess* and then—checking out our guesses—guess again, and so on without end. A religion, or ethical system, or government based on that premise would be a blessing to the planet, maybe to the universe. Imagine thinking, and being surrounded by *other thinkers!* I try to shut down the runaway philosopher's mind; back to what's called reality.

"Honest to God, I'd die if a rat ran across me. I used to be so scared sleeping up here. Then there was that story about rats running across Mother's face one time; I still have nightmares about it."

She puts her hands over her face and shudders. For a long while, when she was a kid, I thought Maggie was only being dramatic when she'd do a thing like that but now I know she means it. She's a very sensitive person, almost *too* sensitive. That's what makes it so hard for us to understand what she's doing now. It's as if she's purposely shut down her receptors, turned off her feelings, is marching through things, people; pretending they aren't there, that nobody counts. I can't let myself think about George and Seth.

Nicole has reached the top of the steps. The ceiling is low here up in the rafters, but she's short enough to stand straight. She's taken off her padded jacket. She stands with her hands on her hips.

"Well, find me a slate, a piece of coal and I'll write you the

Gettysburg address. Where is it I'm supposed to hide the book I borrow so it'll be ruined by the snow and then I can go out and split rails, become the first woman president, maybe emancipate some *real* slaves, all colors."

Mike's standing at the top of the steps—two steps down.

"This is beautiful, Dad. You've worked like a demon. You must know that glass wool is deadly to work under, it gets in your eyes and can cause silicosis if you breathe enough of it. I hope you wore glasses and a mask."

I lie and say yes. I'm too wound up to defend my innate carelessness. Nicole flops out on one of the beds.

"Yeah, this is terrific. It brings back memories of when I convinced Mike and Peg there wasn't really a Santa Claus. Remember?"

Maggie and Mike are looking at her. I am too. I'm anxious to hear what she has to say. It was such a stupid gratuitous cruelty, a violation for all of us. I'm wondering how she feels about it now.

We, none of us, have ever spoken about it since. That Christmas was one of our first at the mill. Bringing off the magic of it all was already hard enough without Nicole's great revelation. She sits on the bed crosslegged-yoga-hippy style.

"I showed them where you hid our presents inside that old Renault in the grange."

She turns her head, repressing a laugh; almost theatrically pretending not to see our reactions.

"Boy, you guys sure didn't want to know but *I* convinced you, I took you out there and *showed* them to you. Gosh, I must've only been about eight and you were ten and twelve."

There's a long silence, Mike and Maggie look at each other again. Nicole's coming on so fast, so mean, I find myself squeezing my lips down hard.

"Willy old boy, keep your cool, hold in there buddy."

Mike comes up the rest of the steps behind me, takes a quick look at the shelves I built along that wall. I went through the books usually spread helter-skelter all over the mill. I separated

Ben-type books from Loretta-type books, then put the rest up here. They used to be jammed and piled along the window sills, three deep; under the bed, on the mantle, in fact, on any flat surface. I'm probably the one in the family who reads the least, me the great humanist philosopher. Maggie and Nicole are Gothic romance addicts, modulated with a few spy or murder mysteries. They both, also, now and then, take on a serious or semiserious piece of fiction, mostly at Loretta's encouragement. My wife is the constant teacher and we're all her most available although inept pupils.

A weird thing with me is, the older I get, the less I read. I try to convince myself I'm thinking, and once in a while I do get something written down, a note, a vague thought, but I haven't published in over five years. I guess this particular elephant has found its final burial ground at the American College in Paris. There could be worse fates. It's better than a junior college in Illinois. It's the most exciting place I've ever taught, with good students and a real international flavor. But I can't help wishing I could do something, anything, more important. Maybe I should work on making up a *new* religion, a really practical religion. One that would *help* people feel more valuable instead of making them feel guilty all the time. Also, it shouldn't be a put-down of anybody else, any other group. I might be able to do that, it could be just my kind of thing; but I'm still too young. Or maybe the Hindus have already done it.

So up here, I tried to accumulate all the books I thought might interest the girls. Also, the books help insulate our east wall, block a few of the holes. Some of our coldest weather comes out of the east.

Mike turns away from the books.

"You know, Nickie, I could've murdered you for ruining Christmas like that. I can still get mad thinking about it. What made you do it anyway? God, I cried all that night. I think it was the beginning of the worst part of growing up. Maybe *you* were ready but *I* wasn't."

Nicole rolls onto her stomach. She props herself on her elbows the same way Loretta did this morning. Except for the size, she looks almost exactly the same as Lor when I married her, only more vital, more animal, less elegant.

It could be a difference in the times they grew up. No. Nicole and Loretta *are* different at some deep level. Nicole is a blend of *my* mother and Lor's sister, volatile, ruthless, emotionally demanding, but incredibly capable. She's a people engineer; the stuff from which competitive success derives. I only hope she marries a good man with a plenitude of tolerance and personal force. She'll make a good wife for somebody like that. God forbid she should ever marry anybody like my father or Mike or me; or worst of all, Ben. She'd wipe up the floor with any or all of us.

Mike's so much like Lor it's frightening sometimes. I'm not sure he has her resilience, her toughness though, but then he's young; he could grow into it.

Maggie's going through the books; pulls out one or two, looks at them.

"It was awful, that night. I cried so hard; then we all promised to pretend we still believed but it was never the same. Mom and Dad knew right away it was over and there was no way to go back. It was like having sex the first time; afterward, sure, there's some romance left but sex always gets in the way.

"Probably the three of us need to grow up, that's what George says anyway, but most times it isn't much fun. I'm still not ready, Nickie, I'm still stuck back there in the Narnian chronicles and Franky Furbo. I'll *never* be ready."

Maggie's to the edge of tears. I figure I can put my oar in this one time. So, out it comes.

"And it doesn't get any easier Peg. I think the growing up Mom and I are trying for now is harder than anything we've gone through before. That's why I appreciate so much the three of you coming down with us for Christmas. A *last* Christmas in our mill like old times is the thing both of us wanted most. Thanks."

There's silence and they look at each other. I know I've done it again, said too much, gone a little too far. As a diplomat, I'd make a great terrorist. Nicole swings around and pushes herself up off the bed.

"Don't kid *me*, Dad; you and Mom are *never* going to grow up. You'll always be drifting back there in the no-man's-land of Franky Furbo. I can't even *imagine* you letting all that go; and Mom will stick it out right to the end with you."

I hope Nicole's right, about the sticking out part, anyway.

We climb down the stairs. Lor has our breakfast dishes cleared and the table set for tea. I wonder how she's going to handle all this. Since Nicole stopped smoking, Loretta, the tea fiend of the Western world, has been drinking herb teas exclusively. We brought down eleven different blends of her tea to the mill.

This is characteristic of the difference between Loretta and me. I, out front, paternal, heavy-footed, heavy-handed, offered Nicole a five-hundred-dollar loan to be forgiven if she didn't smoke for three years. To make the bind even tighter, I put away a hundred dollars for each of the other three kids on the condition she not smoke. It all goes down the tubes or up in smoke if she smokes within three years.

Loretta, on the contrary, quite quietly, without a word, not even to Nicole, gave up her most prized pleasure, tea, as a sort of silent supportive, invisible moral support. I only found out about it from the smell. Tea to me is mostly only colored hot water. I drink it sometimes so I'll have an excuse to dump sugar in it.

We spread around the table. Mike takes my place; nothing meant by it, I don't think; probably something genetic; we both naturally drift to the same place at a table. I jam in beside Ben. He gets up and goes over to the rocking chair by our fireplace.

Nobody comments on the herb tea, maybe they're like me on this. We listen to all the complexities, discomforts, confusion of the air trip. Mike tells how hard it was getting our Capri started in the cold.

"Dad, how long's it been since you last changed oil on that car? It's completely black."

"Okay, Mike, I'll check it when I'm back up in Paris."

Actually, I'll probably change the car before I change the oil. In the junking line-up, it's even ahead of the Fiat. That's the terminal annex to intensive care in the car world, and I'm running out of care, generally.

Then, right there in the middle of a conversation about oil change, while he's still only drunk about half a cup of the herb tea, Mike's red-rimmed eyes start filling with tears. What in God's name did I do or say? If it means so much to him, I'll get new oil, even get a lube job. He pushes his chair back, stands up, the girls look at each other, then back into their herb tea. Lor and I glance at each other, mystified. Ben stays concentrated on his *Guns & Ammo* magazine. The girls brought several down from his Paris collection, on request.

Mike walks over to the fireplace, takes my motorcycle keys from the mantle; moves toward the trap door.

"I'm going over to Geneviève's to let her know I'm here, okay?"

Loretta looks at him carefully, concernedly.

"Will you be home for lunch, Mike? Can Geneviève join us?"

He's almost all the way down the steps, answers with only his red, watering eyes showing through the crack.

"Oh, sure, I'll be back. Geez, it's Christmas Eve. I don't know about Geneviève though."

He's gone, but we can hear him. The downstairs door creaks open. Lor pours more tea.

"I'll set an extra place for lunch, just in case."

We sit quietly, listening as Mike kicks the motor over five or ten times without success. Then we hear the swinging of the big door as he pushes it open and struggles the bike through the mud ruts and out onto the road. There he push-starts it past the mill; it catches and he swings around and roars up the hill toward

Vauchot, adjusting the choke, backfiring as he goes. I'm sitting there congratulating myself for not having warned him to be careful on the icy parts. Would I congratulate myself if he has an accident on that ice? Why couldn't he have taken one of the cars? They're not *that* bad.

After the girls have gone upstairs to arrange their things, Ben and I tie the tree into place so it won't fall over and we start with our electric tree lights. Luckily, I have an extra box of bulbs, because these lights are strung old-style, in series, so if one bulb burns out, the whole string goes dark. We go along, checking, screwing in and screwing out bulbs, progressing up each string till it suddenly lights like light magic, the half-expected shock and surprise of Jell-O jelling, or snow on Christmas morning.

Ben climbs up on the millstone. Because he's so tall, he can wrap the strings over top of the tree and lower them gently into place, patiently untangling the almost invisible green wires between bulbs from the spreading pine tips and needles. We manage to drop four strands of lights at different levels. When we plug in and they all light up, we're quite pleased with ourselves. Ben stares at the tree; his thumbs hooked into his back pockets, shoulders thrown back, back arched, his face wrapped in a self-conscious, unsuppressible smile, the closest manifestation of rapture I think he can allow himself.

Nicole lowers herself down the steps, stops.

"Holy God! Look, these two are wrapping the Christmas tree with colored lights. It looks like Wilshire Boulevard or the White House."

She jumps down the last high step. Maggie is cautiously following behind her, she stops halfway down the steps.

"Oh, Dad! I thought we were going to have a real *old-fashioned* Christmas, with real candles; the kind we used to have in Bavaria."

I reach behind the tree, pull the plug. Ben turns away.

"These are only backup lights, Peg; for after you're gone, when we've run out of candles. You'll hardly be able to see these bulbs and wires with all the Christmas balls and garlands, the tinsel, the candles. You'll hardly know."

Nicole stands with her hands on her hips in front of the tree. "*I'll* know."

"Well, Nickie, these *are* old-time lights; the kind we had when *I* was a kid."

Gosh, she's so hostile, or maybe I'm only supersensitive, nervous. Christmas can be a hard time, a time of unfulfillable expectations.

Maggie comes the rest of the way down the steps. Our Christmas things are spread on the table. Loretta is separating the balls, hooking tree holders into the tops. She's doing it, methodically, almost mechanically; her mind is miles away. It's so sad.

Ben is shining some of the balls with paper towels. Maggie walks past over to the crèche, the little stable nativity scene Ben and I set up in the windows. The figures date back to Christmases twenty years ago. Some of them I carved from wood, some the kids made from carved or cast plaster or soap, a few from papier-mâché; it's a crowded stable.

"Gee, I remember painting this Joseph in Seeshaupt. He still has that constipated look on his face. Is the sheep with the broken feet—oh, there he is. Gosh, I love making a crèche; I don't know why George and I never got one started. George has such a thing about not shoving religious stuff down Seth's throat. I never thought much about it being religious. It was always just fun, playing dollhouse.

"Gosh, Dad. You and Ben have done everything. The crèche was always something Nickie and I did. It was *our* job."

"Take it down again, Peg, put it together the way you want; Ben and I were only checking to see if all the figures were there."

"It wouldn't be the same. We'll leave it the way it is. You and Ben have done a good job."

Nickie moves toward the trap door. She turns.

"You know, it might be fun making all *new* figures; severe modern with a gothic feeling; I might just do that, prove I really *am* a sculptress.

"Come on, Peg, we still have some things in the car; let's go get them. I have the keys."

"Okay, Nickie, but that cellar down there scares me. I thought by this time I'd've outgrown it. I'm not afraid of Phoenix dark, or LA dark, but that cellar, even in daylight, is still Dracula's tomb."

The two of them start through the trap door, Nicole first. I go over and hold it till they're down the steps, then close it. They're chattering away, seem happy enough, but it all feels artificial. It could only be Maggie's nervousness—or mine.

I look up at Loretta in the kitchen; she's signaling me over with her finger, something surreptitious in it. I go close. She whispers.

"Open your mouth."

I open up, thinking she has some special goody for me. I'm ready for almost anything. She holds my mouth open with both hands, looks in deeply, like a dentist.

"Well, I don't *see* any blood. I expected your tongue to be totally filleted from all the biting."

She pushes my jaw shut with her thumbs, gives me a gentle kiss. It's been quite a while since she's volunteered a kiss, large or small; such a nice Chistmas present.

"It won't be long, Will. I'm sure they'll go on up to Paris after our anniversary. Remember, it's difficult for them too; it's hard for all of us. They'd like to be children again for this last Christmas, just as much as we'd like them to be. But we can't hold onto everything. It doesn't make sense."

Is she trying to tell me something?

I hug her, squeeze; look into her soft, brown, vibrant eyes; eyes that welcome then flit away, squirrel-like; a squirrel ducking back and forth in curiosity and fear around a tree. I don't really want to catch her, but I would like to hold on, somehow.

"Maybe bringing the girls down here wasn't such a hot idea, huh?"

I stop, we smile at the accidental joke.

"I think I'll take Ben down with me in the cellar to saw wood. We'll stay out of the way for a while, give you a chance alone with the girls before Mike comes back. Something's going on and I can't figure it, maybe they'll tell you."

"It's most likely only jet lag, dear, then again we're nervous and Maggie's afraid we're going to say something about George and her trouble. Don't worry so. It's Christmas. It'll all work out; let's make the most of it."

"Okay, okay, I'll try, but I do want to show Ben how to help saw wood. This old man is beginning to feel the need for a strong, willing son to back him up. Maybe he'll even learn how to split logs, become president, save some more slaves; after Nicole's finished, that is."

Loretta gives me a soft push out of the kitchen area, turns back to the sink.

Ben could've heard us or not, but I doubt it. He's deep into a book, one of his *Executioner* books again, zapping the Mafia somewhere for the thirty-second time.

"Hey, Ben, could you help me with cutting wood? I'll give you lessons on how to use a saw."

He comes out of his book, slowly, reluctantly; his mind far from the Morvan, Christmas Eve, fireplaces, wood.

"There's already wood cut."

He points, logically, at my precut pile. He doesn't want to, I should leave it at that. I decide on one more try, then I'll cut by myself.

"Come on, Ben, you'll enjoy it. Cutting wood for a fire is a real Christmas thing to do; even *better* than believing in Santa Claus."

I pull on my jacket, hat, gloves.

Ben starts unwinding himself, puts down his book, inserting a bookmarker. Ben never dog-ears books, he uses bookmarkers. The bookmarker can be anything, a metro ticket, a used envelope, an itemized cashier's slip, anything; but once he starts using something for a bookmarker, writes the name of the book he's reading on it, it is assigned for all eternity to that function. He wears out his improvised bookmarkers, they become dirty, ragged, torn, but woe betide anyone who throws out, misuses or even appropriates one of his markers.

Once, I accidentally threw one into a trash can, not realizing what I was doing; just generally neatening things in my usual mother-hen way. Ben rescued it, carefully straightening it out.

"*Dad*, these holders mean a lot to me!"

Ben calls bookmarkers "holders."

"I can look at any one and remember the whole book I read with that holder; otherwise, I might forget."

Now he's standing up. I start into the cellar, he braces the trap door while I climb down backward.

"Ben, you'd better put on a jacket and some gloves; it's cold here in the cellar and we'll need to haul in some wood from outside."

He shrugs and lowers the trap door behind me. I reach the bottom and open our door to the outside, onto the road. The wood is piled right there in front of the mill, beside the doors to the grange. Our girls are over behind the Capri; they don't look up.

I have the woodpile covered with our Ping-Pong table cover. I untie the iced, knotted string. The plastic is rigid, fragile in this cold. It's colored Astroturf green and looks incongruous against our stone wall, in the white, gray, below-freezing cold. Ben comes through the door behind me, wearing jacket and gloves, hunched against the biting wind. He looks over at the girls who are still unloading the car; they don't seem to notice us.

"Ben, you lift on this end while I get the other, then we can fold the cover and put it aside."

We lift together, shake off the frost, snow, bits of wood, twigs. He brings his end toward me, I fold, then refold it, into a pile. The wood is dry and without frost or snow.

"Now, let's carry in ten logs or so to get started."

I grab hold of one by the door. They're split and cut to one-meter lengths, too big to fit in the fireplace; we need to saw each one in half.

Alternately, we carry in the lengths of wood, leaning them against the damp, iced stone wall inside, standing them vertically. Ben consistently takes the largest pieces. Considering his nonathletic pose, he's amazingly strong. When we've lined the wall, I stop; I'm already working up a sweat.

"Okay, now we can get to the cutting."

I take our saw down from the nail on a support post by the mill machinery. It's a saw formed with tube metal into a bow shape with the blade stretched across the space where a drawstring would be on a hunting bow. This is a Swedish-made saw but I just put in a new blade with large, irregular-size teeth called "American style" by the French; it cuts through this wood easily, and will be a good blade with which Ben can start; nothing's more discouraging than a dull blade.

I jam one end of a log between a support for the bottom of our stairway and the stairway itself. The other end I rest on a medium-size stump we've used for this purpose since I built the fireplace. This has been the standard arrangement for wood cutting at the mill over all these years.

"Okay, Ben. Now you steady that end there, keep it from twisting or rolling and I'll show you how to use the saw. That's it; you can sort of sit on it to use your most weight.

"The main thing is not to cut yourself. You need to keep your hands, fingers and legs out of the way. You're not liable to cut anything *off* but you can give yourself a good gash if you're not careful."

I look at Ben. He's watching the saw, my hands, my eyes. Maybe I shouldn't've started off talking about cutting yourself. I want him to enjoy wood sawing the way I do, but I don't want him to hurt himself either. Damn, it's hard knowing what to do.

"Okay, Ben. The first thing to do is judge the middle of the piece and at the same time, pick a spot without knotholes or places where there were branches. I always look for the thinnest part."

I put the saw on the wood and pull it back lightly, it cuts easily into the bark.

"The important thing to remember is, the saw cuts the wood; you only have to guide it, steer it, give it some power; long, easy strokes. A good, experienced man with a sharp saw can cut wood all day without even working up a sweat."

I begin gently pushing the saw back and forth, pulling it the full length of the saw each way. The blade sinks deeper into the wood. I rock the saw up slightly, then down gently at the handle end as I go, not pressing too hard.

"The idea is to keep the saw from binding and at the same time, cut through straight as possible. It's really fun."

Ben has his eyes glued on the saw, his body tense, holding tight. The log is already almost cut through and his weight is starting to bind the saw.

"Now lean back some Ben, so the cut of the saw opens up and I can make the last few strokes. That's it. Hold on to your end of the log when I cut through."

Just then the log breaks. I catch the inside length and Ben holds on to his. I show him how to stack the cut logs on the stairs so we can hand them up when we're finished.

"Okay. Now it's your turn, choose a log."

Again, he chooses one of the thickest logs; slacker he isn't. We wedge it under the stair and I give Ben the saw. I show him how to hold it. I'm surprised to find his hands are shaking. I thought he was taking it all so easily. I don't know why I miss these things; some kind of psychic or emotional blindness.

"Don't worry, Ben. It's the easiest thing in the world. You'll like it."

"I know. But it's the same feeling I had when I first got to shoot my twenty-two rifle. This saw has so much power to cut through hard wood like that and you make it look so easy."

He puts the saw on the wood and pulls back tentatively. It

buries the blade in the bark. He holds his left hand way off to the side, keeps his legs well out of the way. I steady the log and he begins, trying for long, easy strokes but bearing down, rushing it a bit.

"Take it easy, Ben. Let the saw do the work, we're in no hurry at all."

He slows down, a smile on his face.

"It cuts like a hot knife through butter, Dad; I never knew how easy it could be."

Ben loves to use the picturesque clichés he reads in books. Sometimes I think he'll have twenty or thirty in his mind waiting around for the right opportunity. He's rocking the saw now, perfectly, cutting the soft wood on the outside, reserving the hard core of the log for his final cuts. He quickly comes to where I shift and the cut starts to open.

"Now be careful. These last strokes are the hardest. Make sure the saw doesn't bind or snap and that your legs are well out of the way when it comes through."

He carefully, almost expertly, cuts through the log. I catch my end and his falls to the ground between us. He lurches forward to catch it.

"Put the saw down first, Ben, then you can pick up the log."

He leans his saw against the stump and we shove the two cut logs into another space on the steps. I turn around to get another log. Ben reaches for it, too.

"Let me cut another one, Dad. I'm just getting the knack of this. You're right, it's really fun."

I sit on my end of the log. Methodically, he goes through his opening moves of sawing. I know that for the rest of his life he'll cut logs exactly the same way. Ben studiously avoids any change in procedure.

He's about halfway through, when I notice the girls are standing in the doorway. I smile up at them.

"I'm teaching Ben how to saw wood. He's getting good at it; watch."

They have their arms filled with packages from the car, things that must've been in the trunk. I check to see if they want to go up through the trap door, but with their arms so full, they'd be better going around by the dam. Nicole steps down into the cellar behind me.

"So here we see the father-paternity figure passing on the secrets of his manly skills to his young son. How come you never taught *us* how to cut logs? Are we only supposed to set tables, help cook, make beds; woman things like that; is that it, huh? It's not fair."

Oh boy. Here we go. Ben is just about through his log. I rock back to open the cut and he goes through in two more strokes. We catch the ends of the logs.

"Well, Nickie, I never knew you *wanted* to saw wood. I'd've been glad to teach you; I can use help any time I can get it. It just never occurred to me you were even interested. Gosh you and Peg always *hated* it here at the mill."

Ben and I jam the logs between higher steps. I push them to the side in case the girls want to go upstairs that way. Ben picks up the saw again. Nicole reaches for it, he gives it to her.

"Okay, folks; here I go, Paula Bunyan in the flesh. I'll show you how strong *I* am."

She's put her things down on the doorstep. Maggie is still standing there, hugging herself. Ben comes around beside me, leans forward.

"Watch out, Nickie, it's sharp, it can really give you a good gash if you're not careful."

Nicole throws the end of her long scarf over her shoulder.

"Don't you worry there little brother, just watch the logs roll. Timmberrr!!"

"Do be careful, Nickie. The main thing is nice long easy strokes. Strength has nothing to do with it."

I'm holding on to one end, making sure the log's wedged tight. Ben slides past Maggie to get more wood. Nicole starts sawing back and forth with short, quick strokes, her hand much too close to the blade in case it jumps out of the cut. I know she doesn't want criticism, any help from me. She's proving something.

"I'll show you what *strength* is. I'm little but I'm stronger than a lot of men."

"Be careful the saw doesn't catch and jump out of the cut, Nickie, that's the main thing. Your hand's awfully close!"

Her scarf has come back over her shoulder and dangles so it gets snagged by a tooth of the blade, a loop of wool is pulled out, broken. She stops, puts down the saw, stretches the wool to pull the loop back into the knitting.

"Damn! Amy Lou knitted this; gave it to me just as I was leaving, a Christmas present; goddamned saw!"

She unwinds the scarf from her neck, piles it with her other things on the doorstep. Ben passes behind her with a log; Maggie leans against the doorjamb. Nicole grabs the saw again; this time, her hand a safer distance from the blade but still *too* close. I notice for the first time that her pile on the doorstep includes two bottles of Chablis, one of them half empty. Loretta and I bought three bottles of Pouilly-Fumé and three of Sancerre in Nevers so we'd have enough white wine. I guess Nicole's just making sure; she knows Lor prefers red.

"Try easy strokes, rocking up and down as you go, so the saw won't bind. When you see the cut start to open, go slowly, then the blade won't go through and cut you."

There's no response, only a frantic hacking back and forth, almost a caricature of real sawing. Nicole's working her way through this piece of wood by sheer strength and will power. Finally the log splits, breaks, falls. She stands up, the saw at her side, sweat on her forehead.

"There it is; I knew I could do it. See, two logs for the price of one."

Ben takes the saw from her hand. I lift another log in place. I'm hoping Ben won't say anything to antagonize her. Actually he never would; it wouldn't occur to *him*, only to *me*.

"Well, you really cut through it in a hurry. At that rate, in a couple hours, we'd have enough to burn for a week."

She picks up her things from the doorstep, wraps her snagged scarf around her neck. Maggie steps out the door.

"Well, frankly, I'd rather help with Christmas cookies upstairs. This place gives me the creeps; all those wheels, cogs, the wet floor, the wet sawdust. Come on, Nickie."

They leave, going around by the dam. I put Nickie's cut pieces on the steps. Ben's ready to saw again. Maybe I'll never get a chance to cut wood any more; Ben's taking over. I don't think I'm about to cry over it but I think I *could* cry about Nickie if I let myself. We all have to live out our own lives and usually no one can help us. But it can be so hard just to stand by.

Ben and I get fifteen logs cut and pass them up for piling. We have a stack beside the fireplace, now, high as the mantle. I know it's ridiculous but this gives *me* a feeling of security, like a refrigerator full of food.

Lor has been making dough for the Christmas cookies. She makes them from a recipe my mother always used. They're walnut-flavored with a dab of strawberry jam on each one. But first, before baking, they need to be rolled in sausagelike rolls inside waxed paper and put into the refrigerator to harden for a few hours. Snitching some of the batter now, before it goes into the refrigerator, has been a favorite for me and all the kids every Christmas. Lor, who doesn't like the batter herself, has set some aside for us.

My mother used to tell me I'd get a stomachache and pimples from eating raw batter but I ate it anyway, got both pimples and stomachache. I didn't know much about self-fulfilling prophecies then, but this probably qualified.

Maggie's standing by the door looking out on the back porch. The mill is down low enough so you can't actually see out over the dam to the pond from the door.

"Could we go up and look at my property, Dad? You sent me pictures of the work you've done but I've never actually seen it."

As a wedding present, Lor and I gave Maggie and George a beautiful field, about an acre. It slants toward the south and east for maximum sun. On the near, high edge is the ruin of the first house in our town of Moulin de Tonnère. It's even older than the mill itself.

But I mean this was a *real* ruin. Only a few stones actually still stuck above the ground. Originally, it'd been home to the person who controlled our pond for the *flottage*. The *flottage* was a unique system of getting wood that'd been felled here in the Morvan on up to Paris. This was when wood was the main fuel for heating there.

The farmers and foresters would cut and pile it along streams which led to the Yonne River and thence to the Seine. They'd put their mark on each log so it could be identified. At a given signal, the sluice gates of all ponds would be opened; the streams filled quickly and logs would rush the almost sixty kilometers to Clamecy. There, the individually marked logs would be counted and credited to the proper owner.

This house on Maggie's property was lived in by the man who opened and closed sluice gates for several ponds in the vicinity.

We'd been told that, previous to World War II, a woman alone, whose husband had been killed in World War I, raised twelve children in that same house. It's hard to believe thirteen people could live in such a small space.

Unearthing the remains of this house became a minor mania with me, as much an archaeological impulse as anything. Whenever friends would come visit or stay a few weeks, I'd force-labor them into my private folly. We ripped out all the bushes, roots, briar patches first. Then we dug into the space enclosed by the remnants of the walls, piling earth to make a terrace on the downhill side, facing the village; we dry-walled, fitting rocks tightly on the outsides of the terrace walls.

We dug down to the old tile floor and squared the corners. The measurement was exactly five meters by five meters. Even assuming a second floor (and the evidence was there had been one), the total was less than fifty square meters all together, that's only about 450 square feet.

Imagine a family of twelve kids in that small space. This woman must have been the original Little Old Woman Who Lived in a Shoe.

We recuperated the stone lintels for doors and windows, rebuilt these openings; we unearthed the old bread oven; it was made with interlocking tiles, and almost intact.

I gradually started rebuilding the walls, carefully fitting stones like a gigantic jigsaw puzzle, filling in spaces with the dampened earth I'd dug out, mixing it with lime; finishing with a mixture of earth and cement as a natural plaster. It was a great project, wonderfully meaningless, my private Holiday Spa, Vic Tanney gym, Jane Fonda workout, all in one.

After the walls were up eight feet, I abandoned the idea of truly reconstructing the house in the original form and spanned the walls with a series of four-by-ten rafters. I covered these with raw oak planking from the sawmill nearby, to make a terrace on top. I built stone steps from below and now we have a terrific sunning terrace up there.

I also built a waist-high wall around the terrace. There's enough privacy for nude sunbathing and, more important, a reasonably quiet place away from fishermen for sleeping out summer nights. It's also the main launching pad for Ben's airplanes and the stand from which he likes to shoot his .22.

We developed our garden up there because the soil is so fertile and the sun orientation good; the Morvan is not known for quality or quantity of sunshine. I also built a hand pump to bring water for our garden up from the village well.

The best part is that, only a two-minute walk from the mill itself, we have a vastly improved view over the entire valley. Up there, I feel I'm on a flying carpet drifting low over the valley as in a dream. There's magic about the place. As a serious philosopher, I guess I'm not supposed to believe in magic, but I do. I don't think I could face life without it.

So, I'm really anxious myself to show it to Maggie, give her something upbeat to think about, something of continuity, perseverance, rebuilding. I'm still somehow capable of deluding myself into thinking these little, background surroundings can influence behavior. I'm the classic reluctant, ongoing romantic.

We start dressing warmly. The temperature's hovering at fifteen degrees below freezing. I constantly reassure Ben this might be snow weather but I'm beginning to lose confidence, it doesn't smell right for snow. Maggie, who's five-seven, is ducking to get through her own door.

It isn't very impressive inside. I still haven't done anything about the floor. The tiles are mostly cracked and pulling up. I should probably pour a new cement slab and reset the tiles, or, at least, put in a wood floor. I'm running out of steam for the job. There are two hardened sacks of cement and the wheelbarrow's filled with cement-working tools and covered with a tarp. I'm feeling slightly apprehensive, not knowing what Maggie had been expecting. Maybe she thought it was all finished and ready to move into. We haven't even put the door or any windows in the places we've roughed out for them. It's very primitive.

"Gosh, Dad, this is wonderful. If we really get stuck, Seth and I could move right in here. It shouldn't take much to fix the windows, the door and that floor, then we could put a fireplace over there in the corner. We could live here just fine. We'd plant a garden and cut wood for the fireplace and I'm sure George would send us *some* money. We could be really independent."

And she means it! I can see from her face. I can also, for the first time, realize how serious she is about leaving George. If *our* Maggie is willing to try living in a rocky dugout like this, it must be bad. I look over at Lor and she's concentrating on Maggie, eyes narrowed. I'm sure Lor's having the same kinds of thoughts. Neither of us had suspected how desperate things are. Nicole has moved beside Maggie and locked arms with her. It's so great to see them friends; they were so competitive about everything when they were adolescents.

"I'll move in with you, Peg. Between the two of us, we could turn this room into a cozy nest, tell the whole world to go screw itself."

Ben turns away and out the door. This has generally been *his* private place. He doesn't enjoy sun or heat; so, in midsummer, when we might be down by the mill sunning and swimming or up on the terrace here sunning, listening to the portable radio, he'd come down into this room where it's always damp and cool, to sit in the big cut window and read. There's a beautiful view, almost like a painting, through that window. There are hills across the way and it looks directly down onto the field which came with the mill. There's a stream flowing through this field and we can see a tree house I built for Ben, three summers ago, in a tree, on an island, in the middle of the stream.

Loretta and I follow Ben out, the girls file after us, up the rest of the stairs. I always feel an inside lift when I come up here. Maggie's field is cut close and green, thanks to Pom Pom, eater of sugar corn and fruit trees. We go up four more steps, this time wooden steps, onto the platform. This oak-floored surface is ten meters by five meters, a really fine, flat place. Lor strolls across to the edge, looking down toward the village. The girls follow her cautiously. There's a hip-high rail around the entire wooden platform.

It really is surprising, almost frightening, how, with so little effort, we've seemed to go up into the sky. Just then, the clouds open and strong rays of pale sunshine break through to light the whitened landscape around us. Magic *is* the only word for it; shadows of clouds are hopscotching over the patterned hills. Maggie grabs hold of the railing.

"Gosh, Dad, this makes me dizzy. It's like taking off in a 747 or looking down from a *hang* glider!"

I begin to hear my motorcycle coming along the Vauchot hill. The timing's slightly off so it pops, backfires, when you don't accelerate. I watch and catch glimpses of Mike through the trees, then he's visible in the long clear part just before he comes into town. Maggie turns to me.

"There's Mike. Let's go meet him. Maybe he'll take us to his place in the woods."

I look over at Loretta. Again, she seems miles away, not really with us. I try to generate enthusiasm.

"Wouldn't it be fun to pack a lunch and eat out there Lor? Maybe we can even get his fireplace going. I piled dry wood inside last summer when I hiked in and cleared brush. Ben and I put enough tinder in there for us to get a good fire going."

"It does sound like a wonderful idea, Will. But we'd better check with Mike first."

Maggie's face lights up.

"I'd love to see Mike's cabin. The last time I was there, it was only a muddy hole in the ground and some rocks piled in a circle in the middle. He and Debby were working like crazy people on it. By the way, whatever happened to Debby?"

Nicole pulls Maggie by the arm and they start toward the steps.

"Geneviève is what's happened to Debby. Or maybe some Tom, Dick, Harry or Harriette happened to Mike. Nobody knows about those things, big sister."

They both laugh. Loretta and I follow them down. Ben comes behind us. He's walking along reading. This is his way of being here and not here at the same time.

I'm spinning the damned "love" question again. Is it only feeling good with someone, enjoying their company? Or is it more a feeling of responsibility, of caring? How much of it is possession and feeling possessed? I'll never know.

IV

Four Calling Birds

When we get down to the mill, Mike's there and throwing more wood on the fire. He smiles at us, but this is his Buddha beatific smile, nothing real about it. He's being nice, reassuring us that everything's fine, nothing to worry about. His acting skills are about on a par with mine as diplomat. Maggie bursts right out with it.

"Mike, would you take us to your cabin? Dad says there's firewood there and Mom says we can pack a lunch and make a picnic."

The smile disappears. Now he has to really *think*, bear down, decide. I know it isn't so much our going out there he might resent as his going there *with us*. I think his feeling about the cabin is exclusive of our family and inclusive of something personal to himself. It can be uncomfortable. He sneaks a quick look at me, at Lor. Then he looks into Maggie's eyes, sees the sincerity, the honest desire to share in something of his.

"Sure, okay. That'd be fine. But I warn you, it's damp and moldy. Not enough sun gets through all the trees in that wood."

I'm slowly realizing what a wonderful way this will be to spend Christmas Eve afternoon. It can sometimes be a painful time of expectancy, of waiting. We can all take an invigorating hike out there, then come back to bake cookies.

"We'd really appreciate it, Mike, thanks. Lor, you and the girls pack some stuff to eat. Ben, you look for a box of matches and bring along a couple old newspapers to start a fire. We'll all need rubber boots to get across the muddy meadow from the west woods, it'll most likely be iced over but you never know."

I'm into planning a campaign, nobody's paying much attention to me. I haven't been out to Mike's place since summer.

It isn't long before we're ready. We go out, Mike and Maggie in the lead, Loretta and Nicole after them, Ben and I bringing up the rear. The sun has definitely been covered by clouds and some more wind is blowing but the temperature has gone up. *Now* there's some beginnings of snow smell but it's still too cold.

"You might get what you've been asking for for Christmas, Ben."

"I already got it, or I know I'm going to get it anyway, my Russian rifle. I dreamed about that rifle last night. I was shooting little white pigeons with it, like a shooting gallery and they must have been a hundred meters away but I was hitting every one. It was a great dream, they weren't real pigeons, they were metal and went clang each time I hit."

"I mean snow. I think it could start snowing any time now if it only gets about five degrees warmer. We could have snow for Christmas after all."

"Oh, you say that every year, Dad. You're just the perennial optimist."

Another cliché out in the open. I swear it's some kind of game he plays.

The route to Mike's place takes us first up to the next town of Milé, about half a mile along the main road past the mill. Then we cut off to the right and up a hard, frozen, rutted dirt road.

Runnels of ice are frozen in the ruts, cutting from left to right as the path makes its turns and tips on the way up. It climbs fairly steeply for another half kilometer. Then we take off away from it and into the woods, heading almost due south. At the place where we cut off the road and into the forest path, Maggie and Mike are waiting for us. They've each found a stick to use as a staff. Ben's found one, too. It's sort of a family custom. I've been drifting in my mind so I haven't followed through.

Where they're waiting, is one of the largest holly bushes in the whole valley. It's in full sunlight and if there's one place where there should be berries, that's the place. But it's as bare as all the other bushes.

This is just the Christmas without berries. We've had other Christmases when we've really had to hunt for holly with berries but this is the first year I can remember when there haven't been *any*. I don't know if it has to do with the fall and winter not having been cold enough up till now, or too wet, or whatever.

I've been told that holly bushes are male and female; the dark green, pointier bushes are the males, the lighter green, less pointed, the female, but that doesn't fit either. Other years, I've seen some of the most beautiful dark red berries clustered in with some of the deepest, pointiest green holly. Maybe holly has sex, but performs some kind of parthenogenesis, or maybe it's bisexual. That's a nice idea, bisexual holly for a jolly Christmas, make a nice Christmas card theme or a modern Christmas song like the one Arlo Guthrie did with the part "Let's get Santa Claus . . . because . . ."

Mike's staring into that holly bush.

"I can't believe it, Dad. There's not a berry here. This was *always* the last desperation place for berries in bad years."

"Only goes to prove life is not a bowl of berries, maybe, Mike."

Nicole and Maggie fall into each other.

"Oh, please! Somebody stop him! Let's not get Dad started on being witty, Mike. Please! It'll just ruin Christmas to have him tail-ending everything with some way-out, stretched-to-the-edge pun."

Mike's turned and started along the path. I shuffle up to join Nicole and Maggie. Loretta drops back to walk with Ben.

"Okay, I promise. I'll control myself. Whatever it costs in blood pressure rising, in swallowed pride, I won't inflict you with my unmitigated wit. I'll mitigate."

This part of the walk is best. The ground is covered with shades of brown leaves, oak, beech, birch, willow, still somewhat covered with snow in the shadier places. The dark green of holly and some pine trees punctuate the earth colors. There's also the green of moss covering the base of trees and over all the rocks, definitely not the flora and fauna of a desert. The path here is crisp, frozen, crackling mud. We need to walk up on the road edge so we don't slip. We traverse the side of a hill. On our right, there's a bank about four feet high; on our left, a drop down through the thinning forest to a meadow stretching out from town. It's amazing how, with all this cold, on the west and north sunlit hills, the grass is still green; it doesn't look like Christmas at all.

I drop back. The others are rushing forward; even Lor and Maggie pass me up. I'm not tired, only a kind of lassitude falls upon me. I'm enjoying being out here in the woods with my family. I look ahead and know all those people I see are of our blood, come from Lor and me. It's something I didn't think about when we got married. Sure, I knew we wanted kids, but now seeing them; grown-up, regular people, even Ben; each with personal ideas, personal ways; God, it *is* a miracle.

Damn, I hope they all find good mates. Living alone would be the worst thing for me. Despite all the hard parts, the failure, the constant accommodation, accepting the inevitable, living with worry and annoyance; I don't know what my life would mean if we hadn't had a family.

Writing philosophical treatises, even if I did it, would never be enough; it's only a substitute for the real thing.

Now Maggie's breaking out, going it alone, and I think maybe there's something bubbling between Mike and Geneviève for good or bad. But Nicole; she's so hard to please, maybe she does need someone like Mike, somebody smart but with a laid-back approach to life. No, Nicole'd go mad. But it's someone in that direction who will make the best husband for her, someone she can respect and at the same time not feel a need to compete.

The whole idea of love is so complicated, it obviously isn't just sex although sex, passion, should probably be part of it. There's got to be some agreement about the reasons for living. Trust and tolerance are probably as important as respect and admiration or even passion. But there should be a minimum of manipulation, possession, dominance games, competition. Power plays can destroy love faster than anything; slight searching and demands for exclusive attention turn the protective power of love into a cage. These are some of the things I've come to believe but now I'm finding it's not so simple, the animal in us, call it the id, is not easily convinced. Our egos are generally too labile, too fragile.

Nicole stops and pulls out her camera. We've come to Mike's cabin. It's just ahead, almost hidden in the trees.

"Hot shit. I'd forgotten how beautiful Mike's place is. It's the kind of hideout everybody in America talks about when they're spaced out on pot or something. It's like a dream."

Mike stands and watches as she takes one photo, then she walks forward past him for another. It gives Maggie and me a chance to catch up. I look back to Loretta and Ben. Ben is far behind, walking in the streambed. Reaching into the cold water rimmed with ice, he picks up a stone, looks at it, then drops it into the fast-running water. Ben loves smooth, egglike stones; has a collection of them.

We go under some barbed wire to enter Mike's woods. It's about two acres and he has it landscaped almost like a park. The trees he's thinned out are piled around the edges of his property and are dry, so he not only has a fence but an unlimited supply of wood for burning.

There's a small, all-year stream, flowing less than five paces from the porch he's built in front of his door. This door makes the door on Maggie's place look like a door for giants. It can't be four feet high. The way he's slanted his roof lines to fit in with the landscape, it couldn't have been much higher. At a distance, the door is the only really visible thing. Mike's painted it electric blue. The rest is natural tree surface of slashing he bought at the sawmill to use for outside siding, or the gray, moss-encrusted slate of his roof.

Mike goes on ahead and pulls out the key from under a slate where he usually keeps it. I imagine I'm the last one to put it there, back at the end of August. He squats and pushes the key into his padlock. He's fashioned a hasp from two large nails and the padlock's hooked through them. It actually wouldn't keep anyone out, but does signal that the owner would rather not have casual visitors.

However, when we go in, there's a piece of paper on the table. Mike built his table from rough-cut lumber he bought at the same sawmill. There are names of various local kids with signatures, greetings and dates. Mike looks at it and smiles so I imagine he told some of his country friends where the key was. I'm glad somebody's getting use from the place; what a perfect hideout for young lovers seeking peace and quiet, or even *old* lovers, those few who are left.

Maggie's happily immersing herself into the whole cabin. Her head turns slowly, taking notice of the little corner kitchen, utensils hanging on the walls, the food cabinets, the sleeping platform next to the uncut stone fireplace. From inside, looking up, the lath for hanging slate hooks looks like a wooden spiderweb. To really insulate this place in winter, that space under the slate would need glass wool or Styrofoam. But this isn't a winter home, only a great getaway hut for summer.

The rug's spread on the floor. Mike had left it rolled against the wall but when I came out in August it was molding badly.

Maggie looks up at the roof where Mike's built in some windows he pried out from the windshield and side windows of our old Volkswagen. That VW had been the car she and George used in high school; it was practically their private home.

"Gee, Mike. This is a great place. If I had a cabin like this, tucked away, I'd live here all the time. It's a true Franky Furbo house."

Franky Furbo is a character, a smart fox, a mutant fox, smarter than any human. For over twenty years I used him as the basis for morning stories to our kids. I hadn't thought of it before, but there are Franky Furbo qualities to this place, deep in the woods, everything small, simple, practical. Only Franky's house was built into a tree.

I start trying to get a fire built. Loretta finds the broom in a corner and begins sweeping. Ben and I swept the rug in August and maybe some of the intervening visitors did the same, but now there's a soft layer of leaves and debris. Ben begins bringing over light twigs and bark scrapings. He also gives me the paper he brought with him, and the matches. It's going to be hard getting a flame going in the damp, wet-surfaced fireplace.

When I have enough paper and dry shuckings piled, I stack small pieces of wood in a little teepee shape. If this catches I can start adding larger pieces. Maggie and Nicole are sitting at the table behind me; they both have their arms wrapped across their breasts trying to keep out the cold. Coming directly from California sun to a dank, dark wood like this can be a terrific shock to the system. I hope my fire catches; I know it will smoke like hell at first but then, when the flue gets warmed, the smoke will dissipate. At least that's the way it's always been before.

I strike the match. We keep feeding small bits of paper onto the feeble flame. Gradually it starts to catch, twisting fire begins threading through the dry twigs. I work in some more of the dried brush Ben keeps handing me. We both like kindling a fire and the more difficult the problem, the less materials we have, the more fun it is. Our ideal is always a "one-match fire." But this one's going to be a problem. There's too much smoke, there's steam, too, from the wet wood and soaked ashes in the fire pit. But we keep at it; now smoke is pouring into the room, it'll be hard getting enough heat up that flue. We force the flame some by fanning it. I expend most of the dry wood and paper we have, trying to get a hot, high flame going; develop a hot spot.

Ben is down on his knees blowing at the bottom of the fire, a human bellows. I can hear the girls coughing behind me. Lor has stopped sweeping and stands by the door to breathe clear air coming in around the cracks. We either make it in the next few minutes or we'll have to abandon the whole idea; the room is filled with smoke. I turn.

"Why don't you girls take a little walk with Mother over top of the hill, while we try to get this fireplace drawing properly. It should only be a few minutes and maybe then we'll have a nice roaring fire."

Lor pushes the door open a foot.

"Come on, let's go, girls. There's a lovely stream over the ridge there. I'll show you where Mike panned for gold."

Mike, in the meantime, has been out with his saw cutting significant logs for us just in case we do get a fire going. He has some trees nearby, ones he felled in his effort to allow light through to his house. They should be dry now after two years.

But the big if is this smoldering fire in front of us. Ben finds more leaves and grass in a corner behind the fireplace. We put them on and their flare seems to be just the extra heat we need; the smoke reverses itself and starts sucking up the chimney, twirling lines of blue smoke twist out of the room and up. We pile on some finger-thick twigs. They're dry and if we can only keep the fire hot long enough they'll catch. If they get going, then we have a chance. Mike backs through the door, arms full of logs, he drops them on the floor in front of the fireplace.

"Hey, it looks as if you two have actually got something going there. If these big logs start burning we'll be toasty in no time at all."

The jump from finger-sized twigs to wrist-sized ones is treacherous for a minute or two but then they catch.

We nestle one of Mike's logs into the center. I send Ben out for Lor and the girls.

Mike's started to unpack the lunch. He takes down some of

his dishes from the cupboard he built to keep rats and other vermin out of his food. He and Geneviève lived here most of one summer two summers ago; she's a true homemaker and got Mike to install some of the amenities he wouldn't've thought of himself.

The fire's definitely caught and I'm not sure if it's only psychological but the place already feels warmer. I take off my scarf and gloves. Also, a brisk wind has sprung up outside; so being inside and out of that wind makes it seem warmer, too. The smoke is almost gone and it's a quiet joy to be here in Mike's private home surrounded by woods.

I'm just beginning to worry if Ben got lost looking for the women when I see them coming from the direction of the spring. Ben is stumbling along, carrying a leaking wooden bucket, probably filled with that unbelievably clear, almost tasteless water from Mike's shallow spring. Nicole and Maggie have arms filled with pine branches; Loretta has a sprig of holly. I go over to open the door for them. They stomp and wipe their feet on the porch. Nicole comes in first.

"We thought we'd decorate Mike's cabin for Christmas. My big-little brother had a knife so we cut branches from pine trees up on the hill and Mom actually found one branch on a holly bush with real berries. Maybe we're going to have a Christmas after all."

Maggie struggles through the door, hunched over, wet pine branches poking in her eyes. Her cheeks are glowing from the cold through her Arizona tan. She looks beautiful. I can't help thinking of how hard it must be for George losing her. I wonder what I would've done if Lor wanted to divorce me after we'd been married only seven years, when we had little Maggie six years old, and Mike three. Something dumb and desperate probably. It's hard enough thinking about something like that, even now with the kids mostly all grown.

Maggie goes near the fire, turns her back to it, pushes her butt close to the flame.

"Dad, it's so beautiful in these woods. There's moss growing on everything and the trees are magic-looking, without being scary. It's like something from a German fairy tale."

She piles her branches, with Nicole's, along the wall facing the meadow. Lor has strolled through the door in her inimitable gliding way, smiling, turning her head back and forth, absorbing everything as if she's a condemned criminal walking toward the electric chair, looking at this world the last time to see how beautiful it is.

"See my holly, Will dear? It was the only branch with berries on a huge dark green, pointy, absolutely bare bush. It must mean something. It's a gift to us for Christmas."

She's holding it over her head.

"We went up Mike's stream, then doubled back to the spring. Ben intercepted us just as we were going by Madame Calvet's wood. He helped us with his knife, cutting branches to deck the halls and all. Isn't it lovely?"

Ben's come in behind Lor. The bucket is three-quarters filled with water. It looks as if he really did a good job cleaning out the bucket before he filled it. This is such a terrific part of parenting, watching your young gradually learn to do things properly.

"Where do you want this, Dad?"

"Put it over there in the kitchen area, Ben. How was the spring, all filled with leaves again?"

"Yep, but I cleaned them out. The water was so clear it was like air. And those clay pots we made by hand last summer and stuck in the fork of the tree beside the spring are still there. Even all the rain and snow and everything didn't melt them. We should bring up some of this clay to Paris with us. I could take it to school and show it to my ceramics teacher. You know, Mrs. Wright is always looking for new kinds of clay."

"Well, it's too cold now to be digging in clay, Ben; maybe we'll bring some up when we're down here for Easter."

"Oh, come on, Dad; you'll forget. We never do the things you promise."

"You just remind me and we'll do it, Ben. I promise, cross my heart. I'm just getting older and I forget things. You remind me."

Now, Nicole backs *her* butt against the fire. Maggie snuggles beside her. They look frozen. Maggie glances over at Ben.

"It's not just he's getting older, Ben. He never remembers the things he promises, promises don't mean much to him. But he's still a good Dad. Only he's always spinning his head in the clouds about cosmology, time, meaning, reality and stuff like that. If you'll remind him, I know he'll help you get some clay up to school."

And she's right. Maggie wouldn't say it if it weren't true. Honesty and doing the right thing have always meant a lot to her. It must have been difficult for her growing up with a person like me, someone who's never sure what really is and couldn't remember if he were.

It doesn't bother me much any more, I've made most of my excuses. Lor has learned to live with it but for Maggie and Nickie I think it's been hard. I'm the big promiser. If the road to hell really is paved with good intentions I've built myself a Roman royal freeway straight to the nether regions. How do you change what you are?

Poor Lor. When we were first going together, even when we were first married, she was always calling me on what I'd promised, what I'd said. Often I'd wind up saying the complete opposite of what I'd said the week, the day or sometimes only five minutes before. I used to quote the famous line from someone I don't remember about hobgoblins and consistency but it didn't help. Now I think she's finally given up; only rarely does she challenge me in my inconsistencies. Maybe she's accepted that I am a lightweight, perhaps sometimes a likable lightweight, but don't ever *count* on me. I don't count well either.

At least Lor knew something of what she was getting involved with; I hope. Maybe she thought she could reform me, maybe she still does, but I don't think so.

Meanwhile, Mike and Lor are making a beautiful lunch spread on the table. They've found an old tablecloth which isn't too moldy, flattened it across the table to cover the rough boards. They have plates, glasses; dishes they've rinsed in the water Ben carried from the spring. The lunch sack has produced a three-quarter loaf of French bread, some Camembert, tomatoes, hot dogs, butter and pickles. Ben is sharpening sticks to cook the hot dogs. Nicole is pushing the first finished stick into the fire with two hot dogs speared on it.

Maggie and I begin hanging pine branches and more berryless holly around the cabin. The smoke is totally gone and the room's beginning to feel warm. Even Maggie has peeled off her outer jacket and loosened the wool knit cap on her head.

Outside, the wind blows furiously, sometimes it gusts so hard, branches are breaking from the trees. Ben, while sharpening sticks, is standing by the window looking across toward the spring.

"It's started snowing, Dad; it's really snowing! You said it would, and here it comes, we're going to have snow for Christmas."

Nicole joins Ben at the window.

"Oh, come on Ben; you're crazy as Dad. There's no real snow, that's old leaves and things blowing around."

"No, look Nickie. Keep looking. You'll see. There's real snow, it's just beginning!"

"Holy God! He's right. It's starting to snow."

Nicole and Maggie begin dancing in circles like a hoedown, swinging each other around. Ben moves closer against the window, staring out, trying not to see them. Nicole pulls off her scarf and throws it on the floor.

"Come on, Dad, Mom. Dance with us. This is a snow dance. We're going to dance till that snow is so thick we won't be able to see the trees."

Nicole's left the hot dogs she was cooking, leaning them against the stone fireplace. Ben works his way around the dancing and pokes them into the fire again. I grab hold of Lor by the waist, she puts her hands on my shoulders and *we* begin swinging in circles. The room isn't very big so we're bumping into each other. Mike joins to make a circle of three with Nicole and Maggie. And as we swing faster and faster, the snow swirls and increases out the window. Lor starts singing "Joy to the World" and we dance to that. It's the first time I've ever danced to a Christmas carol. Maybe it's the first time *anybody's* ever danced to Christmas carols.

Then Mike begins "Deck the Halls" and we dance even faster; and now we join in one big circle, the five of us with our hands joined, swinging round and round. Mike and Nicole are the leaders. Nicole has us get closer, put hands on each other's shoulders, so we have more space, are better tied together, united. Nicole starts us swinging out our feet, to "Winter Wonderland," crossing them as we change directions. It's almost like Greek folk dancing only we're dancing to classic Christmas carols. Mike keeps trying to pull Ben in with us but Ben only shakes his head without turning around. He's started on a second pair of hot dogs. I think it's overt emotion with which he has trouble, but he'll grow out of it, I hope. It's a serious problem, one I've coped with all my life. I'm like a car with sticky valves. But we're actually having too much fun for me to worry about it much right then.

We finish off with a full version of "Good King Wenceslas," then we're all so pooped we drop on the floor like the end of a ring-around-the-rosy game. We're puffing and laughing. Nicole's the first to push herself up onto her feet.

"I must say I'm warm now. Come on, Ben, move over. Give me one of your sticks and we'll get on with the cooking. I'm starving."

We take turns cooking and eating. We split the baguette to make hot dog–type sandwiches and cut tomatoes or pickles into them along with some cheese. Ben goes and gets another bucket of clean well water and we drink that. The water is so clean, cold and clear it tastes green, almost like a very good Rhine wine.

It's the first time I've been able to taste anything in this water. But now I'm feeling fine-tuned and the taste is perfect with the slightly burned and smoked hot dogs, the ripe cheese, the Dijon mustard.

It's starting to get dark. The wind isn't blowing so hard but the snow is coming down in soft large flakes. Already the meadow is white and, even in the woods, where the trees aren't too dense, there's a light powdering. It looks as if we're really going to have it this year, a true white Christmas Eve; we only have this about one time in three.

We'll almost always have snow sometime during the two-week holiday but not often on the actual day. I'm really happy this is one of the lucky times. I'm beginning to feel things are coming out all right. Even if the rest of everything is a total bust, even if this *is* our last Christmas, at least we had our wonderful Christmas Eve dance at Mike's place. There's no way to plan things.

Finally, we pack up the lunch, put out the fire, and Lor rescues her berried piece of holly. Mike locks the door securely and we tromp off uphill from the cabin to the other way out. I feel sorry leaving the cabin, a perfect place for somebody's Christmas, and no one there. Can a hut, a house, feel lonesome, abandoned?

This way out is on a path most of the way and much easier than through the woods and meadows. It's the way we first came into this place when we bought it and it's the way Mike brought in his building materials in our old Renault when he was doing his construction. It's a rough, rock-strewn road with small streamlets passing over it, or under, through overgrown culverts. It takes good driving skills to get in here. I've done it on a motorcycle but never with a car.

The snow is coming down so evenly and slowly it's as if the sky is breaking into pieces and falling onto us. It's a wonderful feeling. I'm surprised it's snowing because it's still very cold. I didn't know it could snow when the temperature was four or five degrees below freezing and it must be at least that. Nicole and Mike have started scooping up snow for snowballs but this snow is too powdery and they can't compact them into anything. I pick up a terrific walking stick, already carved at one end with small decorations. It could even be a cow prod someone left or lost along the path. So, now we *all* have sticks and I'm hearing again the lyrics of "Good King Wenceslas" in my mind; the part that says:

> Page and monarch forth they went,
> Forth they went together,
> Through the rude wind's wild lament
> And the bitter weather.

Or the part where the page says,

> Fails my heart, I know not how,
> I can go no longer

and the King,

> Mark my footsteps my good page,
> Tread thou in them boldly.
> Thou wilt find the winter rage,
> Freeze thy blood less co-old-ly.

I'm walking along at the rear, stepping in everybody else's footprints when I can, the way you do with stepping on cracks in a city pavement.

We come out with a wonderful view down into the town of Milé where we turned in on our walk out. There are fruit trees in the field on our left and I search for some fallen fruit to make a compote but the birds have gotten them all or they're too far rotted. Each little sickle pear or crab apple is a rounded white bump in the carpet of snow; reminds me of Styrofoam packing.

Ben drops back with me. I can tell by his quiet he's happy to be out, to be walking; to have the snow. I know he's feeling squeezed, pressed by the rest of the family being here, but none of us can have everything the way we might want it.

When we get back to the mill, the fire is almost a goner. The pale sunlight has disappeared in the cloud-covered, snow-filled sky, and it's dark. I switch on the light over our table. Loretta turns the light on over the sink in the kitchen. Ben and Mike try getting the embers of our fire going by turning over the half-burnt logs and pushing burnt ends toward the center. There's a pile of old *Herald Tribune*s and Ben begins tearing small pieces off to rekindle the fire. I can see they'll get it going easily enough.

I open the refrigerator and feel the cookie dough. It's just right for cutting. My job is usually slicing cookies, then Lor puts them in the oven and times them. I'm also in charge of greasing and flouring each pan between batches. Ben's job this year will be stacking the finished, warm cookies gently in the cookie jars and tins without breaking them. Last year he was spreader of cookies on pan and jam dabber. This gives some idea of how much he must be feeling displaced.

The table over the millstone is covered with a fine dust of flour. Our oven is hot by the time the first pan is ready; Loretta lit the oven as soon as she came in. I take off a minute to check our inside thermometer; already we're back up to nineteen. Lor wants to install central heating here at the mill, but I keep putting her off. My excuse is we're only here two weeks a year when we actually need heat; but my real reason is I get such a kick out of fighting the cold, chopping wood, changing bottles of gas, starting fires, watching the thermometer. It gives me the illusion of being in charge of something; of having the elements with which to grapple. Nicole looks up from dabbing jam.

"Come on, Dad. No goofing off."

She smiles. She has one of the nicest damned smiles. But I still can't tell when she's smiling *with* me or laughing *at* me; it's been that way since she was seven. Maybe it's the same smile.

"Just checking how hot it is in here. We've got almost twenty-five degrees centigrade difference between inside and outside right now."

We all stop simultaneously and look out the windows. It's *so* beautiful with a slow, continuous, falling snow. There's that closing-in feeling, the way it is when you get a shot of morphine in a hospital. It not only takes away pain, it seems to give a thick layer of protection all around, like insulation.

Maggie looks around.

"This is really Christmas, folks. I know all this isn't real, how hard it is out there for the whole rest of the world, but it's great to just forget things for a while and pretend everything's okay. By the way, when do we get to taste the first cookies?"

Lor looks into the oven. She reaches in and pulls out a tray.

"These look about right; everybody agree?"

She puts them on the table. The smell goes through the room. We could smell them in the oven, a slight odor of walnut, the smell of hot strawberry jam melting. Mike takes one first.

"I'll be the guinea pig. What can I lose?"

He lifts it off the pan with a spatula, blows on it to cool the hot jam, pops it into his mouth, crunches down. Nicole, Maggie, Ben, Loretta each take one. I pick one that isn't as much done as the others. I generally don't like browned or burnt cookies. I like my cookies soft. I nibble on the edge. You'd just know I'd be a nibbler.

The first Christmas cookie is always special. It's at least half the pleasure of all the cookies I'll eat. After this one it'll only be repetition, filling myself up, indulgence. But this time it's special, bringing back memories all the way to when I was younger than Ben, much younger, and my mother would make these cookies in the tiny kitchen of our row house outside Chicago. I was allowed one cookie before Christmas, one cookie on the afternoon of Christmas Eve.

Time is certainly peculiar. A single cookie like this, with my eyes closed, can make about half a century seem to disappear without a trace. The greatest part of my life goes poof in the delicious wafting smell of a single cookie.

We work into late afternoon, filling tray after tray; Ben stacking jars, then tin cookie boxes, until all the rolls from the refrigerator are sliced and the last tray has been emptied. I look at my watch. It's almost seven o'clock. I think about the concentration of emotion to come between now and bedtime.

Mike rides my motorcycle over to Geneviève's. Although I think he's enjoying himself, he's been uneasy. The age-old conflict between responsibility and pleasure.

We eat lightly for dinner. We know we're going to be gorged at the reveillon. Both Nicole and Maggie'd like to get out of going but it would be such an insult to the village. The whole celebration means so much to them. Life in this valley is difficult so when there's an excuse for a feast, they go all out.

Madame Le Moine has another son who works for a large fish store in Auxerre about a hundred kilometers away. At six o'clock on Christmas Eve, the boss usually tells the employees they can have any shellfish left over because they'll only be rotten by the time the holidays are over.

Christmas Eve, Madame Le Moine's son here in the village, Philippe, and Madame Calvet's son Claude wait on tenterhooks for the call from Auxerre that the oysters, clams and mussels are ready. Then they tear out of the village with classic Morvandeau speed and recklessness to pick them up for the reveillon. As far as I know, this mad event has been going on for at least ten years. On the way back, one of them drives while the other opens about fifteen dozen oysters and clams; cleans maybe twenty dozen mussels. And this is only for the hors d'oeuvres.

I'm not about to tell the girls the main dish of the reveillon will be roast pork from the pig I helped kill only a few days ago at the Calvets'. I don't have to, they probably know already.

It gives me a good feeling to know that somehow I did partially earn the right to eat that pig, if there really is such a right, but I know the girls wouldn't feel that way and it's best I keep it to myself.

Anyway, the feast will finish up with a *bûche de noël* which has been baked especially for our reveillon by the boulangerie of Ligny. In actual cash money, it might well be the biggest investment of all. We'll drink the wine Claude and Philippe bought in barrels and bottled, corked themselves four years ago. We always drink four-year-old wine at Christmas. For serious drinking there will be the *naöle* and usually one "bought" bottle of whiskey.

Nobody drinks the whiskey, it tastes like swamp water beside the power and tang of the *naöle*. Maybe it's the same bottle of whiskey every year. I think they bought it the first year for me because in the movies and TV all Americans only drink whiskey. These people are so damned nice you wind up feeling guilty most of the time. *Rendre service*, loosely translated as "do you a favor," seems to be the favorite local activity.

After dinner, we start trimming the Christmas tree. Nicole's brought along some tinsel, a thing almost impossible to find in France. But this is different than the metallic, heavy glistening tinsel I remember. This is made from a very light substance that moves and blows with every current of air. Nicole takes the packages out of her banana bag upstairs and comes downstairs with them tucked carefully under her arm. She goes over in front of our mirror and holds the packages on top of her head so the strands hang over her face. She brushes them aside and her face shows through the glimmering silver.

"Man, I look like Snow White's wicked stepmother."

Maggie stands behind her. She's holding her hands together; actually, one fist, her right, is enfolded in her left hand. She has a small handkerchief folded tight in that right fist. Maggie's left-handed and for some reason, since she was a little girl, has almost always had a handkerchief or Kleenex balled in one fist or the other. She's rocking at the waist, up and down, laughing.

"No, Nickie, not really; you look like the Frosty Snow Queen; that's what you look like. All you need is a sleigh pulled by wolves and a dwarf to drive you. You're beautiful."

Nicole drapes the silver over Maggie's head. "Nope. You're more the queen type, Peg. Queens are never less than five-foot-three." Lor looks up from arranging balls.

"Queen Elizabeth I, maybe the most important queen in history, was a small woman, Nickie. Maybe you're a queen and you don't know it."

"Leave it to you, Mom. You'll make a queen out of me yet. Thanks anyway—but no thanks."

She goes over and hangs the silver tinsel around Lor's head; stands back.

"Now, that's what I call a *real* queen."

I pull a chair close to one side of the tree, and another to the other.

"Who wants to do top balls? Do we all agree little balls on top?"

I'm only trying to get things started. Lor comes to me with a handful of balls.

"You get on one side, Will, and Ben on the other, I'll hand the balls up. I've got the wire hangers in all these."

Ben and I climb up on the chairs. Even though Ben is the tallest, he does have a deathly fear of heights, so maybe he isn't the best choice. He mounts carefully, slowly stretching to his full height.

"Here, Ben. Put this star on the very top."

Lor reaches it up to him. I lean out and bend the tree top down so Ben can slip the star over the tip. This takes a bit of doing, getting the small hole of the star over the bulbous knob on the tip of the tree. Ben carefully pares the knob off with his Swiss Army knife, then slips it over. Slowly he lets the tip spring back into position and it fits perfectly.

Nicole and Maggie, between and around us, are clipping on candle holders. They also tie on wire hangers with middle-sized balls. We have some nice ornaments for the tree, an accumulation of years. Since we're trimming a smaller tree for the first time this year, we should have plenty. Nickie ties on a bright blue ball and steps back.

"I think I'll supervise this job. Somebody needs to make sure the colors are distributed properly and all the holes are filled."

She walks back to the refrigerator, pulls out her bottle of Chablis, and pours half a glassful. Loretta stands up and starts hanging balls with Maggie. Maggie gives Nicole a quick look, then sneaks one at Lor; but Lor's concentrating on the tree, smiling in that wonderful, all-encompassing, almost moronic smile of hers. It's the smile that should have launched a thousand ships but has only slightly nudged one idiot with neither sextant, compass nor map and four kids who still don't know which way to the nearest horizon. She really *is* too good for us.

Sometimes she must get discouraged but she doesn't show it. Maybe she isn't discouraged; maybe *she* doesn't expect any kind of assured reality either. I'm always trying to read other people's minds and mostly I'm only mucking around in my own. I twist my head.

"Nicole, could you tell me if this ball is better here or there? It's the last small one and I can't really tell from up here."

Ben is lowering himself from the chair as if he's just completed a solo climb of the Eiffel Tower in a windstorm. Nicole points.

"Right over there, at about five o'clock and a foot down from the star, there's a blank space. Here, you should begin putting on tinsel, too, while you're still up there."

She pulls out a small handful of the glittering lightweight tinsel. I take it, look down at Loretta; smile.

"Don't worry, dear, I promise I won't just throw it. I'll place it gently, carefully, with measured grace, one at a time, in the most empty places."

She broadens her smile at me, winks.

"Put them on however you want, Will. I know you'll do it right. You're not as feather-headed as you pretend to be."

"Oh, no, Mum! Don't turn the mad tosser loose. I've watched him with his clots of tinsel throwing it in the air, most of it passing through the entire tree, landing on the floor. Not after I've brought this stuff all the way from San Diego."

"Promise, Nicole. I'll carefully consider each piece as if it were gold; no laissez-faire tinsel throwing."

"*Nickie*, Dad. Can't you remember?"

"Sorry. I was caught up concentrating on this tinsel business."

We get all the balls on the tree. Ben is at the table reading, glancing up once in a while to see how things are going, or to make a suggestion. Lor is putting candles into the candle holders. Maggie is draping tinsel, the last of it, over the garlands. I step back, then go over to our bed in the corner and flop. It all looks so good, everybody's being so reasonable. There's something of static floating in the air but there are no stones, nobody's trying to *make* a scene. I wish *I* could really relax.

I look out the window and it's gloaming dark. I clamber onto my knees on the bed and peer through that west window. Our dim single town streetlight is lit and the snow is as regular and consistent as anybody could want on a Christmas card. The road is thick with it, bushes bend under the weight.

I get up, go over and throw another log on the fire. Our tree is close to the fireplace but I don't think there's any real danger. The tree's green and no sparks can fly out of that deep-throated hearth. But some Chicago fire department creep would have two kinds of cat fits and ring a three-alarm fire. Then there probably *would* be a holocaust; *thinking* things can make them happen. I'm sure of that, sure as I am of anything that is.

Lor begins singing, almost as if she's embarrassed, but everybody picks it up, "Silent Night." We sing quietly, carefully, each of us trying not to play star; but even Ben's with us. We finish with the "Sleeeep in heavenly peace . . ." and there's a pause.

Now my mind is peculiar. Over the years, I've strung Christmas carols out in some kind of special immutable order of which I'm not aware in any conscious way. So, when we come to this part of "Silent Night," my mind automatically switches to "O Come All Ye Faithful."

When the kids were young, and there was no struggle for assertion, it all worked out fine. Everybody seemed glad to have someone start the next song, but now, I'm wary. I don't want to play the heavy father role, not now, especially.

I wait. There's a silence. Then, Maggie, who must be implanted too, does it. "O Come All Ye Faithful" and we're off again. So it is with each song. We sing as we go about other things. Lor's packing away the Christmas ball wrappings and boxes. Nicole is sweeping under the Christmas tree. Maggie is sitting at the table, writing a letter, I hope to her husband; Ben is poking at the fire. Lor brings our advent candles and lights them. Advent doesn't mean much to us, but candles burning in the darkening room do.

I hear Mike down-shifting on the Vauchot hill. I knew he wouldn't want to miss the singing. In a certain way, he's the most sentimental of our children, or it could be Maggie. It's so hard to tell; all we have to go by is how much they tell or show, and that's usually such a small part.

"What's your pleasure?" is an idea that's haunted me these days. What is it that gives me pleasure? What is it I'm waiting for, have been waiting for all my life? What reward, what realization? What's it all about? I've known some moments of intense joy, in the past and in the present. But they always seem to sneak up on me, uncalled for, unannounced. It subliminally reinforces my suspicion that there's nothing, only personal illusions, fantasies maintained to encourage sanity.

But one of the pleasures I sort of looked forward to, expected, when I was in my late thirties, early forties, centuries ago, was that of watching my children grow up, getting involved with their lives; vicariously participating in their struggle to the good life, whatever that may be. But it hasn't happened; one more expectation up in smoke. It's all right if I cherish these *illusions* but I need to be careful I don't hold on too long and get caught with a sour mouthful of *de*lusions. It can happen so easily.

To the extent our kids are independent, as we *do* want them to be, there's no room for Lor and me in their lives right now, except as part of their *illusory* systems; and, at best, we are only some kind of diving board or punching bag—and so it should be.

Somehow, the lines between *wishing* and *having* are forever blurred.

Mike comes up the stairs, covered with snow. It must have been quite a trick, maneuvering that bike up and down those hills. His nose is red, his eyes sparkling; it's almost like having a youthful Santa Claus himself arrive; spreading joy and mystery from the North Pole. He stomps off snow and brushes it from his hair and beard. He sits at the table between Lor and Maggie.

The next song he starts himself, and it's the right one, according to the preordained order: "Joy to the World." We sing with vigor, Mike, still stirred by the snow and his trip over the hill, pounds his hand on the table, keeping the beat, leading us. Life couldn't be nicer. Somehow I wish I could lock all this in an ice capsule, the way those blackberries were this morning, and keep it intact, available to me at will, frozen summer juices.

After the singing, I look at my watch. It's eight thirty. The "midnight mass" in Ligny is at nine. There's *no* way I can justify my desire to go up to that mass. I'm not a churchgoing person. By definition, I'm not even a Christian, or a participant in any dogma; but *something* in me is religious; my pagan concern for the mystic, I suppose. A mass is like the nails in the cross, something real with which to fasten onto a dream, a wish, an ethereal ideal.

But every year here, I go to mass on Christmas Eve. I even did it when it was still held at midnight. It's part of Christmas for me. I like the coming together of people on this night; people who, like me, rarely go to church. We gather in that vault of a tomb-church where Maggie and George were married, where I've helped with the burial of other villagers including Monsieur Calvet and Madame Jourdan. For me it's like saying good-bye to last year, to time, and hello to the new year, whatever it is, another step toward my own disappearance.

My all-time record is broken when four different cars from Moulin de Tonnère and two from Milé stop to offer rides on my walk up the hill. I think they know by now I like this yearly walk, but with this snow, it seems even more unbelievable to them.

And it's really snowing. The road isn't particularly slippery but I'm glad to be wearing rubber boots with a good tread on the bottom. If I were wearing any kind of ordinary shoes, I'd be kicking snow into the tops. It's cold and there's a wind blowing but not much, it's mostly only muffling, dense snow floating down and blowing around me.

I turn the last turn, pass the cross on the side of the road, and see the blurred lights of Ligny. As I round that last steep turn, cars are pulling in and parking on the *place*. The statue of the dead of wars past: for World War I, many names carved in the stone base, a few names from World War II, one from Algeria. The statue is a *poilu*, an infantry private soldier. He stands there in the dark; rust-coated, snow-covered, staring blindly away from the church out at the snow-riven view. He's probably much more "real"; has been seen by more people, remembered, commemorated, than any of those he represents, all long rotted into soil in different spots over the earth. This *poilu* got to stay home, to stand guarding the *place*, the church, his friends and their descendants through time.

I stomp and shake off the snow, take a seat by the side door, about midway up to the altar. It's my usual place; I sit there because I feel I can sneak out if things get too boring.

The priest here is a real loser. I guess this is the kind of place a bishop sticks loser priests. With all the sick and old in the region, he practically never goes to visit or console. He spends his time cruising around in his Simca, visiting all the "notables" within fifty kilometers. He's never without a dead yellow Gauloise cigarette hanging from the corner of his mouth. He talks around it. He lights it about as often as a normal man lights a pipe but can't seem to keep it lit, I think because it's so sodden with spit. He wears dull gray instead of black, is fat, and smells. The *chatelains* and *manoir* owners of the region must dread his arrival.

I don't have that many uses for a priest; but if I could only understand him when he spoke it would help. I thought it was because of the cigarette and maybe he spoke some deep Morvandeau dialect but it turns out *nobody* around can figure out a word he says.

Philippe claims it isn't any accent he recognizes and he heard a lot of accents when he was in Algeria as an infantryman during that particular French crazy time.

Even on the altar, where he *does* take out the cigarette and is *trying* to communicate, it's only a fuzzy mumble. The altar boys, children of Monsieur Pinson, are continually getting confused, crossing the wrong way, not moving when he thinks they should; *monsieur le curé* spends at least half his time, during mass, directing altar-boy traffic. The gospels, the sermon are totally unintelligible. In terms of religious stimulation a person'd be better off staring at a blank wall.

But here I am. I'm doing my usual Christmas-mass-in-the-Morvan meditation. First, I make a little visual tour of the Stations of the Cross. I think of my parents and what it must be like to be dead; I try to feel what it is to be alive, passing along on this magic carpet called time.

Madame Policott, the mayor's wife, has fixed up the crèche and it's directly in front of me. I look to see if any of the personages, the animals, are out of place, or if there are any new ones but all's the same. It's reassuring. I close my eyes and try to push myself back two thousand years, try translocating myself from this wet, cold Morvan to that dry, cold desert. Can't make it.

I'm on my knees so I *could* pass for an intense devout. The blend of smells is one thing I'm here for. There's the smell of camphor in the clothes of the congregation. There's the smell of old incense mixed with new, the smell of whitewash on wet walls—wet and molding—the smell of that mold. God, if I can't step out of the seeming simplicity of being existent here, there's nowhere. Maybe I really am, just *am*.

I stand up, kneel, or sit, according to the path of the mass. I have enough people in front of me to follow. There's no relationship to the sequence of a mass here on this hill and any I've known in America. The great web of the Vatican has definitely failed.

I sing the French Christmas songs, especially "Il est né le divin enfant." After the usual halting start we sing with gusto; our voices and body heat temporarily overwhelm the silence and smells of this doorway to the grave. Then I file up for communion with my neighbors, taking the host in my hand, sacrilege for my youth, and put it to melt in my mouth. The taste is something that hasn't changed. As a boy, I used to think it had wine in it. The practical aspects of Holy Eucharist hadn't quite penetrated. I was ten before I realized that only the priest actually got to take *full* communion, bread *and* wine. But I taste the imaginary wine of my youth in this host and feel it slide across the back of my tongue.

I do some fervent wishing, it could be called praying. I pray we can all get through this Christmas without anyone feeling hurt. Expectations can be so hard; the motions of love awkward, when feelings are so strong. I hope I do the right thing myself. I make strong wishes for Lor and me. I'm not sure what can really be, if anything, but I try. We have so much together, it would be so stupid to lose it all, battered on the irreconcilable rocks of righteousness and pride.

The walk downhill is a marvel. It's not as dark, by far, as the night I was picking holly, or last night, when I cut our tree. The snow reflects, multiplies whatever is coming out of that leaden, heavy, wafer-filled sky. Seven cars pass as I go down and I wave to each of them, trying to indicate in my wave that I'd rather walk. No wonder they think Americans are crazy; it's not quite a random sample they have.

When I get home, everybody's dressed for the reveillon; dressed up, that is, for the Morvan. Mostly this means putting on the cleanest clothing you have, washing your face and brushing your hair. I dressed for church, so we're all ready. Ben, as I expected, has elected to stay home. It's just as well, he'd only spend his time putting up his hand, gently, leaning over a book, indicating that whatever they're serving is not to his liking. For a kid who's grown up almost exclusively in France, he has a very limited palate. Maggie is obviously less than interested in going. Nicole is somewhat overstimulated, cheeks red, quick movements; but I think it's more wine than anticipation.

I should comment here on a rather strange phenomenon of our valley, perhaps it's of the whole Morvan but I think it's only a local accident.

We have an unusual number of eligible but unwilling, unavailable bachelors. They range from about twenty-three, Nicole's age, to over forty. Just in our village there's Philippe at thirty-seven, Jacques, twenty-eight and Clement. With only five houses to draw from, that's a rather considerable number. From Milé, we have two others, from Huis Billard another pair, from Huis de Bras yet another. All of these live within a kilometer of each other.

They have a kind of camaraderie going. In one sense, it's mutually supportive and revolves particularly around hunting and shooting. They go to all the marriages and dance the night through. Regularly, movable dance floors are put up in different towns throughout our region. They go to any of these dances within fifty kilometers. I imagine they dance, they drink, but mostly they laugh with each other.

They'll all come to the reveillon in our town.

I'd hate to be the girl who tries to invade this clique. I don't think any of them are overtly homosexual, no more than *any* male who regularly participates in a bowling league, poker group, or sporting club of some kind as his prime pleasure.

Since last Christmas there have been two losses in this all-male cluster, neither to marriage, both to death. One was a

Carron brother. The two brothers ran a farm up on the ridge of the south hill. They'd lived alone since the death of their mother five years ago. They'd been working together in the fields since before we bought our mill. One, the older, was the more reticent, wearing glasses, sturdy, hardworking, smiling and handsome. The younger—thick enough almost to be called fat, that is, he would be if he didn't work such long hard days—was not handsome. He was the one who talked. There was something of George and Lennie in *Of Mice and Men* to their relationship.

Each was known for his strength and willingness to lend a hand, or help in an emergency. Their names were Paul, the older, and Riri. I don't know what given name Riri comes from; it's the only name I knew him by.

At Easter, Riri, age thirty-five, discovered he had inoperable cancer that'd spread through his body. He went from working in the field to the grave in less than three months. They tell me, at the end, he was only flabs of skin and bone.

Paul, the older brother, now works alone. He nods at us when he passes on his tractor but that's it. He lives alone in the big isolated farmhouse up there on the ridge. Madame Le Moine and Madame Calvet worry about him, how he eats, keeps the place clean.

He's supposed to be here tonight for the reveillon; it'll be the first reveillon or social event for him since his brother's funeral.

As I've already said, the young son of Monsieur Boudine was also recently lost, killed in a motorbike accident. For the last two years he'd been a part of our reveillon. He was always full of jokes; a bright, kind boy. It's strange; this year it's the young who won't be here. In the reveillon group, there are more than five women over seventy, plus Madame Calvet, Loretta and me, hovering around fifty. The established sequences, three-score ten and all are only a consensus reality, not much different from other so-called realities.

I'm hoping Nicole and Maggie will participate in the festivities. Before, they'd been too young, would either not come, like Ben, or leave early. Madame Calvet's daughter Katie, Maggie's age, has borne the brunt of the female role.

Lor is definitely not the type. She'll carry her end of the conversation, the eating, the general laughing and celebrating, but the finale, the part where food throwing starts and wild native dancing begins, is more than she can handle. It's not exactly my idea of a good time, either. I guess, at heart, I'm a citified snob.

The dance they do here is called the *bourou*. It's done to something sounding like old country Irish, Scottish, or maybe Bavarian music. Usually the instruments are an accordion, a violin and something sounding like a bagpipe. The dance consists mainly of stomping.

There are formal face-to-face, leg-over-leg maneuvers, easy to master, but I forget each year and must be retaught; twelve times now. Then there's twirling and swinging, reversing directions to some mystical element in the music; something like square dancing but without a caller.

Anyone who isn't out there dancing, claps and stomps. There's a fair amount of hollering and hooting that goes along with the stomping. I enjoy it for one or two dances, once I get the hang of it, but then the regularity of the music bores me. Although they change the records, it all sounds about the same.

We walk along the edge of the pond using a flashlight. The lights are shining from the Calvets'; I'm hoping no one will bring up my big splash.

It must have been our third or fourth reveillon, when, on my way home, I walked straight into the pond. It was only about three feet deep on this end, so all I got was cold and wet but the village thought it was the funniest thing that ever happened. Loretta was convinced I was drunk and I'd definitely been drinking; the wines are some of the best we get all year, but mostly I was tired and my feet, legs, were numb from stomping.

We knock and enter to the sound of a group-shouted *"Entrez."* Most everybody is already at table. Our places are reserved for us. There's a regular flurry of multiple kissing, wishing of *bon noël*. I kiss more withered skin than most men, except perhaps gerontologists, do in a year. Shaking hands with all these leather-handed, sausage-fingered men is another trial. I've learned to dig right into it; if I linger, or hold back, I get my fingers squeezed to a pulp.

I sit between Madame Le Moine and Madame Calvet. The reason I sit there is because neither of them likes oysters and they keep piling theirs on my plate.

I don't count but I must eat four dozen, that's double my yearly intake. And they are delicious, my favorites, *fines claires*. I also eat a bowl of *moules* cooked in wine, lemon and onions. Then I work my way through two *boudins noirs* and one *boudin blanc*. I'm beginning to see the stuff-point coming and we haven't gotten to the main dish yet. I'll never make it for the *bûche de noël*, never.

I sip more wine, try to settle back, not rush it. I really want to sleep tonight. I want to feel great for Christmas Day this year.

The pork is marvelous. They've cut the tenderloin from right around the spine and made a roast out of it. It's cooked in beer and onions, served with boiled potatoes. It's so good I make a pig out of myself again. I guess that's quite literal in this case. Either I'm making a pig of myself, or, from another point of view, I'm making a pig into *me*. But I go through two helpings.

Next the unveiling of the *bûche de noël* and the bubbly wine. Champagne is too expensive but they have a fair bubbling white wine from near the Loire. We drink toasts. I see that Maggie and Lor are about ready for the furtive departure; already a few bread balls have flown between Philippe and Patrick. It won't be long now until the real bacchanal starts, orgy time in the Morvan.

After the *bûche*, Jacques Calvet brings out five bottles of *naöle* and plumps them on the table. There's enough to fill three or four alcoholic wards right there. Philippe whips out the record player, a tiny portable job, puts it on the table beside a typical Morvanic miniature Christmas tree and fits one of the worn 45-rpm records of the local dance music. It's stomping time.

It's amazing how nobody's shy or embarrassed now. All the wine must help. After Patrick and Jacques have pulled the table off to the side I grab Madame Le Moine's hand and we line up to dance; even at eighty, and after a stroke, she's one of the best dancers in town. Madame Calvet is dancing with Maggie. Paul has been grabbed by Nickie. We're all lined up. The music starts and we step out, stomping, twisting, swinging each other around, bumping into the table, into the grandfather clock. Madame Calvet's daughter, Katie, is leading. She's dancing with Patrick and they're setting a rough pace. Philippe is dancing with Loretta. Nobody's drunk yet but everybody's high enough. I can see Lor is smiling her pasted-on face like somebody in a Japanese No theater production.

We dance three records. Then it's time to crash into the *naöle*. We all *"Salut"* each other again and the men down this poison in a gulp. I sip carefully. Both Nickie and Maggie cough, tears in their eyes. I should have warned them. Lor holds onto her glass, smiles around, but doesn't drink it, surreptitiously lowers it to the table. She looks over at Maggie and they begin moving toward the door. Nickie signals she'll stay on. She has ahold of Paul's arm, as big around as my leg. His face is red and he's smiling a real smile, one he can't get his face around. Philippe puts the first record on again and we're off. New drinks have been poured. From here on, it's a race to see if you fall down from drink or exhaustion first. Some fade out then come back. There isn't as much food throwing this year as usual. I don't know whether this is a sign of prosperity or bad harvests coming. It's like weather predicting with cows sitting or standing. There's supposed to be a relationship, but for the life of me I can never remember what it is.

I poop out a little before one. Nickie stays on. Her face is flushed and she's in some kind of a dancing contest with Katie. They've got those men dancing so they're sweating like the pig they killed. The girls keep creating new steps, new patterns. It's beginning to look almost like rock is working its way into traditional Morvandeau dancing. They're all in a trance; they'll be break dancing to Morvandeau music yet; combined with the stomping, they'll "break" something for sure, like a neck or a leg.

I make it past the pond without falling in. It's still snowing. There's almost eight inches of powder snow over everything. I look across the whiteness of the pond, I bet if I walked into it tonight I wouldn't even sink, could pull off a Christmas Jesus Christ trick, walk across the water, but I'm not ready to risk it.

Inside it's warm. I go over and put a pair of logs on the fire. I snuggle them against each other, then look for the large one I put aside as a true *bûche de noël*, a log to burn through the night. I wedge it into the back behind the first two. It won't actually burn all night but it'll keep things warm and probably keep the fire going till I need to get up for my middle-of-the-night leak. That I'll have to do for sure tonight, after all the wine.

I undress and climb into bed behind Lor. She makes the kind of *hmmm* noise she makes when she knows I'm crawling into bed, closing in behind her; but she's actually deep asleep, I think. I lie there in the dark and feel surrounded, covered by snow. I hope Nickie will come home soon; I should stay awake and wait for her but I'm not going to make it. I'm just about falling asleep, when I realize we didn't put up any stockings. It has to be the first time in over twenty-five years we haven't had stockings hanging over a mantel at Christmas. For years there, it was six different sizes, different colors, and we'd fill them. I used to write long Santa Claus letters in rounded print with snowballs as dots for the *i*s. I'd even write them for Loretta. It's sad how some things come to an end. I need to get myself ready.

V

Five Golden Rings

Loretta

Wouldn't you know, after more than six months, I'd have a period? I don't even have anything here with me. I'll ask one of the girls. Which would be the less embarrassed? Nicole, probably.

Even though the timing couldn't be worse, inside I'm sort of glad. It's most likely the excitement, the worrying, having our family together; the terrible strain of carrying on with things as if nothing were happening when all I want to concentrate on is what's happening with Pete and me. I think sometimes I might be going crazy; I hope I don't say anything in my sleep. I'm that upset.

And the kids seem so vulnerable, so in need of loving, so lost; wanting and not able to ask. Or maybe that's all only me, *my* feelings. I don't know where I am any more, what I *really* want. This body of mine has a mind of its own, or maybe that's my real mind and I never knew it.

After breakfast, I'll ask Nicole for something. She'll think it's the funniest thing in the world, her upper-middle-aged mother having a period. But it feels good to me; as if everything isn't really over; as if there's still some functioning woman in there trying to show herself.

And Will's been acting so peculiar. It's like watching a bull-fighter with his tights, suit of lights, cape and sword, running around the inside of a bullring, ducking behind every barricade, scared to death, while the bull isn't even paying attention. Sometimes living with a dedicated ontologist can be difficult, but this is impossible. He's fighting shadows of shadows. No he isn't. I think somehow he knows and doesn't even know he knows. God, I'm not sure I can hold out.

I hope the girls, Mike, too, leave soon; maybe they'll only stay through for our anniversary; they'll have more fun up in Paris, anyway. It would be best for all of us, especially the way I'm just falling apart. And, I know Will's blood pressure must be soaring. I've absolutely got to talk it out with him. It isn't fair to any of us this way.

Could he possibly know? Maybe he's one of those men who put up with just so much, don't say anything, and then disappear. Disappearing *is* a specialty of his. Sometimes he goes on and on about how none of us could see *any*thing if our eyes were fast enough. He claims we only *seem* to see each other because we can't stop the movements of electrons in atoms, atoms in molecules, all that. He says we're practically empty of matter, more empty than the sky. It can drive a person insane just listening to him.

I'd be all alone then.

Three weeks ago, when Pete told me he was being transferred back to Connecticut, I thought I couldn't handle it. It seemed the thing I most wanted was being pulled out from under me. I thought I was willing to go anywhere with him, do anything; no matter what happened.

But Pete made no beans about it. He has a commitment to Carolyn and his kids. He lost his first family in a divorce and he wasn't about to have it happen again. I think he's suffering as much as I am, but once was enough.

As he pointed out, my kids are pretty much all grown but he has two little ones, one in third grade now and the other in fifth.

Pete's almost five years older than I am. This is his second wife and second family. His other two children are the same age as Mike and Nicole.

One of the things I love about Pete, is he's so straight-out. By nature, he's a decision maker and isn't afraid to say what he thinks. Also, at the same time, he's so committed to what he does. His life is uncomplicated, no shadows, no uncomfortable mysteries.

And he made me realize how, when it came right down to it, I'd never leave my family either.

But, God, it's hard to accept, to give up, after these two wonderful years we've had. Those little bits of time we'd squeeze out of our regular lives for each other, were so intense.

It's hard to know how I'll keep going. I try getting through each day as best I can, making the most of it, trying to forget and not forget at the same time. I don't think I'd ever dreamed what that kind of passionate love could be like.

But, I know, I've *got* to tell Will, and soon. I'm sure these last years have been awful for him, with my heart and mind mostly somewhere else. I just don't know how he'll take it, he's so impossible to predict. How can I ever tell him how much I love Pete, how it started, how it all came about?

Usually in first grade, it's the mothers who come with the children that first day. Pete was the only father. And he wasn't out of place, he didn't get in the way, he was supportive to little Dana, but at the same time let her interrelate with the other children.

He's about the same height as Will, but bald and bearded, somewhat gray, not like a multinational company person at all. He has sharp blue eyes, and a ruddy complexion. He has a separation between his two front teeth. He's definitely burly, husky, almost what you would call a heavy man, but he moves quickly.

He's much older than most of the other fathers, the fathers who weren't there, the ones I wouldn't meet until the first parent conference or open house. I found out he works for IBM; they've already been in Paris a year and a half.

He came often, more often than any of the mothers, so much so, I suggested he be my "room mother." It was the beginning of a running joke. To most of the mothers, usually between twenty-five and thirty-five, I'm sort of a surrogate mother while they're here in France. To the children, I'm more grandmother than mother. I've watched this gradual shift over the fifteen years I've been teaching at the International School. At first, the kids would often slip and call me Mother or Mom, but not much lately. Mostly I'm Mrs. Kelly or "teacher."

He came one day when the children were going off to their French lesson. He invited me for a cup of coffee at a nearby café. I think it's the first time I was ever off campus during school time in all the years I've been there. We got so involved in talking, first about Dana, then about ourselves, that I was late picking up my class from French.

I don't know how he managed it, but he'd come often after that. We'd go for our cup of coffee and talk. I got to expecting, hoping, he'd come. It made me feel so adult for a change; adult and younger at the same time.

He told me how unhappy he was married to a woman almost twenty years younger than himself. He felt he was older than fifty-three in his mind, somehow, and that Carolyn was younger than her actual thirty-five. She was miserable in Paris, wanted to go back to America, but Pete loved it. He'd discovered some wonderful restaurants and wanted to share them with me.

It was so easy. I could tell Will I had a meeting, or was going to visit a parent, and there'd be no problem. I can't ever remember Will asking anything about where I was going or what I was doing, or with whom. Sometimes I used to think he just didn't care, that he wasn't involved enough in our marriage for it to matter, that he was so self-centered, I didn't count. In some ways he was only a shadow of a husband.

A good part of Will's conviction about what the good life is, the way people should live, is: nobody should make anybody else do anything they don't want to do. He's always been this way with the kids. It used to drive me crazy. He just wouldn't give them any direction, they had to figure everything out for themselves. If they really got confused they'd come to me.

Pete and I went to some wonderful restaurants. We even went on the Bateau Mouche one evening. I was scared someone would see us, but Pete kept saying Paris was a big city and nobody would believe it even if they did see us. He had no problem at home, either, because IBM could keep him working any hours they needed. In fact, it bothered him how he had so little control over his own life. They could also move him whenever and wherever they wanted. He said it made him feel like a child.

We'd been seeing each other that way, maybe once a week, for several months, when, one evening, after dinner, while we were holding hands under the table and he'd started running his hand along the inside of my knee and leg, he suggested we go to a hotel.

I was scared to death. I knew I wanted to, but I was frightened. I'd never done, or even thought of anything like that. I was also afraid it would be the way it'd usually been with Will and me, that I'd tighten up and ruin everything. I don't know why, but sex has always scared me, ever since I was a little girl. It's hard to believe, but I never even masturbated. Will wanted me to go see somebody but I was afraid even to do that. I finally went to a woman gynecologist when, after a year, Will and I still couldn't have intercourse. She gave me pills and a set of black plastic penises to stretch myself with until finally Will could actually enter. But it was always painful. Even after I had Maggie and it was easier, I never really liked it. I've always been romantic and enjoyed reading romantic novels but the actual sex act was so awkward. I felt as if my personal privacy was being taken away from me.

"Honest Pete, I don't think it would be such a good idea. We have such a good relationship; I'd hate to lose you."

"How could you lose me? I'm sure we could be even closer. I know we'd be wonderful together in bed."

But I wouldn't go. Maybe I was just feeling guilty but I wasn't ready. I knew I wanted to try sex with him but I was still scared.

In his car afterward we were almost like teenagers we were so excited. He kept pressuring me to come to the hotel with him, and by then I was almost ready to take *any* chances to be close to him, to feel his hairy body against mine, but it was getting too late. I'd told Will there was a meeting after school on "thinking skills" but there's no way I could explain where I'd been if I got home after midnight.

The thing is, Will probably wouldn't ask, might not even notice I was late. Unless we have somebody over, he's always in bed, asleep, before eleven o'clock. Besides, I myself had to get up at seven thirty and teach the next day. I'm terrible with the little ones if I don't have eight hours.

Then, that next Saturday, Pete was supposed to be off in Brussels. I was scheduled to participate in some in-training service classes while Will had three classes and a conference. Ben was going with friends to look at stamps in the Marais, then go to a movie. It was the perfect opportunity. I could count on at least five hours or even more. I knew if he asked me I'd go with him.

I was wearing the sexy French underwear Nicole had bought me the Christmas before. It wasn't black but it was skimpy, transparent, lacy and was a color called wild strawberry. I'd never had underwear anything like it and could never get up the nerve to wear it.

I put on the good French perfume, my favorite, Ecusson, Will gives me every year for Christmas. I'd just had my hair done. I knew I looked good for a woman my age.

We met in the same café where we'd usually meet. It has a hidden corner in back, away from the street, where nobody could ever see us. When I came in, he was already there. He was supposed to have left for Brussels at nine o'clock and now it was nine thirty. I had a hard time getting my breath, my legs were shaking so I could hardly stand up. He kissed me, open, deep in my mouth, then started kissing me on the neck. It surprised me how strong he was, how tight and snug I felt in his arms.

"Not here, Pete, somebody will see. Even for the French, we're going overboard, the guys on the end of the bar there, are watching."

"I have a room, just around the corner, will you come with me? We can spend the night if you can manage."

I was too embarrassed to answer but I nodded. He paid the bill and we left the bar. The hotel *was* just around the corner and there was no trouble with our going up. He lifted and carried me into the room and laid me carefully on the bed.

He undressed me slowly, kissing me every place as he lifted off my clothes. When he had me down to that wild strawberry underwear, he stood up and carefully started taking his clothes off, never taking his eyes from me. I watched his hands as he pulled off his tie, unbuttoned his shirt, unhooked the buckle to his pants. As he dropped his trousers, he smiled, then slipped out of his jockey shorts. He had a huge erection, it was long, not as thick as Will's, and it curved.

He leaned forward and unhooked the clasp on my brassiere. I'd never had a brassiere with the clasp in front, between the breasts, but he knew where it was and just how to open it. His hands weren't shaking and he didn't fumble. So different from Will. He carefully lifted the thin brassiere and I shrugged off the straps. I'm lucky, I still have nice breasts. They haven't sagged and have small pink nipples almost like a girl. He started kissing them and then began kissing me all over.

He did things, to, for, with me I'd never dreamed about, never even heard about. Instead of my body getting taut, it seemed to be resonating, singing to the pressure of his lips, his hands. Then, when he came into me, almost immediately, I had my first all-out orgasm. It caught me by surprise, I wasn't expecting it and

I didn't have time even to think of being scared. I thought I'd have to scream or cry. I twisted and turned, halfway got up under Pete, but he pushed me back down.

Every part of him was wound into every part of me. My whole body was convulsing, shaking, and Pete kept moving slowly, insistently, deeply penetrating me. It came on, wave after wave, until I thought I was going to be swallowed inside out. I began to think how an older woman like me could have a heart attack, but I didn't want anything to stop.

He pressed harder and faster until he too, with a whistling gasp and a groan, stiffened against my body, his legs thrusting his groin deeper yet into me until slowly he started to relax.

We were both soaking wet with perspiration. The bed, the coverlet, the sheets were wet. He rolled me over on top of him to the dry side of the bed. We pulled the covers up over us and both went to sleep. I don't think I could have stayed awake.

The next thing I remember, Pete has his tongue in my ear. I'm on top of him. I get up on my knees straddling him, he cups my breasts in his hands and kisses them, pulls them close together so he can put the two nipples in his mouth at the same time, he rubs his tongue over them. I can feel he's excited again. His penis is pressed against my thigh. I reach down with my hand to touch it. It's stiff, hard. I hold it tight in my hand. I can feel myself going crazy again. Pete sinks into me and I press down on it, then lift until it almost comes out, then push down again. I watch his eyes. He's looking into mine. We go slowly like that. From his mouth and his eyes I can tell when to slow down and when to speed up. I feel as if I'm a *real* lover. I'm enjoying giving him pleasure and at the same time I'm gradually going further and further into myself, feeling the surges of power coming on, almost like having a baby, only without the pain.

This time we come wildly together, we thrash, I understand for the first time how things like love bites and scratches across the back come about. I've seen them on the bodies of people at the beaches and always felt it was some kind of bravado, a mutual macho-macha thing, to make everyone else feel left out. The combination of violence, gentleness, concern and abandon is overwhelming. We go on for what seems forever and at the same time, is no time at all. We sleep again.

When I wake, Pete is standing by the bed beside me.

"What time do you have to be home?"

"We still have plenty of time, Pete. Don't leave me."

"It's almost six o'clock. I'd like to climb right back in bed with you, but can you stay here overnight?"

I jump up and turn on the light beside the bed. My God, it really is ten minutes to six. There's no way I can explain being away for almost nine hours. My God!

I get out of bed and stand beside Pete. He pulls me close to his heavy, hard body, holds me tight, kisses me.

"I think you'd better go. Just say you were invited to dinner by one of the people at your conference. Do you think you can make up something? I'm going to stay here. If you can come back somehow, do. I don't know how it was for you but I never felt so deeply moved in my life."

I knew he really meant it, mostly because it was the way I felt, too. At the same time, I was worried about getting home.

After I dressed hurriedly, we kissed again. Pete climbed back into bed to watch me dress. He got out and came to me; he was still naked and had another erection. He pointed.

"You see, he doesn't want you to go either."

Right there I could have just undressed and gotten in bed with him but my whole life was too much. I couldn't.

During the next eighteen months we took every chance to see each other and every time we were crazy as the first time. It was almost as if it were something chemical, the way it was in chemistry class when we'd take two test tubes with just clear liquid in them and pour them into a beaker and it would start smoking, bubbling and changing color. We were like that. And we didn't lose all the rest of it either, the fun, the joy, the pleasure of seeing each other, of sharing ideas on things. The sex part was separate, something I don't think either of us really expected.

I know I began to look, to be, to feel different. I felt beautiful some days. I began to dress more carefully, to make myself more attractive, and I was radiant when I knew I was going to see Pete. I don't know how Will could have missed all this. Sometimes I used to stand in front of him, and almost plead for him to *see* me, to know something important was happening. I almost wanted to tell him, to share with him my joy. But I couldn't. I guess it proved I never really did believe all the things he said about how people who loved each other would want the other to be happy, no matter what.

Now, I've *got* to tell him. If we're going to be together for the rest of our lives, he has to know this about me. I just don't know how he'll take it, he's so hard to predict. I'll wait till the older kids go up to Paris; I wish Ben would go with them, but that's impossible.

In a certain way, Ben and Will are so much the same, not really facing things. Ben hides behind his books while Will hides in his mind. That is, when he isn't dashing around crazily, straightening things out, mothering everybody, whether they want it or not.

I'm not sure I even know what love is supposed to be any more. Maybe the whole idea of love has always only been a substitute for life, or *live*. About the time one begins to sense a loss of love for life itself; when childhood, play, joy, diminish; we shove *love* in. The words are so similar, both in English and German.

I don't know what Mike and Geneviève are feeling for each other, how much they're using their relationship to hold back the onrush of adulthood. Too often, love becomes an evasion of whatever is passing for reality. Lord, I'm beginning to sound like Will.

Until I met Pete, I'd never been "swept off my feet" by anything. I don't think I even knew what sex was supposed to be like. I knew I was capable of deep feeling; my personal Little Bo Peep was always there; listening, but never abandoning, never forgetting. I have a feeling Will's the same.

I'm not sure any more whose fault it is, either. I don't know why Will could never help me have orgasm, release me to passion. I know Will wanted it, and I couldn't make myself lie. I know it's been mostly me, my problem, but then Will never forced me, never took the initiative. He's always been so tentative, hesitant about everything. Even if I did lie and pretend to have an orgasm, what would it actually mean?

But I always *wanted* to come with Will. It's just that gradually we got so we couldn't talk about it and then, in some strange way, we, neither of us, wanted to talk about anything concerning sex at all.

I'd get excited wanting Pete, but I didn't want Will that way. These last years, Will hasn't even tried, not even an open-mouthed kiss. He's just given up. He holds me tight in bed, cuddles against my back, holds my breasts in his hands, but that's all.

But we have had four wonderful kids. There's very little friction in our lives, no shouting matches. We've, neither of us, ever threatened to leave or *tried* to hurt each other. That's a lot in our times. I'm willing to call it a kind of love.

But if our kids had any idea of the basis for our marriage, they'd probably die. Thank God our parents are dead so we've never had to try explaining any of this to them.

Will's so different from anybody I've ever known. For someone who's so talkative, full of ideas, almost naïve, he can be very secretive. I still don't know where he is in his mind most of the time.

When we first met, I used to think he was only kidding with all this business about reality. He was constantly challenging me, begging me, to tell him something that was real. Then, he'd knock it all to pieces with his existential and Platonic arguments. I learned to hate even the *name* Camus. I finally told him to stop it, I couldn't take it any more and I wouldn't marry him as long as he persisted that we didn't even exist and how our love was an open space defined by our own nothingness.

I'm sure all his nonsense bothers the kids, too. On the one hand, he's always played with them, almost like another kid.

He's told them the most bizarre stories, especially the Franky Furbo business. But he kept insisting Franky Furbo was *true* and wanted them to believe along with him. It was enough to completely ruin their minds.

He's taught them and he's a wonderful teacher. But, in a certain way, he's never truly there. He's like something you catch out of the corner of your eye. When you'd look he'd be gone. I sometimes think he thought he was Franky Furbo himself.

I'm sure he lives in another place, a place of his own he can't share. I guess we all do.

But now I need someone to talk to. I'm afraid if I talk to him about Pete and what happened we'll lose most of what we still do have. On the other hand, maybe something so merely physical wouldn't seem worth discussing to him. He might even lose any respect he does have for me because I've gotten so excited over nothing. No, I'm only kidding myself.

My Lord, these are awful thoughts to be having on Christmas Eve. I'm always this way at the beginning of my period, though, everything looks so black and I get so introspective.

I've got to snap out of it; things are bad enough without one more basket case. If only Pete and I could just have gone off somewhere alone for a last week together. When I told Will in July I'd like the kids here for Christmas, I had no idea Pete would be leaving Paris for good on January first. I'll probably never see him again. God, it's hard to accept.

Something's bothering Nicole, I know. She's been drinking wine in that mad way Lor's sister Nora always did when she was in bad shape. Then, tonight, staying on and dancing with those farm boys. I tried to stay awake, wait for her, like the mother of some teenager. It was about then I realized I might be flowing. I got up and put on panties with paper towels rolled up inside. I hope it's holding, it would be awful starting Christmas morning having to wash, soak and hang up the sheets.

I don't think Nicole was actually having a good time, she was only feeling sorry for Paul and needing something to take her mind off her own troubles. Something's bothering her, all right; I wonder what it can be. And, my goodness, she's taken on so much weight; she must weigh more than Maggie, and Maggie's five inches taller.

Mike, too, something's bothering him. It might only be he didn't do well at school this quarter, but I think it has something to do with Geneviève. He could be letting himself get sucked into the mess of her parents' divorce. I know it's all hard on Geneviève, but there's nothing Mike can do. They wanted to separate and they're young enough to do it without much trouble. Inside, they both might have been waiting until Geneviève and Maurice were old enough to go out on their own. After all, a marriage *is* a contract and any contract can be terminated when it's finished.

I wonder if Will and I will come to that? It's so easy to say the few words that hurt and then there's no turning back. I think that's the way it might be with Will. He'd probably quietly drift away, become even more invisible. We wouldn't need anything formal like a divorce. Pete isn't available, so I'll never marry again.

I wonder how I'd manage. I could probably be quite happy living alone with Ben until he goes off to school himself.

But Ben'd miss Will terribly; he's such a tender child. I watch him and I could cry; it's like watching Will happening all over again. The two of them don't seem to be in tune with this world. I know I'm strange in my own ways; so I'm not complaining.

For me, the best time is spent alone. Even if I were married to Pete I'd need time to myself. Give me a nineteenth-century novel, a bar of Suchard chocolate, some Mozart playing in the background and I ask for nothing more.

Right now, I'm trying to find some balance between three kinds of time. First, my time alone. Then, the time I'm actually dealing with things, housework, shopping, teaching, anything that needs to be done, where the work or the project is the main reason and the relationships with people, though they might be important, aren't intimate; times when I'm playing different roles to different people, when I can't really be myself, or tell anyone what I'm truly thinking.

Then, finally, the part which *is* intimate; relationships with people I love and care about, with Pete, with Will and the kids.

This is the one that's so hard for me. If I care, then I can't let go and allow the ones I love to muddle on, doing dumb things. Also, they can hurt me so easily and it seems they don't even notice, so I'm always on my guard. I *want* to be intimate but I'm afraid. Something in me can't trust the ones I love to love me back if I reveal the way I *really* feel, the way I really am.

It's one part that's so important about teaching. There, I can help those little ones learn to love themselves for the way they are. Already, at that age, the whole society is trying to change them, mold them into something they aren't, for everybody else's convenience.

I have to admit, Ben doesn't seem to need me at all. He's so sweet and hardly ever "acts out" the way the others did, but I can't reach him; he's definitely his father's boy. I think Will put all, or, at least, most of his paternal love into Ben.

It's probably because he realizes he's ceilinged out there at the American College. We're here in France so long now we can never go back. I don't think he could even get a high school job at his age. There isn't much use for a philosopher-ontologist on a high school campus.

Will knows this, although we've never talked about it. He *should* publish, but he hasn't written anything I know of in years now. I keep hoping he's written something, anything, in private, secretly, but I don't think so. He's given up. He's the way I am, he likes teaching and doesn't have time or inclination to do all the research necessary to whip something into form for publication. If he could only write it out, share it, instead of going around spouting about how everything is nothing, ergo, nothing is everything. That kind of talk bothers me.

I know our kids love him, but they're like me, I think, afraid to be hurt. Will can be so cruel without trying, or even wanting to. He's never cruel by attacking. He just seems to wish you away, so you feel invisible, as if you *aren't* any more. And he does it without a word. He projects a psychic blindness or something and you're zapped. At the same time, when he does talk, try to communicate, he's so serious about things that don't mean anything to anybody, it's impossible. At parties, people are always trying to duck him, he can be *so* boring.

I should try to get some sleep. If I don't get at least seven hours I know I'll need a nap and there will be no time for napping when we have to get that turkey cooked and ready.

I wonder if anybody else noticed we didn't put up stockings. It just got overlooked in the rush and when I came home from the reveillon, I was so dead, all I could do was crawl into bed. Gosh, not sleeping on Christmas Eve like this reminds me of being a child, visions of sugar plums dance through my head, only not so sweet.

Peg

That reveillon thing was *too much*. These people here are *so* gross. I don't know how Mom and Dad can take it, especially Mom. Dad has his vulgar side as part of his flakiness, he just slips into whatever's going on, but Mom's always been so careful and elegant; I guess she only puts up with these things because of Dad.

He's always trying to get some hold on life no matter how messy it is. I'm sure he was out there wading in pig gore when they killed that poor animal. I couldn't watch him eat those *boudins noirs.* They leaked blood when he cut into them and the blood was so dark it was almost black.

I don't know what got into Nickie. She usually hates those kinds of macho-camaraderie-type men. And they all act like thirteen-year-olds. Their hands are beat up, with thick fingers, cuts all over and calluses that look like warts; blackened, broken, dirty thick fingernails, some of them starting to curl under like horse hoofs.

How can people live that way? God, if I even get a hangnail or a nail gets ragged or broken, I can hardly cope. People are different I guess; I wish I could let go and not be so sensitive but I can't. I got the pulling back part from Dad, I think, but not the crazy desperateness. I wonder why he's never tried suicide? Maybe he has, Mom would never tell and Dad might not even have noticed or remembered.

George is on my back all the time about my "compulsiveness," but he's as bad as I am. If ever he has to wear a shirt two days in a row, he acts as if he's working in a sewer. If I don't get every bit of dirt out of the collar and cuffs, he won't wear a shirt; even if I've just washed, starched and ironed it. And he *won't* use the wash-and-wear shirts, says he's allergic to them, breaks out all over his back.

There I go again, complaining about George. When I let my mind run alone, it always comes back to the same things. Maybe I'm feeling guilty and making up excuses to make myself feel better. Sharon, my therapist in Phoenix, says, "What we all tend to complain about most in other people are those parts we don't like about ourselves."

That's the whole trouble. I *can't* come up with one serious reason to explain why I want to leave George. There's nothing I can really put a finger on.

At the same time it's everything. It's everything about him, how he brushes his teeth, leaves wet towels on the floor in the bathroom when he takes a shower; the way he eats, talks through his nose, pees hard straight into the toilet bowl so you can hear him all over the house; how he burps and farts, leaves cigarette butts in coffee cups, or books of matches in his shirts so when I wash them it stains everything; everything.

Then I get to thinking how unfair it is. George is doing all the things a man is supposed to do. He goes out and takes bullshit from his boss. He takes on all the worry about keeping his job, getting promotions; he's moving up reasonably fast in a big corporation. He doesn't drink more than anybody. He *does* smoke and I wish he'd stop, *I* stopped when we had Seth, so *he* could too; in fact, he did and then started up again when he got to be section manager.

He smoked for six months without telling me; never smoking at home, but I could tell. When you don't smoke yourself, especially when you're an ex-smoker, you can always tell if somebody else is smoking. It wasn't only in his clothes from other people around him smoking either; it was in his mouth, the way he tasted in the morning; it came out of his pores. I finally had to just out and ask him. He didn't act sorry at all; George hates having anybody make him feel wrong; I guess everybody does.

There are no other women, far as I can tell, but then that stupid company's always sending him off on trips to Houston or Philadelphia. There's no way I could ever know. He didn't tell me about the cigarettes. But I don't think there's anybody. I'd know.

I *do* know he loves Seth and Seth loves him. He's a wonderful father. I wish he were as good a husband as he is a father. I can get jealous just watching them play together. One of the things is, I think Seth is more like George than me. They're the same type. I definitely feel on the outside when the three of us are together, and *I'm* the mother.

God, I hope Mom or Dad won't bring it up. I almost didn't come, I was so afraid they'd make a big scene. They both believe so much in sticking things out through thick and thin.

I know it hasn't been easy for Mom. Dad must be one of the hardest people in the world to live with. He's the original invisible man with krypton rays flashing out of him at the weirdest times. I don't know how she stands it. I wonder if she'd be happier if she'd divorced him when she was my age? It's hard to say. I can't exactly say she's the most unhappy almost-fifty-year-old woman in the world, in fact she's probably happy as any woman can be at that age.

It must be awful to be old. I wish I could do something for her, get her away from this crazy trap they've dug themselves into here in France. I think even Dad'd like to get out if he could figure a way. When Dad's parents died I thought for sure they'd move back to Illinois; he has friends, he could probably get some kind of teaching job there and they'd've had Grandma's house to live in.

Well, if they bring it up, I'll just say I'm not willing to live my life out with a man I don't love, a man I can't even stand to be around, who actually bores me to tears most of the time. I don't think George and I have actually had a conversation about anything important, except maybe my wanting a divorce, in more than four years. The only big thing we did was buy a house and George arranged most of that. Now, I'm the one who has to keep it up, even plant and water the grass, but he made the decision, big-deal businessman.

There I go again. I always spin back to it. I'm so full of anger and hostility. Sharon says it's most likely there for other reasons; reasons having to do with my childhood and relationships with my parents; she said I'm only focusing on George.

Maybe that's it. They did ask us to lead such peculiar lives, isolated from our own country, *never* having a television set, *always* living with a little bit of money, practically starving, wearing used clothes, even passing them on down the line. We were the poorest kids in a school with some of the richest people in the world. And on top of that, we have a Dad everybody thinks is a loon.

I don't think he's actually crazy, he just has all these weird ideas about how only the things you believe are real, and if enough people believe in anything it becomes true. It makes me have dreams of oatmeal, like quicksand, sucking me down under. Then on top of everything he keeps insisting that everything *is* true and at the same time, *nothing* is. And he *really* believes it all. Maybe he is crazy in a certain way. Probably the whole Franky Furbo story thing is the proof.

I think I would have been happier growing up in some little town, maybe a hundred miles from Chicago, and being a cheerleader at football games. Instead I went to French schools eight years, then the International School when Mom began teaching there. My first lover was half German, half Syrian. That gives some idea of what a kooky world I grew up in. We lived in an old carpenter's shop Dad hand-made into a semi-apartment. I couldn't even have my friends come *visit*, it was so embarrassing. He acted as if we were all going to get leprosy when Mom finally talked him into putting in a phone. I guess I *am* full of hostility and resentment.

But I think my feelings about George are separate from all that, though I must admit I might have gotten involved with him because his parents were such big shots, embassy people and all.

And this mill is the *worst*. When our friends at school would be dashing off on ski trips or trips to Egypt or Russia or Greece, we'd be locked in down here with wind blowing through in the winter; rats, spiderwebs; no hot water, no shower, no tub. Then in summer here, everything grows wildly, it's like a jungle, with thousands of wasps, flies, mosquitoes and gnats buzzing around. They're so noisy you can't even hear the birds. That is, except early in the morning when the birds would wake us up before dawn, hollering and fighting with each other.

Dad and Mom swim in the pond; that is, when there weren't any fishermen, but that pond is so mucky you can't see six inches below the surface. I wouldn't even wash my feet in it. It's probably crawling with snakes.

And two days out of three, for the whole summer, it's either raining or clouded over, so you can't *begin* a suntan. We'd come back to school in September, and everybody'd have those gorgeous tans and all I'd have would be a touch of beige and huge freckles.

I'd better get to sleep; this isn't doing any good. Nobody hung stockings on the fireplace. What would happen if I climbed back down these stairs and hung a stocking there on the mantle? Would anybody notice? No, I'm afraid to walk down there alone in the night now.

Another thing we forgot is stone soup. Every year, on Christmas Eve day Dad would insist we make stone soup.

He'd build a real fire in the garden there in Germany, where we always went for Christmas in the old days. Then, when they bought the mill, he'd do it right outside the door up on the dam, where the reindeer with Santa Claus were supposed to land.

We could each put in a number of stones according to our age. I know I used to like it in Germany but never here. We'd search all over for just the right stones, then we'd wash them off in a pot of extra water he had, not the one on the fire. Dad'd look them over, one at a time as if he were examining diamonds, then we could put them in. He'd say some magic words as we put each stone in.

He kept stirring the pot with a big stick, the same stick all the time, he even brought it from Germany when we moved. He had a big old iron pot he got somewhere and that was what he'd cook our stones in. With the fire burning and the water bubbling, he looked like a raggedy druid. The water had to come from the lake or the pond. He insisted water from the kitchen tap would spoil the magic.

Also, before we could put our cleaned, examined stone in, we had to say what it was: a carrot, a potato, or a turnip, an onion or a beet or cabbage. It had to be something. He'd always put in a special stone that he'd searched out ahead of time and washed. It was Mom's stone. That was "seasoning." He'd also have another stone for himself, just one, and that was for "body." Those stones he'd pass around so we could all see them. I'll never know where he got those last two stones. They were always completely different than any stones we could find.

We'd all take turns stirring the soup with the big stick while it boiled. Mom didn't have to do it. She'd be inside cooking "real" soup. She was lucky. In Germany and even here, we'd be out in the snow and freezing to death. The fire heated the soup, not us.

At the end, when we were all almost dead from the cold, Dad would taste our stone soup. He had a wooden spoon he tasted with. He'd blow on it and look around at us. He'd always say the same thing, even before he'd tasted it.

"This year, I think we've made the best stone soup we've ever made. I'm sure of it."

Then he'd actually taste the soup. He'd make all kinds of smacking noises with his lips, saying *hmmm, yumm* and *uhh huh.* He'd tell us how delicious the soup was this year and in a few minutes we could all have a chance to taste it. Every year he'd go on like that and he'd always fool us. We'd beg him for our turn. And every time it tasted the same, like boiled water with a taste of rock or dirt and that was all. I still don't know why he'd trick us like that. It was a terrible thing to do on Christmas Eve, like finding coal in your stocking from Santa Claus. It was so disappointing.

Then, he'd dash us all inside into the dining room where Mom had made us our "real" Christmas soup. It was always more delicious than any other soup in the year. I'll have to ask Mom how she made that Christmas soup. Dad would eat this wonderful soup and keep insisting it was almost as good as our "real stone soup" out there in the garden. And Mom would go along with him. He'd always carry in one cup of "our" soup and pour it into Mom's soup before we ate it, insisting it was just the flavoring this soup needed. Mom would go along with that, too. I think Mom's put up with an awful lot from Dad, I don't know if I could manage it.

But, gosh, since Grandma's died, Dad doesn't seem to do those kind of crazy things any more. I wonder if he tells Ben Franky Furbo stories. I guess Dad's getting older. We all are.

If I leave George, I don't know how I'll make out. It's getting harder and harder to get any alimony and even when you get it, the men won't pay. I know he'll give me some child support for Seth, but that wouldn't be enough. I'd have to go out and get a job, some kind of job where I could be home when Seth got out of school. George and I were married so young, I hardly have any college credits at all, and those are just junior college credits. I don't know how I could work it out so I could go back to school and maybe take a teaching credential. If George would just help me while I did that, it would only take about three years, then I could be independent. But I hate to think of living alone.

I wouldn't really be alone because I'd have Seth. Then again, I might not even have him. More and more the courts are giving custody rights to the man; especially in a case like this, where I don't have any real grounds for divorce.

Some judge *could* give custody of Seth to George if George got married again, and then I'd only have Seth summers or weekends. I don't think I could handle that. And, I'll bet somebody would marry George in a minute if he were free. With his job and his good looks he'll be snapped up in no time and I'll be left alone. Damn, it all looks so black; I really don't know what to do.

I try breathing deeply and resist sucking my fingers. I think Mom's already asleep. I can hear her snoring slightly. I wish I could force myself to sit down and talk to her, tell her all these things I'm thinking. But she seems so far inside herself. She's smiling and doing everything she should to make this a perfect Christmas but I don't feel she's truly with us or actually cares much about what's happening to anybody.

I wonder if she really did ask Dad to have us all come for Christmas. It could have been Dad's idea and he used Mom so we'd be sure to come whether we wanted to or not. It's the kind of thing he might do.

I hope I'm asleep before Dad and Nickie come back. If I have to listen to Dad snoring and with Nickie in bed beside me, I might never manage it.

Ben's asleep in front of the fireplace. I really looked at him when I came in. You'd never know it with the glasses on him all the time, but he's going to be a good-looking guy when he grows up and he's so tall already. I think Mom and Dad are spoiling him but he doesn't seem to make much trouble the way a lot of kids his age do. He's just so separate, weird, like Dad. God, he was sleeping with his hands folded across his chest, you could almost swear he was dead if he weren't breathing. He used to pull the covers over his head to sleep but now he sleeps straight out.

I still suck my fingers sometimes when I sleep, especially when I'm upset. George is always pulling them out and it usually wakes me up. I don't say anything but it makes me mad when he does that; he says I make so much noise *he* can't sleep.

I still suck the same two middle fingers. Sharon says it's because I'm arrested at the oral stage and was surprised when I told her Mom nursed me for nine months. She nursed Mike for over a year and he doesn't suck his fingers or thumb at all. Both Nickie and I are finger suckers but neither Ben nor Mike are. Maybe it's sex-related, maybe women are natural suckers.

I wonder when Nickie and Dad will get back from that reveillon. Mike was smart to just skip it.

Mike

It's strange being so close to home for Christmas and still not actually being there with the family. I knew I didn't really want to go to the reveillon any more than Maggie did and Geneviève just *couldn't*. God, is she ever bummed out and I don't blame her. You hear all the time about people getting divorced as if it's like having your appendix out but that's not the way it's going here.

So now here I am, after a trip of more than ten thousand kilometers and I'm just over the hill not more than three kilometers from where my own family is having Christmas Eve. I wonder what they think. They've probably figured it out, there's not much chance of keeping big emotional changes like this away from anybody who's even halfway sensitive and our family, in general, is pretty sensitive, maybe supersensitive, some of them.

I just *couldn't* leave Geneviève, feeling the way she does. It hurts her terribly to see two people she loves so much, hurting each other, and there's absolutely nothing she can do about it. I'll say, this is turning out to be one tough Christmas.

Her mom and dad are being so polite, so civilized about everything, the way you'd expect intelligent, educated French to be; but, at the same time, there's so much hurting going on. They both have lists of the things they want from this place. As far as I can see, the little bit I've been involved, they both want the same thing, that is, everything. It's impossible. I'll bet, if they'd really be honest about it, they each wish they'd never started this whole divorce business. Neither of them is ever going to get married again, sure, they can live with other people if that's what they want, but why drag the whole state, with lawyers and all the rest, into it?

I don't understand that generation. But then it's happening to my generation, too; just look at Maggie and George, with little Seth caught in the middle. If they keep going the way they're headed, that'll be a catastrophe.

Lord, maybe the beginning to all this kind of trouble is in the very *idea* of marriage. If you think about it, really think, insisting on getting married to somebody else is like saying you don't trust them. Even if you do trust them, the idea is always there, like a poison, to remind you how you started off with some hypocrite church, or some politician; a whole crowd of leeches giving you permission.

If you're going to have children, that's a different thing, some arrangements have to be made so the two of you can give them a chance, help them until they're grown up enough to take care of themselves. It can't be left to the woman alone, the man has to commit.

But I don't thing that's the reason most people get married. Most people get married partly because they begin to think it's the thing they ought to do, or sometimes a woman is tired of her job and wants to stay home, or a man can't really take care of himself and needs a woman to look after him like a mother. And lots of times it's plain loneliness. It can be a drag living alone, eating alone, having nobody to share ideas and things with. But any roommate could do for that; you just have to search around until you find somebody who's compatible, either man or woman.

Anybody who gets married for sex today, has *got* to be nuts. This is for either men or women. It just isn't a good enough reason; it doesn't make sense.

Then sometimes a person, like Geneviève or my grandmother, wants to leave home, get out of the house because it's become too difficult, too painful to stay and they begin to think that by getting married they can start a private nest. But they don't have to get *married*, for Christsake, they can just move in with somebody. But Geneviève doesn't see it that way. She's really a perfect bourgeois French girl. I have to admit it's one of the things I like about her. I've had enough of "way out" women.

Something in me really resisted going to the cabin this afternoon. I've got so many bad memories of that place. Every time I go there I remember all the dampness and craziness that went on. I knew Debby was a bit off the wall, but I didn't know she was so bad she might kill herself. God, was I scared. She'd swallowed about ten five-milligram Valiums while I was out getting wood at the sawmill. When I came back she was practically in a coma. I kept slapping her in the face and throwing cold water on her and she was just slumping down. I rubbed soap in her mouth to make her vomit. I thumped her on the back, but most of all I dragged her through those woods, making her run until she was crying. I was afraid she was going to die. In farm country like this, they'd just never understand; the Morvan isn't exactly Venice, California, or Palo Alto; it's primitive.

When I finally was sure she was okay, I took her back to the cabin. It wasn't even finished yet, only half the floorboards were down, and I wrapped her in a sleeping bag, then blew up the sleeping mat and slipped it under her. I opened my sleeping bag, threw it over both of us and held her, tight as I could. She'd stopped crying but was still shaking so hard it shook me.

That's when I found out this wasn't the first time she'd tried something like this. I held her all night and then in the morning told her I was taking her up to Paris and phoning her parents. I just couldn't handle the responsibility. I knew, also, in some strange infectious way, she was bad for me. She loved to take risks. She'd climb out in the most dangerous places on the framework and pretend she was flying. She was always doing something crazy like rolling all the way down a hill laughing and screaming, right down to where the cows were. She'd spend hours making little figurines or pots from the clay over by the spring.

I know she's a hell of a lot smarter than I'll ever be but she can't seem to put it together. She doesn't want to live enough, not as much as I do anyway. I knew if I lived with her too long I could get hurt.

So, I always have had an eerie feeling about the cabin. I finished the flooring after she left, built a door and a porch, then closed it up. I don't think I've spent a night out there alone since then and that's been almost five years. It was fun living there that summer with Geneviève; she sort of took the curse off the place, chased away the evil spirits.

But, I must say it was great dancing to the Christmas carols with the family. That Nickie is a little bit like Debby, she throws herself into things. Maybe that's part of what they call the artistic or creative personality. But Nickie does something with it, she sculpts. She can be hard sometimes but I don't think she'd ever really hurt anybody, and, in her special way she loves as strong as she lives.

I wonder what's bothering her. She might be having some trouble with a boyfriend or something. She's just the kind of woman who could get all tangled up with some married man, old as Dad, just because he was interesting. It wouldn't ever be anything like Dad, because he's so flaky and she couldn't stand it, but if it were some really deep-thinking guy with all his tools together, she might go for it. I hope not.

Geneviève's turned with her back toward me; it sounds as if she's finally sleeping. I thought she'd never stop crying. If parents had any idea how hard it is on kids, even grown-up kids, like Geneviève, they'd think twice before divorce, unless it's something absolutely exceptional.

In front of them, Geneviève keeps her spirits up. She definitely doesn't want to take any sides, or be around when they start ripping into each other. But when she's alone with me, it all comes out. She says she'll never understand what happened. They always seemed so stable, the way parents are supposed to be. She's not sure if it was only because she was too young or if it really happened the way they say it did. As far as I can see, from what Geneviève's told me, her mother got caught up in the "lib" thing. She felt that Maurice, that's Geneviève's dad, had always been the big shot and treated her like a little girl. She told Geneviève he had some kind of "guru syndrome," loved and understood everybody and told them how to live their lives.

Well, Maurice *is* a bit like that. He does have a beard and a wonderful smile. He's the kind of person you like to talk to, he's a good listener. But what's so bad about that? A woman should be glad to have an interesting husband instead of just some other clod. But Valentine got involved with an old boyfriend, one she'd dated before she met Maurice, and they started an affair. It was all so stupid. She told Maurice. He was willing to put up with it for a while but then Valentine wanted a divorce. She was going to live out her childhood dream. In a special French way, Geneviève's mother is terribly naïve, a real romantic.

But now it's just sad. Valentine feels she's ruined her life and Maurice has found a young girl who likes, appreciates, his "guru syndrome." In my opinion, she's a real nerd; but she plays up to him and he loves it.

So, now, tonight, out of the blue, Geneviève tells me she wants *us* to get married. From all that's going on with her parents, I'd think that was the last thing in the world she'd want. We've been going together for almost three years now and we've never even talked about it, we've just had a great time. I never knew anybody who likes most of the things I like and is such fun.

I think she just wants to get away from home. When I was in America and I got her letter saying she couldn't come join me on the trip we'd planned, I knew something was wrong. I'd really been looking forward to those deserts and the sun, clean and hot. So I got worried about her. I knew she wanted to take this trip as much as I did. It was almost all we wrote about in our letters, besides the usual things.

I could've just said I couldn't come, but I *did* come so that must mean something. Now, I'm not sure it was such a good idea. After she asked like that, while she was crying, I couldn't say no. Boy, I really have to do some thinking.

What am I going to do? Hell, even if I cut out of the PhD program, I still need another year to finish my master's and get a teaching credential. In my field as a high school teacher, I can have four months' vacation every year nobody else ever gets. But I'd dread having to live all my life out in America. Hell, I'm more French than American and I know Geneviève would die if she had to leave France and live in California or somewhere like that. The French just don't export easily.

So, I said yes.

The question is, how in the hell am I going to manage this? The first part is I have to tell my folks. God, Dad's never going to understand; but then, in a certain way, he doesn't seem to understand anything or even want to. It's as if all he's trying for is a life without too many waves. He's wading through his imaginary universe smoothing things out, worrying things away.

That seems to be *his* answer. It will be harder for Mom. She has such high expectations for me, I know.

One thing I can do after I quit school, is go work for Monsieur Costa on the Rue Main d'Or in the Eleventh, in Paris. I've worked summers at his shop before and he said any time I wanted to be his apprentice, he'd take me on. I'm pretty good with my hands at that kind of work. Being an *ébéniste* isn't a bad job and I love working with wood.

I'm probably up a blind alley as a scientist anyway. I know for sure I'm not maniac about it the way some of the other people at school are. I might have more imaginative ideas but they go after the smallest things, so carefully, without seeming to think much. Can you even imagine an imaginative paleontologist? I'm a real fish out of water in most of my classes. I learn as well as the next one but old rocks have lost their charm for me.

Monsieur Costa only uses his atelier in the daytime. He has his own apartment in the Twentieth. But his *bail* is a *bail mixte*. That means it's legal to live there as well as work. There's a john and a sink already. I could bring in a folding bed instead of that beat-up old couch he has by the window. If he'd let us stay there nights, we could make it okay.

In exchange, we could sweep the place up, wash windows, things like that; we could pay the electricity and gas bills. Monsieur Costa might go for it. Geneviève could get a job, too, so we'd have enough money until I was ready to set up my own shop. Maybe, in time, I could buy Monsieur Costa out when he retires. He's getting old, he should be ready to retire soon. Somehow, some way, we'll work it out.

Shit, I'll never be able to explain all this to Mom and Dad. It even sounds nuts to me. I'm probably only inching my way into all this. I'm not thinking. I'm not even actually sure whose idea it was to get married. Geneviève was crying so hard and I hate to see or hear her cry; I got all mixed up. I'm not sure of anything.

Damn, I always swore it wouldn't happen to me, here I go down the same dead-end path Dad took. Even if I stay on at school and take a credential, it'd be the same thing. I'd be stuck in some high school somewhere teaching twenty-five hours a week and no place to go. Without a PhD you can't get any college jobs.

To be honest, right now, I'd be happy having a spot like Dad's. Sure, he's stuck there at ACP but he has a job, he's teaching something he likes, he only teaches about fifteen hours a week and, most of all, he's in Paris. But it's just luck he got that job, he could never get it today and I, sure as hell, couldn't either. Paleontologists are about as much in demand as ontologists.

But, shit, I'm twenty-five. Dad and Mom were twenty-two and twenty-one when they got married. Dad's parents were twenty-one and nineteen. People get married young all the time.

We can't have any kids for a while, but we can wait; for Christsake, Geneviève's only nineteen.

I don't see Dad giving me money to continue school if Geneviève's going to be living with me. I don't know why I think that, but I'm pretty sure. He's always been that way. It's always been, if you earned money and were living in the family it went in the family pot and then if you needed some you asked. I'm sure that if you get married, then he feels you've made a decision on your own and it's your responsibility to work it out. Look at Peg and George. They really had some hard times there at first. He probably gave them a little help, but not much. If I did stay on in California that year, Geneviève couldn't work; for one thing her English isn't good enough.

God, it's quiet here in Geneviève's room, and cold. She fixed it up last summer so she'd have a private place when everything was so crazy-hectic. Her parents weren't talking to each other and they kept talking to Geneviève and she'd pass on the messages. It was enough to drive anybody bananas. Besides that, her mother was crying all the time.

This is the old stable part where they kept the cows when this place was still a working farm. There's the smells of hundreds of years of cows still deep in these old stones. Usually I like that smell, but tonight it makes me think too much of how it must have been with Joseph; Mary pregnant, them not married, and they're in an old cow barn, almost two thousand years ago.

Geneviève has thick rugs on the floors and macramé things she wove herself, hanging along the walls. It's so dark, I can't make anything out, but I know they're there. She's the kind of person who can take almost any place and make it comfortable and homey. I really do need somebody like that in my life.

Geneviève moans and rolls on her back. I hope she doesn't start crying again. I push up on my elbow and stare at her. This could be my wife for the rest of my life. I can just make out the cheeks and hollows of her eyes in the gloom.

Upstairs it's all fancy. Before everything fell apart, her parents worked like slaves turning this old *mas* into a masterpiece of French country gentleman–style living. They all did. They preserved the natural beams and then smoothly plastered the stones between them. They built a raised fireplace where the old cooking hearth used to be.

It's all neat, clean and beautiful, almost like an apartment in Paris. In Paris, people're always trying to have *poutres apparentes*; exposed beams, and rustic things all around. Then when they come into the *real* country they try to make everything look like Paris. Even the French do crazy things that way.

I've got to say, my parents are either smart or lazy when it comes to fixing things up. Our place is still an old mill, with the millstones still in place and natural stone, even on the inside. It isn't as comfortable, and the carpentering is sort of "rough and ready," but it's still part of this Morvan life.

And upstairs here, now, there's virtually nothing of Christmas. You'd never know, from looking, that there was anything to celebrate. Come to think of it, there isn't.

But, even on other Christmases, there wasn't much of a Christmas feeling here, just fancy thin candles and maybe a piece of holly carefully arranged in a vase on the table, no Christmas tree. The French aren't really much for Christmas, especially

French intellectuals of the left, the way Geneviève's parents are. Anything that even smells of religion or religious practice is out.

God, my family goes about Christmas with both feet and arms. I think they've built in every Christmas custom anybody anywhere in the world ever thought about. Mom does a whole thing on December sixth with Niklaus-kommt-ins-Haus, German-style, and then again on January sixth there's the Epiphany witch and the Three Kings. Every night, from the first of December to Christmas Eve, we sing Christmas carols around advent candles, lighting one more candle each week until the big night.

Then, there are advent calendars. We had them when we were little kids before anybody except the Germans had ever heard about them. I remember they were so beautiful, with twenty-four little windows we opened every night after dinner before singing Christmas carols. Every window had a picture in it, angels or candy canes, or snowmen. It was like Chinese cookies only with Christmas pictures. We'd each have our own and Dad would line them up in front of candles so the open windows were almost like stained-glass windows. It was truly magic. My dad's a specialist in magic, that's for sure.

I think those nine years we went to Bavaria for Christmas started it all. I don't remember any Christmases before that. Then we came to the mill and brought most of that German Christmas feeling with us. We added some French things as well, then.

Boy, I remember how bad it was the first year I was away from home, living in a dorm at UCLA, for Christmas. Just about everybody else left to go home, but going home for me was a very expensive proposition and our family doesn't have that kind of money. I'll tell you it's hard mocking up a Christmas on your own in an empty dorm. I bought a tree on Christmas Eve for practically nothing and smuggled it up to my room. I cut out paper ornaments and colored them; I had some candles and I sang Christmas carols. I picked out some of the carols on my guitar. Outside it was a balmy evening so I pulled the drapes. Then I read out loud to myself the story of "T'was the Night

Before Christmas." Finally, I went to sleep and when I woke up, I was almost disappointed there weren't any presents under my tree. I think I half expected Dad to jump on Franky Furbo's trained eagle Bimbo and fly to California in the night with a whole lot of presents. In my deepest unconscious, I probably *was* looking for Santa to make a special trip.

I wonder what kind of Christmases Geneviève and I will have with our kids. She'll just have to get used to living with a Christmas freak. I'm not about to sit around in a bare house with no pine boughs draped all over everything, without Christmas cards hung from strings and a big, homemade wreath hanging on the door. I'll never be satisfied sitting around quietly, drinking champagne out of long-stemmed glasses, or whooping it up at some wild reveillon. No matter where we live, Christmas is going to be old-fashioned. I even hate those Christmas carols like "Rudolph the Red-Nosed Reindeer," or "White Christmas." There should be a law against song hucksters mangling Christmas.

Christmas is a private family time, that's all there is to it. It takes somebody in the family to make it all come true. I guess with us it was mostly Dad but Mom makes a lot of it, too. Dad is always holding onto things, trying to make it all stick together, keeping up some kind of continuity; at the same time he can go for hours ranting about how there's nothing. But he's great with Christmas. It must fit his crazy world somehow.

You should hear him go on about Wheeler's worm holes, with other universes on the other side of them and about entropy. He can even get all worked up over the validity of the pathetic fallacy. God, poor Peg used to just stick her fingers in her ears and close her eyes. I wonder if all philosophers are as weird as Dad.

The reveillon at the Calvets' is probably over. I bet Peg and Nickie hated that. I usually have a good time. Holy puke, I wonder if anyone will notice; I left without hanging up my stocking. Usually Mom reminds us, maybe I just wasn't there when she did, this time.

Nickie

I don't know if I can hold back any longer. I'll try swallowing slowly sixty times, that usually helps. Boy, the combination of wine and swinging in circles with those cowboys has turned my stomach upside down.

Nope, I've got to make it down those rickety stairs somehow. I definitely don't want to wake Peg. She needs her sleep, she told me how lots of times she doesn't sleep more than two hours a night; worrying about George and Seth, the whole thing.

The swallowing isn't helping; it's getting worse, my mouth is filling with spit, and the more I swallow, the more spit there is.

I slide out carefully from under the covers, holding onto my stomach and mouth at the same time. I could just let fly in that portable bidet Mom left for us up here, but that'd make a lot of noise and stink. I just *have* to make it down somehow.

I'll need both hands holding onto these steps, it's practically a ladder. Wow, what a mess it would make if I upchucked from here on the top step all over the living room. Ben'd probably die from pure shock and horror.

I step down that long, last, bottom step. I know I'll never make it across the room to the toilet. It's time for the big effort.

I move the butane bottle that's holding the door shut against the wind, and walk out into the snow on the porch in my bare, well-stomped feet. I lean over the edge and let fly into the frozen pool at the bottom of the fall from the pond. I can hear it hit but I can't see it. I heave three different times, and, for a minute there, have that empty-head feeling I get before I faint. I look up and breathe deeply.

After that first spontaneous upchuck I reach back and close the door behind me with my foot. I don't think I woke anybody. My feet are going numb from cold, but I feel better; having those feet so numb already from stomping isn't all bad. I scoop a handful of snow into my mouth to wash out the sour taste. At least getting sick woke me up.

It's still snowing and there's an ice-cold wind. I don't know why Mom and Dad come down here every Christmas. There are so many great parties and things going on in Paris. They must have some masochistic streak; more likely, they're victims of Dad's impossible illusions, and Mom's almost as bad as he is in her own way. They actually *believe* in Christmas; all the good cheer, yule logs, hall decking, Santa Claus; the whole crazy, cockeyed lie.

I know I'm going to have to talk with them before I leave. I'll try it out on Mom first. We don't have much time. Peg wants to be up in Paris the evening of the twenty-sixth; she has a date with an old French boyfriend; maybe checking what it would be like to be single again. I don't know what Mike wants to do; maybe he'll stick it out down here with Geneviève, or maybe she'll come up with us.

Driving down in the car, it was sad watching Peg's face while Mike told us about Geneviève's parents' troubles. She turned stony-faced, white, and didn't say anything, just looked out the window. For her, it must be like looking into some crystal ball, seeing her own future.

I hope she knows what she's doing, but from where I am, George isn't all that bad. No, that's not true. I, personally, want some truly interesting dude as father for my kids. I want somebody I can admire and respect. I don't care if he's eighty years old or ugly as sin; it's his mind I care about. If I'm going to risk my life, look like a ruptured tire for nine months and then spend twenty years raising a kid, there's got to be some possibility it's going to be a special person. After all, having a baby *is* the ultimate artistic creation; you'd be dumb to get into it without using the best materials possible. Having a child with most men I know would be like trying to sculpt the Pietà with Play-Doh. That's why I'm so hooked on Spike, I guess. I love even imagining what kind of kid he'd make with me.

He has everything. He just doesn't want to be a father and he'd never do anything like get married. But God he's exactly what I want. He's all male, a wonderful lover; tender, sensitive, talented. Damn, is he talented.

I think I'm finished upchucking. I open the door carefully, close it and slide the butane bottle quietly in front where it was. It sounds as if everybody's asleep. I sit down in the rocking chair beside the fire. It's blazing merrily. I look down at Ben, he's dead to the world. I sit there rocking quietly and try to put my head together.

I met Spike when some of the people at La Jolla said they knew a "real" sculptor who lived out near La Mesa in the desert. We all knew the classes we were having there as art majors had nothing really to do with sculpting. We were only pushing materials around, playing with plasticine or papier-mâché, making all kinds of junk sculpture. The damned studio there looks like a dump, everybody dragging in broken washing machines or cars and welding them together and polishing them or painting them. Other people were gluing or hammering bits of plywood together and painting them gold or black. God, I've had Louise Nevelson right up the nose. I always thought sculpting was taking a hammer and chisel and just cutting away at a hunk of wood or a rock. Not at La Jolla, it's some kind of kindergarten project gone amok. Everybody's trying to please the teacher and he doesn't know any more about real sculpting than I do.

So we all jumped in Harry's Land Rover and took off. He's the only one who'd ever been out to see this guy before. He said he came on him when he was trying out his four-wheel drive by driving down an arroyo.

We get out there, really up a small canyon in the middle of nowhere and I can't believe it. He's built this place with a combination of adobe bricks and cement blocks. But these cement blocks aren't ordinary cement blocks you'd buy. He's made them himself with forms he designs by cutting into the sand. He has actually built a studio way out there in the desert which is a sculpture in itself.

There's an old flatbed truck with no fenders and no hood parked beside his place. When I first see him I almost laugh out loud. He's only wearing a pair of cutoffs, cut so short the pockets hang down so you can see them, and big heavy hiking shoes without socks. He's covered completely with white dust. I thought he'd painted himself white.

Only his eyes are pink and darkish showing all through the dust. He also has a pair of goggles shoved up on his head. He has his hair cut so he looks almost bald. He has a heavy short-handled sledgehammer in one hand and a cold chisel in the other. This, I knew right away, was a real sculptor.

I might have fallen in love with him even before I got out of the Rover. I didn't know then if he was twenty, forty or sixty, and I couldn't care less. It turned out he was twenty-eight. He just stood there as we, all five of us, piled out of the Rover into the sand.

He recognizes Harry, and is nice enough, but I have a feeling we're interrupting something. He's only being polite until we go away. There's no one else there. He's way out there in the middle of the desert, alone. He gives us all drinks of water from jerry cans he has stacked in a corner. It's warm. He sits down with us but he never puts down his sledgehammer.

In the middle of the floor is a huge piece of stone, it's really a river boulder from the streambed. He's cutting the spirals of a snail onto it, more or less following the contours of the stone. The small head or foot of the snail at the bottom is already roughed in. In a certain way, it looks like some of the big fossils I've seen in paleological or anthropological museums. He's going along with the stone but is making it something personal to himself. I point.

"Wow, that's really something. Did you find that boulder out here?"

He looks over, puts down his glass of water. Where he's been drinking, it's flesh-colored from the stone dust being washed off.

"You mean Roscoe? Yeah, ain't he somethin'? I keep finding faults in the stone and I'm scared to death I'll get it all cut then have the head fall off. Those antennae are going to be tough. I

think I'll have them curled up the way they do sometimes. I
wish I had some snails out here for models but it's all too dry.
I got into this project when I hauled this rock home and haven't
been to any place cool and wet enough since then to find any
snails."

He looks right at me while he says this. His look isn't penetrating or anything like that, it's only calm and you can almost
feel the fires inside him. I realize the gray of his eyes is almost
exactly the color of the stone he's carving.

We look around some more. There are all kinds of crazy things.
There are animals and human figures curled up, sometimes only
one but most of the time two or three. Some of them are life-
size.

They aren't all carved out of rock. Some are castings from
cement. He shows us how he does sand castings with cement.
He makes a mold directly in the sand, wets it to make it stay
the way he wants, then lines the down side with Saran Wrap to
hold moisture. The one side is the way he molds it in the sand,
the other side, the top part, he molds with cement to the general form, then carves when it's dried just right. I never heard
of anybody working that way. One is a curled-up figure and
looks almost as if it's a mummy somebody dug out of sand or a
fossilized body from Pompeii. He also shows us the beginnings
of a mold he's making for a giant bear.

"That one's going to take at least six sacks of cement. I use
about five to one for these things. It's hard to find stones I can
move with my hoist and truck that are big enough but not too
big. I've carved some right in place when I couldn't resist. This
bear here, Shorty, I'm going to paint and push him up to stand
beside my door. That should scare anybody away who might
want to rob or mug me."

He laughs. I couldn't even think of anybody who would have
the guts and be crazy enough to try mugging him and there's
nothing to rob, nothing anybody could carry away anyhow.

He explains how he mixes something like gesso with plaster
of paris and glue. He coats the cement statues with this when

they're dry. That's the surface he paints on. Those pieces he shows us are incredible. He paints as well as he sculpts. Harry says something about gilding the lily, that maybe just the honesty of the cement is enough.

He looks at Harry, smiles. By the way, his name is Spike Tate. I'm sure Spike isn't his real name but it fits. I never did find out his real first name.

He picks up his cold chisel again. He walks over and stares at his snail.

"I don't know about that, Harry. The old Greek and most of the Roman statues were painted. The paint just wore off and we've all got an aesthetic about sculpture based on faded, washed-out stone. And it's a great feeling, painting sculpture, no faking shadows; no illusions of space. It's much more real than regular painting, the statues seem to come alive."

I have to agree. They aren't hoked up like some wax museum but are more real than ordinary statues. Some of the animals he does are bigger than life and some of the people, smaller. But the ones he paints are special.

He starts chipping on his snail. It's obvious he's given us as much time as he wants. I hate to go, but I don't want to be a nuisance.

"Okay, everybody, let's go. We should leave this madman to his work."

I head out to the Rover, the others follow. He comes to the door of his place and watches us. As we drive away, he waves his hand with the chisel. I know he's waving to me.

For the next weeks, everything I do seems so superficial. I dream about Spike Tate. They're very sexual dreams and I haven't had sex dreams since I got old enough to go out and get some of the real thing. After two weeks pacing around and feeling lost, I dig up the nerve.

First, I borrow Amy Lou's car. I tell her I'll be back next evening. Early in the morning I sneak out and walk all around campus until I find about ten big snails. I pack some bread, ham, cheese and a bottle of wine in a backpack along with a canteen of water. I'd marked our way back in the Rover, so I know just where we came out onto the road. I find a place near there, park the car, lock it up and sling the pack on my back. I'm wearing jeans and a T-shirt, no bra. It's hot.

I get started trekking into the desert at about eight in the morning. When I say I got up early, I mean early, besides I couldn't sleep and that's when I knew I'd find the snails. There were always shiny snail paths over all the paths at school, so I knew they were there.

I'd tried to spot some landmarks as we were coming out in the Rover but there was a lot of dust. I figure if I find the arroyo, I can just follow it up and can't miss. It takes me about two hours hard hoofing before I spot his place. Boy, if somebody wants to be alone, this is the place. It's only April, but it's hot. I come in as quietly as I can. He isn't working on the snail. Then I see him mixing cement around the side. He's filling in the mold of that giant bear he'd shown us. I get quite close and I'm standing there when he looks up and sees me. He leans on his shovel and looks around.

"How in hell'd you get in here?"

"I walked."

"You walked from La Jolla?"

"No, I borrowed a friend's car and parked it up on the high-way, then walked in."

"Damn, you could've gotten lost. It's easy to get all twisted up in a desert like this where everything looks about the same."

He's really staring at me now. I begin wishing I hadn't come. I know if he asked why I came, I couldn't answer. Instead, I slide the pack off my back, reach in and pull out the snails.

"Here, here are some models for you."

He leans the shovel against his hand mixer and comes forward, takes the snails from me. He peers into the jar.

"Boy, these are beauties. This is really nice of you, thanks."

He carries them into his place and I follow him. He puts them in a place between two jerry cans of water.

"I don't know how long they can last out here in the heat where it's so dry."

I've cut holes in the lid so they can breathe, if snails breathe. He scatters water on the top so it seeps down into the jar.

"God, I don't know what they can eat. There isn't much in the way of snail-type food out here."

He begins to have the anxious, interrupted look again. He looks over to where he was working.

"Do you mind if I go back to work for just a little while, I have the water with the sand and cement in the mixer and I have to turn it before it begins to set. Also, I have to finish pouring that whole beast or I'll have a dry layer in the middle and it'll never hold together when I push it up."

He goes out past me. I follow. I sit on a pile of cement sacks covered with a piece of plastic and he throws more shovelfuls of cement into the mixer, then begins turning it by hand. God, it's great watching his muscles work. He's slim and his muscles are stringy but he must have thin skin or something because every muscle stands out, thin strands of muscles in his arms, his back, legs, even his neck. I assume there's skin, from the places where sweat has run and I can see dark through the coating of white. It looks like the same white coating from two weeks ago. I don't imagine he has much water to spare for washing up.

He dumps that load into his mold and gets down into it, shaping the figure. He's already above ground level and as he shapes, he pulls sand up from the sides to keep the cement from running. It's really quite a technique.

"Would you like me to start filling the mixer again while you're doing that?"

He looks briefly over his shoulder.

"It's hard, I warn you. But that'd be great. It'll speed things up."

I work with that shovel for three hours. The only rest I'd have is when Spike would mix and pour the cement. It's almost impossible what he's doing. I don't know how he can keep it all in his head. We hardly talk. He's so totally involved with that bear and I'm just about pooped out. After he's poured the tenth load, he stands up, stretches his back, walks around his bear and looks at it from all angles. He reaches down and cups some of the cement with his hand to push it into place. He's working with bare hands in the cement.

"Well, that ought to do for now. Let's take a break. I never thought I'd get that Shorty bear so far along this morning. Thanks again."

He looks at me and smiles. I must look a wreck. Ordinarily I'm a heavy sweater anyway, but I never sweated the way I do this morning. My T-shirt is sopping. I see him looking down and sure enough, my nipples are standing out like Juneberries.

"Come on inside. We can have some water to cool off."

I reach down and pick up my backpack. It's red hot, I should've left it inside. The wine, a good Chablis, is going to be warm as piss, or warmer. I follow him.

Inside, he clears off a place on the floor with a twig broom. He bangs two beat-up pillows against each other so dust flies, then puts them on the floor. He goes over and fills two big glasses of water. I don't really see anything to eat in the place. There's no fridge. I start unpacking the lunch. I pull out the wine. He squats across from me and stares.

"Wow, I haven't seen food like this in a while."

"Do you have a bottle opener around here?"

"No, but I can get the wine out of that bottle."

He brings over his sledgehammer and a nail. I hate to think what he's going to do to my fifteen-dollar bottle of Chablis. He drives the nail into the cork with the sledgehammer. Then, somehow, he manages to pull on the nail at an angle with a pair of pliers and out comes the cork making a nice little pop. I've spread out the sandwiches. He pours his water into himself and I empty my glass. He pours the wine.

I hold out my glass to clink and he's bringing his glass to his mouth. He catches my eye and makes a slight motion toward my glass. I say *"À la votre."* He closes his eyes and it's beautiful to watch the way he enjoys that mouthful of wine. It seems almost five minutes before he opens his eyes again. He looks at me smiling.

"That's the first guzzle of wine I've had in almost three years. It was worth waiting."

He looks down into his glass.

"When I was about twenty-five, I was really into wine. I could have been on the edge of becoming alcoholic, I think. Now, I can't afford the stuff and I feel better, but this wine is something else. In those days I just slugged it down for the effect, now I've learned to really savor things, let them happen to me."

We eat the sandwiches and it's the same way, he takes each bite and chews it forever with his eyes closed. When he swallows, I swear I can see it go clear down his neck. One reason is he has his head tilted back as well as having his eyes closed. He makes sure his mouth is completely empty before he takes another bite or a sip of wine. That meal, just two ham and cheese sandwiches apiece, with the wine, takes an hour and a half to eat. I try slowing down to match him but I can only chew something so long then I've got to swallow or it gets disgusting.

After we're finished, and before he can get away again, I make my proposition. I ask if he'll take me on as a student. At first, I don't think he heard me. He takes another sip of wine.

"Your name is Nickie, right? I think that's what Harry called you."

I'm surprised he remembers.

"Nickie, you don't know what you'd be getting into. First, I'm not a teacher, I hate teachers and I hate teaching. The way I live here, no woman would put up with it. I don't want you trekking in across the desert every Tuesday and Thursday or something like that, either. I hate schedules. I have no toilet, no running water; that piece of flattened out, raggedy foam rubber over there is my bed. I don't always sleep in it. I have my work to do and there's just not room for anything else."

He looks at me, his head cocked like a bird. I look back at him. He's getting that "interrupted" look again.

"Why don't you give me a try? You don't have to teach me, give me lessons, or anything like that, just let me watch you work and work a little myself. I'm tougher than I look. I'm not afraid."

"You ought to be. How do you know I'm not another Charles Manson, seducing pretty young girls to come out here in the desert and live with me? I could have the hills around here filled with women I've raped and killed. Did you ever think of that?"

There's nothing to say. I look into those pale, gray, hot, slate-like eyes. For the first time I can understand those Manson girls.

"Nickie, I go into town once a month. I just go to the nearest town. I buy a sack of soybeans, a sack of rice, a sack of flour, a sack of sorghum, about ten sacks of cement, some oil and two dozen eggs. That's what I eat. Not the cement, or maybe I do, sometimes. I don't have much money and I don't sell my work, I don't even try. I could use the money but it takes too much time.

"The little money I need, I earn going around doing odd jobs in town. They all know me there and I'm a good worker. Usually, in two or three days I can rustle up enough to keep me for another month."

He stands, stretches. We've wiped out the bottle of wine. I stand, too.

"So, that's it, the 'unwelcome mat' is out."

"I didn't say that. I'm only trying to tell you the way it is. If you can pay me enough to stay around here so it saves me going into town working dumb jobs, it'd be terrific for me. Just don't get in my way. If you could sort of push things around here without disturbing too much, that would be great, too."

He smiles.

"If you learn to do that, live in a sculptor's space without being a menace, you'd've learned a lot. I warn you, I'm not Charles Manson, just an ordinary garden-variety man when it comes to sex, but if you stand around with those lovely tits sticking out, you're going to get fucked. If you don't like that, then you'd better get back to La Jolla and stay there."

He starts out the door past me, going out to work some more on his bear. I stand in front of him and rip off that dripping T-shirt. I stink but no more than he does.

"I think I could handle it."

And he starts handling me. That's how it got started. Would you believe, in the middle of the most wonderful fuck I've ever had, he gets up, takes one of those jerry cans, and bare-assed, goes out to sprinkle water on that bear.

I drove the car back to Amy Lou, packed my things, went down to the registrar's office to tell them I was dropping out. I had to see a counselor to explain why. I made up some lies about my family in France needing me.

I pulled out all the money I had in the bank; what Mom and Dad had sent me and what I'd made last summer cocktail waitressing. There was almost two thousand dollars all together, my whole wad. I took it out in twenty-dollar bills. Then I got Amy Lou to drive me out to where I could hike in again. I had a lot of personal stuff and stashed it under some mesquite about fifty yards from the road. I could come back to get it a bit at a time or maybe Spike would drive me back. I put what I could on my back and took off. Amy Lou was convinced I'd flipped my lid, and I guess I had.

It was just as bad as he said. It was always hot in the days and cold at night. Even though I took that dirty piece of foam rubber out in the sunlight and beat it to death, it still smelled of sweat and rubber. I cooked with a skillet over a fire in back. I tried every combination of rice, soybeans and sorghum I could think of. He didn't even have salt or pepper, no coffee.

Spike just pees whenever the time comes. Sometimes when he's in the middle of something hard, he doesn't even stop, just whips it out and sprays over whatever he's working on; says it gives personality to his sculpture. Okay, but it also smells to high heaven. He insists when you've lived in a desert long enough, the fact that your body can shoot out fluid is almost miraculous, something you really get to enjoy.

I'd go outside to do my business. But I did get so I didn't mind, especially at night with those incredible clear skies.

Spike does his share. He scrounges up and chops wood; builds the fire. He washes the clothes. He does this by stomping them in a cement depression he's made in the back. The problem is water. He claims this method uses the least. After they're done he spreads them out on the bushes and they smell clean and full of sun.

Actually there aren't that many things to wash. He has three pair of those super cutoffs he made from worn-out-at-the-knee Levi's he'd bought at the Salvation Army. He doesn't wear underwear. I have underwear, jeans and a few T-shirts. I get so in the heat of the day I go topless, it's lots cooler and my nipples even begin to tan. We wash our dishes and pots with sand.

There isn't all that much sex. Spike is like a man possessed. Sometimes he falls asleep at three or four in the morning, right in the chips where he's been chopping away for ten or twelve hours. Sometimes I can drag him to bed but sometimes he's like a dead man and I can't budge him.

I never do figure out just what he's trying for. He won't talk about it much.

He shows me how to use a mallet and chisel and how to sharpen the chisel. He gets me some medium-sized stones, weighing over a hundred pounds each, and sets me cutting. The first time we go into town, I buy gloves because my hands are all cut up and bruised. I can see it won't get any better, either. Spike, after all these years, always has terribly beat-up hands, as if he's been in some kind of deadly fist fight.

I found that, in a certain way, cutting stone is like a fist fight, or at least what I think one would be like. After a while, you get so you lose all sense of time, of pain, you struggle to make that damned stone into what you want. It's a question of dominance.

I stay out there with him five months. One thing I'm learning is I'll never really be a sculptor. The shit they were giving me at La Jolla was awful but is about what I can handle.

Spike is gentle about this, but even I can see it isn't there. I'm becoming good at cutting stone but somehow I can't conceive in three dimensions. Spike seems to *become* the stone and in some weird way the stone becomes him.

We do manage, with the help of the winch on the truck, to get that bear out of its hole, dragged over and stood up by the door. Spike spends a week cutting the rough edges. Then he gessoes it and starts painting. He paints two more weeks. When he's finished, it's alive. It's more than a bear, it's all the power and glory in nature. That's what Spike can do, transcend ordinary things and make them extraordinary.

I begin to want his baby in the worst way. I've been on the pill for three years and I want to get off it and just be a real woman. All the talk I've listened to and all the things I've said myself, since I was sixteen, about being my own woman and living my own life, seem to be melting off me out there in the desert. I'm beginning to be like some kind of squaw, and the worst part is I like it.

I tell Spike, after we make love one night, that I want a baby. He's on his back and I have my head on his chest. He doesn't move. It's like that a lot of times, you aren't sure if he's heard you because he can be so long answering. Finally, he runs his hands through my hair.

"If you want a baby, Nick, that's okay with me. That's your business; my business is making sculpture. I can't be a father to it, there's no room, I don't want to be a father right now. Those stones, those rocks out there, are my children. I'd feel as if I were abandoning them. You understand?"

I understand and know he isn't bullshitting me. There's barely room in his life for me and that's crowding him a lot. I lay awake all that night trying not to cry.

In the morning I tell him I'm leaving. He's working on an enormous, almost vertical piece of stone. It took us two days to haul it in from higher in the arroyo. He never will tell me what he was carving until I could start to see it myself. He said the sculpture has to do the talking.

He stops, hammer and cold chisel in his hand, the way he was the first time I saw him. Sweat's running down his body.

"If this is what you want, Nick, okay. You can stay around here's long as you like; that's okay, too. Whatever you want to do. I'll miss you."

I think that last sentence is the only time he lied to me.

We piled my stuff on the truck and he drove me all the way to La Jolla. We didn't talk much. There wasn't much to say. He left me off at the entrance to the school. I knew Amy Lou would take me in. It was just a few days before the next quarter started. He swung the truck around and waved as he drove away. I watched him go and knew how much I wanted something of him, anything. It was then I decided I'd have a child by him somehow, sometime, no matter what.

I got in on a late enrollment and started classes. It all seemed so tame, worse than before. Every day I wanted to go back out to Spike, but I stuck it out. When I read the letter from Dad asking if I could come for Christmas with the whole family together, and he'd pay the way, I began planning and investigating. I phoned and was surprised to get Dad. I asked if it was all right if I brought a boyfriend for Christmas.

"Just as long as you bring yourself along, too, Nickie. I'll tell Mother. I'm sure it will be okay."

I'd found that with a university charter I could get two round-trip tickets for the same price Dad was sending for regular air fare.

My folks had no idea I'd been out in the desert with Spike those five months. We don't write a lot in our family and Amy Lou had picked up my mail and was holding it for me. It was when I picked up the mail that I found Dad's letter. He'd written it a month before.

First I went to the Salvation Army and found a reasonably good piece of foam rubber six inches thick for only ten bucks. It was hardly used. Then I bought a bottle of wine and rolled it tight inside that foam rubber. I used rope to make a sort of sling so I could carry it on my back. Amy Lou agreed to drive me out to the take-off place from the road but she was really disgusted with me. I'd told her everything that'd happened, but the way Amy Lou felt about men, she couldn't understand.

It's really a hot hike in. I get there and Spike isn't there. The place is a real wreck when you just take a casual look at it. But now I know. Everything has a place. Spike isn't neat but he's orderly. His food, his tools, all the things he needs are carefully stored. He just doesn't do ordinary straightening out, cleaning up, dusting, anything like that.

The truck is gone so I figure he might be up the arroyo somewhere hunting stone. Or, he could be in town. I decide to wait anyhow.

While I'm waiting, I neaten things up. I roll up his old foam rubber pad with the rope I used to carry my new one in, and make a sort of chair from it. It's the only thing like a chair in the place. I spread the new pad in the place where the old one was. Boy, it really gives me pleasure just looking at it. I hope Spike won't feel I'm trying to run his life for him, that was one thing we'd have arguments about. Whenever I changed anything, moved even a box or the water cans to another place I had to tell him beforehand. He says he could work in that studio blind because he knows where everything is and when something changes he doesn't feel the same. I take the chance.

I stash the wine in the shade between jerry cans of water. It isn't exactly cool but it's cooler than anyplace else. I'm already sweating like a pig.

I'm just trying to build a fire to cook something for dinner when I hear the growl of that truck transmission coming around the curve of the arroyo above me. I'm so nervous I can't keep still. I want to go out and meet him but I make myself stay still and sit on the new chair I've just made from the old pad.

I listen as he pulls on the brake, slams the door and crunches across the stone chips surrounding his place. He's walking over toward the jerry cans when he notices me. He just stares. I stand up.

He comes over and takes me in his arms. I hold on for dear life, his dear life and mine. I'd almost forgotten how he smelled. If somebody could bottle that smell and sell it to men, women would go crazy.

He pushes me away with his hands on my shoulders. He still hasn't kissed me.

"What a tremendous surprise. You're looking great, Nick. I was just thinking about you. I'm up there about three miles carving, or helping the water carve, a huge ovoid boulder with a hole in the center, almost like a lopsided doughnut and I got so horny working I started remembering all the great times we had."

He looks up toward the place where his pad usually is.

"Holy shit. Look at that. This place is turning into some kind of luxury palace."

He looks down at the old pad where I'd been sitting.

"Jells hells, we've even got a chair; think of that."

He looks around sniffing, checking all his storage places with suspicion.

"And you've even cleaned up this den of iniquity. I'll be darned."

I go over and pull out the bottle of wine. I hold it up.

"That looks mighty good, Nick. But right now, that new bed over there looks even better. How about it?"

I walk into his arms again and he carries me over. We're so wild getting undressed, I get a cramp in my foot trying to push my shoe off without undoing the laces. But I don't feel anything except Spike. He's like a crazy man. He's the way I thought a man should be who lives all alone out in a desert without a woman. He almost scares me. Maybe he is Charles Manson and I only made a miraculous escape the first time.

When we finally slow down, absolutely exhausted, I crawl over and get the wine. This time I brought an opener. I slowly open the wine while he watches me. We take turns drinking out of the bottle directly, slowly, savoring, enjoying; interrupting each time as Spike recovers. We still aren't talking much. I'm waiting for the right minute, when he brings it up himself.

"So, are you moving back in with me, Nick? As I said when you left, you're welcome."

"It's not so simple, Spike."

He has a mouthful of wine in his mouth. He swallows it slowly.

"Nothing ever is."

"Spike let me be serious for just a few minutes then that'll be all, okay?"

He takes another mouthful and nods, staring up at the corrugated metal top of his house.

"I still want to have your baby. I know there's no room for me or for a baby in your life here. I understand and I respect that."

I wait. He's still holding the wine in his mouth, still staring at the corrugated metal.

"I'd like to have our baby on my own. I wouldn't have it here, I'd have it in France with my parents. Then I'd come back to California and let the state take care of me as a single parent. I've checked it all out and I could get by fine with what they'd give me. You know I can live without much money."

He swallows, looks at me.

"You're crazy, Nick. I could never be part of anything like that. You know you'll just trap me somehow. You know how I am. I don't even want to let anybody have my boulders I cut. I could get all caught up in being a father and lose control of my life. You know that."

Somehow I'm blowing it. I try to start up again but I'm having a hard time not crying.

"Okay, let's forget about all that for just now. I'd want to talk to my folks first anyway. They deserve at least that.

"But there's another thing. My dad sent me money to come visit with them for Christmas. We used to have our Christmases in an old valley with more stones than you could ever carve. I'd like them to meet you and you meet them. We could go up to Paris and you could see Maillot and Rodin and Houdin, all the sculptors there. I found out I can get us both charter tickets for the same money my dad sent me. What do you think?"

I'm sure he's going to take another swallow of that wine so I lift it from his hand and pull a good swallow myself. I lie back and wait. He's quiet, waiting in his usual way. I decide I can wait until tomorrow if he wants to. But he starts talking.

"I'll start at the back, Nick. I don't want to see those sculptures, those old cities. I have nothing to do with all that. I don't really think I'm a sculptor anyway, I'm a cutter of boulders and a caster in cement. My things have nothing to do with what's in museums.

"I'm sure your folks are nice people but I really don't want to meet them. I have a hard time meeting and dealing with people. That's what I like about my boulders, they don't move and they are consistent. Besides, I couldn't leave all this. Some nut could come out here with a sledgehammer or dynamite or something and kill everything I love. I'd be worried all the time."

I think I knew it would be like this. I swallow the wine I've been holding in my mouth while he talks.

"So, okay. You don't want to be a father and you don't want to come to France with me. I understand, I really do. I think you're holding on to yourself, the madman in you, with those stones and I also think you might be the most important artist of our times. I could never forgive myself if I did something to break up this wonderful creative world you've made for yourself."

And I know I'm believing this as I say it. But what I'm not saying is he's going to be a father whether he ever knows it or not. *That* can't hurt him.

He looks at me. I roll on top of him, tip the last mouthful of wine into his mouth.

"That's all you get, buddy. Now, let's fuck. You don't have anything against us fucking do you? That's not going to get in the way of your boulders. Just let me come out here and climb onto this nice soft pad once in a while with you, okay?"

He pulls my face down to his by my hair and puts his lips on mine. He forces that wine into my mouth and we both try to swallow but almost drown. We laugh and, as far as Spike's concerned, that's the end of it.

I look up and the fire is practically going out now. I turn one big log over and it glows. I haul two logs from the pile and stack them on the glowing one. I blow and little bits of fire catch. I wish I knew more about starting fires, we all just let Dad do it. Both Mike and Ben know how. Either there's a strong strain of sexism built into this family or there really is a difference between boys and girls, men, women. When I was out there with Spike, he always made the fire, too; so it isn't just our family.

I go out into the grange and drag back the big banana bag. Lordy, it's heavy. Thank God, I'm feeling much better, but my feet are still numb partly from the snow, partly from the Morvandeau stomp.

Wow, that dancing was really something. It was great having men really appreciate me. They'd almost drool when they touched me, or looked into my eyes. They didn't seem to even mind all the extra weight I put on either. In fact, they seemed to like it; big tits, like a good cow.

When I came back to civilization after Spike, I ate like a pig. Maybe I was trying to get pregnant on food. Maybe I was making up for all those soybeans and sorghum meals. I don't know, but I put on twenty-five pounds in four months.

I know I could get any one of these farm guys to go through the whole routine, marry me, the works; but that's dumb, like buying a horse when there are automobiles. And I've been spoiled by a diesel truck. Here, I'd wind up milking cows and herding sheep in the cold and rain for the rest of my life. That's not what I want either.

That's the trouble. Peg and I have been brought up in this

weird between world. I seriously want to do something important with my life, make it real somehow. I thought I wanted to sculpt, but now I know. Whatever it takes to be an artist, the controlled craziness, just doesn't run in our family. Maybe Dad's an artist without an art. Or his art could be going invisible, changing in a split second, confusing himself and everybody else about what's real or not. My God, between Mom and Dad, we certainly got hung up.

There's Mom, upright, two feet on the ground, even while Dad's saying there *isn't* any ground. She's always organized, always seems to know where she's going, how to get there. She knows how to get things done. Then, there's Dad, programed failure, the floppy philosopher. It would be great to sculpt a real philosopher's stone. Spike would like to try that, just his kind of thing.

Still, in some weird way, Dad's sensitive, intuitive, intelligent, responsible. What a waste. He's always building things, making nests, trying to help Mom, doing his share of housework. He's practically a househusband and at the same time he does a job. He's spoiled us all rotten. There *aren't* any men like that. I don't even think *he's* like that. It's all part of his crazy game, a game where only he knows the rules and he keeps changing those rules all the time.

Including Spike, the men I keep meeting are *either* sensitive, intelligent, interesting, vital men, *or* ordinary, nice, turn-me-on-turn-me-off studs who want to hold a steady job, have children, fight to be a success.

There don't seem to be any blends. I think that's what happened to Peg. She married somebody who'd do the second part, but now she wants more excitement, somebody with wild ideas, imagination. I should introduce her to Spike. Oh no! After one day out there in that desert, she'd run screaming back to George. I keep trying to tell her the right mixture isn't around any more; something happened.

So, you get your choice. Either you have a baby on your own

from an interesting man you really respect, or tie up with some plug who'll be there through thick and thin, even when you don't want him any more. Big deal choice.

I finally get finished with the things I have to do. I hope everybody likes what I got them.

I climb up the ladder, slide carefully into bed. There's no warmth left, but I can lay my head back and it doesn't spin. Somehow, I did manage it. I think I'm about ready to relax, finally, and I'm going to sleep when, out of nowhere, I'm crying like a baby. Here I am crying, alone Christmas Eve, just when I thought I'd be the most happy.

I wipe away the tears, but they just keep leaking out the sides of my eyes; down my face and into my hair. I hold back on the sobs. I don't want to wake Peg. I don't want to talk with anybody, don't want to try explaining anything or listening to anybody else. There's got to be some mystery in this life, or what the hell is there?

Here I've been, fighting it all my life and now I want mystery more than anything else. I'd like to be able to believe without proof. Anything. It could be because I know a little bit about something now. If you're going to be an artist, you have to be good at believing, believing in something, or nothing; it doesn't matter, but believing. I've forgotten how to believe, knocked it right out of myself on purpose. How dumb can you get?

The world looks so crappy. If I could only have one human being all to myself, it would at least make some kind of sense. Maybe jollying yourself along is all there is to it. Ho! Ho! Merry Christmas!!

I've got to get to sleep, tomorrow's going to be insane around here.

Maybe I'm crying for joy, but it doesn't feel that way. I could be crying for joy and not even know it. Dad would approve of that.

Ben

It's still dark but I've been asleep. I look over and see Nickie putting some wood on the fire. I hope she does it right; I don't *ever* remember her putting wood on a fire. She does it fine and I close my eyes to see if I can slip into the space between being awake and being asleep. I watch through my eyelids as fire starts burning under the new logs.

Heck, this is really only a *pretend* Christmas. There are no stockings hanging, no surprises in the morning. Presents are under the tree but I know what all of them are and Santa Claus didn't bring any. If there's no scariness, no surprise, it really isn't Christmas.

I was so scared, so excited, I never used to sleep Christmas Eve; I guess I actually *did* sleep because Mom and Dad always managed to arrange Santa's presents under the tree without my knowing, but it seemed as if I'd been awake all night.

Damn, I hate growing up. I don't mind getting bigger, getting stronger; or my penis growing and hair on my legs or my mustache and beard growing. That's all fun; like watching baby birds in a nest or tadpoles turning into frogs. But *becoming* a grown-up doesn't look as if it's fun at all.

Nickie, Maggie and Mike don't act happy. All they seem to be doing is proving to each other how great they are. They always look to see if everybody else is seeing how grown up they've become.

Nothing is natural. Gosh, this Christmas, even Dad is like a grown-up. He doesn't have time to play with me; he's only running around straightening things up or sweeping, or getting stuff for somebody else or pretending things aren't happening.

Making cookies was fun, that was real, but I hardly got to do anything important. Nickie and Maggie and Mike did all the best parts. No, this year it's only a pretend Christmas and how many Christmases are left for me at home?

To be honest, practically nobody at school knows how to play any more either. They think I'm crazy when I bring one of my models and fly it on the football field. I'm sure they want to play with me but they're afraid somebody will think they're acting too young. Not even Serge. Before, I could always get him into a game of Battleship or something but now he's afraid to play with me because the others will laugh.

All the kids at school think of, is playing at being grown up. They're either smoking, or chewing tobacco to look like big-league baseball players, or talking about how much beer they drank over the weekend and how lousy they feel or about stealing liquor from their parents, or smoking pot.

The boys talk about girls; which one they felt up here, or there, or in the bushes and who lets you *do* it with them. I guess the girls are talking about the boys, too, which ones have the biggest muscles or the longest penises. I don't know.

Then it's everybody always pushing each other around and taking those crazy karate or judo stances. None of that's *really* playing, it's only pretending to be grown-ups, *crazy* grown-ups. Nobody laughs except when they're laughing *at* somebody.

And the girls don't think of anything except how they look, who's got a date for the dance or to a movie. I'd really like to know some *serious* girl who's smart, someone I could *talk* with. Half the fun of reading is sharing with somebody what you've read or what you're reading. The only person I get to talk with about books is Dad and he doesn't read much any more. Mom's books just don't interest me. They all only seem to be about getting the nice, poor girl married to some rich squire or a preacher.

Then again, a lot of the books I like, Dad doesn't want to read. He won't read any of the war books or that kind of thing. The most I can expect is he'll read some science-fiction book with me if it's by an author he considers good, like Heinlein or

174

Clarke or Asimov. Pretty soon there won't be anybody in the world left for me to talk with.

It seems people forget how to have fun when they're about thirteen. Everybody gets so competitive; and everything is only for show. Even Mike. He and I used to play sometimes, but now he's all the time with Geneviève. He's gotten serious as the rest. He hardly ever laughs and he used to have a good laugh. It was fun just hearing him laugh.

I can't remember Peg or Nickie ever really laughing, they laugh as if they're in a play and the line in the play says *Laugh* so they laugh. They laugh *too* hard, *too* long. I wonder if it's really as awful as it looks to me.

What I'd like to do is just keep living here at home. I'd stay here and let them take care of me until I'm old enough and have my doctorate or something, so I can earn money. Then when Dad and Mom are too old I'll take care of them. That seems like a fair enough deal. I don't think I could ever stand being a father myself. Even that damned little Seth drives me crazy. Tiny kids like that are so noisy; they don't understand when you want to be alone to think or read.

I'll grow up, get to be about six-foot-three or -four, so nobody will push me around. I'll grow a nice full black beard and keep wearing glasses. I don't want to get contacts. I *like* staying behind my glasses, I feel safe. With them and the beard I can be practically invisible. Maybe I'll get to look like President Lincoln, only I won't be president of anything, only president of myself.

To be perfectly serious I'd be happy living all my life here at the mill. That would be my idea of the perfect life, living here with stacks of dry firewood, simple food and books. I'd take long walks and do some shooting up on the hill. I'd make model airplanes to fly up there too and maybe someday have one of those ultralite planes with pontoons. I could take off and land on the pond.

There's no place I really want to go, but it would be nice to look down on things as if I were a hawk, seeing our whole valley from up in the sky; but then I can hike up a hill to see that.

Well, this is Christmas Eve but it doesn't feel like it. Maybe next Christmas will be better. I'd hate to think that all the Christmas Eves from here on will be like this. No, we won't have it that way; we'll make them good the way they used to be.

VI

Six Geese A-Laying

I wake before I open my eyes. I lie there, anywhere, anytime. Am I truly fifty-two years old, thirty years married, the father of four children, a teacher of philosophy in a foreign land? Or am I actually seven years old and all the rest is a dream?

Until I open my eyes—move—feel my body—do some reality check—either can be true. Even when I do open my eyes it doesn't prove anything. Opening them can be a dream as well as all that follows.

My same old spin starts again. If I could only convince myself that something is, that something exists. This time I find myself up the old rut of God.

Almost a thousand years ago, Anselm in his proof of God's existence posited God as "a being than which no greater being can be conceived." At the same time, God is supposed to be noncontingent, immaterial, infinite, nontemporal and unconditioned. All we know, perceive, or experience of the things in this world is contingent, material, finite, temporal, conditioned. *But* God is everything. He is the cosmos and more, yet, he is incomparable. He is not cause or effect, and at the same time he's supposed to be superior to the cosmos. Superior implies comparison, doesn't it? I'm too dumb to be an ontologist. Sorry, Anselm. But I do believe in the existence of God or some power I can't know. It's just the basis for my belief is so personal, I can't share it.

If God is everything, then he is also nothing, because nothing is something. Even if nothing is nothing, God has to be that, too. However, Kant insists that existence is not a predicate and adds nothing to the perfection of the subject. Therefore, an existent object has no more perfection than a nonexistent one.

So, there I am again, nowhere with nothing. At the same time I'm sure somehow that everything is, in one way, nothing. Therefore nothing has to be everything, even *without* God, but it can't be nothing *or* everything without God.

Somehow I've got to keep my mind on things, keep it all from slipping away. I've got to take one thing at a time, help hold on to some order in this constantly changing cosmos. If we can't end entropy, at least let's let everything disappear with order and not chaos. I've got to believe it's all there, that should help. The secret is in there somewhere. I'm sure all life is somehow one vast self-maintaining system, each part part of every other part; all of us one spirit.

I smell the fire. I smell the permanent, residual damp mold smell of our dirt-filled stone mill walls. Probably it's not a dream. Probably I am a late-middle-aged man waking up for another Christmas. Another Chrismas where I'm supposed to be in charge, make it go, help this be an event of happiness and joy, no matter how I might feel myself.

I open. It's still pitch dark. Is it possible I've only been asleep a few minutes and it isn't Christmas yet?

I slide out the end of our bed, carefully, not to wake Lor. It's hard to realize we'll be married thirty years tomorrow. People say "That's thirty" when they mean something is ended. I think it comes from newspaper printing. I hope it isn't true with us.

It's no longer only a matter of sticking it through. There's something positive in our momentum now, something I think we both feel is worth preserving, at least I hope so; sometimes lately, I catch Lor looking at me as if she doesn't know me or, at least, wishes she didn't. I can understand that, too.

The fire's still burning. Somebody must have gotten up and put wood on. Maybe it was Ben. No, he almost never wakes in the night. It could've been Nicole when she came home from the dancing, or maybe she isn't home yet. My watch is on the dresser so I don't know what time it is.

I push the hollow burned-out logs close to each other, half rotate them and throw two more over the fissure between. That should make a good flame in a few minutes. I go across the room and look at the thermometer in the flickering light. It's already nineteen; that fire must have been burning hot all night. I check the two butane burners, they're glowing away merrily.

I tiptoe back, pick up the pocket flashlight from beside Ben and get a good hold on my pajama pants because, in addition to the bum clasp, the elastic is shot and they tend to fall down. I peer between the drapes at our outside thermometer. It's minus twenty! That's thirty-nine degrees difference centigrade inside to out. Having so many bodies giving off heat in this small space must have something to do with it, or maybe all my spreading of cloth over the glass wool upstairs has increased our insulation.

I look under the tree. I don't want any candle wax dripping on the presents. Ben is fast asleep. He breathes so deeply, yet so quietly.

There doesn't seem much in the way of presents. It looks a little bit like everybody else's Christmas.

I'm going through my usual Christmas morning guilt trip, wondering if we've gotten enough. There's probably *never* enough. Even if we were suddenly millionaires I probably couldn't buy enough so on Christmas morning, at this critical moment, I wouldn't have the feeling I'd missed something, failed somehow.

I slide on my slippers and pull a sweater over the top of my pajamas. I wrap my belt around the outside of my sweater to help hold up the PJ pants. I always wear a wool hat to sleep down here at the mill in winter. I pull it tight down over my ears. The head of our bed is right against that cold west wall with the window directly over it. There're bitter cold zephyrs of wind blowing in through chinks between stones.

I carefully climb the three steps; open our door into the upper grange. Holy God, it's cold. The light's on in the bathroom. I take a strong, quiet, long whiz and let in water to flush. It's amazing the water in the bowl hasn't frozen; must be because the toilet's been flushed enough to keep the water moving. I left the water running slowly into the sink and I could hear it when I woke up, so the whole system isn't frozen. At least I don't think it is. I hope not!

Mike and I have spent many a cold morning downstairs with a butane bottle, a long hose and matches, blowtorching the copper pipes all the way from where the water comes out of the ground, then along the outside, into the cellar and up to the sink, trying to get the damned ice in the pipes to melt. It makes a hard crackling, sliding noise when the ice starts moving so the water flows. It can sound like the most beautiful music possible.

I flush. I empty the little pan catching that leak behind our toilet from the toilet tank. This leak might be what kept things from freezing out here.

Now comes the hard part, going down into the cellar to get those presents I hid. I figure nobody would be looking behind the mill machinery for anything; but, gosh, it sure isn't much. I've got the waffle iron; *that* I managed to keep secret. Loretta pretended not to notice the Moulinex food processor but she must have seen it when we went through the line at Carrefour; she's a regular Sherlock Holmes by nature.

I've got a little bottle of perfume, Ecusson; I had a friend buy it for me in Paris at the duty-free shop before we came down, but she knows about that, she should know; I always give her the same perfume for Christmas, it's a tradition with us.

I can open a bottle of that perfume and smell Loretta; it's the way a smell of honeysuckle can make me remember summer, or floor wax or those Christmas cookies can turn me into a child.

I don't have anything for Mike. I *could* give him the electronic Battleship game I bought for Ben. It's one you rig up with lights and batteries so it makes a simple game into something more exciting. It's a game I know Ben likes to play and Mike used to play a lot. It's an awfully childish toy for a twenty-five-year-old, though; it's even childish for a *fifteen*-year-old, but what else. He did catch us by surprise.

What's left for Ben? He has his rifle coming but he's already seen that. I could give him my motorcycle. He'll soon be old enough to ride it legally, and down here nobody pays much attention. The thing is, he's never shown any interest in motorcycles or even bicycles; sometimes he'll ride on back with me, but for him it's only another way of getting from one place to another, no thrill.

I lower the trap door quietly over my head. Wow, it's more than cold down here, it's so damp it almost sears my lungs. The water that's leaked in under our door and through the bottom of the wall has frozen. I don't ever remember the water down here freezing. This must be the coldest Christmas we've ever had. I should move the wine and soft drinks upstairs before they freeze and explode.

I realize I haven't looked outside to see if it's still snowing. I peer through our cellar window, directly onto the road. It's hard seeing past all the leftover summer cobwebs. This is one window I didn't get to wipe off and shine in my mad cleanup.

I brush a clear spot in the windowpane. There's snow all right, about a foot thick of untrammeled, deep, quiet snow but it isn't snowing now. I stand on that iced granite floor, peering through my little peephole and shivering. I get a strange surge of black-gray through me, like death. It's calming, not frightening, and for just a moment I feel separated from everything.

It's hard pulling myself away from the wiped-away place in the window.

I step carefully over the grain hopper and back behind the gigantic cogs which years ago turned those millstones. My packages are there, a bit snow-dusted from where snow blew in through a hole in the wall for the shaft of the mill wheel. I lift them out.

We have nothing for the girls. All we have are those portraits we've commissioned. It's the best thing we could think of. Lor's written little notes to each of them which we both signed and then we slipped twenty dollars in with the notes. It's money we have left over from our last visit to the States two years ago.

I feel good about the portraits. Jo, a longtime friend, will be doing them. Both the girls know him well and like him, I think. It'll be a good experience for them to sit in his cozy warm studio and talk with him during the painting. Jo's a good man with whom to talk.

One amazing thing is how much Jo loves people. He loves them more than anybody I've ever known, and he loves them the way they *are*. At the same time, somehow, paradoxically, he loves them as they could be. He sees with love and believes what he sees. This can be anything, not just people; a landscape, a still life, or an old gas box in Paris. He puts himself and his personal belief into each painting and it becomes more *real* than anything real *ever* is. When I look at one of Jo's paintings, it's as if the merry-go-round of life stops and I can truly see, calmly and clearly, for a change.

I pack the presents under my arm and scurry upstairs. When I push that trap door open, the warmth feels like life itself. The smell of burning wood is mingled with warm stones into a special smell.

I change the name on my Battleship game to Mike. I only hope Loretta has gotten some little extra surprise for Ben. She must have; she always does. She surprises us all every year with something special. Surprises me practically every day; a totally unpredictable woman. What's so strange, is that nobody else seems to see this part of her.

I warm my hands over the fire; it's burning well. I use the ski pole we use as poker to push a log closer in back, up against the big yule log. It's only then I notice the stockings. How could I have missed them? Maybe they weren't there. I can't believe what I see!

They're hanging all across the mantel, from one edge to the other. They glow brilliant red in the flickering light of the fire! They're giant-sized and knitted; there's a name embroidered on each one. There's even one for Mike—and one for Geneviève! I stare and can't integrate it. They seem to have appeared suddenly out of nowhere!

I feel like a child in my joy. It's *really* going to be Christmas. These stockings will make up for anything. I stand there and glow inside. The firelight, the magic, radiating from the stockings into the dark, stops me dead still. I turn and look at my watch on the dresser; it's seven after seven. It's Christmas morning!

I know I'll never sleep but I crawl back in bed and wait for the light. I married the right woman all right. How could I have been so smart so young? And how did she manage it with those stockings, with all that's been going on in *her* life? Maybe she had them mailed down from Paris to Madame Calvet and then picked them up when we got here, maybe even at the reveillon. And I wonder who she got to knit them? Could be Madame Sybella, the Italian lady upstairs in Paris; she's always knitting. Once Lor asked her to knit some little bed stockings for her and stockings for Seth.

Boy, what a great idea this is. I wonder what she's put in them. I really *do* feel like a kid waiting on Christmas morning for the light; I'm so excited. I'll never sleep.

I think about getting up again, lighting all the candles on the tree and breaking out with my own loud, not quite true, version of "Joy to the World." But Ben looks so beautiful sleeping in his deep sleep before the fire and everybody was up late; we can all use the extra time in bed.

I carefully slide over and cuddle with Lor. She mumbles in her sleep. I want to wake her, celebrate with her, alone, the wonder of what she's done, but that wouldn't be fair either, so I only squeeze her to me and kiss her on the shoulder through the flannel of her nightgown.

I've just drifted off when Ben's watch alarm starts beeping. He has it set for seven twenty-five, the time he gets up for school in Paris. I always hear it from our room there; it goes off five minutes before our clock radio. It never wakes Ben and it doesn't wake him this time either. I listen to its two-toned *beebeep* for thirty seconds, counting as I usually do until it shuts off.

I turn my head on the pillow to look up through the small skylight in the roof. The heat from the inside melts the snow on the glass so I can still see through. It's probably a terrible heat loss but it does lighten the room. The walls are so thick we don't get much light from the other windows. The sky just doesn't want to lighten; it's a dull, deep lead color out there above that skylight. I can't even pick out the branches of our birch trees hanging over the mill roof.

I find myself holding my breath and listening for the scampering of tiny hoofbeats and I *do* hear something. I think it's only ice cracking under the snow against the slate; it can't be trapped dormice.

Usually, I try not to stay in bed after I'm awake. It's the time I can have my most depressing thoughts, thoughts about emptiness, meaninglessness, nothingness. These are, in a sense, the tools of my trade and I can deal with them in the abstract but not on an early winter morning.

But this morning I'm having no trouble. I'm happy, glad to be alive, for what it is; content with cuddling tight to my wife, feeling her warmness, aliveness; smelling her personal, familiar perfume. The mystery, the wonder of life itself pervades, overwhelms me.

I hear one of the girls moving upstairs. I listen, wondering if it's one of them getting up to use the portable bidet.

Then, I hear the motorcycle. It's got to be Mike coming over the hill from Geneviève's. He's crazy driving that thing through this snow but he's good on a bike and he can always drop it. I untangle, get up on my hands and knees in bed. I kiss Lor gently on the shoulder again. I shake her lightly.

"I hear Mike coming, Lor. I think it's time for Christmas. Your stockings are absolutely beautiful. I can't even imagine a more wonderful Christmas surprise. I'll light the candles."

Lor looks at me in the dark, her eyes still sleep-fogged, not focused. She smiles, pulls my head down to hers, kisses me lightly, puckeredly, on the lips.

"Merry Christmas, Will. What stockings? Would you put on some water for washing up?"

She stares up at the still dark skylight.

"Isn't it terrible we forgot about the stockings? I didn't even notice until I was crawling into bed and I was just too tired to do anything about it."

I climb out over the end of the bed, stand up, look down at her. I slide my slippers on again. I still have the sweater and belt on. So Lor's going to play Santa Claus all the way; including me. That's really nice.

I go over to the mantel where there are matches. I light the candles, first our advent candles on the mantel. That mantel looks spookily enchanting, mystically magic with those stockings. Beside me, in the dark, I can almost see Santa sitting in the rocking chair smiling, the fire flickering makes him twinkle.

I begin with the highest candles on the tree. They glitter against our colored balls, reflections on reflections; they start the new lightweight tinsel moving with their heat. I can't help thinking how great it would look with colored lights, too. We'll wait till the girls are up in Paris.

Loretta is out of bed and has on her robe. She's standing with her mouth open, staring across Ben at the stockings. She was the star of her high school play but I'll bet this, right now, is the greatest acting of her career.

"My God, Will! They're beautiful; where did you ever get them?"

She walks around Ben, reaches out, handles, turns, hefts each stocking in turn as I did, reading the names.

"But these are *handmade*, Will, and the names are perfectly embroidered across the top. They're *absolutely* gorgeous."

She comes to me under the Christmas tree. I'm holding a lit candle in one hand but she comes into my arms and holds tight onto me. I blow out the candle over her shoulder so I won't light her hair. She's crying. This is carrying things a little too far. I'm liable to start crying myself, that'd be a fine way to start Christmas.

"Come on Lor; you don't have to *cry*."

"Oh Will, you can be such a beautiful man sometimes. You have these wonderful, crazy ideas in that unreal, nonexistent, hopelessly meaningless head of yours. But this is the most incredible thing I've ever seen. I'll bet you've been planning and working on it ever since summer when you asked if I wanted the kids to come for Christmas. I'll never forget this, no matter what else happens."

She pushes herself back from me, stares into my eyes. Her crying face breaks into a smile.

"Excuse me dearest. It's always this way with me. At the most important moments I have to 'go.' But I'll be right back; just stay where you are."

With that, she eases out of my arms, walks past the lit tree and me, up the steep three steps into the grange.

"Brace yourself, Lor. It's glacial out there, but the toilet is working, for some reason it didn't freeze. Is it okay if I continue lighting the tree?"

She tosses a quick smile over her shoulder.

"Don't forget the hot water will you dear?"

She's carrying a wad of paper towels with her. Are we running out of toilet paper again? Maggie once complained to Loretta how we were always running out of toilet paper when she lived at home. Now, Loretta is usually at least ten rolls ahead. It's hard finding places to store the stuff.

I walk over toward the kitchen. Lor is acting so strange. I know she's terribly upset about everything, we both are; but this is crazy, pretending she didn't make the stockings, then crying and running off like that, most peculiar.

It'd sure be nice if I could be a little bit *more* sensitive, or a little bit *less*. All that crying didn't really make much sense; Lor hardly ever cries. Usually she's worse than a man about not crying, not showing emotions.

Maybe she really *did* have to go to the bathroom. That's usually more *my* problem mornings but everything at the mill is different this year for some reason.

I fill the kettle, my usual style and right to the top. I light the biggest burner and put the water on, a bit spills and sizzles in the flame. I'm the kind of person who's impressed with how wonderful a match is, how it lights so easily, how I can turn on the gas and the gas lights from the match, quietly, consistently to heat water that I didn't even have to go out and pull from a well.

Somehow I never grew up in my mind properly, there's a great clot of child still left in me. The ordinary things of life I should get used to, still seem like miracles. But then probably I'm not really noticing the real miracles happening all around, things I don't even know about or can't get myself to believe. I hardly ever feel I'm living the same life in the same world where every-one else seems to be. I'm some kind of alien.

Maggie is coming down the stairs. She's wearing a pair of bright red and white candy-striped flannel pajamas tight at the ankles and cuffs. She takes the last long step to the floor. She even has red furry slippers.

"How do you like me, Dad? Do I look like Mrs. Santa Claus? I wish Seth were here."

She looks at me. She stops; staring.

"Oh my God! You look like a pirate who got lost on skid row. Where'd you ever find such a crazy costume?"

"You're beautiful, Maggie. You're just the thing to jolly up a dark, cold Christmas morning."

I'm waiting for her to notice the stockings. She goes over and looks at herself in the mirror over the wash table. Ben's opened his eyes. From any other movement you wouldn't know he'd wakened. He slowly reaches over, picks up his glasses and watch from the table beside him, slides on his glasses and peers at his watch-calculator using the light from the tree.

"Is it Christmas?"

Maggie comes back over to him from the mirror. She's tied a soft piece of red wool in a bow around her hair. It looks lovely, it matches the stockings. She leans over Ben and impulsively, nervously, gives him a quick kiss. He's vulnerable, helpless.

"Of course it is, silly. What other day did you think it could be?"

I hear Mike opening the downstairs door, stomping up the steps. He pushes the hingeless trap door open with his head. He's wearing a red-orange motorcycle jacket and a black wool hat with orange stripes. He must have borrowed them from Maurice.

His face is redder than anything he's wearing. He also has a sack swung over his shoulder, so he looks like a Hell's Angel Santa Claus. He maneuvers the sack with him through the trap door.

"Merry Christmas everybody! Where's Mom? Where's Nickie?"

From upstairs comes a slurred, sleep-filled voice.

"I'm right here in bed, Mike, where any sensible person should be. What's this business of getting up before the sun even comes over the hill? You all must be crazy."

Mike pulls off his hat, his jacket, hangs them on the hanger by our door out to the pond.

"You know it's a family Christmas tradition, Nickie. We're

always up early. We never stay in bed until the sun comes up, we might miss old Santa himself. We've got to keep up the traditions."

Boy, is Mike ever right there. Over the past twenty-five years, every Christmas Eve, long before morning, there's been one after the other of them popping into our bed asking if it's morning yet. When they were young, this could start early as eleven o'clock, Christmas Eve.

I guess it's the same in every family but with ours it's always seemed exaggerated. We hear Nickie shifting in her bed.

"Okay! Okay! I'll be right down. What time is it anyway; five in the morning?"

Ben sits on the edge of his bed. He looks at his watch again.

"It's precisely seven thirty-four; I believe we can say it really *is* Christmas morning."

He swings his feet out of bed and into his gunboat, size-thirteen bedroom slippers. He gathers his clothes and starts toward that cold toilet room. Before he goes, before I can stop him, he turns and looks into the fireplace then up at the stockings. He leans forward, peering.

"By golly, I do believe Santa Claus really *did* come! *Look* at these stockings, they're gigantic! And they're filled to the top!"

I'd begun to think nobody was ever going to notice, but I didn't want to say anything until Lor came back. She should be here to enjoy the pleasure all her work and planning will give.

Mike and Maggie have stopped and are staring. They're in total shock. Their mouths are actually open. Just then, Lor opens the door from the grange; she still has tears in her eyes.

As Loretta stands at the top of the steps, Mike and Maggie move toward the stockings in stately unison like a pair of bizarrely clad altar boys.

Nickie is coming down the steps from the sleeping loft. She's wearing her waffle-patterned long johns and is carrying some wrapped packages against her breast. She uses her other hand to hold onto the rail coming down. On that high last bottom step she stops, stares along with Mike, Maggie and Ben.

"Oh my God! What happened? Where'd all that come from?"

The shrillness, the loudness, the vehemence in her voice is in stark contrast to the almost holy reverence of the other kids. Nickie sounds as if she really *is* delivering lines in a high school play. She comes down that last step, looking down. It's a long reach for her.

Loretta still stands at the top of those three steps to the bathroom, tightening the belt on her robe.

"My goodness, everybody, it all looks so beautiful. It's such a wonderful thing having the family home for Christmas.

"Right now, I'm trying to put this scene in my head to last my life through. Would you look at those stockings. Hasn't your Dad made us the most magic Christmas anyone could ever imagine?"

There's a still quiet in the room while only the fire crackles. Nicole, slowly, quietly, bent over, holding her presents, her hair in a tangle, puts presents under the tree, reaches over and strokes one of the stockings, the one with my name on it.

"How'd you do it, Dad? I *know* you can't knit; I tried to teach you once, remember? And who'd you get to knit them for you? I know you're the disappearing man and secretive as the devil, but how the hell did you manage it? Wow! They're marvelous!"

I figure it's gone on long enough. I can't really understand what Loretta's trying to do.

"Now, *wait-a-minute* everybody! *I* didn't knit those stockings *or* fill them. You're right Nickie, something this big is *way* beyond me. I wish I did do it, I wish I could've. I wish I had the imagination to even *think* of an idea like this. But, I didn't.

"Think, kids. Who is it who reminds you every year to put up your stockings? Who makes sure you have a pair of nice, clean, long ones here when *we* always forget?"

I stop and look around at all of them and then we turn in unison to stare at Loretta standing there at the top of the steps.

"This year it was *Mrs.* Santa Claus, not me. And she's been trying to pretend it's me, even to *me* when we were *alone*. Come on down Mrs. Claus and take a bow. This is the most amazing surprise you've ever pulled and I'll admit you've pulled a few good ones in your time. Come on now, 'fess up."

We all break into applause, even Ben. I'm surprised to see the beginning of tears in his eyes under his glasses. I don't think he even knows they're there. Mike reaches up to give Loretta a hand.

"Hooray for Mom, the original Santa Claus."

Maggie reaches up toward Loretta with both arms open.

"I should have known. Mom, this is really just too much. You've already spoiled us for real life, both of you, and now this, the ultimate Christmas."

Ben pushes up his glasses by the center piece with his thumb. He's still holding his clothes in his arms.

"Yeah, thanks, Mom. But I can't help wishing it really had been Santa Claus. Wouldn't *that* be great?"

Nicole looks up at him, puts her hands on her hips, and shakes her head.

"Boy, Ben; you really are a simp!"

Loretta is *still* at the top of the step. She didn't take Mike's hand when he offered. She has her *fists* dug into *her* hips and is standing with her feet about shoulders' width apart, very unlike her. Lor usually takes very ladylike poses. Mostly, it's trouble when she stands like this. What can it be?

"Okay, Will. This is *too much!* It's fun playing Santa Claus and everything but you *always* overdo it. Every year you'd be outside in the snow chewing up carrots and spitting them out. Then you'd be stomping around in boots and with those reindeer hoofs you'd carved from a stick and kept in the attic of the grange all year. Then there was the year you bought the big black leather belt and left it on the table *after* you'd stuffed yourself with cookies and milk the kids had left Santa. If the real Santa drank as much milk and ate as many cookies as he does here, he couldn't get down chimneys anywhere."

We're listening and it *is* like a play, with the candles on the tree lighting her from below. Her red toweling robe glows in the dark exactly like a Santa Claus suit, almost as red as those stockings. I put my hand out to help her down the steps.

191

"Come *on*, Lor. Stop trying to beat me at my own game. *I'm* the fantasy and irreality specialist around here. The kids are all grown up now, even me. We only want to thank you; all you've done is just too marvelous to pass off as if some mystical, mythical Santa Claus did it all. Come on now."

Loretta leans back against the door; she doesn't take my hand.

"Will, this is *so* embarrassing. How can you be this insensitive? Don't you *see* how it makes me feel, having *our* kids think *I* did this when I didn't? It also makes me feel stupid and not a real mother. Maybe a *real* mother would've. You know I can't knit any better than you.

"Listen, I want to ask all of you one question."

We wait. She has tears in her eyes again but these are a different kind of tears. These are angry tears and at the same time sad tears.

"Have I ever lied to you?"

"Not that I can think of, Lor."

"Well, I'm telling you now, I did *not* knit those stockings and I didn't have anybody knit them for me either. I did not buy whatever is in the stockings. I had nothing whatsoever to do with any of this and *you* know it. I wish *you'd* 'fess up before you ruin everything by being silly."

She takes my hand and comes down the steps into my arms. The kids are all quiet.

Ben snaps out of it first. He leans under the stockings and pushes the logs in the fire closer to each other again.

"Then it *must* be Santa Claus. To be honest, I've had a suspicion all along that telling kids there isn't any Santa Claus is only a cruel joke parents pull on kids to force us into growing up. It's probably the same kind of thing as making us go to school whether we want to or not, brushing our teeth, cleaning our fingernails, taking baths, taking piano lessons, swimming lessons, tennis lessons, horseback lessons; being quiet, not running; all the things that make a child stop being a human being and turn him into a grown-up."

Ben, having delivered this monologue in a near monotone, gathers his clothes tighter and heads toward the toilet room to change. I lean over and pull out the plug to the electric heater.

"Turn on the heater in there, Ben, or you'll freeze. It's at least minus ten degrees outside this room."

"That's okay. I don't feel the cold unless I want to."

He pushes open the door and goes out. Nicole puts *her* hands on *her* hips again, cocks her head.

"That kid's weird. How can you *not feel* the cold? I think he might almost be worse than you, Dad. He has no idea at all of what's real. But I do and I'm freezing even in here; move over somebody and let me get close to that fire."

I start folding up Ben's portable bed, haul his mattress under the steps to the sleeping loft. I'm beginning to wonder which of the kids put together this wonderful Christmas surprise with the stockings. I don't think Lor would lie to me; at least not about a thing like this.

When I come back, all three kids have pulled chairs over from the dining table and are huddled around the fire under the tree. I stop a minute and just look at them. Lor has moved into the kitchen area and turned off her boiling washup water. She pours some of it into the washbasin. Nicole looks around at me.

"Come on, Santa, pull up a chair and get warm."

"I'm okay, Nickie, there isn't enough room anyway. Besides, I'm not Santa."

"Oh come on. We all know Mom isn't lying, so it *has* to be you. You're the great liar in this family. No, that isn't quite true either. How can a person lie when he doesn't believe there's such a thing as truth? If nothing is real, then truth isn't even real. You could probably do all this and maybe not know you did it because doing it might not seem real. It could even be it isn't important enough to remember."

Mike pushes his shoulder gently against Nicole.

"Aw come off it, Nickie. What is it you want, some kind of

IBMer for a father? Far as I'm concerned, Ben's most likely right. Santa made one last special stop here and left these stockings. What's the difference if it's Mom, Dad, Santa Claus or the Easter Bunny? Why fight it? I say, let's open up those stockings and *see* what's inside."

Maggie leans forward, looks over at Mike.

"We'd better wait for Ben. He'd be terribly disappointed. You know I've been thinking about what Ben said, too. He's not all wrong, Nickie, it's only another way of looking at things."

Loretta finishes brushing her teeth. She's the only person I know who brushes her teeth both before and after breakfast. She's finished her washup but she's still in her nightgown and robe. She comes around to the fire.

"Mike's right. Let's stop playing detective and see what's in the stockings. I'm dying of curiosity. I wonder just what Santa's brought us. I know I could hardly think of a single thing to buy anybody, or even anything I'd buy myself."

Mike lifts and loosens his stocking from the cup hook it's hung by. Those cup hooks are there year round. It's where we dry clothes in wet weather, bathing suits when it's sunny, or warm stockings when we ice-skate on the pond. They've also been used to hang Christmas stockings every year. Mike spreads his stocking on the hearth of our fireplace formed by the projecting apron of the millstone on which the fireplace is built. He looks up.

"Hey, look; there's even one for Geneviève! That Santa really knows where it is. Yaaa hoo!!"

We have a family tradition of opening presents one at a time so everybody can enjoy. It also prolongs the whole Christmas rite.

I'm watching the candles on the tree. They're about burnt down so I get another packet of candles and start replacing the stubs as they get down to the metal holders. Nickie takes me by the arm.

"Come on, Dad; forget the candles; enjoy Christmas with us."

"Gee, Nickie, it won't be right with a tree and no lights."

I push in another fresh candle. Just then, Ben comes down

the steps, dressed, his pajamas folded in hand. Nickie looks up at him, then at me.

"Okay, okay, you two can turn on your newfangled electric lights if you want; but come on, join in the fun."

"Those lights are *not* so newfangled, Nickie. I brought them here from home in Illinois. They're from *my* parents' house, the house where I grew up. These are the exact same lights I had when *I* was a kid."

"Just so long as they don't blink like some kind of neon sign, Dad."

I lean over and find the plug for the lights. I push it in and the tree radiates the multicolored, clear-toy, candylike glow of my childhood Christmases. It looks wonderful to me. Lor comes over and takes my arm.

"I think it's the most beautiful tree we've ever had, Santa, darling."

She smiles into my eyes. I look back into hers. Everyone's crowded around Mike. Sticking out the top of his stocking is a man like a home-baked gingerbread man, only it's Santa Claus. He has red icing with white trimmings for the beard, the cuffs and trim on a Santa suit. I look and see there's a Santa peering out the top of each stocking.

Tied to his hand is a small sack, puckered and pulled tight at the top. Mike carefully opens the sack and inside is a piece of folded paper. The paper is yellow and crinkled at the edges.

Mike slowly unfolds it. Lor lights the yellow silk-shaded lamp hanging low over our dining room table.

It's a Santa Claus letter. That is, it's a letter like the ones I used to write to each of the kids every Christmas. I look carefully and it's written in *my* own *personal* Santa Claus writing; big, rounded, leaning-back calligraphy with huge snowballs for dots over the *i*s.

Mike looks back at me smiling and points at the letter.

"Now we know. Come on Dad. I don't know how you managed all the rest of it, but you've got to admit this is a dead sure giveaway."

I move closer to Mike. I reach out for the letter. There are strange shivers going up my spine.

"Let me see that, would you Mike? I can't believe this!"

He hands me the note and this is what it says:

Dear Michael:

I hope you like the presents I brought you. Do have a Happy Christmas and be kind to your brother and sisters. Also be nice to your parents.

Remember I love you and I am thinking of you all the year. Please tell your parents I miss the cookies and milk. My reindeer would also like carrots next year. They work very hard.

Have a very merry Christmas

Love
Santa

"This is a forgery! Who's forging *my* Santa Claus Christmas letters? It took me twenty years to develop this personal style of writing."

Nicole leans back and lets off one of her false laughs.

"Hey, maybe *this* is the original. Maybe Santa decided to take a hand in this after all. Actually, *you're* the one who's been the forger. You're the one who's been trying all these years to make everybody believe Santa wrote those letters when maybe he didn't."

I look even more closely. If I didn't know, I'd swear I wrote this myself. Maggie comes next to me and puts her hand out for the letter. I give it to her.

"You're right. This is a real honest-to-goodness Santa Claus letter. Nobody could ever fake one of these. You know, I still have all the letters I got from Santa for every year since I was only five years old and couldn't even read yet. When Seth's really been good, I sit down and read them all through to him. He loves those letters as much as I do, it's like messages from outer space.

"Last year, I tried to write one myself. I thought it would be easy because I'm left-handed and from the look of those letters I was always convinced Santa was left-handed, too. But it was hard. After about ten tries, I was almost ready to write to you, Dad, and ask for one to Seth and me. George acted as if I were crazy. Gosh, it's awful making a *real* Christmas on your own."

She hands the letter back to Mike. She looks me deeply in the eyes, she's so shy she hardly ever does that with me or with anyone.

"Come on Dad. It has to be you. Nobody else can write Santa Claus letters."

"Except Santa Claus."

I smile and look back into her eyes. I generally have a hard time, myself, looking into people's eyes, especially people I love. I have trouble deciding which eye to look at and I don't know how to look at two eyes at once without both eyes getting blurry.

I think I'm also afraid I might fall in, get lost in somebody else's nothingness. It's hard enough living with my own.

But this time it's comfortable for us both. We shift simultaneously to watch Mike; he's pulled out a cylindrical package wrapped in beautiful Christmas paper.

"Now, what the heck can this be? Old Santa's getting awfully mysterious in his old age. Maybe it's some of that magic stardust Franky got for him to spread on the runners of his sleigh so he could fly fast."

He unwraps it and turns the cylinder from one end to the other; then looks into the hole on one end.

"Holy Jehoshaphat; it's one of those kaleidoscopes and the pieces inside are all true transparent colored glass, not plastic!"

He holds the kaleidoscope up against the Christmas tree lights and turns the cylinder slowly.

"It looks like Chartres or Sainte Chapelle. Wow! And with the tree lights it's magnified so it's psychedelic. I can't believe it!"

We all take turns and I don't think I've ever seen anything so beautiful. Ben's never seen a kaleidoscope and doesn't want to stop looking.

"Now, *that's* real magic. Don't anyone tell me how this thing works. To me it's just magic and I want to keep it that way if I can."

Mike's already digging further into his stocking. He brings out a large magnifying glass in a leather case. He puts it up to his eye like a monocle and stares at the rest of us.

"Well, Watson, I'm not sure just what the nature of this mystery is but it mystifies me."

He laughs his bubbling laugh, then goes over to the Christmas tree and focuses on one of the bulbs.

"Just the reflection on this bulb fills up the entire glass!"

By now, we're all crowded around him. It looks as if the things inside the stockings are as interesting as the stockings themselves.

Next he pulls out an old-fashioned pair of fleece-lined natural sheepskin slippers. They have a bunny's face on the instep, exactly like the kind I used to get as a child; the kind Lor and I have looked for every Christmas and could never find. Mike holds them out for all of us to see. He jumps up and down in glee just like a little kid.

"Wow! Look at these. I swear they're handmade!"

Lor leans forward.

"Let me see those, Mike. Are you sure they'll fit?"

"Of course they'll fit, Mom. Santa knows everything, even my size-nine-and-a-half foot."

Mike keeps taking out presents, each one more exciting, more original than the last.

There are crystal prisms of all shapes, heart, diamond, round, oblong and even one on the end of a glass wand.

Then, as we each open our stockings, we find many of the same presents Mike has but special presents for each of us.

There's a rock hammer in a beautiful leather case for Maggie. It's the perfect thing for someone whose major was geology. There's also a full set of woodworking tools for Nickie.

"You tell me *how* Santa knew I wanted to try woodworking. This is really getting *most* mysterious."

A telescope is in Ben's stocking, a Moroccan leather-bound set of the Narnian Chronicles in Maggie's. There are napkin rings with all the kids' names on them in Lor's. I'm still wondering who arranged all this. It's easy for one part of me to be like Ben and just give Santa his due; but another part really wants to know *what's* happening, *who* bought all these wonderful presents. Who had that kind of money, let alone imagination?

It takes us over two hours opening and being amazed. Each of us receives a plug-in, rechargeable flashlight.

For Lor, there's a leather-bound set of Jane Austen. She's still looking at me as if I'm the one responsible. She also got another bottle of perfume, this time it's something called My Sin.

There's one other gift which makes everything else seem somehow insignificant. In each stocking is a small jeweler's box and in each box is a ring. The ring is a gold signet ring exactly the same as the one my mother bought for my father before they were married, over fifty years ago, and which my father gave to me before he died.

It's the ring I lost last summer swimming in the pond. I was really brokenhearted. I spent that entire summer diving, sifting mud through screens, and cursing myself for being so careless. How could I lose something which had been so carefully worn all those years? I felt like the flat tire or broken gear in a time machine.

But these rings don't have my Dad's initials on. They have our family name beautifully engraved within a circle. The rings are all very simple, neither feminine nor masculine. The only difference, one ring to the other, is the size. I'm about ready to slip mine on when Nickie says:

"Hold it everybody! I think Santa wants these rings to be part of a ceremony or ritual of some kind. Maybe we can do a family marriage. We should all stand in a circle, each of us putting a ring on the finger of the one next to them. Okay?"

She doesn't give us time to answer, she's pushing us into positions.

"Now we'll do this according to age. You stand here, Dad."

She stands me in front of the fireplace. We're all being taken into Nickie's staging.

"Mom, you stand here on Dad's right."

Lor picks up the box with her ring from beside her stocking. The whole table and some of the chairs are covered with gifts. Next, Nicole puts Maggie beside Lor. Lor looks at me smiling. She's beginning to catch on to the idea and likes it. Then it's Mike. Nicole takes Ben by the hand and pulls him so he's between her and me. It looks like a bunch of half-dressed druids preparing for some kind of ceremonial dance. Nicole smiles around at all of us in the light of the tree.

"Okay, does everybody have their ring?"

We all nod, not quite in tune, a bit amazed by it all.

"Now, take it out of the box and hold it in your left hand so you can slip it on the right hand of the person to your right.

Everybody should be putting a ring on somebody younger than they are except Ben, who closes this circle, and puts the ring on Dad; and we should all do it at the same moment.

"Whoops! Wait a minute! Everybody has to give their ring to the person on their left or the rings won't fit."

We all exchange rings. Nicole gives hers to Ben. It's wonderful how everybody's taking it so seriously, even Ben. We're intimately into the fantasy of Christmas.

"Now, Dad, will you say something appropriately mysterious and mystical. See if you can freak us out the way you always did when we were kids."

I feel on the spot but this is the kind of thing I like. I hold up my ring, turning slightly toward the Christmas tree. The others do the same.

"In the name of this tree, symbol of all nature, which we have taken from the forest and brought into our home to help us celebrate the birth of the sun for the new year, may we be blessed as a family, as a small forest of people reaching up and searching for peace and love in this world."

I'm not sure I said what I really meant, but I turn and slide Lor's ring on the ring finger of her right hand. On her left hand she wears the wedding band she's been wearing for one day short of thirty years. Each of the others does the same. Mike slips his ring onto Nicole's finger.

"Gee, I wish Geneviève were here. I wonder if there's a ring in her stocking."

Lor looks at me then at Mike.

"If there isn't you can always buy her one if you want, Mike. I'll lend you the money."

After all the rings are on and we're staring down at the magic of them, we still stand there, not knowing what to do. Mike starts off,

"Six golden rings . . ."

We all join in and lightly, without rush, sing out the rest of the song; one number in advance until we finish thirteen. There's a brief pause and Nicole picks it up, creates,

"Thirteen babies bouncing . . ."

We all laugh and joyously, dancing, finish out the song, going back down the line to the beginning, ending with two partridges and leaving it at that. We've been walking sideways slowly around in a circle until I arrive again with my back to the fire.

We break up the circle and everybody starts looking at the other presents under the tree. I go over and turn up the butane heater some. It's stopped snowing but boy, is there ever a lot of snow. I'm watching when Lor whispers into Nicole's ear. I figure it has to do with some other Christmas present so *I'm* surprised when Nickie leans back and breaks into one of her false laughs.

"*Oh come on Mom*, you've got to be kidding!"

Then, they both go upstairs to where the girls have been sleeping. What could it be now? Honest to God! I seem to live in a mystery. When I was a kid there was a radio show called "I Love a Mystery"; I *used* to love it, but now I've been living with mysteries so long I can't really say I even *like* them.

So everybody's there waiting to continue Christmas while Lor and Nickie are upstairs. Maggie looks at me and does her version of a French shrug. Mike and Ben are on their knees beside the millstone under the tree looking at the presents, trying to pretend they aren't waiting.

Upstairs there's whispering. At first it almost sounds as if they're arguing, and then there's some silence, then more whispering. I decide to say something, somebody has to.

"Hey, what's going on up there? Come on, it's Christmas. We're all waiting."

Loretta pulls apart the upstairs curtain and looks through it. That upstairs is more or less a balcony with the end over the living room closed by drapes.

"We'll be right down, dear. You can all get along without us if you want. We won't be a minute, honest."

There's something in her face, her voice, that spooks me. It's the look she had on her face when she called me home on emergency that time Maggie swallowed chlordane. It's the look she had when she got the letter from her mother saying her father had died; not a telegram, a letter. Her face is gray-white, collapsed, but she's wearing her calming, captain-going-down-with-the-ship smile. Oh God, what can it be now!

We stand around like stuffed toys for another two or three minutes. The candles, the second ones I lit, are already half burned down. Then there's a noise and I see Nickie's feet on the top steps. She peeks at us from there. She's smiling; a younger, more aggressive, more positive version of Loretta's smile. Loretta follows her down, carefully holding up her robe so she won't trip.

Nickie insists Ben open the Atari set. Nickie and Mike show him the directions; they *did* get exactly the tapes he wanted. He settles back in a corner and concentrates on assembling it. Too bad we didn't bring down the TV so he could hook it up, but with that Fiat, I couldn't've squeezed in a Walkman radio, let alone a TV.

Mike's created handmade presents for everybody. For Loretta he's made a matchbox holder out of wood to hang by the stove. He even brings in a hammer from the grange and nails it up for her. It's for kitchen matches. He's painted it with flowers of the Morvan and varnished it, but *not* the striking surface.

Loretta shows her appreciation, kisses him, but she's way off somewhere.

For me, Mike's made a leather holder for my Swiss Army knife. He's decorated it with a leather tool so it has flowers embossed down the side. The same flowers as on the matchbox holder. He's made puppets for Nickie and Maggie. They walk when you manipulate a four-string wooden cross over them. Maggie's is a duck and Nickie's is a chicken. They walk them around the floor while Mike demonstrates. Nickie walks hers across and up onto the washstand in front of the mirror so it can look at itself.

"See, that's you. That's me. Chicken!"

For Ben, Mike's made bookmarkers, hand-cut, designed,

painted. There are twenty of them, each with a title and author of a book Mike has read and loved. Ben is entranced, shuffles them like Tarot cards. I know that by Easter he'll have read all twenty of those books, including *Zen and the Art of Motorcycle Maintenance, Sometimes a Great Notion, On the Road, Crime and Punishment* and *Steppenwolf.*

Loretta kisses me when I quietly give her her perfume. The waffle iron is an instant success. It's agreed we *must* have waffles for breakfast. Loretta gets out her cookbook for a recipe, Mike reads the directions for making waffles. Loretta is also happy to have the Moulinex processor but there's no song and dance pretending she doesn't know we bought it. We're all still stunned and mystified by these magic stockings and I can't help but wonder what could've happened up there between Nicole and Loretta.

Then, suddenly, but quietly, Lor leaves and goes to the toilet room. She's gone for at least five minutes in the middle of all the Christmas unwrapping. It isn't like her.

When she comes back, she has a somewhat better smile; she hasn't been crying; she also has a present wrapped with a big ribbon. She hands it to me.

"Here, dear. I think this might be as much for me as it is for you."

I don't usually get presents. I carefully open the ribbon, unstick the bits of Scotch tape holding the paper in place. Loretta's wrapped this herself; I know her style. I open the box and it's a pair of pajamas, a pair that's tight at the wrists and ankles, almost like a jogging suit only lightweight and dark brown. I hold them up against my chest, over my four-year-old flannel pajamas, my sweater, my belt, my beginning pot belly.

"Now, ain't I something!? I look like a French advertisement for men."

Loretta looks over at me from the sink where she's washing her hands.

"I must admit, dear, I'm tired of seeing you stagger around

in the morning holding onto the belt of those tattered PJs. I'm throwing them out right now."

"All they need is some new elastic, Lor; there isn't even a hole in them, see?"

I put my new pajamas on the table. I look down at my old ones.

I hadn't been noticing. They *are* ratty-looking, the nap of the flannel is mostly worn off and the check pattern has practically disappeared, faded. These things happen without my noticing. I've been wearing these pajamas all this time as if they were new; they were *still* new in my eyes, my mind's eyes I guess.

"I'll go right up and change now, Lor. Merry Christmas. We can tear up these old ones and your kids at school can use them as paint rags."

"No, Will. I wouldn't do that to those dear children. We throw them out, into the trash can. It's the Christmas present I want most from you."

"Okay, okay, I got the message!"

I scurry up to the toilet room and change into my new pajamas. They fit perfectly and don't bind anywhere. The waist's a bit tight but then all my clothes are tight in the waist lately. I guess I'll have to admit I'm not a thirty-three any more.

I come back down to clapping, cheering; whistles from Nickie and Mike.

We open the rest of the presents and as each present is unwrapped I throw the paper, the boxes, into our fireplace. This is another tradition, one *I* started, maybe dangerous, but exciting. Christmas morning can look like a cyclone hit if you don't keep ahead of things. Loretta and Nickie have begun the waffle making, Mike lending technical assistance. Maggie and Ben are setting the table, our first and our last table setters. Ben even sets himself a place at table.

The true feeling of Christmas pervades. Those stocking presents, especially the rings, did it. I pull out our heater plug in the corner and go plug in the heater for the bathroom. It's well over twenty in this main room and probably warmer up where the girls will dress. But we'll all appreciate some warmth in that icebox of a toilet.

I take out our envelopes with the notes about the paintings by Jo Lancaster and the twenty-dollar bills. I pass them to Loretta and she gives them to the girls. They seem pleased. I hope it isn't too selfish a present. After all, they won't have that much time in Paris and might not want to spend any of it posing.

I've made a special envelope with a fifty-dollar check for Mike. I smuggle it to Loretta for her to write a note and sign, too. Then I take it over to him.

"Now this is just for you, Mike. It has nothing to do with tuition or plane fare or anything. This is extra, just to buy something you want for Christmas. You kind of caught us by surprise, wonderful surprise, I admit, but we're still off balance."

He opens it and looks at the note, the check. His eyes start filling with tears. He turns away, walks to the tree, stares at it, wipes his eyes with his sweater at the wrist. I watch him, feel myself deflate.

God, it's only fifty dollars. What's *he* got to cry about? Did I do something wrong again? I don't know whether to go over, put my arm over his shoulder, say something; or pretend I'm not noticing. Lordy, the whole place is filled with emotion. I'm beginning to feel like Ben, as if it's too much, too much for me to handle. I'll be bursting out crying myself in about two minutes if I'm not careful. Maybe that's what I really should do anyway.

Mike turns away from the tree, goes over and kisses Lor from behind, on the shoulder. He comes and shakes my hand.

"Gosh, thanks, Dad, Mom. I can sure use it; but I don't deserve it. I feel like all I do is take things from you that I can never pay back."

I'm stumped. This situation is beyond my noncreative skills. But something has to be said. Nickie saves me.

"Don't you worry, Mike. You'll get to pay back. You know how Dad is, he never loses. In the end, you'll pay somehow or another. Don't you worry about it."

She puts her arm around his waist, stands beside him, sticks her tongue out at me, smiles.

That gets us past it. The waffle iron turns out to be a great success. It makes waffles fast as we can eat and *that's* impressive. Loretta fakes our syrup the usual way, melted brown sugar with maple syrup coloring and flavoring.

After breakfast cleanup we all dress for the cold and go outside. It's clear and freezing. Mike tries the pond and finds it's solid. Loretta holds her hand over her mouth while Mike jumps up and down on the ice showing how frozen hard it is. Even Ben finally ventures out on the snow-covered ice. The ice is so hard, and the weather was so cold when it snowed, that the snow sweeps away easily, leaving very clear, invisible ice.

Lor comes out with all presents wrapped and ready for Katie's little ones at the Calvets'. It's past ten o'clock now but there's still no sign of life there. We decide we'll wait till later; they probably danced, ate and drank until six this morning.

Mike gets a broom and starts sweeping the ice. Nicole goes downstairs and brings up our ice skates. They've been down there unused for over four years. It turns out there's a pair that'll fit Mike if he only wears one pair of stockings, one pair fits me, and there are two pair to share around for Maggie, Nicole and Lor. We clean them off, cobwebs, spiders; rub off the rust; dust them, oil them with salad oil and put them on. All this we do inside by the fire.

I get the push broom from the cellar and another broom from up by Maggie's place so there are three brooms. Mike, Nicole and Maggie start sweeping clear a place for skating. It's amazing how fast the snow piles up and gets heavy; but we work hard and in fifteen minutes have a good ten-yard by ten-yard space cleared. There are no skates to fit Ben, nothing even close. If there were, he wouldn't wear them anyway.

I'd almost forgotten how much fun it is to glide over ice virtually without friction. Loretta and I skate together cross-handed. She has a hard time keeping her ankles stiff. She's always had weak ankles; even on those wonderful winter days in Bavaria when we'd skate almost every day, her ankles would buckle.

Mike decides to go get Geneviève. He mounts the motorcycle with his skates still on. I guess he can shift in this snow with ice skates, and brake, but I don't know how.

In about five minutes he comes back. He couldn't get enough traction to climb the hill up to Vauchot.

Nicole, Ben and I have pushed the snow back more so now we have maybe 150 square yards for skating. Nicole and Maggie are skating together. Mike starts tying a series of short rope lengths he's cut from the support for our volleyball net. He ties them around the wheels of my motorcycle. It's so cold I don't know how he can tie the knots.

But he gets them all tied, then rolls the bike out onto the ice.

"Come on, Dad! I'll give you a ride."

I skate over; grab hold of the luggage carrier. He starts slowly, slipping but getting enough grip to pull me. His feet are out on both sides to balance the bike. He pulls me out of the cleared area into the part of the pond with untrampled snow. After I get through the piles we've made, the snow gives some resistance to my skates but not much. I slide along; it's like skiing in deep-powder snow; snow's flying out around me. Mike's hollering and hooting as we go. This should surely wake the Calvets.

Out by the pond's end, he puts one foot down and swings the bike, with me, around in a quick turn. I let go and glide slowly to a stop, knee-deep in bulrushes. He waits. I skate back and grab hold again. We gain speed till we're at the edge of our cleared area, where I let go and spin turn to a stop beside Lor. Mike jumps the bike up over the pond edge onto the dam.

"I'll be right back. Geneviève'll love this."

He goes along the dam and carefully turns downhill onto the road. I hope he can go downhill as well as up. I hope he can go uphill all the way to Vauchot without wearing out his ropes. Hell, he'll manage somehow.

Nickie and Maggie have started rolling snowballs as a way to clear the pond. The snow is a bit dry for this, but the sun is out strong now, bright blue sky, and the snow is getting softer, heavier so they can make the balls. They start with little snowballs and quickly have balls big enough to sit on. The snow still picks up clean from the ice and our skating space is getting bigger all the time.

Nickie's sitting on a big ball she's just rolled. She's sweating and has her scarf off, her down jacket opened. She's indefatigable.

"Wow, have I got a good idea."

She looks around as if she's measuring the pond. She pants, gets her breath. Maggie's just finished a big ball and rolls it up next to Nicole. She sits on it. I don't think I remember Maggie ever doing anything so physical. She pulls her hat down over her ears, takes off her woolen gloves, shakes off the snow, rubs her hands together, blows on her fingers, puts her gloves back on. She looks at Nicole. Nicole has started laughing. I can't tell if it's a real laugh, but then who am I to judge whether somebody else's laugh is real?

"Look. We've got all this raw material; let's sculpt a life-size crèche right out here on the ice. Mike, Ben and I will be the sculptors. Dad, Mom and Maggie can be the haulers of snow. We'll build something out here that'll be competition for Chartres, Fatima, Lourdes, Nôtre Dame and Saint-Denis rolled into one.

I refuse to respond, but I'll go along if the others do. Ben's gone inside. Lor looks at Maggie then at me.

"That sounds like a wonderful idea, Nickie. I can't think of *anything* more Christmasy. You're a genius."

"Well, Mom. It's about *time* somebody recognized that. I'm the creative personality type, that's what all those crazy tests at La Jolla tell me. Why do you think I'm an art major? I used to think I was going to be the first important woman sculptor in this dumb world.

"Okay, let's get to it everybody. Dad, can you lift that ball Peg just rolled over there on top of this one?"

Maggie and Nicole stand up. I get behind the ball, at least three feet in diameter, and with Nicole's help, I muscle it up the side and onto the other ball. Nicole starts patting snow into the crack between the balls, patting and firming the snow.

"Okay, this will be Mary."

She moves over a foot or two and scrapes a place on the ice with her foot.

"The crib will be here. Do you still have that old sawhorse you used to use?"

I nod my head. It's down in the cellar.

"Okay, we'll stand that upside down, packing snow around the bottom of it, to make the crib. We'll let Mike make the baby. That's *his* specialty."

What's she mean by that? Is this some kind of hidden message? Is that what she was talking about with Loretta up there? Is Mike pregnant, is it Geneviève? I'm spinning again. I try to shake this new one off my head. She probably only means he painted the baby in the little crèche all those years ago.

When Mike and Geneviève come back, he's as excited with the idea as Nickie. It's really great to see Geneviève. She's all the best of the French rolled into one person, small, vibrant, quick eyes, quick hands, and intelligent. She and Mike made their first real contact here at the mill on his twenty-first birthday. We had a party. What a great twenty-first birthday present. Lor and I talk sometimes about what wonderful grandchildren they could give us.

We do the four-way kiss all around, her cheeks are smooth and cool. She holds on when she kisses, most French don't. Mike goes inside with Geneviève to show her her stocking; I'm sure to see if she has a ring. I want to follow them but when I look at Lor, she shakes her head slightly, no.

We roll more snowballs, Nickie is sculpting away using a garden trowel. In about five minutes Mike and Geneviève come out. Geneviève is entranced, looking down at the ring on her finger. She's speaking earnestly to Mike.

"But, Michel, there is no Santa Claus, no Père Noël. That is a story for children. Who could do all this, buy such wonderful gifts? I don't understand."

Mike smiles and puts his arm around her. He yells to us out on the pond.

"Poor Geneviève here doesn't believe in Santa Claus, what do you think of that?"

Geneviève steps down onto the pond. She's so lovely. She comes toward me. I'm just finished rolling a snowball.

"You shouldn't have done this, it is too much, but thank you. I love the ring very much."

She spreads her fingers, looks down at it. It fits.

"Don't thank me, Geneviève, or Santa might get mad and then everything will disappear, vanish into thin air."

Mike helps me roll my snowball up onto the other one.

"That's right, Geneviève, it happens all the time."

Nicole sends Mike down to find the sawhorse. He and Geneviève pack snow around the bottom and damned if it doesn't look like a typical manger in a crèche. Nickie has a special eye for seeing things. It must come from somewhere but it isn't from either Lor or me; we're both observers but neither of us is particularly aware, especially *I'm* not. Geneviève keeps talking to Mike in French about the gifts, about Père Noël. She just can't figure it. Her logical French mind can't let it alone.

Maggie and I have a great time rolling the huge balls of snow and lifting them into place. We're both sweating like pigs and our gloves are soaking wet but we're caught up in the whole artistic inspiration. Lor's coaxed Ben out and even *he's* involved. His specialty is faces, or at least Nicole lets him do that part because it's the most interesting. She's shaping beautiful figures with flowing robes. There's Mary first, then Joseph, surrounding the baby. They're actually somewhat larger than life-size but a bit more stubby. It's hard to make snow hold together when the forms are too thin. Behind, Nicole's finished two shepherds with a cow on the ground beside them. This cow is definitely life-size and takes six snowballs in itself. There's also a donkey and two sheep. Each of them is stretched out lying on the ice with head up, facing the manger. There's no way to make thin legs and have them stand. Actually, it makes the whole ensemble more effective with only the mother, father and two shepherds kneeling around the baby, then with all the animals down on the snow around them.

Mike's done a wonderful job with the Christ child. He does *this* face himself and it's absolutely angelic. Maybe that's a put-down for Christ. Should it be messianic, like Rasputin? It's the only figure with a halo. He's made the halo from a piece of rubber tubing looped over the head and stuck into the snow "straw" under the baby's head then packed with snow.

Now Mike and Nicole insist on doing the Three Kings. Maggie, Lor and I are pooped. Lor goes in to start preparing Christmas dinner. It's already almost three o'clock. Still, no one is moving over there at the Calvets. They must really be zonked.

Under persistent prodding, and madmanlike sculpting by Nicole, Mike, Geneviève and Ben, we do it. This has become an obsession. But it is fun; I can't think of any time in my life I've been so involved with such a monumental project; it's taken on a life of its own.

This is a Christmas I'll definitely remember all my life; even with all the complications, the mysteries, the worries, it's the best I can remember, even better than any in my childhood. I never would've believed it possible. And I know, it's almost to the extent it's *been* complicated, incomprehensible, mysterious, that it's good.

We've just finished the last wise man, this final one built on the dam itself, as if he's only now arriving, when Madame Calvet opens her door to shake out a tablecloth. She's still in her blue housecoat, the same housecoat, or one like it, she's worn all the twelve years we've been coming to the mill.

She stops as if frozen; takes two steps down the steps, staring; then turns and runs back into the house.

"Katie, Claude, *venez voir! Venez voir ce qu'ils ont fait!*"

Nicole and Mike have attached the garden hose to the outside spigot at our place and are gently spraying the snow sculptures with water. The temperature's still way under zero and as the water falls, the ice freezes, giving a smooth glasslike coating to the work. It really is beautiful. Maybe because it's ours, something we did together, but it rivals for me some things I've seen in Rome or Florence. There's a naïve simplicity, a massiveness of form, a unity of material which gives it sculptural magnificence. The light's already beginning to wane on this short winter day and a pinkish glow from the west turns the figures to an almost lifelike pink.

Mike is pulling Geneviève with his motorcycle over the practically snow-free pond on ice skates. She's never ice-skated before and is continually falling down. She's being pulled along on a cord Mike now has attached to the carrier of the bike. Their screams and shouts, laughter, are in strong contrast to the solemnity, the dignified silence of the figures. What wonderful sounds, real Christmas music to my ears.

But I'm frozen, so are Maggie and Ben. Nicole seems beyond all fatigue, all cold, everything. She's putting on the other skates to join Mike and Geneviève. I walk down the steps carefully on my skates. I go inside, sit in a rocker by the fire and take them off; my feet luxuriate in the freedom and warmth. I go over and help Maggie off with hers. We hang our coats and gloves from the cup hooks on the mantle to warm and dry. The magical stockings along with the *real* Santa presents are spread on our beds now. Ben hangs his gloves and coat on the hooks, too. He slides into the rocker where I was sitting. Loretta is working in the kitchen area.

"Will, dear, would you mash the dressing and stuff our turkey? I know there's a certain way you like it and I never seem to get it right myself."

I wash my hands at the sink. There *is* a distinct way I love turkey dressing. I like it to be so mashed it all becomes unified, the bread pieces, the celery, the seasoning, the chestnuts, the apple, all one thoroughly mixed mess. There's only one sure way to get that effect and this is by putting in both hands and squeezing, squeezing till no particles are left hard and unintegrated. It's a gooey business but I enjoy it, probably left over from my anal childhood repression. Smashing that dressing is most likely first cousin to my need for order.

I get it properly squished and stuffed in the turkey. I sew it up with string and make a ball of some extra to put in an aluminum foil wrapping beside the turkey. There's never enough dressing for me, especially when it's soft and moist like this; it compensates for the dryness of turkey itself.

Soon the turkey is in the oven; potatoes are oiled, ready to go in forty-five minutes before the turkey comes out. Loretta suggests a long before-Christmas-dinner walk. She's been simmering the real cranberries I luckily found at the Marché Aligre in Paris; with them, we're making genuine cranberry sauce.

All we need do now is wait. I check the butane bottle but it's still heavy with liquid gas. We won't run out mid-turkey; that's happened before.

"Okay, who's going with us for an appetite-sharpening walk?"

Lor's pulling her coat off the hook. She has on her hat and gloves. I'm more than a little fatigued but this is another tradition, the before-Christmas-dinner walk. But we've never before created a whole stable full of people and animals, just *before* cooking. Maggie stretches her legs.

"I can't make it. I'll fall asleep over the food. Suppose I stay home and baste the turkey every half hour?"

Nicole is flopped out on our bed; her face is pale but she's flushed around the eyes.

"Count me out, too. I'm taking a nap. Or, that is, I think a nap's going to take me."

Ben's leaning over the fire, pushing sticks around.

"I'll stay here and tend the fire. I want to read the book Maggie and Nicole gave me."

They gave Ben a huge book on the history of aviation. It

must've cost fifty dollars and has hundreds of color illustrations, every major airplane since the invention of flight.

They had a crazy story to go with the book. Nicole stored the book up on the overhead rack of the train from de Gaulle Airport to Paris; it slid out and almost emasculated a young French man in the seat beside her. Nicole said you never saw a more surprised, scared guy in your life. He jumped out of his place and hobbled to the toilet in back of the train, probably checking to see if he was still intact. Then he changed his seat.

Mike is taking off his skates, sitting on the millstone under the tree, Christmas balls banging against the back of his head. Geneviève is standing beside him.

"Geneviève and I are driving over to her place to see how things are going. We'll be back for the big dinner. What time do you think we'll eat?"

Loretta looks at the little Swiss cuckoo clock without a cuckoo over the thermometer.

"It should all be ready at seven thirty."

Nicole lifts her head off the pillow and says in a sleepy voice— she's almost gone—

"If you don't make it, I eat your share."

With that she drops her head back. Mike stands up, his shoes on. He takes the bike keys from the mantel. There's still one hook left there without steaming clothes. I throw two logs on the fire.

"Okay, we'll go alone. Ben, be sure to look up from that book every once in a while to make sure the fire's burning; it's our main source of heat. The temperature's going to drop from now on as it gets darker."

"Okay, okay. I'll be sitting right here. You know I'll keep it burning. I've *never* let the fire go out."

He's upset, all right. He's hardly ever so touchy; is usually easy to get along with. I turn to Lor.

"Well, dear, I guess it's just the two of us. Which way do we go?"

"I'd like to see some cows and lambs in a barn. Let's walk by the Pinson place, then down that old deep-cut Gallo-Roman road and back out on the Vauchot road above Maggie's. Okay?"

I nod and we walk out, carefully closing the door. Ben comes over and pulls one of the gas bottles in front to keep it shut. I check the temperature, it's four below. I thought it would be colder than that.

We go up on the dam. Claude, Philippe, Katie, Pierre Rousseau and the two little girls are looking at our sculpture. Pierre comes over and shakes my hand. His voice is low, almost as if speaking in a church.

"Ah, ça c'est quelque chose. Est-ce-que c'est vrai que vos enfants ont fait cette miracle?"

I smile and tell how Maggie, Loretta and I only rolled balls while Nicole, Mike and Ben made the figures.

The crèche is gorgeous now. The deep lowering now pink sun casts long shadows, pulling the figures into an even tighter unity. It's a shame we can't make something permanent out of it. It's then I remember the camera and film I bought for Lor. I excuse myself, go back inside, pushing aside the butane tank. The new camera is still unwrapped under our tree. I suspect Lor is quietly doing the same thing as Ben, saving some of Christmas till later when it's calmer; but she's always been slow opening Christmas presents; nibbling away at Christmas. I come back out and give the package to her. Lor's talking to Katie and the little girls. They're walking around between the statues.

Loretta looks at the package, at me.

"Do I really have to open it now?"

"You'll be glad if you do."

She pulls at the ribbon, it falls away. She unwraps the box and sees it's a camera. She smiles at me.

"You know I can never make one of these things work, Will. But you're right, we should have some photos of this for later."

She hands me the box. I take out the camera, open the box

of film, snap film into the camera, and explain how it works. Nothing could be simpler. To illustrate, I put the camera to my eye; there's just enough light. I push the button. There's the whirr of a Polaroid; exposed film slides out and I rip it off. I hand the film to Loretta and we all crowd around in slowly dying light as the image gradually appears. The magic of this Polaroid almost outstrips the statuary. We all ohh and ahh in two languages.

It was a lucky shot. The figures are clear. There's a mystic aura of permanence, of immutability. At the same time, there's a sense of the basic humanity intrinsic to the tableau. There's also an air of spiritual symbolism.

I have a hard time getting Loretta to take her eyes away from the photo and try some shots herself. She lines one up as I remind her to hold the camera still and to keep the camera level when she pushes the button. Those are the only uncontrolled variables with this camera: it does everything else itself.

She wants to watch this film come to life but I force her to take the rest of the roll, from different angles, some up close to particular figures, before the light fails; it's dropping fast. I take each photo as it comes out and hold them all in my hand, spread out like a deck of cards. The village crowds around. When she's shot the last picture she comes over to join us, her face animated, joyous. Some unmitigated Christmas feeling has snuck up on her. Then, as the photos become visible, each one better than the last, incredibly transcendent, we're both entrapped in a particular moment; enveloped in the *right now* in an existential sense; removed, living fully in our joy. We pass the photos around, Loretta turns to me, speaks in English.

"Will, that's the nicest present you could've given me. If we throw the camera away now, whatever you paid was worth it. I'll always treasure these photos, they somehow say something about what I've hoped our life has been all about. And to think, *our* kids, all of us, made this come to life."

I put the camera back in the box along with the photos and

leave it on the edge of our porch. Nobody will steal it. I can't think of anybody within twenty kilometers who would steal anything from anybody.

We start off toward Huis de Bras. As we trudge up the hill, after we go over the bridge, I can feel a change in the atmosphere. It has nothing to do with the weather, although something is happening with the weather, too; clouds are building up. I'm talking about Loretta. She's shifting emotional gears, speed-shifting, from her euphoria with the photos to something heavy. I wait. There's nothing else to do. My experience is, you can't hurry these things and if you try it's almost always a catastrophe.

"Will, I've something to tell you and I don't know how to begin."

Oh boy! Here it comes. I wait, my heart quickened. Maybe I should run away. No, I'll have to face this finally, share it. I take a slight cushion shot; a beveled effort to distract.

"Is it about Mike? Is Geneviève pregnant?"

She looks at me. There's fear, shock in her eyes.

"What makes you think that?"

"I don't know, I'm only guessing."

"It's Nicole. This is what we were talking about while all of you were delayed with Christmas present opening. I had one of my rare periods and asked her for a pad. She started talking just then, she needed to talk. That's what took us so long. We were both sorry to hold you all up, but there was no way to stop it."

"You mean *Nicole's* pregnant?"

"No, not really, but she *wants* to be. She wants to have a baby."

"Well, that's easy. Just find the right man, do the right thing, and if she's lucky, she'll have one. What's so terrible about that? Has she found the man yet?"

"Yes, she has the man in mind, a sculptor in California; the one she wanted to bring here for Christmas. This man doesn't want to marry her, doesn't want to be a father. But Nicole still wants to have a baby by him."

"That's nuts!"

"She wants us to help her so she can have this child."

"I give up! Help her! How can *we* help?"

"She'd like to live here at home for the last three months of her pregnancy, have the baby at the American Hospital where Ben was born, on our family Social Security. Then, when she's on her feet, she'll take the child back to America, try to make it all work out somehow."

"Great. And how's she going to live?"

"Don't get mad at *me*, Will. I'm only telling you what *she* told *me*.

"Nicole says there are a lot of single parents in California and they get help from the state; I guess welfare, food stamps, child care, MediCal; those kinds of things. I don't really know. She says there are even communes of single parents who look out for each other, if this man won't help her. Can you imagine our Nicole living like that?"

"I can't imagine *any* of it. It's all so unreal, it makes reality look like a mirage."

I must admit I'm not totally, completely overwhelmed. I guess I should be, but I'm not. This *is* the 1980s, 1984 has come and gone. Those wild kinds of things are not quite as crazy, as impossible, as they used to be.

We walk along some more. I'm having a hard time putting thoughts together in my mind. I can't handle so many changes; none of any of it makes sense even in a nonsensical world.

Lor looks at me, smiles her mystery smile, but there's pity, kindness, understanding in it. If it weren't so cold, if she weren't wearing slightly wet woolen mittens, I think she might even reach over and stroke me kindly on the face the way you would a horse before a difficult jump or a dog after he's fetched.

"Will, can't we help her financially those first six months when she needs to stay home full-time with the baby? Think of it, we'd be grandparents again."

I do a quick mental calculation. That's at least five thousand dollars right there.

It's getting out of the improbable, impossible, into the totally fantastic. Where in hell, with *our* family, did she ever get such an idea? Lor's looking at me again. She stops, turns toward me. I stop. She puts out both her hands to take mine. We're at a break in the hedgerow; I look over her shoulder at rolling white fields; two hawks or crows are barely visible swooping through the valley. I look into Lor's eyes. They could use her as a model for Saint Philomena or Saint Theresa, one of those long-suffering types.

"I'd like us to take the baby if she decides to go back to school, Will. I think it would be better and I'd like to do it. I have a sabbatical due me and I'd take it."

Wow! She's done it again. How can a man live so long, thirty years, with a woman and know so little about her? No, that's wrong. I would've known if I'd taken time to think. What I don't know is *myself*.

"My God, Lor! You're crazier than Nicole. I'm over fifty years old; we could never handle a tiny baby like that. We'd go crazy. Then, what if Nicole meets a man she wants to marry, who wants to marry her, there's a good chance he won't want her kid by this other guy. We'd be stuck with it. I'll have to work until I'm seventy-five getting this one through college. I'll never make it. I'm not sure I'll even make it with Ben."

"Come on, dear. You're younger now than you were when Ben was born. Age is more a matter of what you have to do than anything else.

"If we wind up raising another child it wouldn't be so bad and it might be good for us. Besides, I know my Nicole, she'd never abandon her baby; she probably won't even listen to my idea. But I'd like to offer, if you agree. I think, more than anything else, she wants our moral support; wants to feel we're with her no matter what she decides."

I'm stumped again. I know what's bothering me but I don't know how to say it. It's the old problem. I'm afraid of guilt. The idea of being or feeling guilty can make anything good in me, any truly generous act, shrivel in seconds. I've got to say it.

"Okay, Lor. I hear you. In some ways, I even agree with you, but think of this. Suppose in two, three or five years, some man comes into Nicole's life she really wants to marry and he won't because of her child. Suppose, as a result, Nicole winds up an alone woman, no mate, locked in by this decision. Is she going to ask *us* why we didn't stop her now, explain to her what might happen? Is she going to blame *us* for it?

"When I think of all the things we've done so far with the kids, doing what seemed right to *us* at the time, and, now, I hear how *they* feel about it. I've lost confidence.

"I'm getting tired of being wrong all the time. Somehow, it doesn't seem to affect you, you ride over things, but I'm not like that. Maybe I have some prideful, false idea about myself, want to be loved by everybody; I don't know; but right now I'm worried about how Nicole will bawl us out in five or ten years. I'm *that* selfish if you can believe it. I suppose being kicked in the face is part of being a successful parent but I'm not good at it."

I know I still haven't said what I really feel or mean but it's close as I can get, for right now. Lor, for one of the few times in our marriage, is crying. This is twice in one day. Our whole life is mixed up. There are tears rolling in the cracks made by all those smiles, real smiles and false smiles. I can't stand this. I look away.

"You poor dear. Don't you know they love you deeply, Will; that's why they have to hurt. They feel violated by your love; the *way* you love them, so crazily, so totally, so personally.

"They feel sometimes they have to fight back just to survive. It's all inside twistings, things we don't understand, feelings we only guess at."

Why does it seem so hard to me? What will Lor think of me when I do what I have to do? Will she be happier?

We stand there. I'm trying not to think. I feel some of the tightness, the blocking inside me softening, loosening. We start walking again, holding hands. I usually don't like walking holding hands in public, but right now it feels fine, maybe it's because we're wearing gloves.

The dark is coming on more seriously. The darkness of trees against the sky, against the snow is becoming general, more violets, deeper shadows, less varied. The death of night is coming to this Christmas day. But it *isn't* getting colder. The snow is going mushy under our feet. Instead of squeaking or crackling it's squishing. I look up at the sky, it's gray now with fast-moving clouds almost like a summer thunderstorm building up lumps of clouds in the waning light. I look down at my feet when I talk.

"Okay, Lor, but *you* tell her. I'm not sure I can trust myself. I might either start bawling or get so tongue-tied I'll ruin everything. They're used to it, you know, I'm the invisible man, on purpose, I guess."

We walk along some more. We're on the main road up in Vauchot; dark stone houses on each side of us, a light showing now and then through a shutter. I look over at Lor who's watching me.

"You're right, Lor. It could be fun having a baby in the house. It'd be fun having you home for a year being full-time housekeeper, mother and wife again, like old times. And think of it, at the same time, we *would* be grandparents. Think of that, Granny. But Lor, think, be honest. Is that what *you* really want?"

Lor swings forward of me and stops so I walk into her arms. She puts up her face and we kiss, kiss hard enough so her hat falls off into the mush. I feel what's almost like rain on my head. We break away; I pick up her hat, brush it off, slide it onto her head, she tucks in her ears. I check to see if anybody's been peeking out of shutters, maybe calling the local vice squad or *huissier.*

"We'd better get down to that turkey and those kids, Lor. I wouldn't doubt it's going to rain. If nothing else, you can say the Morvan has weather, just about any kind you can think of."

We start off walking fast, then skipping. It's quite a trick skipping in slush and we keep falling into each other. By the time we get to the hill going down to our mill we're both puffing and we start sliding in the melting snow. Loretta has on crepe-soled, après-ski boots and they slip whether she tries or not. My old gum boots with tread give us both some traction if I hold her close.

It's after six when we get home. Nicole is still asleep on the bed. Maggie is just closing the oven from basting the turkey. Ben has dismantled and is cleaning his gun on the table, the same table to be decked with our Christmas meal. He looks up.

"What time do we eat?"

Loretta goes over with Maggie, checks the turkey, great smells come out of the oven. She takes the butter-soaked cloth from the turkey's breast and starts nestling potatoes around the sides of our turkey inside the pan. She closes the oven.

"Okay, Ben. Time to get all your gun stuff off the table, Christmas dinner is about to begin."

They start putting out the plates, knives, forks. We're setting for both Mike and Geneviève, even though they aren't here yet. I'm feeling light-headed; displaced. I look at Nicole sleeping, her mouth slightly open, on our bed and think of her as a mother. She's smart and all but I just can't imagine her being consistent and long-suffering enough to mother a child. Probably incipient mother juices will gush to the fore.

I try to help with the setting but between Ben and Maggie, with some special advice from Loretta, it's going along fine. They're warming the plates on the butane heater. I'm just beginning to hear the sound of my motorcycle with Mike and Geneviève slipping down that hill when Nicole rolls over and opens her eyes. She sits up, yawns, then swings her legs off the side of the bed.

"Gosh, it looks like Santa's workshop here. What work have you got for a tired little elf?"

Loretta comes over and takes Nicole's hands to pull her up.

She gives her a hug. Nicole falls into it but seems confused; maybe she's only sleepy.

"Nickie, would you help with the cranberry sauce? As far as I can understand from this cookbook, we make part of it with the berries, then take some of the sauce to make the smooth jellylike kind. See if you can figure it out. I can't find my reading glasses and the print's too small."

Nicole and Lor open and stare into the steaming pot of cranberries. My job will be carving the turkey, so I stretch on the bed where Nicole just was and gather my strength. Her warmth radiates into my back.

Then I get the idea to put new candles on the tree and light them while we're eating. I roll out of bed and open two new packs. I pull out the old stubs and push in the new ones. It's hard to make them stand straight when the branches bend, also the holders blend in with the tree so they're hard to find. I forgot *my* glasses too, in the rush down from Paris. God, I hate being dependent on them after a lifetime of good eyesight.

Mike and Geneviève come clomping up the staircase chattering away. I hope he cleaned some of the slush off the bike. It'll rust the chrome for sure and then, when it dries, be a regular devil to get off. But that kind of thinking isn't in Mike's way of life; in fact, I know he *prefers* driving a motorcycle looking as if it just came through a wild motocross meet in the mud. It's probably the modern version of macho. The way we used to roll up the sleeves of our T-shirts over our shoulders, pretending we were Marlon Brando or James Dean. I really enjoy riding my bike when it's all shined, even the spokes; I feel as if I'm on a new Christmas present, riding it for the first time; some kind of childhood throwback.

Geneviève goes over to help Lor and Nicole; Ben is back pushing wood around in the fire. He throws on another log. I'm pretty sure I've gotten all the candle holders filled.

At quarter to seven, I pull the turkey out of the hot oven. It looks perfect. Lor has the carving knife and fork on the table and a large plate on which I'm to pile the cut meat. Nicole puts the two versions of the cranberry sauce in the freezer to cool and takes out the cold white wine we'll drink with our meal. She masterfully curls the metal foil around the cork, pulls the cork quickly, adroitly, hangs it in the curled metal. She worked as a cocktail waitress two summers and this is one of her residual skills.

I cut into our turkey at the leg joint and juices flow. I take off the whole joint and separate the thigh from the upper leg on each side. In our family, we leave these dark meat parts as units and don't slice them. I cut off the wings the same way. Now I have a basket case of a turkey. I sharpen the knife on our round, old-time sharpener; I've never yet mastered the easy back-and-forth sharpening motion of a butcher but I give my personal imitation. I don't learn these kinds of things easily.

I start cutting slices of white meat in long, dry, textured slabs. This is something I *can* do. I get more than ten slices from each side of the breast. Then I go around picking out all the best little hidden parts of meat that usually get missed in a casual carving. I've piled the white meat on one side of the plate and dark on the other. With a turkey, though, it's practically all white, even the thighs are white, just a little less dry.

Then I cut the stitching and scoop out the stuffing. Lor has a hot plate for it and has already put the stuffing from the aluminum packet in it. I scoop out the last bits from the front and back packing places. There's a good pile and it smells wonderful, not too wet, not too dry. My mouth is watering. I snitch one of the small tenderloin delights from the back of the turkey. Whether I'm carving a turkey, a duck, a goose, a chicken or even a guinea hen, I always exact this piece as my toll. It's tender and filled with taste. The first bite of anything is always the best so I savor it slowly, trying to let it come into me, become part of me, help me enter further into the wonderful meal I'm hoping this will be for all of us.

When I turn around, everything is in place; I help Lor into her chair, another Christmas tradition, then seat myself. Everybody else slides into their chairs. Twice a year we say grace in our house, Thanksgiving and Christmas. Although Loretta and I both come out of a Catholic tradition we don't like using the formalized "Bless us O Lord for . . ." formula and prefer a more natural, again, maybe pagan, appreciation for the bountifulness of this earth. I look around and Mike gives me the eye, showing he wants to do it.

Nobody else seems to be objecting so I nod to him. Our family tradition is hands flat on the table beside our plates and we look into each other's eyes as grace is said, then we lift our glasses and clink them in a toast. Nicole is just finishing pouring the wine around. Mike is leaning toward Geneviève, apparently explaining what's going on. He stands.

"I'd like to say how thankful I am to be here today. It's great being with my blood relatives and sharing some of the bounty from this lovely earth. If there *is* someone or some force responsible, I thank it. I'm part of this group because my parents conceived us to share in their love. I thank *them*."

He looks at both of us. It's embarrassing. I can see he's going to have my problem of not knowing what's enough. I keep my eyes on him but it's hard. Tears are welling up in me and I see them rolling down Mike's cheeks. He reaches his free hand over, his glass in the other, and pulls Geneviève up out of her chair. She has her head bowed in humiliation or embarrassment or in restrained joy.

"Now, Geneviève and I want to announce we're going to continue the natural and best way to be thankful for the world and life; by sharing it; hopefully someday sharing it with others of *our* combined blood. Merry Christmas to all of you, too."

He extends his glass to clink. We've clinked glasses of milk, of apple juice, of Coca-Cola, of chocolate milk and now it's wine all around. Pandemonium hits. It's just sinking into my thick skull what he said; they're going to get married or at least something like it.

Nicole, who's sitting next to Mike, jumps into his arms so he tilts his glass and pours cold wine down her back. She doesn't seem to notice. Then she grabs hold of Geneviève and squeezes her, pulls her away from the table, dances her around. Ben gets up and leaves the table. Lor walks past me and gives Geneviève, then Mike, a big kiss and hug. I stand there looking down at the food, thinking it's all going cold; wondering if we should put some of it back in the oven; thinking how far *out* of things I really am.

Mike is looking up from the women surrounding him. I stand and walk around the table, past Ben in the rocking chair. Mike's taken my usual place. I put out my hand, put my other hand on his shoulder.

"Congratulations, Mike, and you, too, Geneviève. I hope you'll be as happy for as long as Mom and I have been."

I lean down and sneak in a kiss on Geneviève. She's tiny, smaller than Nicole. I guess I'll have some short grandchildren, but then one giant in the family is probably enough.

Lor comes and puts one arm around Mike and the other around me. She looks from one of us to the other.

"It'll be wonderful having two married men in the family. You know, Mike, your Dad and I were already married and I was pregnant when he was your age."

That was for me. And it's true. But then young people seem younger these days. What she isn't mentioning is I already had my credential and had a job teaching in a junior high school. I was earning the grand total of $527 a month but, in those days, the middle fifties, it was enough to support a wife. I can't help wondering what Mike has in mind but I keep smiling.

Nicole's still holding onto Geneviève for dear life. She's babbling away with her in French. My own accent is horrible but I understand everything.

"God, Geneviève, you're so lucky. You might just be marrying the last really interesting man in the world who will actually *marry* anybody. I hope you know *how* lucky you are; and if you change your mind let me know; I have nothing at all against a little incest."

Mike picks it up.

"Okay, Nickie. You're second in line. If Geneviève ducks out on me, I'll look you up."

I can't let Nicole catch my eye. If I do she'll know I know. What a hell of a spot to be in, wanting a baby and not having a man to pitch in; needing to have parental help. For someone like her it must be hard. I begin to know what Loretta's been trying to tell me.

During all this, besides the wonderful dinner getting cold, Ben grumbling into the fireplace, Maggie's been standing aside crying. The tears are running down her face and she's sobbing. She's somebody else at whom I can hardly look.

I can't help but think of the wonderful fun we had at her wedding here in the mill. I forged a baptismal certificate so George could marry her in the church on the hill. Maggie has no religious pretensions but she wanted a real old-fashioned country church wedding with all the trimmings. My sister and her husband came. Joan, my sister, helped Maggie sew the wedding dress. An old friend of over thirty years, Syl Bernstein, whose daughter Maggie was flower girl at our wedding—we named *our* Maggie after her—played his violin for music at the mass. We sang songs from *Fiddler on the Roof*. I cried ridiculously when they played "Where Is That Little Girl I Carried?" The recessional was the theme, "Sunrise, Sunset."

Then, after mass, we had more than fifty village people dancing and stomping in the grange till I thought it was going to collapse. As a magical part of the celebration, a herd of cows, for the first time anyone can remember, wandered into our pond and got stuck in the mud; the men all ran off to help.

The scariest thing was that as we walked in full regalia down the hill from the church, my friend, Syl, playing his violin during the whole walk down, we started hearing shots being fired. Every time we passed a house, a fusillade went off, it was like a war. It turned out to be an old Morvandeau custom, the men running ahead and hiding behind barns shooting off guns as the wedding party goes by.

Later, I just managed to thwart another regional custom. In the lower grange, under where the dancing was going on, the men were building a fire and were preparing to throw on wet straw and firecrackers. It took quite a bit of talking to convince them the bride was nervous and wouldn't like it.

Now I'm standing here, smiling, not looking at Maggie, not looking at Nicole, not looking at Lor. I can hardly look at Mike either. He's wearing his Siamese–Cheshire-cat smile. It's the smile he wears when he's both embarrassed and guilty at the same time. His lips are thin, upturned, covering his teeth, and I swear his blue eyes cross like a Siamese cat's when it's about to pounce. It's a smile I've learned to recognize. When he smiles like that, it's time to say nothing and get *out* of the way. It's a version of his Zen-guru smile, hostile, *determined*, content.

Since I'm not looking at everything, maybe it'd be better if I were blind. Maybe if I were blind, I could write like Homer. No, I'm definitely not a Homer, more in the line of a pop fly to the pitcher with the bases loaded, automatic out.

I'm beginning to feel it's time to play father.

"Okay, everybody. Let's sit down and celebrate the great occasion. The food's getting cold."

Nicole picks up her glass.

"First, *I* want to make a toast."

We all pick up our glasses. It's a start toward eating, anyway. Nicole looks around at all of us, each directly in the eyes, in turn. She doesn't ever have to go blind.

"To fertile women and marrying men."

We drink a sip. We're all back at the table now, still standing; that is, everyone except Ben. Maggie pushes forward her glass. Her eyes are still wet and she has a mushy Kleenex to wipe her cheeks. Her voice is low, choked.

"To long happiness and a marriage like Mom and Dad's."

We all take another sip. I can feel we're getting into a Russian diplomatic toasting situation. We're *all* going to be making toasts. I turn my mind to what I can say that won't be too hypocritical, something I can live with. I try not thinking of how cold the food's going to be. Lor is ready for her turn.

"To long happiness, health and a marriage, not like *ours*, but original, complete and unique to your lives."

There's a moment's silence. I try to figure what she means. It's like translating the Delphic oracle sometimes, just figuring out Lor. It's my turn. Ben is still ignoring the whole process.

"To life itself, whatever it is, and to our mutual enjoyment of it."

That's about the level of my creativity.

Mike turns to Geneviève. Her face is red, there's sweat along her upper lip.

"Oh, no, Michel."

That line could be French or English, only a matter of spelling, inflection. Mike encourages her. She holds up her glass.

"I hope Mike and I will be happy together a hundred years— and never fight together."

She turns toward Mike, questioning.

"Is that right, Michel?"

Nicole goes over to Ben, pulls him by the arm.

"Come on, Ben; your big brother's getting married; can't you wish him happiness on this great day?"

Reluctantly, he lets himself be coerced from the rocking chair to the table. He keeps his eyes down. He holds his hand out without a glass, palm up, like a salute in one of David's paintings.

"Okay, to happiness. And when are we going to eat?"

It breaks the tension, the emotion-cluttered atmosphere. We all sit down. Somehow the food isn't as cold as I thought it would be. Probably all that plate-warming helped, maybe the intensity of what had been happening made time seem to stretch out the way it does sometimes. In fact, the food is just right, the dressing, the gravy, the turkey, the potatoes, the cranberry sauce are all perfect, warm but not so hot you can't get the full flavor. I thought I wouldn't have any appetite after all the adrenaline spilling up and over things, but I eat like a horse.

The table conversation is lively with Maggie and Nicole pumping Mike and Geneviève in English and French for details. How did they make up their minds? When? Do they actually want to have a ceremony? If so, church wedding, the way Maggie did, or what?

The main thing I get out of it is: the wedding will be soon, a civil wedding only and they'll be married in France. At least it gives Mike French citizenship if he wants it; but I still don't know how they hope to live. Geneviève says something about getting a job in the post office but that's all. Is Mike going to stay in France? And, what kind of job can he get? I worry too much but I can't help it. I'm a worrier. So?

I try eating slowly, not bolting the food. It's so easy at a big feast like this to rush through things. We finish off with pumpkin pie, a surprise from Maggie and Lor. It's made from canned pumpkin Maggie brought with her from America. Maggie's pleased as a child that we all like it.

"I figured what's a Christmas dinner at home without pumpkin pie? I was probably thinking of Thanksgiving but it turned out okay, huh?"

We all help with clearing the table. Even Ben helps by shaking out the tablecloth and placemats. Actually we're getting in each other's way more than anything else.

I go up as if I'm going to the toilet but go on out the side door of the upper grange and onto the dam.

It's incredibly warm. A south wind has sprung up so the snow is starting to melt seriously. In the dim light, our crèche figures are smoothing out, softening, beginning to take on a slightly Henry Moore-ish quality. The ice still covers the pond but I wouldn't think of walking on it. I go out and along the dam, down to the road. The town is quiet. There are some lights at the Calvets' but I don't see any light coming through the shutters at Madame Le Moine's. I stand out in the middle of the road and stretch. I feel stuffed and overfed. I feel depressed, it could be only the south wind, it affects me that way sometimes.

I stroll into the garage to see if Mike's taken off the ropes or not. He probably won't need them going back over the hill if things keep melting like this. I squat beside my bike in the dark and feel the tires; the ropes are in tatters, some of them have gotten tangled around the axle. It could be dangerous.

I search out the big flashlight I keep down here for emergencies. I flash it on the wheels; this is going to be some job. I find a knife and an old pair of pliers. I start trying to unwind the rope, then realize it will go more easily if I pull the bike up on its stand and put it in neutral. I'm just doing this when I hear a sound of someone squishing in the mud outside and hear the latch on the door pushed down. The door opens and it's Mike.

"Christ, Dad! You don't have to do that. The ropes started fraying on our way over from Geneviève's but we were so late for dinner and were so excited I figured I'd come down later and cut them out. I don't know *how* it is you always guess when something's wrong and jump right in there trying to make it right. It must be some special skill, or magic."

"I could do without it, Mike. My mother was that way; she'd know when I'd blown something before I even knew I was going to do it. I was convinced she was a witch."

I straighten up and Mike starts pulling at the rope, spinning the wheel at the same time to let the rope untangle. It's all grease-covered and frazzled into strands. I kneel down on one knee and begin cutting away at the ropes still attached to the wheels. We work quietly. I know I should be saying something, maybe only acting out my Dagwood role, but at least saying something. Come to think of it, I don't know the names of Dagwood's kids. I know the name of the dog, Daisy, and those kids have been around as long as I have but I don't know their names. That must mean something, doesn't it, Doctor?

"Do you really want to get married, Mike?"

He doesn't look around, reaches in to fish out a deeply bound length of rope.

"Whatta you mean, Dad?"

"I mean is Geneviève pregnant and you're only carrying through?"

"No. It's nothing like that."

I cut two more ropes from the front wheel. It's practically impossible to untie them; I guess Mike used square knots.

"Where are you going to live, Mike? How? I hate to be so fatherly but I *am* the only father you have; somebody has to do it. I have to, if it's only so I can live with myself after all is finished and done. I never felt I talked to Maggie enough about her marriage; she just made all the decisions and now look what's happened."

Mike's working in a squat. He can squat the same way my father could. He'll squat by the hour working on the side of a motorcycle and I can't squat more than five minutes without getting cramps. It's one skill which skipped me, a generational overflight. He turns and looks at me.

"Don't worry about Peg. She'll be all right. Maybe she and George made a mistake, that's all."

I have the strings cut and I stand up. Mike adjusts the flashlight to concentrate on the other side of the wheel. I pick the light up and straddle the bike so I can beam it directly on the spot. Both of us are only wearing sweaters but it isn't cold.

Steam vapors rise with our breathing, mostly only humidity. Mike sits now straddling the bike from the rear with the wheel between his legs.

"I'm quitting school, Dad; so you can forget sending on the tuition check. Geneviève and I are going to live here in France. She's found a little apartment in the Twentieth, for only six hundred francs a month. I think I can get a job helping old Monsieur Costa in his shop and he'll probably pay me four thousand a month as an apprentice; with that, and Geneviève's job at the post office, we should be able to make it okay. I can probably get a *carte de travail* if I'm married to Geneviève."

"Is that what you want, Mike? Your grandfather and great-grandfather, most of my uncles, were carpenters; it's a hard life and you never really make any money.

"Look, Mike, all you have to do is stick it out two more years; then you'll have that academic union card, a doctorate. It's something I didn't manage because *I* married too early. I hate to see you making the same mistake. It can change the quality of your whole life."

"Your life doesn't look so bad to me, Dad. If I can have half as good a life, I'd be satisfied."

Have I said enough? I don't want to argue; I just want to help him see all sides of this. Nobody can know the insides of somebody else's life. I'm shocked to find he thinks mine has been so *great*. Holy God!

"Look Mike. If you go back to school for only *one* year, you can take a teaching credential and probably a master's. With that you can get a job anywhere in the world, even here in France at the International School where Mom works, or the American School. We could carry you and Geneviève financially for that year, somehow, if you want to. It could make such a difference in the kind of life you live.

"The main thing is: Do you really want to get married? Are you doing this because you feel sorry for Geneviève, with her family breaking up and everything? We want to help but we don't want to if it only digs you into something you'll regret later, the way it is with Maggie."

Mike pulls the last of the greased ropes out of the axle. He checks the front tire, too. He stands up, stretches his back, lifting up on his toes, yawns. Maybe he's trying to let me know he's tired of our talking, wants to get out of it. No, it's only tension.

"Dad, were you all *that* sure when you married Mom? Did you *know* you loved her but were worried about how it would work out with the two of you being so different? Mom had a crummy background she was trying to escape, didn't she? Were *you* worried about whether you were only feeling sorry for her, wanting to rescue her from things, protect her from the world?"

He pauses. I unstraddle the bike, turn the flashlight onto the floor. How could I have such a smartass for a kid?

How does he figure these things out? His life is bound to be better than mine; I hate to think how little I knew about my parents when I was his age. They were only biological background; I had no idea of where they were coming from until I was forty-five and they were dying.

Mike opens the door to let some light in from the street before I turn off my flashlight.

"Well, Dad, that's the way it is with me. I think I'm sure sometimes and then I'm sure I'm wrong. All those things you mentioned come to my mind. I can't guarantee anything about myself *or* about Geneviève. It's a risk but I think I'm willing to take it.

About going back to California and trying for a teaching credential, I'll talk to Geneviève. I can't make those kind of decisions that have to do with *our* life, by myself any more. I think it's terrific of you to offer but shouldn't you talk to Mom about it first? It's her money, too, isn't it?"

"Mike, when you're married thirty years you're past having to talk about these things; you just know."

"That's what I mean, Dad, see?"

He pushes wide the door. I turn off the flashlight, hang it on the wall over our water meter. We step through the door into the mush. We walk around the house and up onto the dam. We both stop and look at the slowly melting figures on the ice, then go inside.

The greater part of the cleanup is finished. Lor's just dumping the dishpan in the sink; Maggie and Geneviève are chattering away in French and drying the last of the dishes, putting them in the closet. Nicole looks up at us as she wipes off the table.

"Well, you guys timed it right. Just eat and leave the mess for the women to clean up. That's typical."

But there's no bitterness there; she's smiling. Mike hangs his coat on the coat rack.

"We were out fighting polar bears and wolves, Nick; there are packs of them roaming around here. We tried a little hunting for meat but it was too dark."

I notice then how I forgot to light the candles for the dinner. Now's as good a time as any. I go over and get the matches from Mike's Christmas match holder.

Nicole is putting the table cover back on and shifts our holly from the millstone table to the eating table. I want to light the top candles first, then work my way down, trying not to miss any. It can be uncomfortable reaching over a lit candle to get one you missed. Nicole comes over with me, lights a candle on one of the candles already lit, and lights along with me.

"Dad, do you really want your electric lights on? It's okay with me. I was just being ornery."

"No. They're only backup, Nickie. They're okay for when we run out of candles or I'm too lazy to go around putting in new candles and lighting them. We'll stick to the old-fashioned way."

When the last are lit, we step back to look for missed ones and to get the effect. The rest of the family is sitting around the table, chairs pulled out so they face the tree. Ben is in the rocker, without a book, dividing his time between the fire and looking at the tree.

Mike starts off singing "Away in a Manger"; then we sing the song that has the same tune as "Greensleeves." It's the one I can never remember so I fake most of the words. Lor and Nicole are the ones who remember things, so we follow along with them. Mike and Geneviève move over to the bed and she stretches out beside him with her head on his chest. None of these songs mean anything to her.

I break in for the next one with "Il est né le divine enfant," she looks over at me quickly, smiles, and sings along with us.

It'll be nice having her in our family; the whole business about gaining a daughter isn't just bullshit.

We sing until the last candle burns out. All of us watch as if we're watching someone die, while it struggles, the last flickerings, flaring up, then dying down and finally failing. At last the lights on the tree are finally extinguished and we sit for several minutes with only the fire burning, reflecting from the Christmas tree bulbs. It's a fine end to a good Christmas day.

Soon after, Mike and Geneviève decide to head back for her house. I could feel she was getting nervous, worried about her parents. I tell Mike he can take the car, the road's so slushy they'll get all wet on the bike. I give him the keys.

"Don't forget, no third gear, tricky brakes, slipping clutch, window doesn't close."

"So what else is new, Dad? Have you ever owned a car that was actually legal? I don't think I could drive a vehicle without at least three serious things wrong with it."

He reaches with his free arm and gives me a hug. He speaks in a low voice, just above a whisper.

"I'll talk things over with Geneviève about what you said. Thanks again for offering and don't forget to check with Mom."

Early on, Maggie and Nicole climb upstairs for bed. It's been a long day and nobody got much sleep last night. I know I'm dragging. Ben pulls out his cot, his mattress, and sets himself up in front of the fireplace. After the girls are upstairs, I plug in the Christmas tree lights and they give a nice warm glow with the light from the fire. Loretta is already in her dark blue flannel nightgown. When Ben goes up to the toilet to change, I quickly shuck my clothes and pull on the new pajamas. What a great Christmas gift. I'm just sliding into bed when Ben comes down from the toilet room. He has his clothes folded in one hand and some wrapped Christmas packages in the other. He places the packages under the tree then slips into his sleeping bag, puts his glasses, his watch, on the table and stretches out. Ben is obviously intent on having his own private Christmas.

I wonder what he's gotten us as presents. I wonder if he has anything for Mike, Nicole and Maggie. I doubt it. Tomorrow will probably be real Christmas Eve for him. I hope the other kids' feelings aren't hurt if they find out. I'm trying to decide if I should get up and pull the plug on the Christmas tree lights, when I drop off to sleep.

VII

Seven Swans A-Swimming

I wake up in the dark. I mean I *really* wake up with my eyes
open as if someone's shaken me. I don't have to go to the bathroom so it can't be late. Everybody's sleeping. I can hear the
contented breathing from upstairs and from Ben's cot. I lift
myself up to look at the fire; the last log I put in is three-quarters
burned away. I should throw on two more logs but it's warm
outside, it really isn't necessary. I lie back. I try to see what time
it is from my watch but the combination of dim light and dim
eyes defeats me. I have that feeling you get when you know that
even though you're tired you aren't going to sleep. Some little
machine in my head is running like crazy.

I finally decide to get up, take a drink of water, flushing out
some of the dinner wine from my body, throw on the logs, and
take a pee, just to be sure. Maybe I'll make it through to morning
that way.

I move against the wall, pull the covers off me from the side,
then carefully slide down and out over the foot of the bed. I don't
think I wake Lor. First, I drink two glasses of water so cold it

makes my teeth ache. Lor warms it to brush her teeth and never drinks it straight from the tap, even in summer. She decants it into a pitcher and lets it *chambrer*.

I throw on two considerable logs; we're beginning to work our way through what had looked like an inexhaustible supply. We're running out of wood and I'm running out of days, maybe nine thousand left if I'm lucky. I decide I'll go outside to take my leak, so I slip my feet into our slippers by the bed, get the little hand flashlight, lift the butane tank quietly from in front of the door, open the door; close it behind me as firmly as possible and turn on the flashlight. I piss over the edge of the porch and into the flowing, no longer frozen, waterfall.

I carefully make my way up onto the dam. I flash the light onto the space where we built the crèche. It's like watching the sinking of the *Titanic*.

The shifting of the ice might be what woke me. The figures, melted almost to unrecognizable globs, are still above water but the slab of ice they're built on has broken away and is tilting so water is slowly rising, engulfing the figures. Two of the three Magi are already underwater, balls of snow floating in the murky deep; the other has melted to a formless lump on the dam. The water is slowly, remorselessly, moving up on the other figures as the ice tips, the water mounts. I watch as first the forward shepherd, then the baby in the crèche, are inundated. The sawhorse floats, snowballs float. Quickly, easily, Mary, Joseph, the animals are tilted into the water. Within ten minutes it's all gone.

I'm feeling cold. There's a warm wind blowing but I'm cold anyway.

I carefully go down the steps; aware of my own fragility, how easily I could slip, fall, break a bone. Death sneaks up on us imperceptibly. It seems we can fight it off, exercise, eat the right food, jog, run, do yoga, but you can't fight a tiger with spitwads. I flash the light on our thermometer. It's ten degrees *above* zero Celsius. I flash it on my watch. It's exactly midnight.

I'm feeling shaky as I slip off our wet, cold slippers and ease myself back into bed. The bed is still warm. I'll never be able to explain to Lor how I got the slippers all wet. We share them. We have the same size feet. I should maybe get up again and put them by the fireplace to dry. No. I can't; I'm too shaken up. I know I'm not going to sleep. Loretta rolls over and puts her hand across my mouth. I kiss it, her fingers feeling like elongated lips.

"I'm sorry, Lor. Did I wake you?"

"No, I was awake."

"I went outside."

"I know."

"I got our slippers wet."

"I figured as much. Don't worry about it."

"Do you think I should put them by the fire to dry?"

"No. Don't worry about it. It doesn't matter."

She's lying on her back. I can't tell if her eyes are open.

"I watched the crèche sink into the pond. The ice tilted and it all just slid in; it was like watching a boat sink."

"That's too bad, dear. I was hoping it would last until the girls had gone. They worked so hard."

I feel she must be half asleep; her voice is so low, so calm, so clear, even more than usual. I should shut up and leave her alone but I feel so alone myself. I roll over and put my arm across her, she turns her back to me and pushes her rump against me.

"Happy anniversary, Lor."

"It's not until tomorrow, dear."

"But it's already tomorrow, it's past twelve. We've been married for thirty years. Who would ever believe it?"

"I would. But we got married in Illinois and that's seven hours behind us and besides we didn't get married until nine in the morning. It's sixteen hours until we make it. Thirty is a big number."

Now I know she's really awake, you can't do those kind of calculations half asleep, or maybe she's been doing a personal countdown.

"I've talked to Mike. His idea is to try getting a job with Monsieur Costa and live in Paris. He wants to quit school."

"If that's what he really wants, I guess there's nothing we can do. I never actually believed he wanted to be a paleontologist anyway. It's so unlike him. I think he just got all caught up in some complicated accident."

"Yeah, maybe. But I'm worried he doesn't really want to get married. He could be going into this the way he got into science, more or less by accident, just taking the easy way."

"That's the way almost everything happens, dear. Stop fighting so hard; you've got to let things happen that have to happen. There is *no* master, great predictable plan. You need to have more confidence."

I roll onto my back again. Loretta stays on her side, her face away from me. I hear the trees beating against the roof. If I don't get them cut, they'll loosen some slate for sure. Maybe before we leave I can get Ben to hold the foot of the ladder so I can climb up there and cut some branches. I want to talk to Lor some more.

"I tried convincing Mike to stay on and take his credential, at least. That way he can get a teaching job somewhere, maybe at ISP with you. I told him we'd help support the two of them while he did it. Is that okay with you?"

"Of course, Will. Whatever will help them get on their own feet, have a happy life. Nothing else matters."

She rolls onto her back. It's a dirty trick. Now I've got her awake and staring at the ceiling. I hope she doesn't notice those branches. I can't let it go.

"But then I got to thinking. If Nicole has her baby and we support her through that and you take off on sabbatical at half pay, and who knows how Maggie's going to manage if she divorces George, with lawyer's fees and all; then, with Mike and Geneviève on top; I don't know what we'll have to live on ourselves."

Loretta rolls over toward me, gets up on her elbow and throws her arm across my chest. She gives me a kiss on the cheek, then a light one on the mouth.

"It'll all work out, dear. Stop worrying. I'll bet your blood pressure is soaring right now and lying awake, not sleeping, isn't helping. We don't have a real worry in the world. Everybody is healthy. That's the big thing. So far as money is concerned, we have the money in cash fund from selling your mother's house when she died. That'll be more than enough."

I sit up. Lor rolls back. I lean over her.

"But, Loretta, that's *our* nest egg. That's really all we've got in the world beside this mill. You must be kidding. It's the *only* thing we have to fall back on in our old age."

Lor smiles up at me. Then she puts her hands behind my head and pulls me down for a nice, soft, deep kiss. We haven't kissed like that in a long time. I'd almost forgotten how nice it is, what a soft but firm mouth Lor has. She looks me in the eye.

"Listen dear. Despite my recent relapse, a residual accident of the body, we have nothing to do with eggs any more. That part of our life is over. We have our nests, this mill and our apartment in Paris. With our long-term lease we can always manage the rent of the apartment. We don't have any problems with a nest so we don't need a nest egg, a nest nor an egg.

"But our kids do right now. I can't think of a better way to spend that money than investing in their eggs, their nests. I think your mom and dad would feel the same way. They earned that money by hard work and if they could speak now, I'm sure that's the best way they could think for *their* money to be spent."

So, I missed it again. I don't seem able to figure these things out for myself; somebody else always has to explain. I cuddle close to her.

"How can you stay married to such a jerk, Lor? I haven't given you anything I promised. You married somebody who was going to be a famous philosopher, and now you're stuck here in a foreign country away from our children, our only grandchild. You have to work to help us keep our heads above water. You really got a bum deal. I say now and I mean it as I've said every anniversary since the beginning; even though we're still, by the twirling of the earth, your private calculations, fifteen hours away from the actual moment: Do you want to call it off? By any standard I can think of, you've been short-changed. Why not get out while you can?

"From what I've read in sex literature, Johnson and Masters would condemn us to twenty years of touchy-feely sessions and sensitivity training. You sure you want to go through with this?"

At first I can't tell if she's laughing or crying. Her whole body is wracking, shaking. Then I realize it's a combination of both. I hold her closer. When my face touches hers, I know she's been crying, her cheeks are cold, slippery wet.

"I'm here, Will. I've never known a nicer, kinder man than you. Not many women can honestly say that about their husbands. I'm trying, I'm hanging on with both hands; please, just give me some time."

There's nothing more to be said. We hold tight and I think she goes to sleep in my arms. I unwind myself and stretch on my back. It's as if I've had an orgasm; I feel undone inside, slowly melting, drifting. My mind has stopped spinning and is gently touching on thoughts, delving into them not dwelling on them. It's a good feeling. Do other people have many moments like this? It's so unique for me.

I shift, turn on my left side, stare at the stone wall in the dark, watch the stones lighten, glow pink-orange in the reflected firelight, dropping to gray-blues, dark ochers of the natural stone in the unlit flickers. I know I can only stay up like this, on my left side, back to Lor, a few minutes. If I stay any longer, I'll wind up with lower back pain. If I fall asleep this way, the back could easily go out and that would *really* ruin Christmas. But it feels so good, forbidden fruit, up on this side. I'll give myself just a few more minutes as a Christmas-anniversary present.

One thing I'm convinced of is you can't love others unless you love yourself first. That's a big part of my trouble. Somewhere along the line I lost confidence.

Every kind of love, if it's more than mere respect, admiration or passion, has some mystical quality by which one feels, participates in others' feelings; their joy, sorrow, ecstasy, despair.

You're happy if they're happy, you cry if they're sad. But to do this, you must have personal experience with these emotions.

I roll onto my back, stare at the log slashing of the ceiling and wish I could love like that. I sleep.

When I wake it's light. The snow's melted off the skylights and I can see the branches of our trees blowing lightly. The wild winds of last evening seem to have abated.

I look over and Ben's already up; his cot, his mattress tucked away; the fire's blazing strongly. I hear Lor working in the kitchen. I also hear the girls upstairs giggling and moving things around. Lor looks over at me.

"So, you're awake at last!" She looks at her watch. "Well now, in just six more hours, we'll be married thirty years."

I hold my watch at arm's length and squint. She's right; it's almost ten o'clock. I don't remember having slept this late in years. I jump up and begin straightening the covers, making the bed. I feel very refreshed but slow. I fluff the pillows and smooth the brown bedspread, then back off the end of the bed. Loretta puts her arms around me from behind.

"Happy anniversary, Will. There's water to wash with before the girls come down. They're going to drive up with Mike and Geneviève to Paris. Then, Mike and Geneviève will drive back down here again in a few days. They're all looking forward to having some fun in the good old city of lights."

She seems so lighthearted. I'm still slow, just coming around.

I hurry my washup. I stink from all the nervous perspiration yesterday, so I give myself a brisk rubdown with warm water and soap. I use one of the glove washcloths Lor bought each of us for Christmas, then I spray myself with some of the perfume I gave Lor. I'm a natural Indian-giver.

I quickly slip on my second-best clothes. I'm pulling on my shoes when the girls come down the steps. Nicole stands at the bottom while Maggie passes the bags down.

"Hi, Dad. We began to think you were dead. Did you get a good sleep?"

"I guess so. I don't remember a thing. I was thinking and suddenly it was as if somebody hit me over the head; new version of the Japanese sandman, he karate chops with a sandbag."

Maggie comes down the stairs, jumps the last long step. "Happy anniversary, Dad. I already said it to Mom. I can't imagine you being married thirty years."

Nickie piles their things on top of the trap door to the cellar.

"We thought we'd have a kind of anniversary breakfast, then take off."

She goes over to the refrigerator and pulls out a bottle of champagne.

"See, we even snuck this into the refrigerator last night. We do things right."

She's wearing the same outfit she drove down in. They've got that long ride up, with the window stuck open, but this time it shouldn't be so cold. Ben goes over and takes his two presents out from under the Christmas tree. He puts them at the plates set for Lor and me.

"These aren't Christmas presents, these are anniversary presents. I'm still too young, in my opinion, to give parents Christmas presents; besides, anniversary presents are more important."

Lor comes over and gives him a little hug, not enough to embarrass him. She slides a waffle onto my plate.

"Come on, Will, start eating. Ben, we'll open the presents when we drink the champagne, okay?"

"Sure."

Lor keeps bringing waffles out and we keep eating them. We're about halfway through when Mike and Geneviève roll the Ford in front of the mill and stomp up the steps. They're chatting gaily, it seems so carefree and joyful. Has it always been this way and it was only my own personal dark cloud which made it seem so heavy?

"Hi, everybody. Sorry we're late. We had a hard time getting away and we slept late, too. Actually, mostly we slept late."

They take their places. Lor has a slight backup in waffles so she sits down with us. This is really more fun than going to Madame Le Page's for our anniversary dinner as we planned. It's more light, more like our wedding. Our wedding breakfast was at ten thirty in the morning at a hotel in Chicago looking out over Lake Michigan on a very cold, sunny day after Christmas Day.

Nicole opens the champagne. She pours expertly without spilling a drop, moving from glass to glass in turn until they're all full. They're ordinary wineglasses, not champagne glasses, so it's a good trick. She even pours one for Ben. We lift our glasses, they look at me. I look at Lor, she nods to me.

"Okay, but there's only going to be one toast this time. I'm running out of emotion."

I hold up the glass, look all around.

"To the past thirty years, not so easy as some of you seem to think; but worth it. Marriage is not a bowl of cherries or a bed of roses or anything else. It's not just a bed either. If it's anything it's a mutual support and admiration society of two."

I hold out my glass to clink and we clink all around, even Ben. We sip at the champagne. It's excellent, just cold enough, dry and with the flavor of dried grape stems. Ben sniffs at his, takes a small drink, wipes his nose, puts his glass down.

"Open your present, Dad, will you?"

I put down my glass and pull the string from his awkwardly wrapped package beside my plate. I carefully open the paper, shake the box, listen, the way my dad used to open packages, smiling all the while. Will Ben and Mike do the same thing to their children? I bet they will.

When I open the box, it's almost too much. I've been holding back my tendency to cry, to spread my emotion all over everybody. I thought the good night's dead sleep had put my frazzled nerves together but my eyes start filling as I lift Ben's present from the box. How could he know? I never said anything.

I turn it upside down, then right side up. The snow falls slowly over the stylized snowman. He has a broomstick, a top hat, black coal spots for eyes and a carrot nose. Everybody applauds. Ben is smiling as wide as I've *ever* seen him smile.

"Well, when I bought it, you kept promising me it was going to snow. Now we've had some real snow and built some real snowmen so maybe this is just extra.

"Open yours, Mom."

Lor dexterously opens her package, no nonsense but no rush. She opens a package as if she's a film running backward of somebody wrapping a package, step by step in the reverse order it was put together. She lifts out an old-style stereoscopic viewer, with a slot on the side for slipping in the slides. There's a box with about twenty pairs of slides. Ben reaches over and lifts one from its niche, slips it into the slot on the side of the viewer. A wondrous smile comes over Lor's face.

"It's beautiful, Ben."

Ben kneels beside her, adjusts the knob on top.

"See, Mom, isn't it just like really being there? It's more real than real."

Lor passes it to me. I'm seeing a sepia-toned view of camels standing in front of pyramids. It's like looking into the past. I take the viewer from my eyes. It's beautifully made, each slide is glass, mounted in a wooden frame. Ben is so excited his hands are shaking.

"I found it at the Marché Aligre. Because I looked at it so long, the man sold it to me for half the price he told me at first. You know, this is the first time I've begun to know what fun it is to be Santa Claus myself. It really helps."

Lor kisses Ben on his soft-haired cheek; he flinches some but tries not to.

"Thank you, Ben. It's a wonderful present. I intend to spend hours looking into it, myself, seeing the magic, and I'd like to share it with my little first graders. I know they'll just love it too. Is that all right?"

He nods.

I've been giving my snowman a shake once in a while, watching the flakes come down, remembering the last few days, the dance in Mike's cabin, the building of the snow crèche, the sinking and sliding of it off the ice, the battery in the Fiat. This is the perfect souvenir of it all.

Mike stands up with his glass in his hand and raps the side of a dish with his fork. We all look at him. He's very serious.

"And I'd like to unannounce our wedding. Geneviève and I have decided I should go back to California, get my credential while she works in the post office here. She'll live with her mother and save money. We're *not* unannouncing the *marriage*, only the wedding. Next Christmas maybe we can reannounce the wedding."

I look quickly at Geneviève. She's smiling up at Mike. I wonder how they worked it out. I hope I didn't stick my oar in too fast, too hard; that this is really their decision. I find myself running up the same old guilt path.

Now Nicole is rapping on the edge of her plate. Her face is serious but edging on a smile.

"And folks, I'm going back to school. Then I want to study stone cutting with the man I'd hoped to bring here to join us this Christmas. I hope I can talk him into something permanent. No Virgin Mother business for me. I've seen what happens to Virgin Mothers; everything melts away, the ice tilts and it all sinks slowly under water. I'm going to go after my man, make him know how much I love him and bring him into our family somehow, even if I have to hit him over the head with one of his mallets or drive a cold chisel into his heart, like killing Dracula.

"I'm sure he'd make a wonderful husband and father. You'll all like him. He really knows what love is, he's just been wasting it on a bunch of rocks and cement. He could probably carve the whole Morvan into one gigantic sculpture, make this place famous."

I glance over at Lor. She's smiling and it looks from here like a real one.

We sit down and finish drinking our champagne, finishing off the last of the waffles. The girls shuttle down their luggage. Mike and Geneviève go out to see the sunken crèche. Lor and I hover over the trap door. When it closes, Lor comes into my arms. We stand like that and the trap door pushes open again. It's Maggie, she closes the door behind her. She looks at us; we still have an arm around each other.

"Mom, Dad. I hope you don't mind but I've definitely made up my mind to get a divorce. It's weird but in a strange, backward way, watching you two together helped me make my decision even though I know you don't want me to divorce George. He and I can never be the way you two are.

"I feel terribly sorry about Seth, he and George love each other so; I hate keeping them apart but I need to live my own life my way. Mostly I don't want you two worrying. I'm a big girl, I'll work it out."

She started fine but by the time she's finished, tears are running down her face faster than she can wipe, even with two Kleenexes. She goes back down through the trap door. Lor and I follow.

When we get to the road, our Capri is loaded with luggage and Nicole is squeezing into the back seat. Maggie pushes in beside her. Geneviève climbs in beside Mike.

We all know we're not up to a big good-bye scene so we're rushing it.

Mike starts the car and turns around. They wave out the windows and we watch as they head up the Vauchot hill toward Geneviève's place to pick up her bags. I hope that old car holds out with all the load.

God, there I go again. So many of my big worries have been wiped out just like that and now I'm starting new ones. It's a disease. Lor is leaning against me, her hand on my shoulder.

Is this the time? I look around to see if we're alone. Ben's nowhere to be seen. I don't think he even came down to say good-bye. I hope the other kids were so anxious to get started, to get away, that they didn't notice.

I turn my head down to look at Lor. She's still staring at the curve where they went up the Vauchot hill. God, I hope I can get through all this without hurting her, without having her think I'm being mean or selfish. I'm not so sure of myself any more. It's eating away everything about me that I've always valued. I feel I'm becoming like everybody else.

I've gone over it all a thousand times in my mind trying to make it come out right but now I feel as naked as the first minutes I knew.

I pull away from Lor and hold her by the shoulders, looking into her beautiful fading-fade-away eyes. In many ways, she's lovelier than when I first met her at Evanston. Her eyes blink, she smiles one of her automatic smiles that doesn't hide her sadness, her wariness. Her voice is low, controlled, so different from what I'm feeling inside.

"Wasn't that a lovely thirtieth-anniversary celebration, Will? Weren't the kids wonderful?"

I still search in her eyes, looking for something to help me; I'm beginning to lose my nerve. Maybe I should wait a little more. But I don't want to go back into the mill, our Christmas home, until all the poison is out of me. I feel if I keep waiting too long I'll never be able to say what has to be said and we'll live our lives around it the way we've been doing so far and Lor will just drift farther away from me.

I wonder if I can trust my voice. I feel solid inside and at the same time empty.

"Yes, Lor, they were great. I don't think any of them really suspected this could well be our last Christmas and anniversary together. I kept trying to tell them but they weren't listening."

Lor's smile slowly vanishes. The color is draining from her face so her eyes seem to glow, lustrous in the cold light.

"What do you mean, Will? I'm sure some other time, maybe even next year, we'll have them all together with us, maybe even Seth."

"I'm not talking about them so much, Lor. I mean us."

I wait, take a deep breath. I can still back off but I go on.

"It kills me to say all this, Lor; but I know about you and Pete. I'm terribly sorry."

Her face has turned gray as the slush pushed up on the side of the road. She's continued to stare into my eyes but tears slide out the corners of hers, run down the outside of her face. I'm still holding her by the shoulders. We're still, silent, looking into each other the way we haven't in years.

For some reason my eyes stay dry. I can't cry. Maybe because I've thought about this moment so long, so often, dreading it, avoiding it, wishing it away, pretending it isn't. But now it's happening and inside I'm feeling a release, a knot melting, falling away. Lor opens her mouth to speak twice but says nothing. She finally manages.

"Please, Will, can't this wait? Let's go inside."

"I'm sorry Lor. If we go inside I'll never be able to do this, inside is so much *us*, everything we've been, I couldn't. Don't you understand?"

"All right, Will. I'm sorry you couldn't have waited just a little longer. I've wanted to tell you about all this myself, to try explaining, now you'll never be able to believe that. Probably I'm the one who waited too long."

"I believe you, Lor. I always believe you. You know that. It's the way it's been with us."

We're silent some more. I pull Lor close to me. I can't look into her eyes any more. I hold her tight. I can feel my throat tightening and know I'm going to cry so I'd better hurry.

"Now *you* have to believe me. You know how I first suspected there was something, Lor? God, it's so like me! I was lecturing to a small seminar one Saturday afternoon when, suddenly, it was as if the ground shook under me. I had to stop and sit down. I was astounded to find I had an erection.

"This whole experience lasted only a few minutes. I don't know what my class thought. I thought I'd had a mini-stroke or a slight heart attack. I considered going to the American Hospital for a checkup. I meant to tell you. But I forgot all those things the way I do. You know the way I am.

"That was May eleventh, just over a year and a half ago. Does that date mean anything to you? Knowing what I know now, I think it's when you had your first orgasm, the orgasm we tried so hard for all these thirty years."

Now Lor is sobbing against me. I hold her tighter. She's so limp I feel I have to hold her up. She doesn't respond except to nod her head against my shoulder. I try getting myself together enough to go on. It's even worse than I thought it was going to be. I take a deep staggering breath.

"It happened several times after that, usually on Saturdays, or days you stayed late or went to a meeting. It was never as strong as the first time and I wasn't scared. In my usual stupid way, I never put it together with you. I thought it was maybe part of male menopause or something like that. It was the erection out of nowhere which always surprised me and my testicles would hurt afterward. I don't have random erections any more these days."

I wait. Lor still says nothing. Now comes the hardest part.

"Then, one day when you weren't home, a woman called. Her name was Carolyn, she was crying and said she had to talk to me. It was Pete's wife. You know how I feel about multinational company wives but she sounded so upset I agreed to meet her the next day after my Saturday class. I knew you wouldn't be home, you never were any more. It was the Louvre, or some special exhibit, or the Orangerie, the Comédie Française, shopping, the Opéra or something. I could feel you were happy so I was happy too, but I did miss you.

"She came up to the apartment. She had some letters from you to Pete. You'd mailed them to his office. I don't know why he brought them home. Probably they were so beautiful, so full of love, he wanted them near him. I would have. Carolyn wanted me to read them, she said they were love letters, dirty letters. She was absolutely raging mad, quivering in her anger, her face white through her makeup. I said I wouldn't read them. They were your personal letters to Pete. It was wrong for anyone else to look at them.

"I'll admit I was hurt. But I wasn't surprised. Deep inside, I felt your joy, your satisfaction over the past two years. One part of me realized you'd found someone you could love the way you could never love me. That part was happy for you. You've got to believe that."

I try to push Lor away so I can look into her eyes but she pulls tight to me. I want to put it all together in my mind. I don't want to talk about it ever again.

"Anyway, despite all my arguments, Carolyn showed the letters to Pete. She told him she was going to get a divorce and take away the kids if he didn't ask for a transfer immediately and stop seeing you. She was going to the school and show them the letters. She insisted some of the things you said in those letters would make it so you could never teach school to little children anywhere again.

"Pete asked for his transfer. I know he's been seeing you since but I didn't tell Carolyn, of course. Besides, she'd never believe *how* I knew. I talked her out of going to the school with the letters. It wasn't hard, her own pride stopped her more than anything I could say. I made her promise not to contact you, not to make any scenes. It worked out better than it might have."

I can feel Lor stiffening in my arms. She's becoming rigid. I hold her tightly but her arms drop to her sides. She won't look at me. I'm doing exactly what I didn't want to do, hurting the one I love most. But I'm almost finished, I have to go on. I don't want to hurry it, but I don't want to drag it out either.

"Now I knew what it was I had been experiencing. It was hard to accept at first. It came rushing in on me so I could hardly work some days. I watched you and so much made sense now, things I hadn't understood before, the way you dressed, did your hair, even the way you walked. I truly knew for the first time, emotional, psychic, mental jealousy. Sometimes it was hard not to be physically sick, vomiting, thinking about it. I also knew I had to talk with you, get it out in the open, share what was happening to us. I wanted so much for you to tell me yourself. I wondered what Pete was telling you, how much you knew."

There's still no response from Lor. She's still standing stiff, holding herself away from me but still in my arms.

"Lor, I love you. I know you've been suffering terribly. I understand how you must really love Pete. I know you'd never hurt me unless it was something profoundly important to you. I know, in your own way you love me. I have to know that. I know it must be hard for you loving me sometimes. I don't have good ties to this world. I spend too much time dashing around trying to put things in order, trying to make things make sense, making a fool of myself, trying to believe in all the reality everybody else takes so easily for granted."

Now Lor leans back and looks up into my face again. Her face is flushed, her cheeks shining with tears. She's shaking her head back and forth, not fast enough to be a definite no, not slowly enough to be just an expression of disbelief. I look over at Madame Le Moine's. The shutters are still closed. If anybody's looking we might only be sad because the kids left.

"Look Lor. This isn't easy for me to say, but I mean it. We were going to spend a lot of money on Nicole, now we don't have to. Why don't you use that money and take a sabbatical. You deserve it, you're overdue.

"If you want, go to Connecticut, talk it out with Pete, with Carolyn. See what can really be and what can't. I want you to do everything you can to be yourself again, to be the woman I've loved all these years. I want you to do this not just for you, but for me, for our whole family. When you know what you want, what can be, what can't, then we'll work it out somehow. I'm convinced it'll be better for everybody that way."

Neither of us moves. Lor has stopped shaking her head. She's stopped crying, too. I'm almost finished.

"Lor, all I know is I don't want us to go on the way it's been these last years. I don't just mean the sex part, I mean the not sharing, the secretiveness, the both of us always pussyfooting around, pretending things that aren't, pretending things that are. It's not good for us and I don't think it's good for Ben either. I'm sure all his reading and being so apart is not only something genetic from me but his way of not knowing, of pretending."

Lor's hands are still at her sides. I pull back, let her go, reach down for her hands—they're ice-cold. I look long into her eyes. They're empty now, flat, stagnant brown. It scares me.

"Lor, I want more than anything else for you to be happy. If staying with me, away from Pete, makes you unhappy, then how can I, in conscience, believing the way I do, convince myself that I love you truly? Do you understand? I'm asking you to do this, painful as it might be, for me."

Now tears are welling up in my eyes, tears of self-pity, of joy that it's done, of shame at what I've done, at my loss? I don't know. One of my problems is I'm never sure.

Lor looks at me directly. There's strength and at the same time a question in her eyes. She stands apart from me, pulls her hands away.

"Will. This is all so terrible. First, I want to say I love you and that I'm deeply sorry for what happened. I'm sorry you had to find out about it the way you did. It must have been miserable for you. How could I have been so blind not to see it?

"There's no sense trying to explain what it was like between Pete and me. It's like trying to tell someone else about a dream you had which was so real, so intense that no words can begin to describe it and at the same time it seems to fade away somewhere almost as fast as it happened.

"I know you didn't want to hurt me, it's not in your nature. But you did. I didn't know any of this. Pete never told me. I didn't know about Carolyn finding my letters. I didn't know he *asked* to be transferred. The memories I've been holding to my heart of him, of what we were to each other are fading, more, being erased, by this deception. Do you understand what that means? I feel betrayed. I never thought I could be more unhappy than I was before, but I am. I could die."

Her voice is so intense. I'm more than crying now, I'm sobbing like a baby. I want to hold onto her but she keeps apart.

"The only good thing that seems to have come from all this is that I don't have to feel guilty about *us* any more. I mean the guilt I've felt for thirty years about our not having a real sex life, about my not responding to you. I thought it was all my fault, now I know I *am* a sexual person. In some way we, you and I, aren't matched to each other, it's chemical or something. I guess that's what they mean when they say people are sexually incompatible. I think we are. I married you because you were one of the only men who didn't scare me, because you were gentle, never put any pressure on me. You never made me try sexual things I didn't want to. The very things that annoy me sometimes now, your preoccupation with theory and concepts, were attractive. I felt I could live with you. I don't know why *you* married *me*."

"I married you, Lor, because I loved you. I wanted you for my wife and I wanted to have children with you. I knew you were very shy and modest and that attracted me, too. I liked being with you."

Lor bites her lip. I know from long experience that she's about to say something she's afraid will hurt, but that she has to say. It's almost as if she's punishing herself in advance by biting herself, or maybe she's trying to stop her mouth from talking.

"Will, I think you're afraid of sex, of me, of sex with me. I don't think you have a strong animal drive or id or libido or whatever you want to call it. It seems I need a man who does. Pete was that kind of man. He'll probably have another woman in bed with him, besides Carolyn, before he's a month up there in Connecticut. He's that way. I know that now, I think I always knew it. Maybe I'm just a slut, a slut schoolteacher, perhaps Carolyn was right wanting to take my letters to the school. I enjoyed being a lover, making love with passion beyond reason. It made my life so exciting I could scarcely think of anything else. I'm sorry, Will, but that's the way it was. That's the way I am, I guess."

She looks down at her feet. Then she looks up at me again.

"But I love you Will. I love you for all the love you can give, for the way you love our children, for the same reasons I married you, because I like being with you. But that isn't going to change our sexual problem. I'd like to think we could have good sex together now but I'm not so sure. I'm sorry, Will, both for you and for myself. It isn't your fault and it isn't mine. It just isn't there.

"I think you should do whatever you think you should do. I can keep on teaching, thanks to you. Ben can stay with you or me or whatever he wants. We can go on living together or live apart. Whatever you want. I'll tell you I'd like to continue living with you, try to bridge what's happened here, but I'll understand if you don't want to. It's your decision."

She looks at me for another minute, searching my eyes.

"Excuse me, Will. I can't keep this up, I feel as if I'm going to faint. Also, I left the tea water boiling on the stove, and I don't want to burn down the whole mill, do you?"

She turns away. I watch as she gracefully steps over all the sticks and debris left from where we hauled the logs inside for cutting. She opens the door, goes through and closes it again without looking back. I listen until I hear her lower the hingeless trap door back into place.

I start around the mill, up toward the dam. My legs are shaking and I'm cold. I zipper the jacket I threw on before we came outside. The sky is lightening and there are patches of blue, the clouds seem to have slowed down and flattened out. We could have cold weather again, but it doesn't look like snow.

I stop at the edge of the pond, just outside our door. The ice is almost completely gone. I look down. For some reason, the water is incredibly clear. The ice-water-soaked snowballs are still floating like giant mothballs. The piece of rubber tubing for Christ's halo rests lightly amongst the rocks on the bottom.

I put my hands in my pockets and feel something hard. It's the stone, that third stone, the stone I didn't throw on the morning of Christmas Eve, my stone not thrown.

I take it out; it's smooth and flat, warm from being in my pocket. I nestle it in the crook of my index finger and cock my thumb behind it. I hold it there for just a moment, stare at it, then flip it gently out, like an aggie marble, in a slow arc and into the water. I watch as it settles, swinging back and forth to the bottom.

I look out across the pond. There are no maids a-milking, but then I don't need maids or milk. There are no swans a-swimming. There's only one fat, drifting, gray goose, paddling happily around out there by himself.

Nine drummers drumming
Ten pipers piping
Eleven ladies dancing
Twelve lords a-leaping.

Twelve lords a-leaping
Eleven ladies dancing
Ten pipers piping
Nine drummers drumming
Eight maids a-milking
Seven swans a-swimming
Six geese a-laying
FIVE GOLDEN RINGS.

Four calling birds
Three French hens
Two turtle doves
And a partridge
In a pear tree.